A FEW
GOOD
MEN

BAEN BOOKS by SARAH A. HOYT

Draw One in the Dark
Gentleman Takes a Chance
Noah's Boy (forthcoming)

Darkship Thieves
Darkship Renegades

A Few Good Men

To purchase these and all other Baen Book titles
in e-book format, please go to www.baen.com.

A FEW GOOD MEN

SARAH A. HOYT

A FEW GOOD MEN

A Baen Books Original

Baen Publishing Enterprises
P.O. Box 1403
Riverdale, NY 10471
www.baen.com

ISBN 13: 978-1-4516-3888-2

Cover art by David Mattingly

First printing, March 2013

Distributed by Simon & Schuster
1230 Avenue of the Americas
New York, NY 10020

10 9 8 7 6 5 4 3 2 1

Pages by Joy Freeman (www.pagesbyjoy.com)
Printed in the United States of America

To Glenn Harlan Reynolds, a not-so-secret Usaian whose blog and writing have helped keep me both sane and informed for the last several years.

Acknowledgments:

I asked so many people to read this book before I had the nerve to submit it, I'm guaranteed to have forgotten some—now almost a year later. If your name was dropped, don't feel your contribution was ignored. I will catch you on the next book.

I'd like to thank, among others: Dan Hoyt, Amanda Green, Sean Kinsell, Kate Paulk, Eric Scheie, Francis Turner, Sanford Begley, Pam Uphoff, Rowan Larke, Tedd Roberts, Lin Wicklund, Courtney Galloway, and Edie Ostapik.

A FEW
GOOD
MEN

THE MONSTER

Carry Me to the Water

THE WORLD CELEBRATES GREAT PRISON BREAKS. THE FRENCH territories still commemorate the day in which the dreaded Bastille burst open before the righteous fury of the peasantry and disgorged into the light of day the innocent, the aggrieved, the tortured and the oppressed.

They forget that every time a prison is opened, it also disgorges, amid the righteous and innocent, the con artists, the rapists, the murderers and the monsters.

Monsters like me.

My name is Lucius Dante Maximilian Keeva, Luce to my friends, though I killed the last one of those fourteen years ago.

I was born the son of Good Man Keeva, one of fifty men who control the immense territory and wealth of Earth between them, and have for the last three hundred years. As good as a prince.

But for the last fourteen years, my domain had been a cell, six by ten, with a cot attached to the wall, a fresher in the opposite corner that served to have a sort of vibro-wash and clean one's clothes, and to take care of the other necessities of the body, all in one. At the foot of my bed there was a dispenser through which a self-opening can of food and a container of drink came through every so often. I thought it happened three times a day, but I couldn't swear to it.

I couldn't see daylight from my cell. But cans arrived three

3

times for each period they kept my lights turned on, so I considered that a day. And I kept count by saving one of the cans and scratching it on the side with the lid. Three hundred and sixty five days made a year with the usual adjustment. And I had fourteen of those to the day when freedom came, unexpected and terrible.

It wasn't strictly true that I hadn't seen another human being in fourteen years, not after a couple of days or so of questioning after arriving here. Once, in the middle of the second year, I'd got very ill. Who knows how, unless the food was contaminated. I'd caught an infection that wouldn't let go and wouldn't be cured by any of the usual means. They transferred me to a secure hospital ward for two weeks. A very secure ward, with robots as caretakers and doctors who saw me only remotely, at least after I regained consciousness. I retained a vague memory of having been touched while only semiconscious. Touched by human hands.

But after I became conscious only mechanicals touched me. Still through the window, made of transparent dimatough—I know, I tried to break it—I could see people coming and going. Men and women walking around, free, under the sun or the rain. I remembered them very clearly, each of their expressions, their clothes, their movements. I'd spent years remembering and making sure I didn't forget that there were real, live people out there. Even if I was as good as buried alive.

Twice more I'd been hospitalized, when I'd tried to commit suicide. And one of those times I'd been attended by humans, while they sewed the open cut on my face, from having got the cot to drop on my head. I remembered that touch too. Because down here, in the artificial light or the dark, it was easy to imagine there was nothing else. Nothing but me, all alone in the world forever.

A world and a monster. Forever.

Fourteen years after my arrival in Never-Never, I was exercising. I'd found that just lying around and sleeping made it difficult to sleep and all too easy to stay up all through the time my lights were off, thinking of ghosts. I'd tried that for three years. Now I exercised.

I partitioned my day, so that in the morning—or right after the lights went on and I ate the first can of food—I cleaned myself, removed my beard with the cream provided, vibroed my one, faded yellow body suit, thrice replaced, but still much worn and now tight, and put it on, because it gave me the illusion I was still part of the world of living humans, and that someone, somehow, might see me and care how I looked.

Then I sat down and used the gem reader some kind soul had slipped into my cell through the food dispenser almost at the beginning of my captivity. I used it through gems totaling about five hours, and then the second food ration was dispensed. And then I exercised.

Back when I was the pampered heir of Olympus Seacity, I'd been provided with exercise machines, and hired trainers. Turned out you could do just as good a job, or perhaps better, using your body as a counter weight and resistance. If you had five hours and nothing else to do.

Oh, I used my bed in exercises too. It used to fold up, but since I'd almost managed to kill myself by getting the bed to fall on my upturned face, they'd fixed it so it was permanently attached to the wall, permanently down, and couldn't fall. Not even when a man who must be six seven and close to three hundred pounds—I had no way of weighing or measuring myself—pushed himself up from it by the force of his arms, over and over and over again.

I had my palms spread flat on the bed—at about the level of my pelvis—and was using my arm strength to push down on it and pull myself up, while bending my knees, till my feet left the floor completely for a count of twenty, then down, then up again. I was on my hundredth rep of the day, counting aloud: fifteen, sixteen, seventeen—

Boom.

Boom is not the way to write it down. It was like a boom, a crash and a whoosh all in one, deafeningly loud.

I let go and found myself cowering under my bunk, my back flat against the cold, smooth wall, my head bent, my arms around my knees. Instinctive. It is instinct to try to make yourself small and unobtrusive. Not that I was ever either.

My mind ran through what could have caused the boom.

The first thought was that it was impossible. Had to be. There was no way—no possible way—that there could be that type of explosion anywhere near me.

The prison which had been my home for so long was called

Never-Never because it was the safest, best guarded and most absolutely secure prison in the history of mankind. It was impossible there had been an explosion there. And if there were, it would do nothing but drown all the prisoners, because as I remembered from when I'd been transported here in the dark of night, Never-Never was underwater, sealed into the base of a seacity. Most people didn't even know it existed.

Yet there were other noises from outside. Noises I wasn't used to hearing. Normal prison noises—cherished as random diversions from an otherwise monotonously ordered day—were distant conversations, too distant to hear the words, and sometimes the sound of muffled footsteps walking by, outside my door. Sometimes, rarely, there was a scream, perhaps as a new victim was dragged down to this antiseptic isolation. Unlike prisoners of an older era, we didn't even have rats as consolation.

Now the screams came one after the other. There were drumbeats of running feet. An odd sound scared me, for a moment, until I realized it was laughter. And then there was ... singing?

My mind raced, making my heart race, and not all the will power in the world could bring me out from under my cot. Until I saw the water.

At first it showed as a filmy sheen under my door. I blinked at it. Sweat stung my eyes, and I was sure that it was a mirage. Although Never-Never was under the ocean, I hadn't seen water except in my drink dispenser for fourteen years. The fresher was strictly vibration only. At a guess, long before I'd been brought here, some clever soul had filled up the waste disposal hole with cans, by keeping five or ten of them, stopped up the space under the door, perhaps with the blanket—then filled the cell with fresher water.

Now the only way to commit suicide by drowning would have been to block the hole, stop up the crevice under the door, then piss enough. Supposing drink hadn't been controlled, I didn't think even I could muster enough desperation for that.

So when the water first came in, it took me moments to believe it—dozens of minutes of my staring in disbelief, while it crept under the door, in increasing quantities, till it lapped at my bare feet, cold and wet. I put out a finger, dipped it in the water and tasted it. Saltwater. There was a hole in the prison. A hole that let in seawater. I reacted.

Or rather, my body reacted, which means it did something stupid, as bodies will when you're not paying attention to them. I jumped up, cracking my head—hard—on the cot, then bent again and scrambled out from under the cot, on my hands and knees, splashing in what had to be, now, two inches of water.

My heart beat hard, and my throat was trying to close in panic. Never-Never was completely under water, even if the entrance was up above the water line, a narrow, well-guarded hole on a seacity floor. The explosion could not have been at the main entrance or no water would be coming in. That meant it had to be in an underwater wall, somewhere.

Never-Never had seven levels. Seven circles of hell. I was on the sixth down. If I understood the organization properly, and it was entirely possible I didn't, this level housed the most dangerous prisoners. The level below me contained only torture cells.

I'd been taken to them for two days when I'd first come to Never-Never. I'd never understood what exactly they wanted to know or what they thought torture would accomplish. Maybe they just liked hearing me scream.

I tried to remember exactly how long it had been from boom to water under my door. The water was now up to my ankles, and I couldn't think clearly. It felt like the explosion had simultaneously taken place several years ago and only a heartbeat away. But the water was now above my calves, which meant the hole had to be nearby.

Someone would come, I told myself, swallowing, imagining the cell filling with water to the ceiling, drowning me. They'd come before I was floating lifeless. They'd never let me commit suicide, and they weren't about to let me die now.

Yes, I'd tried to commit suicide before, but you need to work yourself up to a certain pitch of despair for that. I wasn't there now. I had a brand new data gem, slipped in yesterday's otherwise empty mid-day food can. It claimed to be ancient novels from the twentieth century. Thirty of them. I hadn't even looked at the gem at all. I'd been saving it, reading my old gems: history and science, music and language, and saving the new one like a rare treat. New ones came in seldom and irregularly. I'd gladly forego a meal a day for a gem, but I never got that. This was the first new gem in three months. And now I'd die without reading one word of it.

I lurched towards my cot again. I kept the gem reader—a cheap, tiny unit of the sort you used to be able to buy for a couple of cents anywhere—and the gems in the crevice between bed and wall. Not exactly hidden. Either the cell was wired for sound and sight—and it probably was or else how could they stop all my suicide attempts in time?—and they didn't care I had it, or else it wasn't and they didn't know. No one ever came in to inspect, so no one would find it otherwise. But I kept it there so it wouldn't fall and break. The gems were my only connection to other humans: to their words, their minds, their thoughts. If I lost them, I would quickly lose whatever grip I retained on reality.

Perhaps I had, I thought, as I grabbed the gems and the reader, and wrapped the whole thing, tightly, in my coverlet. Perhaps this was all a hallucination. The coverlet ripped easily but I'd found in the past, when I'd spilled drink on it, that it was completely impermeable. Like water proof paper. I was thinking that neither gems nor reader were designed to be exposed to salt water. And if I broke them, new ones might not be provided.

Though they had to come from someone within the system, they couldn't be exactly official or else they'd not be sent inside otherwise empty food cans.

I wrapped the whole as tightly as I could, ripping the coverlet and tying it over itself. The torn strips weren't sturdy enough to hang oneself with, but they worked for this. I slipped the packet inside my suit. The water was now up to my knees.

Splashing, I drew myself up to my cot and stood on it, my hands on the ceiling for balance. That would keep me safer longer and give someone time to rescue me.

They would come. They had to come. After all my clever attempts at killing myself, they weren't going to let me die like this.

A voice screamed something outside the door. No, wait, sang. Then there was...

A flash of sound and light that glared through the hole in my door where the lock used to be. I blinked.

When I opened my eyes again, the door was open, and above the ripple caused by the door opening, standing on a broom—a little antigrav wand, forbidden for transportation in all civilized lands—was the most unlikely angel of deliverance I'd ever seen.

Setting All the Captives Free

ANGELS SHOULDN'T HAVE FACES THAT LOOKED LIKE THE RESULT of an industrial accident—perhaps an encounter with a giant cheese grater—one of their shoulders shouldn't be hunched on itself, and the entire left side of their body shouldn't droop and sag as though the muscles and bones holding it had been semi-liquified.

They shouldn't have a only a few straggles of long brown hair that looked like the rest had been plucked by a blind man wielding tweezers.

And—mark me, I'm not an expert on theology, but I'm still fairly sure of this—angels should not, under any circumstances, be singing *Women of Syracuse* at the top of their lungs while standing on a broom.

Women of Syracuse was a listing of the acts supposedly performed by these willing ladies for varying quantities of money, and, let me tell you, some of them were so inventive that even I found them odd-sounding. I'm quite sure, for instance, one's ear is not built for that.

I blinked stupidly. My savior gave me the sweetest smile I'd ever seen, despite its necessarily lopsided nature. He waved cheerily and moved on, still standing on the broom even as it sped off. Of course—I thought—angels could stand on brooms. They could fly, so if they lost the broom it wouldn't be a big deal.

9

And then I realized that the door was open and that the water level was still climbing, slowly, very slowly.

I jumped from my cot, and the water was just below my knees as I half ran, half lurched out.

My rescuer was moving from cell door to cell door, as the women of Syracuse found ever more unlikely things to do to their gentlemen friends. His burner flashed at intervals. Yells and strange inhuman-sounding laughs echoed somewhere.

The hallway had grav wells at either end. As usual, one would be rigged to go up, the other to go down. Water was pouring in a torrent through the downward one. And I was going to the upward one.

I ran towards it, then stopped just short of the grav well field.

In my mind, Ben's voice came, clear as day, *That broomer will free the people on this level, but what about the poor bastards in the cells below?* And in my mind, Ben crossed his arms and looked his most stern.

So, Ben has been dead for fourteen years and really shouldn't be talking to me like that. But this never seemed to matter to him and anyway, whether he talked to me or not was a matter between myself and him and none of anyone else's business, right? What's a minor insanity between friends?

I can't, I told him. *See the way that water is pouring? The antigrav wells are actually pulling the water downward as fast as possible. Down there, the water will be up to my neck. And I'm tall. If anyone was there, they'll be dead for sure. Now or soon enough.*

Yeah. Think about that, he said. *Think about the "soon enough."*

And I did, though I didn't want to. I remembered being down there, strapped to a chair, or strapped to the wall, while they did unspeakable things to my body with instruments no sane human could even conceive of, much less use. And then I imagined water pouring in and not being able to escape, not being able to swim, while the water climbed, climbed, climbed.

It's none of my business, I said. *I am a murderer. A monster.*

In my mind, Ben's mouth twitched with the beginning of a smile, and his dark eyes wrinkled slightly in amusement. *Now, Luce,* he said.

Which just goes to show you the damn bastard didn't play fair. He never did. Even dead fourteen years, dead at my hand for fourteen years, the stubborn cuss insisted on thinking the best of me. And now, as always, I couldn't disappoint him. Death would be easier.

My body didn't want to want to go to the lower levels. Bodies aren't stupid. They know their business is survival. I tried to overpower it with my mind, but the body would have won. Except the mind had Ben on its side and even my body wasn't able to resist the irresistible force of his belief in my non-existent goodness.

I lurched around, unsteadily, against the shrieks from my body that I should save myself, and ran to the grav well. I dropped through it, water pouring down with me, soaking my hair and clothes, and hopefully leaving the gem reader dry. Hopefully. Because when I was caught, I wanted my damn gems.

And if I just did this, Ben assured me, I wouldn't have the ghosts of the dumb bastards down here keeping him company in my head. That was incentive enough.

There were four cells down here. I remembered that from when they'd dragged me down there to torture. The nearer one was open—the door hanging on one side and blown on the other.

On the water here up to my chest, someone was floating facedown, a middle-aged, well-dressed man. I splashed over and turned him face up, then let go. First, he was Good Man Rainer. Second, there was a burner hole in the middle of his forehead. The Good Man Rainer was dead. The man who'd first sent Ben and me to jail. My mind couldn't process it and neither could Ben's ghost, who frowned distractedly but said nothing.

The next cell was still locked and it occurred to me, belatedly, I didn't have a burner. *He'll have it*, Ben said. Obviously talking about the corpse. *Remember all the bastards have burners on them at all times for self-defense.*

I told him he could search the corpse himself, but he only smiled at me in that irritating way he did when he reminded me he had no more existence than any other figment of my imagination. All I can say is that my imagination must be against me.

Trotting back against water resistance was not as easy as it seemed, and I had to swim to get a good grip on the late, departed Good Man Rainer. I might never have found the burner in time, if I hadn't got lucky. It was strapped under his pant leg, to his all-too-cold ankle. I grabbed it and sploshed back to the first cell.

Using a burner under water is always a crap shoot. You shoot and, if it's a cheap burner, it won't even produce a beam. If it's a slightly better burner, it will sort of work and shock you right back through the water. But this must have been one of the solid state ones, equipped with a laser for underwater work, because it beamed, white and hot and true, and burned the lock right out. And then nothing happened. The door didn't spring inward.

The water pressure is holding it, Ben said. *You'll have to kick it in.*

Ghosts have absolutely no sense of reality. Probably comes from not existing. To kick something under water is about as easy as to kick something in low grav—an experience I remembered from an all-too brief visit to Circum where some areas were kept at half-g.

You had to get a good hold on something. All I could get was a sort of hold on the door frame. Fortunately I'd spent the last fourteen years exercising insanely.

I got hold of the frame and kicked at the door with both feet. It opened enough to let the water flow out some and then it opened fully.

The occupant of this cell was beyond human cares. He was strapped to a chair, and floating, chair and all. And if he wasn't dead, he should be. I was no more prepared to give him regen for his eyes or to stop the blood spreading in billows in the water around him, than I was to fly. And if he wasn't dead, he'd be dead in minutes, one way or another. He was unconscious, so there was no suffering I must stop as I'd once stopped Ben's.

I turned and swam back to the next cell where I burned the lock, kicked the door in. And found myself assaulted by a madman, wrapping his hands around my neck, in what seemed like a creditable attempt at strangling me.

A good slug with the back of the burner would have coldcocked him, but then I'd have to save him. So, instead, as he scrambled for a good hold on my neck, hampered by my hand in the way, I hauled back and slapped him hard across the face, then took advantage of his confusion to point him towards the upward grav well. "That way," I said. "Go."

It was iffy whether he would, but he shook his head, then turned and swam that way. Leaving me to swim to the last closed cell and repeat the door-opening procedure.

This time I faced a young man, probably twenty-two or so, the age I'd been when they'd brought me here. Actually, he looked a lot as I had at that age, with smoothly cut hair—though his was brown—and, from what was visible of his sleeve, wearing a high-quality suit. And he was clinging desperately, with an expression of terror in his eyes, to the light fixture directly above where they normally strapped prisoners to the wall. His head was tilted back to keep his nose above water.

He stared at me as though seeing a vision of perfect horror, which I probably was. Don't know. I had been fourteen years without a mirror. I pulled myself up so I could talk and said, "Come on!"

And he tilted his head back more and spoke, the words intercut by chattering teeth. "I ca-can't. Ca-can't swim."

Damn. Yeah, I could go and leave him here to drown. He was going to slow me down, and frankly I had to leave fast. The few inches of air up there would soon be closed off by water, but I couldn't leave him here to die. I just couldn't. Ben wouldn't ever let me hear the end of it, and worse, he might acquire a buddy with brown hair and chattering teeth.

I must have expressed myself loudly and profanely. You spend too much time alone, you forget that there are thoughts that shouldn't be expressed aloud. My companion looked even more terrified and tried to shrink from me.

"Don't be stupid," I said. "Try to breathe when your head is above water, because I can't promise it will always be." And I grabbed him by the back of his suit. Expensive material ought to hold.

Then I took a deep breath, and plunged my own head under for faster speed towing him. I hadn't swum at all in more than fourteen years, and certainly hadn't swum towing someone. Halfway through the hallway, I surfaced to breathe. My charge, white as a sheet, seemed to be managing to keep his own head in the air by treading water. Good. I plunged under and dragged him again.

All the way to the antigrav well, which sucked us all the way to the upper floor.

The well was, of course, slightly dislocated from the well on the next level, so you wouldn't accidentally go all the way up. So we stumbled off the well field, sideways, and into the field of the next well, having no more than time to register that the water here was up to our knees. Then up again, and the water up above our ankles. Then up again, and the water covered our feet. I stared at the other grav well at the end of the corridor, ignoring the people swarming around.

There were broomers everywhere, some of them women. And there were fights going on between broomers and guards and, in a couple of instances, prisoners. But I just looked at the downward grav well at the end and determined that no water was falling down through that. That meant there was no water in the level above. So the hole had to be on this level, right? The hole was my chance at escaping. I wasn't about to try to leave through the main entrance. I wasn't that stupid.

A quick look, to see where the hole would be, brought an even quicker decision that it would be on the side where there were more broomers and fewer guards. Stood to reason, since guards were pouring in from above.

I grabbed my charge's wrist and pulled him in the direction where there were more broomers, and I told him, my voice little more than an exasperated puff—it's not easy running and towing a full grown man, even if he's smaller than you—"Come this way, ignore the broomers."

He hesitated a moment, then followed me. I was coming to terms, as he splashed behind me, with the thought that I'd have to tow the kid behind me no matter how far the surface was. Couldn't leave him here. He seemed about as capable of survival as the drowned baby rat he resembled. Twenty-one or twenty-two or around there, certainly not as much as twenty-five. His face was too rounded and soft for that, and his skin seemed smooth and flawless like a girl's. And he could be my son. Well, he could have been if I'd ever done anything that could have led to a son. And I didn't think so, not even when drunk out of my mind.

But he could have been. And I was the adult here, which meant he was my responsibility. What kind of species would we be, if adults didn't take the responsibility for juveniles?

Your father's species? Ben said in my mind, which only goes to show you that ghosts don't get out of breath or tired, no matter if the head that they're haunting feels as though it would very much like to have a good bout of unconsciousness.

I ran down the hallway towards where I hoped the source of

the water was. First there were ever increasing numbers of broom-ers, all of whom ignored us. If I'd had a little more breath, I'd have slugged one and stolen his broom to pull us to the surface. Except I was fairly sure I owed my freedom to them, and I refused to slug my saviors. Monster I might be, but there were limits.

Then there were no more broomers, as they were all behind me, and I could see the hole—a jagged tear in the wall of Never-Never, through which water poured. And one of the mysteries was solved for me, because someone had slapped a manhole underwater seal on the opening. Because it wasn't precisely the same shape as the opening, it allowed water to rush in around the edges. But it wasn't the torrent it would have been, had the hole been fully open. Which explained why even the lower level wasn't fully filled.

I turned to the kid behind me. "Take a deep breath. I don't know how far down we are, but the broomers came that way, so it can't be too far." I neglected to tell him that the broomers had brooms to tow them down, and therefore would have trav-eled much faster than any swimmer could. "I'll take you to the surface."

But even as I heard him draw breath, a man came through the membrane, then another. I jumped back and—this shows you how ghost-bullied I was—stood in front of the young man, as my mind realized that these men in stylish, dark suits, who clipped their brooms to their belts with military precision as they landed on this side of the membrane were not your average broomers.

In fact, they were a paramilitary unit, and only one of those deployed with brooms, so they could target problem spots in no time.

They were almost mythical, only I'd seen them once before. Scrubbers. The Good Men's secret service of last resort.

Out of Hell

SCRUBBERS WEREN'T SPIES AND THEY WEREN'T EXACTLY A MILI-
tary force. What they were was the Good Men's ultimate weapon
in opinion control. Whenever an incident occurred which might
cause public opinion to go out of control, Scrubbers were sent
in to deal with it.

Their normal approach was killing everyone and making the
bodies disappear. If you were really, really lucky, you might have
some DNA and a few scuffle marks left when they were done.
Theirs was the only avocation in which disposal of dozens of
bodies wasn't rare or incidental but a core part of their mission.

I'd met them before, once. I'd escaped with my life, barely.
Ben and I might be the only ones of their targets to ever do so.

But Ben and I had ended up in jail. That led to all the rest.

Now, my blood ran cold, and my entire body seemed to tighten
in a knot. I'd escaped that one time, but this was death. Death
for me, death for the kid I'd rescued, death for the broomers
who'd set us free. Nothing would be found of us.

And then I lost my mind. Or at least my mind let my body
spring free.

I can't explain my capacity to move really fast, and I've never
found any reference to this from anyone else, not even in the
copious literature and history gems someone had snuck to me in

the depths of Never-Never. For a long time, I'd thought it was illusory, but both in the last incident with the Scrubbers and in the many incidents that Ben and I had been involved in in our first year in a common jail, I'd found that my ability was in fact true and it could be summed up as this: When in danger or great fear, I could sometimes move at a speed above normal humans. Fast enough above normal humans that I could win against great odds.

There were six men, which was the limits of even my ability, particularly since the front one was drawing a burner, no doubt to cut us down. And I didn't want to kill. I didn't want any more deaths on my conscience, but I also didn't want to die. And I couldn't let them kill the kid.

I sprang. Kicking the gun from his hands, I punched him hard enough to shove his nose in, then flung myself sideways towards his burner because it was easier than drawing mine. I must have moved at a speed that his comrades found hard to perceive, since their burner fire followed me down, but didn't quite catch up with me. I heard the kid give a sort of gasp, and hoped it wasn't loud enough to call attention to him.

And then I was flat on my belly, with the gun in my hand, and cutting down the Scrubbers in a long, continuous scything. I didn't even have time to set the controls on the burner and it wasn't set to heat, but only to the penetration where it works like a blade. Bodies fell, cut in half. Which was good, because they were wearing the large oxygen tanks people use when they will take brooms underwater, where the mere oxygen concentrator on the broom won't be enough. And if I'd hit them with heat-burn, depending on what the tanks were made of, I'd have either blown us all up or ended up with a lovely rocket effect. But it poured out blood and guts in plentiful supply.

The kid must have been shocked enough by the sight that he didn't move. Which was bad, because the last of the Scrubbers jumped, before the beam reached him, and got behind the kid, his burner to the kid's temple. "Surrender your burner or your son gets it."

And damn it, I didn't have time to argue genealogy, any more than I had time to set the burner to burn, instead of cut. So, instead I removed my fingers from the trigger for a moment, aimed it at the man's head, faster than his eye would be able to follow or—I hoped—his hand react to, and I shot him neatly in the middle of the forehead.

It was the equivalent of running a sharp, lance-long needle, through the middle of his head. Blood and brains erupted, then poured. He spasmed once. Fortunately his hand moved from its position at the kid's temple, so the shot went straight down the hallway. Someone screamed down there.

But I was already reacting. Reacting to the falling Scrubber, reacting to the kid's turning very pale, and his eyes trying to roll up into his head, as the blood of the scrubber poured over him. Good thing we were about to go out and into seawater, right? It would get rid of most of the evidence.

I sprang, pulled the corpse away from the living boy, administered a calculated slap to the kid, and told him, "Buck up. We don't have time for nonsense."

All I can say is that he must have been raised by as strict a man as my father. His reaction to the slap and the voice of command was to come fully awake immediately, steadying himself. "You—" he said, his voice unsteady. "You killed them all."

"Yeah, kid," I said. "I'm a murderer. Why else do you think I'm in Never-Never?" As I spoke, I was unhooking the broom from the dead Scrubber's belt, and cracking the shell over the remote sensing-and-controlling unit, but not over the unit that transmitted the ignore codes.

To explain: every government broom—or military broom—came equipped with a unit that would allow your superiors to call you in, or at least bring the broom in if needed, as well as allow them to tell where you were at all times. There was another and separate unit—and I only knew this from having taken these brooms apart—that simply broadcast a code which told local authorities to ignore this broom.

Broom riding was illegal in every seacity and every continental territory, but it was routinely used by two sorts of people other than illegal broomers: people escaping flyers that were about to crash, and police or agents of the Good Men. The first type of broom had a beacon that called for the authorities to help. The second had a hush-up-ignore code. This code was generic. It wouldn't identify the broom, just let local authorities know that as far as the Good Men were concerned, it would be better for everyone to pretend the broom wasn't really there.

I left that in place because I'm not stupid, but I crushed the locator and remote with the butt of the burner. I could do a prettier job, I could. Given tools. But I didn't have tools. And I wanted the kid out of here and safe.

"Have you ever ridden a broom?" I asked.

He looked at me as if I'd asked him if he'd ever drunk the blood of a newly killed infant. "No!" Probably outraged at the idea of doing something illegal.

"Do you know how to?" I asked, and then realized how stupid I was being. Of course he knew how to. Every kid old enough to drive a flyer—which in most places was around fourteen—was required to learn how to ride a broom, since it might be his only escape from a crash, and his only hope of getting to civilization again, depending on whether he was flying over a wild zone or the sea.

"Uh...I learned...I mean..."

"Yeah," I said. "Look, this broom is a little more powerful than the rescue ones." I fumbled with the nearest dead Scrubber, and got the mask and the oxygen tank. I strapped the tank to the kid's back. "You can go higher. And faster. I don't know how far you need to go. I want you to put this on." I handed him the mask and goggles. "And I want you to hold onto the broom for dear life, and aim it up out of the water. Then stabilize and try to get to the nearest landmass or seacity where you'll be safe."

"I have friends in every—"

"Good for you." I left him holding the broom and the mask and goggles, and stripped the Scrubber who had held the kid hostage. He was the only one with an intact suit, since I had cut the others in half. Damn it. I had to learn to plan better. At least the kid wasn't wearing a prisoner's uniform.

I was, and I was also barefoot. Which meant I had to have the suit. "I don't have a suit you can use, kid," I said. "So just try to land on whatever seacity this is located in, if you truly think that there is someone who will take you in here."

"We have people in every seacity," he said. Right. From his expensive suit, he was probably a merchant's whelp, and they did tend to have vast and interlinked families.

"Good," I said, as I slipped the suit on, zipped, and turned my attention to the other brooms. The suit fit like a tourniquet and the seams were close to splitting. The dead Scrubber had been tall and well built but I'd always been outsized and now was even more so. No matter. I wasn't likely to sire any kids anyhow.

I realized the kid was still there, staring at me, as I crushed the locator and control unit on the first broom. "Why are you still here?" I asked him. "Scram. Go. Make yourself safe."

He blinked at me, as I grabbed a second broom and beat its locator out of it, then clipped it to my suit. "What are you waiting for?" I asked him.

"You...saved my life."

"Oh. And?" I hoped he didn't think this made me responsible for him forever.

"My...my name is John Jefferson."

"Ah. Good for you." I beat the brain out of the sixth and final broom, clipped all but one of them—besides the one the kid had—to my suit. Unless things on the outside had changed completely in the last fifteen years, brooms like this, with the chip disabled, were worth their weight in poppy juice, and little less in more complex designer compounds.

The kid hesitated one more second, as I collected burners and clipped them to my belt or slipped them into as many pockets as I could. Burners, too, made good trade coin, besides being good to keep you alive.

He put the mask and goggles on, slowly, looking at me in appraisal. Then he lifted his hand, his thumb and forefinger held in a circle, the other fingers up in that moment solving for me the puzzle of what a nice boy like him was doing in a joint like Never-Never.

The gesture was the benediction of the Usaians, a religious sect that seems to have its roots in a mythologizing of the old country that used to occupy much of the North American territories. I'd learned a lot about that country in the gems my unknown benefactor had provided.

Without giving me time to react, the kid faced the membrane and turned the broom on. He punched through the membrane with force, allowing a little water in, and left me to wonder if Usaians reproduced by fission. They seemed to be everywhere if one looked carefully enough.

The entire incident, subduing the Scrubbers and getting the kid out of there couldn't have taken me more than five minutes. My muscles ached in the way they did when my super-fast mode had been activated and was starting to subside. There was a good chance what had confused the kid was that I'd talked too fast also. Sometimes I wasn't aware of it.

I hesitated for a second considering whether to shout to the broomers and warn them more Scrubbers might come, then realized I was being an idiot. Chances were that the authorities would give Scrubbers a little time to clean up a problem this size. A glance down the hall told me broomers were now going up the antigrav well to the next level, a lot of prisoners with them.

Strength to their burner arm, Ben said in my head, and for once he was only echoing what I thought.

I put on the mask and the goggles, grabbed one of the brooms, activated it, and punched through the membrane into freezing ocean water.

Stranger in a Strange Land

I RAN OUT OF WATER BEFORE MY LUNGS BURST AND EMERGED into air, gulping and sputtering and making a noise that sounded all too much like a whine.

They say riding a broom is like walking. Once you've learned it, the body remembers, and you can default to it without thinking.

It must be true, because I was terrified, my mind frozen in the grip of gibbering fear, but my body somehow leveled off the broom, so I wasn't flying straight up to nowhere, but flying level, at about the normal altitude for a broom over the sea, slightly lower than flyers, where you could pass more or less unnoticed to traffic control sweeps. Or where they could at least pretend they didn't notice you.

Meanwhile, my eyes were trying to make sense of what they saw. I know this sounds odd, but it took me time to figure out what part was the sky and what the sea, and the immensity of it still seemed unbelievable to my brain. After the tiny confines of my grey cell, with its safe walls, for so long, this seemed dangerous. I felt exposed, like a man does when he's naked in a crowd, or standing alone and unarmored in front of guns.

I kept feeling as though I would fall, not just down from the broom, but sideways too, and maybe upward. I mean, there was no stop there, nothing to hold me in place. I could float away like a balloon into the shining blue and—

23

I think it was that image of me floating away like a balloon that brought me to myself. It was so ridiculous, and so completely unlikely. I took deep breaths and tried to relax the grip of my hands on the broom, because I was holding it so tightly that my knuckles not only shone white through the skin but hurt as if I were about to break them.

Instead, I set about getting coordinates on where I was. Having broken the locator chip, I was left to figuring this out by memory. The landmass directly to my right, the landmass over Never-Never, which I'd never been able to identify the night they'd dragged me here—still in shock at Ben's miserable death and beaten to near unconsciousness—was unmistakably Syracuse Seacity. That meant my home, the home of my childhood and the seat of my father's cursed rule, Olympus Seacity, would be north-northeast and about three hours.

Which was fine by me, because I wasn't going there. There wasn't enough money in the entire Earth to pay me to confront my father again. I remembered what he had said, as he pronounced verdict on my first conviction in the council of Good Men. I couldn't believe he didn't also know about what had happened to Ben and my transfer to Never-Never. If I met Father again, I'd have to kill him. If not for my false conviction, if not for the death of my lair mates, if not for Ben's death, then for having forced me to stay damnably alive through each of my suicide attempts.

The technology they'd employed, particularly to save me from the last one, five years ago, was expensive enough that the order to use it had to have come from my father, heartless bastard that he was. Oh, I missed Max and I'd like to see my mother again, at least once. But seeing Mother and finding out if Max even knew I existed anymore, since my little brother had been all of three when I was arrested, would wait. There were better ways to die than walking straight into the lion's den and demanding he eat you. And Father would be looking for me right about now, or in a couple of hours, as soon as he realized I'd escaped. He'd be looking for me to slam me back in prison. Because he wouldn't allow me to die, but he also wouldn't allow me to escape. I suspected he kept me alive to keep Mother from getting too upset. But he wouldn't ever again recognize me as his son or allow me freedom. And it wasn't even because of the supposed murder or the real one. Father took having someone killed as his prerogative. That would not be enough for him to cast me away. I could never figure out why he had, unless he hated me like fire.

So, no Olympus for me. What other seacity could I go to? There was always Liberte, only a few miles south from here. I thought I would go there and land somewhere in one of the lower-priced areas. I thought some of the fences I used to know would still be operational and I could get rid of my burners and brooms.

But then an odd thing happened. Flying there was easy. It was early evening and I saw no more signs of life than the occasional shadow of a flyer overhead, or a boat in the water, far below. I became better used to the expanses of sea and sky and got misty-eyed at the sun, setting in a glory of gold and red to the west. I thought that even if I got captured tonight; even if they hauled me back to the cell again, I'd have the memory of this flight, the memory of sunset and sea, and the tang of salt in my nose to take with me to captivity. I touched the suit over where the gems and reader sat.

As the skyline of Liberte became visible in the horizon, I had a momentary pang for the society of humans. There were humans in Liberte. Not many of them. I don't think the entire seacity ever had more than a million inhabitants. It wasn't really a seacity like Syracuse, or even Olympus, colonized in levels and populated by both rulers and bureaucracy and workers.

Liberte owned another seacity whole—Shangri-la, which had been a mobile seacity in the old days—and Shangri-la was the working seacity, with industry and farming all around it. In Liberte the apparatus of state and its functionaries resided, and the island, carefully landscaped in slopes and terraces, looked like a garden, carefully cultivated from its Good Man's residence at the summit to the white sand beaches disappearing into the carefully kept-clear waters.

This is not to say the island didn't have a seedier part. Of course it did. Not only did the maids and gardeners have to live somewhere, but cheaper restaurants and hotels will appear to cater to them, and other service industries of a less strictly approved of kind will spring up, unbidden, to cater to all classes of inhabitants.

For a moment I was taken with a physical, almost aching, craving for that type of service, or to be honest, for someone I could pay enough to let me hold him through the night. Just the idea of warm body in my arms appealed to me with the same intensity as food appeals to a starving man.

When I was a child or a young man, I didn't particularly like to be touched. Oh, I endured it from some people, my mother most of all, since she liked to hug me and brush my hair with her fingers. And later I enjoyed it from lovers.

But I didn't know it was possible to crave just the touch of human flesh, of human warmth, even when it didn't mean sex or even affection—just the idea of being held by another human made me ache with need.

I managed to get within sight of the shores of Liberte.

And then the sound hit me. I can't explain it. It was, I think, the sound of any inhabited area.

Music and voices, the hum of flyers, the roar of the occasional boat beneath, whistles and honks, all melded and fused into a low roar. It should have been welcoming and familiar.

It should, but I'd spent fourteen years hearing nothing but the occasional distant, echoing voice, too far away to be able to identify the words. The noise made me shake. My hands clenched very hard on the broom again.

I told myself I was being an idiot. But my body clenched and my mind panicked at the thought, at the idea of all those people—all of them near me, moving, talking.

I couldn't. It was too much. Too much noise, too much movement, too much light.

The broom had somehow turned itself around and I was headed out to open ocean, and Ben protested in my mind, *Luce! You have to conquer it. You can't live on open sea.*

And I tried to tell him I needed more time, I needed more courage, I needed—

Meanwhile I was flying fast, fast, away from the city, away from all the cities. Away from humanity.

After a while I saw a small islet in the ocean. I flew over a small group of isles, and found it. Though it wasn't small enough to be underwater at high tide, it was small enough that I doubted there had ever been a human habitation there. Fishermen from the nearer large island might come there if there was good fishing around it, but—as I drew near and realized how craggy its sides were—that was unlikely, since mooring there would be a right bitch. Perhaps courting couples flew out there now and then to picnic, but I doubted that too. As I got nearer and saw it was little more than black rock jutting out of the sea, with some mosslike growths in its lowest spots, and a lot of seagulls gathered on it and flying around it. Their cries were deafening in the air.

I stopped on the highest crag, and sat on it, watching the sun setting. *You have to face civilization sometime,* Ben said, and he was right, of course, but sometimes a man needs time and space to deal with things.

All right, he said, as though it were a great concession. *This night then. At any rate if people are looking for you, this is safer. No one who knew you will imagine you just veered off to sleep on a crag in the sea.*

I found a spot where a piece of rock kind of overhung me, anyway, on the reasoning that I didn't want anyone overflying the islet to see me lying there and come down to investigate. But the true reason—it being nighttime and the islet having no lights, and travelers in flyers not being likely to look too closely below—was that I couldn't face the idea of sleeping uncovered and open to the sky above. I was afraid I'd wake up dreaming of floating away into the blue.

As I was half asleep, a smothered laugh shook me. I'd dreamed of sleeping in warm, living arms, and here I was, wedged in rock, cold, alone.

But in that space between awaking and sleep, I heard Ben's voice, *You always have me.* And I fell asleep to the feeling that he was right there, with me, under that rock.

Don't Look Now

I WOKE UP CRAMPED AND SHIVERING. LIGHT WAS SHINING IN MY eyes, and I was shaking. My head felt achy and my eyes gritty, as I blinked dumbly at the rock and sand in front of my eyes, pelted by a steady fall of rain. I was wedged sideways into a narrow crevice in black rock, with more of the rock about a foot above my head. And my nose was full of sea and sand, my ears full of the seagull screams that filled the air.

Moving brought protesting aches from joints and muscles and my body felt like it would never be warm enough again. Despite the insulating qualities of the Scrubber suit, it had been thoroughly soaked in saltwater by the time I crawled in here, which meant it had leeched the cold from the rock and right into my flesh and bones.

Now it had dried, in sea-salt patches, though as far as I could tell at least the blood and brains of the last occupant had been thoroughly washed away. I wondered if the kid I'd freed had made it somewhere safe, or if he'd got himself recaptured and imprisoned again. But I'd done what I could for him, and hanging out with me wouldn't have made him any safer.

If I knew Father, and I did from my escapades when I was much younger, right about now he would have figured out I'd escaped Never-Never and he'd be screaming bloody murder, wouldn't he? And when Father screamed, things got set in motion, starting with his henchmen, who would be looking for me high and low. There was only one of me, and Father had a lot of henchmen. Sooner or later, they'd find me. Unless I was very careful. It would have been harder to be as careful and as ruthless as I needed to be while protecting a hapless kid, who was little better than an infant when it came to saving himself. Hopefully he'd found shelter with other Usaians, who indeed existed in every land and seacity, though the religion had been illegal for at least a hundred years and I suspected for longer than that.

And besides, you couldn't wait to get rid of human company, Ben said in my head.

I shrugged. I would have to brave human company this morning, at any rate, because I was starving, and I wasn't willing to live on fresh killed uncooked seagull or even seaweed—all this isle was likely to offer in the way of breakfast.

Crawling out cautiously into the pelting rain, I was surprised to find it only a little cold, though that made sense, since it had been early winter when I was captured, and it was fifteen years later, just about. I breathed the sea air for a while, feeling the rain caress me and washing away the salt from my suit and hair. I tried not to think of what I looked like. A hand run casually across my cheeks informed me my beard had come in, as it usually did over twenty-four hours, forming a sand-papery texture and probably—hard to tell without mirrors—a visible fuzz on my skin. Being blond it wouldn't be too visible, I told myself, and as disreputable as I was likely to look, I wouldn't be going to any part of any town where that would stick out. At worst people would think I was a junkie who had given up on his appearance. Plenty of those in any of the seedier areas of seacities. No one would notice, much less try to interfere with one of them.

I ran my fingers through my hair. It is straight, and it had grown over the last fourteen years, to just touching the end of my spine. My choices for managing it had been to either let it grow as it had, or to rub the same cream on my scalp that I rubbed on my beard. I didn't fancy a completely bald head, so I'd let the hair grow. Normally I combed it through with my fingers in the vibro, and then tied it back, making a knot out of it. I now did that, with a little more difficulty since there were salt tangles in it, and tied it low at the base of my cranium.

Then I checked all my possessions and braved myself to face the fleshpots of Liberte. Right now the kind of flesh I was most interested in was a slice or two of beef and maybe some eggs, but fleshpots, a word from a religious book in the reading gems, seemed an appropriate term, nonetheless. They'd be teeming with all-too-corporeal humans, a strange and alarming idea for a man who'd consorted only with a ghost for fourteen years.

I'd had time to get used to the idea—or at least that's my explanation for why this time I managed to land without turning tail and bolting. I was still spooked—I still felt out of place. I still wanted to cringe and hide. But I'd stand my ground.

It reminded me of when I was seven and Mom had insisted to my father that I be allowed to attend a big party the estate was giving for all the children of retainers, functionaries and servants. It had been a fateful party, in a way, because at that party I'd met Ben, who was exactly my age, and we'd found out that we lived a stone's throw from each other, since his family's relatively modest mansion was just across a side avenue from the palace. As it should be, since Ben's much older brother and guardian, Samuel, was the main manager of my father's properties and general factotum of his business and household. From there to one or the other of us studying how to get over the wall with the complicity of guards who had doubtless been told by my mother to leave us alone, was a matter of days, and after that we'd been inseparable.

But part of the reason that Ben and I had taken to each other initially was that we'd both been hugging the fringes of the crowd, feeling strange, out of place and more than a little scared in the middle of that crowd of shrieking, running, talking children.

I was then an only child, and would be for another eleven years, before Max was born. Given my birth status and the care that Father had with me—which even then seemed to be more concerned with keeping me alive than with keeping me in any way happy, or well educated, or even obedient—I was rarely allowed to see children, and I'd never been in the middle of a large group of them. Mine was a solitary childhood, carefully watched by nannies, and more exactingly educated by Mother, who taught me herself, as well as hiring tutors to teach me what she didn't know. I'd enjoyed myself, in my own way, with reading and virtus programs, and playing in the garden, and I didn't realize it wasn't normal to have no friends beside a rather dumb blond setter dog.

Ben, in turn, was younger than his brother by more than twenty years, the last child, born of a second marriage, in a family of hereditary retainers to the Keevas. His life probably wasn't as solitary as mine. He was allowed to play with a few of the better born children in the city. But like me he didn't attend learning programs, and he didn't meet up with any large number of children at one time.

Entering that room, with a hundred and some children screaming and running and fighting and laughing, had given me an instant panicky feeling of being outnumbered. I'd ensconced myself at a corner, with my back protected from any sneak attacks and stood there, shaking, terrified that anyone would try to fight me or, even worse, talk to me.

No one did. I guess they'd all been warned I was the Good Man's son. No one even got near until Ben had come, sidling along the wall, his back against it, looking about as scared as I felt. And because he looked scared, I could talk to him, and eventually find out he wasn't the frightened mouse he looked.

I hadn't felt so scared since. Eventually I'd found my way out into the world beyond my father's walls. No matter how little he liked having me out of his sight (and he didn't like it at all), I'd not only learned to navigate occasions of state, banquets of Good Men, and the company of their heirs, but I'd on my own—with Ben's complicity, of course—found my way to the lowest dives in most seacities: the hangouts of working men, and the hangouts of men who didn't work at all. Pubs and taverns, diners and broomer lairs, fences and dealers of smuggled goods. At one time, if the place opened off a narrow street populated by workers and those who labored in the gray and black economy, it would have been my natural habitat and I'd have moved through it as contentedly as a fish in the sea.

But now I clung to the walls and walked looking straight ahead. I wasn't bothered, anyway. Men my size rarely are, and I suspected my fear was translating itself into a death-glare, threatening bodily harm to anyone who came near or even looked at me twice. People gave me embarrassed looks, or glanced quickly away.

The first fence I knew in Liberte was gone. The place where it had been had become a restaurant, advertising "cheap steak," so

I didn't think they still operated. And if they did, I wasn't likely to know how to go about signaling what I wanted.

The next one I remembered, Lupin and Sons, was still the same dive I remembered, a narrow hole in the wall of a shop, the shop window filled with dusty bric-a-brac, in a pile and in no particular order, antique candlesticks and modern cheap power pack holders mingling with old clothes, boots that looked like they were walked into holes before being put on the shelf, and, disconcertingly, a stuffed squirrel, which had been there at least sixteen years. Its little beady glass eyes glared resentfully from under a layer of dust and cobwebs. For reasons known only to someone I hoped never to meet, it had been outfitted in miniature broomer kit, and was holding a tiny toy burner in its clawed fingers.

The operators didn't recognize me as I came in, which was odd since the man behind the counter was old Francois and his helper was his son Louis who was about my age and now had a receding airline. I knew they hadn't recognized me because they both stared at me and I saw Louis's hand move beneath the counter, doubtless reaching for the burner he kept there. The stories I'd heard was that no one tried to rob old Lupin's twice. And since they kept the police properly bribed, their business remained profitable and stable.

I said the words I had learned eighteen years ago, and which I hadn't had to use since, since after the first few trades they'd known me. I'd sold clothes here, as well as some minor pieces of jewelry. My own jewelry, my only source of money, since Father kept me short of cred gems. "Robespierre sent me."

Louis didn't relax, or move his hand from under the counter, but Francois stared at me, with a slow intent look, then held onto his son's arm, as if to prevent him drawing, and said something quickly in the old French patois that is still used *en famille* in Liberte.

Then he said, looking up at me still, "It's been a long time."

I swallowed hard. "Yes," I said. "But I'd like to do some business."

He inclined his head. For a moment I expected him to tell me that they didn't want my business. I wondered if the wanted bulletin for me had already gone out, and if no one, not even the demi-monde, would trade with me. But then Francois looked up and said, "Show me."

I showed them. Four of the brooms and about half the burners. I don't know what it says about their business that they didn't even ask me where I'd got those highly unusual brooms, or those weapons of such high range of fire, and so completely blank of all identification. Instead, they looked each piece over carefully, noted the dents where I'd disabled the tracking chips, and then old Francois made his bid, higher than I expected, "Five hundred narcs."

I was so shocked, as I'd been expecting something closer to fifty, that I almost forgot I was supposed to bid him up, which of course I did. You wouldn't want to take the first price he offered. You couldn't, without making him suspect there was another tracking chip in there, one designed to get proof of his misdeeds.

I bid in at twelve hundred and we settled at eight hundred. I had no idea what prices were like now, but this should allow me to get other clothes, if I weren't extravagant, and to get myself cleaned, and probably to live for a good week. I doubted I had a week with Father on my trail, but if I were still free by then, perhaps I'd have a better idea of what I could do with myself.

At any rate I made a mental note that Francois paid a lot more for brooms and weapons than for jewels.

I half expected to find that the price of the things I needed had crept up and out of sight too, but when I bought a used but in good condition suit from Francois, he charged me only five narcs, despite its being good material and Francois knowing how much I had in my pouch. I kept the boots, which were seawater stained, but in good condition and nondescript. The broomer suit to go over my street clothes was only fifteen narcs, despite being leather and insulated. I rented a cube and fresher in the next building—by the hour, no questions asked, but the fresher was a water-powered one, the soap was good and if the building was mostly used by prostitutes, they were clean prostitutes—the whole cost me only two narcs for the hour.

The steaming hot shower felt like heaven on my salt-covered body, and I washed as I hadn't in years. I decided that I didn't care if vibro fresher sessions made you as clean or cleaner than water, they didn't feel that way. And I liked feeling clean.

I opened the sterile toiletries pouch that came with the cube, and got beard-cream, and a comb. There was a mirror just outside the fresher, and for a moment I felt like I was staring at a total stranger. Oh, I'd seen myself before, of course. But not my face. Not face to face. Not to stare myself in the eyes. And seeing my face and my body, facing me, realizing it was me was an odd experience that brought with it a sense of disconnect.

I hadn't grown since I'd been in jail. My height was the same, or just about. Everything else was different. I knew my body had changed a lot since then, mostly because of my rigorous exercise program. I'd acquired definition and slabs of muscle, but my mental image of myself was still of a tall, lanky young man who'd grown too fast to fill in. A twenty-two-year-old with ribs you could see through his skin and a thin face with terrified eyes. Which didn't look at all like the thirty-seven-year-old in the mirror, facing me.

I'd untied my hair before climbing in the shower, and now, as I combed it free of tangles, I was glad it hadn't started to recede yet. It had been fifteen years since I'd seen myself in the mirror, and a receding hairline might have killed me. There might be white in the hair, though I couldn't find any. At any rate, it wouldn't be too visible among the golden blond mass.

I found a proper tie for it this time, a scrap of black ribbon that had tied together the toiletries in their pouch.

The biggest difference in me was the scar that went from just under my right eye, cut across my nose and all the way to the left ear lobe. That had been from the suicide attempt in which I'd tried to crush my face in with the cot. It had worked so far as to crush my nose. I remembered gasping desperately for air as I drowned in my own blood. But when I'd awakened my nose had been regened. I never figured out why they couldn't regen away the scar. Regen sometimes failed to work on some things, and perhaps that was all that had happened. I'd known it was there, because I could feel it with my fingers before. Mind you, it wasn't very obvious, just a faint pinkish line, but it made me look vicious and battle-hardened. The other scars that couldn't be regened, a mass on my right wrist, from when I'd managed to gnaw through to the vein, the low, semicircular jagged scar in my lower abdomen from my previous encounter with Scrubbers, and the myriad small, odd scars from the tender mercies of Never-Never torturers would be hidden by the suit, which I pulled on.

It was a little tight. Not too much. My mental image of myself might be that of a twenty-two-year-old stripling, but I'd guess that old Francois had only shown me what might have fit me—and fit me it did, a well-made tunic and pants in serviceable blue cloth, which hugged my body like a second skin. I slipped on the new broomer suit—another five narcs—not that I intended on flying just yet, but it would keep me from being asked too many questions. I'd made sure it was black with no markings, so no rival lair could take offense at my being in their territory. After I'd put the boots on, I was ready to face the world. Well, at least that part of the world outside the doors, which I navigated by clinging to the walls, and sliding from hole-in-the-wall shop entrance to hole in the wall shop window, until I came to a diner.

It was the sort of cramped place that serves all meals at any time. They catered to working people who worked in shifts on the few algae farms nearby, and who might well be having breakfast at sunset. This being neither sunset nor sunrise, nor the noon hour, the clientele was sparse and quiet, mostly one or two people per table, and a few at the counter that ran the length of the diner, facing the automated kitchen. I'd heard some of these programmed the robots to carry on conversations with the customers, though it had always evaded me why anyone would want to carry on a conversation with a thing that looked like a metallic column with arms that ended in pincers and spatulas and whatnot.

This wasn't that sort of establishment. The tables didn't even have an interactive surface. Ordering was by means of punching buttons on a little plaque beside the table and popping your credgem into the little circular slot, then out again. And the drinks didn't arrive via a chute on the table, but by one of columnar robots delivering it. And the robots didn't chatter, so the customers had to provide their own conversation.

I sat at the corner table, my back to the wall, and listened to the desultory conversations, mostly from those sitting at the counter. They were the conversations people anywhere will have. Jobs and love affairs, how good or bad the food is, and how expensive things had got. Not that my meal was that expensive, though certainly, guns and stealth brooms seemed to be out of sight—though those weren't mentioned by anyone.

My food was decently cured ham and eggs, cornbread muffins, and coffee black as my soul. I ate and drank with relish, since the food provided in Never-Never might be nutritious and have all needed vitamins and minerals. Certainly, I'd never gotten ill because of any lack in it, but a man does get tired of green salty mush and pink sweet mush with no other taste.

After a while I started feeling as though I must have a target on my back. It wasn't what anyone said. It was what no one said. No one mentioned the break out of Never-Never. Fine, I could even understand that, to an extent, since after all Never-Never was a secret prison. I mean, even I hadn't been sure it existed, even if I'd heard rumors, until I found myself in it.

But still, the Usaian kid couldn't have been the only one who'd escaped. The broomers had penetrated it, and I suspected even though any number had been recaptured, surely a good number of prisoners had made it out. Many of these men would have been put away for a decade or more. How could they reappear whether their story was believed or not, without its being in the news, somewhere? By now, surely, some of these people would have heard of it. Particularly since most escaped prisoners, like me, would make a beeline for this sort of neighborhood.

But there was nothing. Just talk of everyday, humdrum events. And I wanted to bite my nails. It ruined my enjoyment of my third cup of coffee. There was only one reason I could think of for this kind of silence, and that was that Father meant to entrap me—to get me feeling safe, to...

But that didn't make sense. This wasn't even Father's seacity. Here his power was at most limited by whatever influence he might have over Good Man Jean-Batiste St. Cyr. I didn't remember the two even being particularly friendly. My father associated with Good Man Sinistra and Good Man Rainer, mostly. Not St. Cyr. Which was why the joint raid on our lair had shocked me so much.

By the time I'd finished my food, I was dying for news. Daily news, the sort of news that would be available. Oh, they'd be censored. Most news outlets had been throughout the centuries except for a mythical time, in a mythical place. But you still could glean a lot from what was said. And what wasn't.

I looked in the menu, hoping to find it, and there it was. In the better establishments, even fifteen years ago, you could call up the daily news on your table top for free, but in this level of establishment, you had to pay for your news. I guessed it kept the price of food lower. I ordered up a newsreader, loaded with the news of the last year—because if I was going to read, I might as well get myself up to date. I ordered the cheapest one, reading and not virtus, and the robot delivered a small, square, greasy unit, which I wiped with a napkin before activating it.

The holographic letters formed in front of my eyes, though they'd look unreadable to anyone else, mere shadows on my face.

There was nothing in the reports about my escape, or anyone's escape, or any prison. There weren't even any bulletins for any escaped persons. There was talk of rebels and attacks by something called Sons of Liberty, which sounded like a pretentious name for a broomer lair. Then I found an article where they were identified as the fighting arm of the Usaians which almost made me wonder who was crazy. The Usaians were religious nutters waiting for their prophet to come back, when their land would be restored to them by miraculous means. I'd never heard of their doing anything related to violence. From the stories, though, maybe that unrest justified the price of burners and brooms. At least I was going to assume the usual censure applied and that the Good Men were not as blameless in the face of ruffians as they made themselves appear. So...a low-level civil war was going on.

I flipped backward through the date pages, trying to find the date of this rebellion and what might have sparked it. And froze looking at the news a day back, feeling as though I were dreaming, because the headline was *Good Man Keeva Found Murdered*.

For a moment, I rejoiced, thinking the old bastard was dead. No wonder he wasn't chasing me. But then I thought of Mother and Max. Max would be very young. Eighteen? Nineteen? Around there somewhere. Had he inherited? Was he prepared for it? I didn't want to take the rule away from him—I doubted that I could make a claim, with my criminal record and all. Too easy to discredit. I was sure the old man had written me out of his will. If Max wanted to rule, he was welcome to it, but on the other hand was he ready? Or was he scared? And would he greet his older brother come back from the dead, as friend or foe?

My mind in turmoil, I read on, and froze again. It wasn't Good Man Dante Keeva, but Good Man Maximilian Keeva who had been found practically dissected, in such a way forensic investigators were sure he'd been kept alive until the last possible moment while his body was taken apart piece by piece.

I stared at a holo of Max just before his ascension to the honors of Good Man, which apparently had occurred a year ago. A picture of my face as I remembered it, but perhaps more open and happier than I'd ever been, smiled back into my eyes. He'd been chubbier than I'd been. Not fat. Just better padded features, the ruddy tan of a healthy, outdoorsy young man and a smile that could drown out the midday sun.

Something like a tidal wave of grief hit me, submerging me. Oh, Max, Max, damn it. In my mind, he was a little boy, of four or five, playing around me, trying to get my attention, clambering onto my lap to be read to. Falling asleep in my arms at the end of the day, while Mother smiled at both of us, a happy protective smile.

How could this happen? And why? And what must Mother feel? And why would the best one die young, while the irredeemable son would stay alive, persist in living despite all?

I realized there were tears dripping from my chin, and wiped them, hastily, with my sleeve. This was neither the time nor the place to engage in public displays of grief. A large and intimidating man in broomer leathers I might be, but if I sat here crying like a little girl, people would get the idea I was an easy mark. Besides, something my father had trained me in, despite all, was deportment in public. The Good Man was the face of his territory. He should display neither happiness nor sorrow, neither confusion nor embarrassment. He should be always impassive, confident and composed, so the people knew he wasn't one of them: not a simple mortal man, at the mercy of his emotions, but someone born and bred to rule. Father said that that feeling of separation was better protection than all the bodyguards in the world.

I got the tears to stop after a while. I tried to retreat into my mind, to achieve that state in which I'd convinced myself that Ben's voice, his memory in my mind came from elsewhere, that they were in fact his ghost. But Ben wasn't there. And if he'd truly been a ghost, wouldn't he have told me Max had died?

I bit the inside of my cheek till that pain distracted me from the less physical pain.

What to do now? I had half thought of hanging around in this kind of area, until I could afford surgery to change my features, and then perhaps get some manual labor somewhere, until I could acquire some useful occupation. Any useful occupation. I liked learning and had a turn for organizing things. I'd been sure I could support myself.

But now everything had changed. My father and Max were both gone. The article said that the Good Men would gather shortly—perhaps as early as a month—to decide who got Olympus.

This had happened five or six times in history. A family died out without descendants and another Good Man annexed their territories. It was what happened with Shangri-la. What it meant in practice was that the city left leaderless became subjected to the other city. Its hereditary retainers were despoiled of their positions and, over time, the absorbed territory lost its economic status and its wealth, as the absorbing territory claimed pride of place and everything of any value.

Ben's family were second only to mine in Olympus, but that wouldn't last. Not if another Good Man took over. And they weren't the only ones. There was a never-ending hierarchy under them, most of it hereditary. They'd immediately become subordinate to even the lowest servants of whoever took over. Their homes would be taken, their possessions looted. And though it was never mentioned in the news, and would be denied if it had been, there were stories one heard. Intrigues and assassinations. Even the widows of Good Men weren't safe. Anyone who might wield the smallest amount of power by tradition or custom would be despoiled, reduced, removed, until the people were left leaderless and ready to accept the new leader.

My life wasn't worth much. And my rule would be worth even less. I'd never been trained in it. But if I claimed the isle, I could protect Olympus. Now that there were no other candidates of the blood left to rule, no one could really dispute my right.

I could at least protect Mother and our retainers. And I could find out who had killed Max. I read the description of how they'd found him and shuddered. If this had been done by the Sons of Liberty, they'd answer to me. I'd personally destroy them one by one.

The one thing I knew for sure was that Max might look like me, but, having known him when he was very young and unable to disguise what he was, I could tell that there had been no malice in him. I knew he could not possibly have grown up to deserve this fate. And I would find the ones who had killed him and I would relish wielding the power of the Good Man of Olympus if it meant I could torture them as they'd tortured Max.

I stood up from the booth and got ready to claim my inheritance.

Long Live the Good Man

OLYMPUS SEACITY IS, PERHAPS APPROPRIATELY, MORE VERTICAL than most seacities, climbing up to a high summit where my ancestral palace was, occupying the center of carefully tended gardens, surrounded by high walls. Around it, in almost defensive array, stood the mansions of our favored retainers.

I knew several ways into the palace. Ben and I had started getting around security, probably with Mother's behind-the-scenes help, when we were very young, but by the time we were teens, we knew how to exploit real security flaws.

There was a way to go around the back, over the wall, into the trees in the garden, and then to a spot where there were no cameras, and from there to my room. For a moment I considered it, but it would be insane.

If anyone in there remembered me—well, the retainers would and I hoped Mother did too—most would think I was long dead. One doesn't come back from the dead by sneaking into one's old room and pretending to simply have overslept by fifteen years or so.

No, when returning from the dead it behooves the newly alive man to make as much of a splash as possible. Knock on the doors, rattle the windows, demand that his shocked retainers put silk attire on his back and rings upon his hands. At least that's how every fairytale treated the lost prince.

41

I didn't know how I'd deal with it, if the front gate had been closed, but it wasn't. Even stranger, the guards normally stationed at it didn't stop me, or even look at me twice as I walked up the long drive that led to the front door.

I'd heard it said that some Good Men's palaces were architectural witnesses to hereditary madness. Syracuse's for instance is almost a declaration of paranoia in cement and stone, with staircases that lead nowhere, sudden drops at the end of a passage, and all the style and taste of a brothel. A cheap brothel.

Our family's madness seemed to be of the more controlled kind. The kind of control in a fist that clenches tight over the levers of power and will never let go.

It was rectangular and sprawling, and perfectly symmetrical, its front displaying a broad, white dimatough staircase leading to a shining door that looked like crystal, but was translucent dimatough.

I'd never seen the door closed during the day, but it was closed now. Maybe this explained the gate being open, or the inattention of the guards. Or perhaps it was that they didn't have anything real to guard anymore. After all, the Good Man was dead. Both of them. But I wasn't going to think about that, because this truly was not the time to cry over Max.

Instead, I gritted my teeth and walked straight up to the door, and thumbed the comlink lever next to it. Looking through the slightly green-tinted sheen obscuring the doorway was like looking through a heavy sheet of falling water. It took a moment for anyone to respond, and I thought when they did that I'd ask to speak to Patrician Isabella Keeva. Best to be admitted to Mama's presence, and explain everything to her, then let her make the announcement to the family and get the lawyers to deal with the legal issues.

I wasn't sure how Mother would feel about me, but grieved and horrified though she might be, I couldn't imagine a time or place where she wouldn't love me or be on my side, even if I'd turned into a monster.

But when a voice said, "What do you wish?" creakingly, from the other side, my body apparently had different plans from my carefully thought out ones. I heard the words that came out of my lips in utter disbelief, "This is Good Man Lucius Keeva. Open the door."

There was a long silence, then an almost scared squeak, all the stranger since it sounded like it came from a grown man. "What?"

"I am Good Man Lucius Dante Maximilian Keeva. Open the door."

From the scuffles and sounds and the shifting shadows and movements on the other side, the squeaky-voiced man called a hysterical woman, who called a booming-voiced man, who in turn called another man, who called a woman, who called another woman.

As the discussion on the other side reminded me of nothing so much as three catfights going on all at once, another voice came in. At first I couldn't hear it at all, just the sort of vibration that indicated someone was speaking in normal tones and at a reasonable volume in the middle of the cacophony.

Strangely, this caused the other voices to stop, and I heard what seemed the last words of his sentence. "No, he's not dead. Yes, of course it could be him."

The squeaky-voiced man said in the tone of someone accusing someone else in a crime, "He looks just like Patrician Maximilian Keeva. Older."

"Yes," the controlled, patient voice said. "He would. About eighteen years older."

And even through the door, attenuated, I'd recognized the voice. It was Samuel Remy, Ben's much older brother, my father's steward and man of affairs, and the only person who'd ever treated me like a son.

I heard locks slide and bolts pulled, and wondered why they were barricaded in the house. Then I remembered the seacity was up for grabs, and it wouldn't be the first time nor probably the last that a Good Man solved that kind of issue by force, ahead of official meetings and declarations.

Finally, a pale face looked up at me. It was endowed with two dark eyes, and the hair above it was mostly white, but I remembered it mousy brown, and the face found a place in my mind as Savell, my father's butler.

"Hello, Savell," I said, smiling. "It's certainly been a long time."

His eyes widened at me. Whatever instrument he'd seen me on before—I seemed to remember a holo viewer just inside the door, to screen visitors, though the door was never closed and anyway I didn't open the door myself, ever—must have failed to get the full effect of my scarred face, my bulk, and my attire. Now he gave me a quick up and down look, and seemed just a little scared.

But my manner, cordial but distant, had been perfect to etiquette, and that probably helped him steady himself, because he swallowed once or twice, then flung the door open, and stood straighter, saying in perfect butler-mode, "So it has, sir. Welcome home."

I stepped into the front hall of my ancestral home. Like the outside, it was of classical design and might have been more at home in the eighteenth century than in the twenty-fifth—or even the twenty-second, when it had been built. Oh, the yellow and black tiles, laid in squares on the floor were probably dimatough, rather than marble. And the high vaulted ceiling overhead was probably poured dimatough rather than plaster, the same way that the massive chandelier hanging from the middle of it was probably transparent ceramite rather than crystal, but it was the sort of home that a well-to-do Englishman of the eighteenth century would have recognized.

Only even I had trouble recognizing my retainers. Not that they had changed. The two women hugging each other and looking at me as though I were holding burners to their heads were, I was fairly sure, the housekeeper and the second floor manager. The man with his mouth wide open and the sort of look like he expected me to pull out a weapon and mow him down, was the chef. Behind him, holding a rolling pin as a defensive weapon, was our baker. Other people in various positions of defense or incredulity were known to me as household personnel. The lanky blond man against the wall, turned pale as milk, with most of his fist crammed in his mouth was a total unknown, but—from his grey pants and shapeless grey tunic—was a secretary or clerk.

In the middle of all this, Samuel Remy looked odd by looking perfectly normal and perfectly calm. "Sir," he said. "Welcome home. It is a relief to find you are alive and able to assume your place."

"What if he isn't?" the chef said.

"What?" Samuel asked, wheeling around on him.

"What if it isn't him? They do wonderful things with surgery, you know? I wouldn't put it past—"

Samuel inhaled, noisily, and I thought he was going to scream, but when he spoke, his voice was perfectly composed. "What test would satisfy you? I recognize Patrician Lucius, but if you don't..."

I understand he's much changed. So, what test would satisfy you? Would it be proven he's himself if he can open the genlocks? As we know all males in the line have close enough DNA to do it."

There were scattered nods of agreement, though the blond man by the wall scrabbled with his feet at the floor and managed to get yet more of his fist into his mouth, which didn't stop something much like a shriek from escaping.

Samuel Remy looked at me, and I saw he was trying to phrase this as a polite request. I decided to make it easier for him. "I don't mind, Sam," I said. I'd never called him Sam, but my father had, and it seemed like I should. "Will my father's office do? Is it locked?"

"Yes, sir."

I turned to the third hallway on the left, figuring this was part of convincing them I was really myself, and walked down it. This floor was mostly service areas, offices, administrative rooms and public areas: the ball rooms, the dining room that got used only for official receptions and, at the far left, my father's offices and those of the people who worked closest to him.

Walking down the high, ceilinged hallway, I felt my throat close. The holos on the walls were those my father had favored. For all I know those holos had been the ones that had hung on those walls since my first ancestor had taken possession of the house. They displayed peaceful meadows and the occasional flight of birds.

They should have soothed and comforted me. They should have. But they didn't. Instead, I felt that this had all been a mistake, or perhaps a trap. My father had arranged for me to be given a doctored gem reader. I would walk up to his office and the door would open, and he'd emerge. And behind him would be guards, ready to drag me back to the lonely, antiseptic confines of Never-Never.

I don't know if any of it showed, but I know I was holding myself steady and normal-seeming with all my will power. I suspect my step acquired a mechanical, artificial rhythm as I led the small throng of servants along the hallway, past various doors, to the last one. It was closed. Which meant, I thought, that Max hadn't gone off knowingly or willingly with whomever had killed him. Because no Good Man thinking he might be away for more than a few minutes would leave that office locked. Particularly not when he was the last survivor of his line. That meant someone would have to blast through the genlock to get in. And no one would. Not until the Good Men decided which of them was to take over. Doing otherwise would mean hell to pay.

That meant that if anyone else—most likely Sam Remy—had papers or work in there, he would have to wait in abeyance until the new owner of Olympus took over. And then the Olympus functionary would have to submit to whatever the new Good Man thought of his unfinished business. A bad business all around— one to which no Good Man should subject his loyal servant. Not a Good Man interested in the loyalty of his servants, at least.

The door, black and unreflective, didn't open as I approached. Blindly, trying not to think of what would happen if somehow my genes didn't open it, I shoved my finger into the soft grey membrane of the genlock.

A deep click sounded and the door opened slowly inward. I had a moment, nothing more, to register that the office looked exactly as it had under my father, meaning that Max either had lacked the time or the interest to redecorate, then I turned around to face the crowd of servants.

Sam Remy was the closest, bowing. He reached into his pocket and brought out a small box. "Sir," he said. He need not say more. The box he was extending to me had a large, golden K on the lid and I knew it. It was the box into which every night, before going to bed, my father had sequestered the signet ring of the Keevas.

I hesitated a moment, then took the box, opened it, and took out the ring, as I said, as casually as I could, "I assume the police returned it?"

Was that a momentary hesitation? He shook his head and I got the very strong impression he was trying not to look at someone. But I didn't know whom. I just got the impression he was exerting the strictest possible discipline over his eyes. "No, sir. Your brother disappeared from his bed."

Ah! Max had been enticed away. Honeypot then, most likely. It happened. Though Max should have known the risks as well as I did. At least I didn't have to worry about whether the ring, which besides a signet was also a data gem that contained a lot of the needed information and codes to run my territory, had been corrupted.

When I looked up from slipping the ring on my finger, and noting in some surprise it fit perfectly, the household was bowing to me. More people had gathered than before. I never understood how news passed around the house, but clearly they had heard. And Sam Remy was gesturing wildly at a young man who stood at the edge of the crowd, looking up at me with an unreadable expression.

Sam hissed, "Nat," which should not be a word that could be hissed, and gestured more wildly.

The young man, the same who had been doing such a creditable job of stuffing most of his fist in his mouth, now approached, reluctantly, doing as much of an impression of robotic walking as I must have done on the way here. He stopped next to Sam, who bowed just slightly, in that sort of bow people give when indicating this is a formal occasion, and said, "Good Man Keeva, this is my oldest son, Nathaniel Remy."

Nathaniel was so pale that he might have been cast of the same white dimatough that imitated plaster on the ceiling. He was taller than Sam by a head. His hair was the sort of pale blond normally described as white-blond, a color not normally seen in anyone over two years of age. His features looked older than he could be. Because if he'd been in his late teens when I'd been arrested, I'd have known him well enough. In fact, I seemed to remember that Sam's marriage had occurred when I was twelve or so. I remembered my mother talking about it. And Sam was not the type of man to have a son outside marriage. I had a vague idea of his having a son and a daughter, five or maybe six by the time I'd been arrested.

But Nathaniel looked at least late twenties, more likely early thirties, and not easy ones. There were no wrinkles on his skin, mind, not even the sort of very fine ones I'd traced on my own face yesterday, in front of the mirror. But he looked like his face was all angles and hollows, the sort of sculpted, spare features that you didn't get before your late twenties, or later than that. Or perhaps he suffered from bad insomnia.

It was his eyes that stopped me cold, though. They were haunted and strange, as though he were looking at some horror no one else could see in my face. But in shape, in dark color, in the way his eyelids opened very wide for a moment as though he tried to but couldn't absorb the reality of my existence, they were Ben's eyes, staring at me from this stranger's face.

I became aware that I'd stared at Nathaniel much too long and possibly too intently, and that he was staring at me in a definitely odd way, somewhere between fright and hatred, with his throat working, as though he were fighting hard not to make a sound.

And Sam looked from one to the other of us with a puzzled expression.

I managed enough control over my wayward body to say, stiffly, "Pleased to meet you, Nathaniel. Am I to assume you have been trained in business and are your father's assistant?"

"Not business primarily," he said, but his voice came out squeaky, as if he were a too-young boy just at the age when voices change. "More law, though I am learning the business administration from my father as fast as I can."

"I see," I thought. So, crazy and a lawyer, par for the course. And of course his eyes looked like Ben's. They would. He was Ben's nephew. Which probably explained the hatred in his eyes. He probably knew I'd killed Ben. Fine then.

Something like a wave of mingled nausea and grief hit me full force, because I hadn't been back in this house without Ben, and it felt like Ben had just died, all over again. "I . . . I will look forward to working with you," I managed, then looked over Sam's head, at Savell who stood by, hovering. What I wanted to do was run through the crowd, screaming, run away from all this, from the servants staring at me, from the much-too-full hallway, from the press of bodies, their smell, their heat far too close after my life as a recluse. From Nathaniel Remy's all-too-explicable hatred. But I couldn't. The Good Man might be an absolute dictator—most are—but he's also a prisoner of his house and position.

My throat had constricted, my body hurt with the effort of my holding in place, but my voice sounded calm and composed in my own ears. "Savell, if you would order a bath run, I need to change into"—I looked down and made a small self-deprecating shrug—"more appropriate clothing."

"Ah, sir, of course, only—" He looked like he was about to say something, then bowed. "Of course, sir. I shall order your room cleaned and prepared."

"Forget it. I just need a bath. Now."

There was scurrying and moving, as Savell clearly gave instructions to his underlings by gesture and look.

And Sam was still there, still staring at me. Something in his expression was unreadable. I thought I saw surprise and a faint disgust, but most of all there seemed to be pity. Why he should feel sorry for me was unfathomable, but I was sure that he felt it nonetheless. "Sir," he said, "you will need to speak to Nat. There are legal issues which must—"

"You mean someone will dispute my right to be the Good Man?" I asked, and hoped my voice sounded more incredulous than I felt.

"Oh, not that, sir," Sam said. "But we must make sure everything is watertight all the same. And as quickly as possible. Before the council of Good Men meets."

I realized what he meant by that. The retainers had been living in fear, as I expected, of someone taking over and what it meant for them and the seacity.

"Nathaniel"—I said, and spared that worthy what I hoped was a withering glance—"can come to me in half an hour." I wanted to meet with him about as much as I wanted to saw off my head with a rusty saw. But I supposed there was no avoiding it. "I must have some privacy, first. And my mother? Has anyone told her I'm here?" I was surprised she had not come running yet. Perhaps she too could not forgive me. Perhaps even she hated me.

Nathaniel seemed to go paler, but it was Sam who answered, steadily, "The Lady Isabella passed away, sir. Two years ago."

I looked at him and I know my look was disbelieving, even if I didn't mean it. "What?"

"An accident, sir. Her flyer caught fire. She didn't escape in time."

And then I did run. I ran, most indecorously, between two flanking rows of retainers, back to the front hall. I pelted up the stairs, as I did when I hurt myself in the garden, when I was little, and ran up the stairs to my mother's comforting lap.

Only I ran past the rooms that had been hers, and down the side corridor, to what had been my own bedroom. I went in without even thinking, and then stopped, because this room didn't look at all like mine.

It looked like my father's.

Clothe Him in Silk,
Cover Him in Gold

NATHANIEL CHARGED INTO MY ROOM AS SOON AS I CAME OUT of my bath, while I was still mother-naked, and completely vulnerable. My fault.

It wasn't just that I hadn't locked the door—I'd spent so much time locked from the outside, it never occurred to me that someone might want to come in to my room. And besides, I'd grown up with retainers coming in and out of my room to lay out clothes or clean something, more or less at will. The Good Man or even his scapegrace son could never lock the door without interfering with the smooth running of the household.

But that wasn't the problem. The main problem was that I had dawdled and not just because I'd cried in the bath, where no one could see me, overcome suddenly by the loss of my mother on top of what felt, irrationally, like the recent loss of Ben.

It was that I'd also wandered around the room in a daze for a while before bathing. I suppose I should have expected it to have changed. But I didn't.

Olympus tradition is different from that of most of the other houses I've heard about, where there is a ruler's room and an heir's room. Instead, the house has assigned rooms for each person and the person remains in his own room, regardless of his position.

On the other hand, when I'd left, Max had been in the nursery.

51

And I'd guess they'd moved him into my room when he'd reached the age to leave it, at six or so. No reason why they shouldn't. I'd certainly not been expected to return.

But instead of the furniture Mother had picked for me, the warm smooth pine shelves and undecorated bed, the low dressers and the comfortable chairs, I was faced with an ornate, heavy and dark wood bed, curtained in dark blue; with pastoral holos on the walls, with carved, polished trunks and dressers. It made the room look exactly like my father's when I was little, and I can honestly say if this was Max's taste, I didn't think highly of it.

There was only one piece of art that I didn't remember as something my father would surround himself with. It was a damn good likeness—I presumed of Max, or perhaps of my father when he was very young, wearing a casual coat and pants, and with a setter dog at his heels. Done in pencil on paper, it had an archaic look and the lines of it were pure and clear in a way that was highly unfashionable in the holo-enhanced art of our day. There was a spareness to the line that didn't in any way make the work look cartoonish, and which made me think that the artist was a professional. However, it wasn't signed. I looked. Which was bizarre since having a piece in the Good Man's private quarters would make any artist's career soar.

Whichever it represented, Max or my father, it confirmed for me how startlingly like them I looked, and how different all the same. My face was battered and scarred in a way neither of theirs had been, and over the years of my captivity it had settled into bitter lines.

It had been a while before I tore myself away to get in the bath, and even longer to get out. And I did take a bath, in the deep-sunk marble bathtub, instead of just a shower.

When I came out, water-wrinkled, I rubbed myself with the towel kept in the warming shelf, and wondered how I could have forgotten how soft towels are. But I had. The softness against my skin sent unexpected shocks of pleasure through my body and I smiled to myself, thinking that next I would become a serial towel abuser.

Outside, in my room, someone had laid out a suit that made me raise my eyebrows. Really? Was that what they were wearing? It was gold and blue and more ornate than anything I would have seen in polite society before.

And that was the moment, as I stood there frowning at the suit, thinking it would make a very funny contrast with my scarred features, that Nathaniel Remy burst into the room.

Burst is an advised term, though he wasn't a large man, and I'd never think of him as a particular attention-getter. He was tall. I'd guess six two or so, probably enough to appear very tall to most people, but his build was—much as his father's and Ben's for that matter—lean and long-legged. With pale hair and pale skin, dressed in dark colors, he looked like he should have faded into the background—a dry little clerk going about an uninteresting dry little life.

But as my door burst open, he came in with his fists clenched, his face taut, and his whole body giving the impression he was a powder keg all too eager for a match to set it off.

He closed the door behind him as I turned to stare, so surprised that if he'd taken a burner to me, I'd not have reacted even in time to dive for cover. Fortunately he didn't, though his eyes looked like he'd like to.

Looking up at me, he brought his pale eyebrows down over his dark eyes, and said, with the type of finality that implies both that the person spent a considerable time thinking of what to say, and that he's afraid of being challenged, "I'm here. But you needn't think... You needn't think..." His eyes flashed inarticulate hatred.

I never was an angel, even before I was responsible for the deaths of anyone. Ben and I had run a broomers' lair together, after all.

I will grant you we were the sort other broomers called play-broomers. Unlike them, we didn't live outside the law, we only visited there in our spare time.

Other than riding brooms, in situations not of an emergency nature—a serious enough infraction in most territories and seacities—we had committed few crimes. We had stolen from a drug transport once, and we'd engaged in territorial fights, like any broomer lair. And never once, in those circumstances, had I ever seen anyone stare at me with so much hatred. Not even my father when he sent me to jail.

It made me feel defenseless, unprepared. I thought that this was Ben's nephew, that this man had Ben's eyes, and that he hated me. And why shouldn't he? Whether I'd killed Ben to halt his suffering or not—that had just been the last step in my involvement in Ben's life. There wasn't the slightest doubt in my mind that if I'd never got involved with Ben, Ben would still be alive, probably Sam's right hand in administration and a fond uncle to this young man.

The idea of that alternate future; the image of Ben mature, assured, respected, made my throat close and my heart shrink, which in turn made me unable to speak.

And it allowed Nathaniel Remy to close the space between us, an inarticulate growl emerging between his clenched teeth and turning into words. "You!" he said. "You needn't think you can fool me. I don't care what my father says." His voice wavered and he stopped, looking startled, not so much at the wavering, I thought, as at the idea he'd talked at all. If it were possible for a man to stare in bewilderment at his own mouth, he'd have done so.

But slowly, he focused on me again. I'd often heard hate described as fire, but I'd never before understood. Now I felt as if, if I stared hard enough at Nathaniel's dark eyes, I'd find a red pinpoint of smoldering hatred in them. "If you hadn't got yourself put away, *safe and cozy*," Nathaniel said. "You'd be dead and Max— And he—" a watery sound drowned his words, even though his eyes were dry.

It wasn't funny, but the wrenching of my feelings away from Ben and to Max was so startling, the juxtaposition of Never-Never or even the jail before that—where I'd had to fight tooth and nail to keep the slighter-built Ben from being beaten or worse—and *safe and cozy* wrenched a surprised laugh from me.

Nathaniel was standing maybe two steps from me, glaring up. At the laugh, he started and jumped, as though I'd slapped him.

His bunched fist shot forward too fast for me to react. It caught me hard on the mouth, and sent me reeling back a step, but not far enough that his left fist didn't catch me again.

My mind had figured it out by then. I didn't know why Nat Remy hated me, but surely he had plenty of reason.

And I didn't know what he thought he was doing, but some things I did know. I knew this was a man in the grip of such a powerful emotion that it had to have totally overpowered his mind. I knew he wasn't thinking of the penalties for striking the sole, despotic ruler on whose good will his life and the lives of his relatives depended. And I knew he'd forgotten my very existence was his and his family's only bulwark against destitution and maybe death.

And I knew too that he was Sam's oldest son and that Sam loved him. That much had been obvious in the way Sam looked at him. And I knew Sam was one of the few—perhaps the only man left alive—for whose good opinion I still cared.

As Nathaniel raised his foot to kneecap me, my mind got hold of my body and I went into my fast mode. I couldn't allow him to injure me. I couldn't allow it, not because I didn't deserve it, but because all Good Men united in punishing crimes against one of them. It was maybe the only thing they all agreed on. And if Nathaniel seriously injured or killed me in a way Sam couldn't cover up, Nathaniel would die for it. And Sam didn't deserve that. Not over me.

I dove away from where his foot would have hit, and behind him. Taking advantage of his being off balance, I grabbed both his wrists, secured them into one of my hands, while my arm snaked around him and pulled him tight against me, I pushed him up against the wall, pinning him.

The man didn't know the meaning of quitting. Or the meaning of self-preservation. He jerked his head trying to hit me, and his attempts to kick backwards made me shift my hold and make it tighter, all the while trying to ignore that he was warm and alive because this was not what I'd thought of when I'd imagined holding someone warm and alive in my arms.

It would have been easy to kill him or incapacitate him from this position, but my purpose was not to kill him.

Not knowing what else to do, I just held on tight, breathing as steadily as I could. I don't know how long it took, but eventually he stopped trying to attack and began to shake like a leaf in a wind storm, his teeth knocking loudly together.

I recognized the reaction because Ben had had it too. It was the whiplash of the berserker. Nathaniel, like Ben, was a ber- serker, and when a berserker fit was cut short, he got hit with a near-painful reaction. Ben had never gone berserk at me, but he'd gone into that state a few times in broomer lair fights and had to tamp it down.

Nathaniel had also gone heavy in my grasp, and I thought the reaction probably made him weak enough he couldn't harm me. I also knew the only way to bring Ben out of one of these, and there was a chance it would work on Nathaniel too.

I saw the drinks table to my left, went over to it, and grabbed a bottle at random. It didn't matter what it was, provided it was alcoholic.

Ben thought the alcohol worked because of its effect on the ner- vous system. I thought it worked because it made him concentrate on the burn of alcohol. By the time I got back to Nathaniel, he was in a heap on the floor, shaking, his hands over his face.

I treated him exactly as I'd treated Ben in the same circumstances. I uncapped the bottle, pulled his hands down and shoved the bottle at his lips, then tilted. Most people will drink rather than drown. He did, taking three startled gulps, before pulling his head back and taking a deep breath.

His shaking lessened and he took another breath, then he reached for the bottle from my hand.

Yes, I did think that it might be used as a weapon, but I was now forewarned and, anyway, I was faster than he was. In the event, he did nothing but take another swig of the bottle, swallow, then look at it and say, in startled shock, "Gin. I don't drink gin."

I couldn't keep the laughter in, though I tried, and he looked at me as though seeing me for the first time. The bottle fell from his grasp. It didn't break, but it rolled sideways, spilling liquid on the carpet. His mouth fell open. His throat worked.

"You," he said. "I . . . Damn. I . . ." He covered his face with his hands, then lowered them and looked resigned but not scared. "I attacked you, Good Man Keeva, and I want to make it clear that I'm acting on my own. Neither my father, my mother, nor any of my siblings, nor any acquaintance or friend or colleague or teacher incited me to do this. It is my fault, my fault alone." He stood, and faced me, managing to look dignified. "And I will repeat this statement as needed."

It was, in the circumstances, as noble a speech as I'd ever heard, and he stood with his shoulders thrown back, his head held high, ready to die alone for a moment's fury. He was an idiot, but a gallant idiot.

"Very likely," I said. "But you forgot to exonerate one person. I would swear you had nothing to do with your own actions, either." And, to his startled look. "How long have you been holding back the berserker fit? Since I came in the door?" And, because I'm not a genius, but I can think through cause and effect, and I remembered the horrible description of Max's death through torture. "You and Max were friends, weren't you?"

He took a deep breath, nodded. I turned my back on him, deliberately, and walked back to the drinks table. "What do you drink?"

"Nothing. Not at this time of morning. My father would have

my skin, and besides..." He sounded surprised. "I don't think I've eaten in...over a day."

"I imagine," I said. "With the search for Max and then their finding him murdered." I found the soda dispenser, filled a glass of soda water, and took it to him. "Drink," I said, "or you'll start hiccupping in no time."

"I cut your lip," he said. His gaze arrested on my lip. "You're bleeding."

"You did?" I wiped at it, leaving a red streak on the back of my hand. "So. No big deal. I've done worse to myself."

He took a sip of the water. "Any other Good Man would have had me—"

"Not a sane Good Man," I said. "Grief and shock hit you too closely together. You weren't in your right mind." Which was true enough even if he did have one, which, of course, I couldn't know. "But for the record, I didn't maneuver or intend to spend a year in a prison for violent criminals, and fourteen in solitary confinement in Never-Never."

"Solitary?" he asked, clearly surprised.

"Yes, and I didn't do it just to escape the Sons of Liberty."

"The Sons—" he sounded startled. "No. Is that who they say did it? Killed Max, I mean? Well, for once..." He trailed off. "No. I know you didn't—" he stopped. "Fourteen years? And you're still sane?"

"Functional," I said.

He blinked at me, then looked me up and down. "You're naked."

"Astonishing powers of observation," I said. "No wonder you're a lawyer."

He shook his head. "You should dress. And I should...I meant to ask you about Goldie."

"Goldie?"

He gestured towards the drawing on the wall, the one I'd admired before. "That," he said, "is Max and Goldie. Goldilocks. Goldie for short."

I looked at the portrait. I looked at the dog beside the person, whom I had to assume now was Max.

"Max's dog?"

Nathaniel gave a sort of exasperated little huff. "No, I— Oh, never mind. I thought...Yes, Max's dog. I...I'd like to keep him, but..." He floundered.

I turned towards the bed and said, "Am I really expected to wear that? Has the style changed that much in fifteen years?"

He looked towards the bed, too, and made a sound. Then shrugged. "Your father's tastes ran to rather more gaudy than... than fashion," he said. "And I'd guess they haven't had the time to get your clothes from storage or..." He paused, looked stricken. "They might no longer exist."

I opened my mouth to ask him why my father's clothes would be in this room at all, and if my father's clothes wouldn't have been disposed of, as well, since Max had succeeded a year ago, but I couldn't because he'd walked past me to the closet and thrown it open. "There should be something. They're never *that* thorough," he said. Then he shut the door with a bang and started, with strange enthusiasm, opening drawers under the closet. "Ah," he said, in a tone of satisfaction. "This drawer is all Max's." He brought out a, dark, soft-looking suit, and threw it at me.

As I caught the pants midair, the tunic fell on the floor. I grabbed it, one-handed, and tossed it on the bed. The type of fabric was non-wrinkling. I started pulling the pants on and felt disapproval from somewhere in Nathaniel's direction. I looked up and at him, and he held, in his hands, just taken from the drawer, a pair of underwear. Oh.

I pulled the pants off, and extended my hand for the underpants. "I'd forgotten about the niceties," I said. "It's been fourteen years with only one suit, nothing else to my name. I suppose I should wear socks and shoes as well."

It didn't get a smile from him, just a tight nod, and when I looked up from pulling on the pants that felt like a second skin, he handed me socks and a pair of dark slipper-shoes, the kind one wore when one wasn't going to do much walking over rough ground.

I was about to ask him how and why he seemed to know where everything was in this room, but I never did, because he glared at me as if I'd done something wrong. "You'll have to have suits made. That is much too tight. You're bigger than Max." And then he said, "Perhaps they still have your clothes in the attics or something. Sometimes I think nothing gets thrown away in this place."

The chuckle at the idea came out despite my best intentions. "My clothes? From before I was arrested? They'd fit worse than this. I was twenty-two and skinny."

"Twenty-two." The though seemed to stop him and he looked at me, as though to make sure I wasn't lying, then shrugged. "Sorry. No one ever told us that. As far as I remember, you were, well...old."

I didn't remember him at all, though now that I made an effort I conjured up the image of a small, pale shadow trailing Max, an older boy who mostly watched from the sidelines and rarely spoke. "I would seem so to a six- or seven-year-old," I said, drily. "At any rate, if you wanted to tell me you wanted to keep Max's dog, fine."

"My father says he's technically yours if you want him," Nathaniel said, with far more emotion than seemed to be warranted. "He says you like dogs."

"I like dogs," I said. "And cats. And hamsters. And I once was very fond of a tarantula spider. But I don't like fish except on the plate." I looked up to meet with total confusion in the dark eyes. "Right. But, just because I like dogs, it doesn't mean I need Max's. If he's used to you now, that's fine. Is he used to you?"

Nathaniel shrugged. "You can always get another dog," he said. "I'd hate to disrupt Goldie's life again."

"I can always get another dog," I agreed. I hadn't had a dog since the scene when my father had got rid of my dog when I was ten. "Was that all you wished to tell me, Nathaniel Remy?"

"No," he said. He looked guilty. "The dog is not—never mind. I'm sorry, it seemed the most important thing. I...I have no idea what came over me."

I patted his shoulder once. Once, because by the second time, he'd sprang away from me.

"Grief acts in strange ways," I said. And I hoped I was telling the truth and that his behavior was the result of grief, because I wasn't prepared to tell Sam Remy that his son was completely insane and would need serious treatment, or perhaps to be confined in a nice cell where he couldn't hurt himself.

Nathaniel looked up at me a while longer than made sense, frowned, nodded. He ran a hand across his forehead. He was wearing a heavy silver ring, which probably explained the cut on my lip. "Yes," he said. "Yes, I suppose it would. But...my father sent me in to discuss with you the legal strategy for presenting your claim to the Council."

"Your father doesn't think that anyone can dispute my right to rule."

Nathaniel shrugged. "My father doesn't think anyone can

dispute it successfully. But my father hasn't examined the law. He's simply speaking from custom and logic. You're the last of the blood. By blood, Keevas own Olympus. There is no possible claim that outstrips yours. But there are some small issues we should sweep out of the way first."

"Of course," I said. "I'm sure my father disinherited me."

He shook his head. "No. He simply superseded you with Max. You were the heir, after Max. No. What I mean is, though it is irrelevant now, because the Good Man can't be guilty of any crime, you...have a conviction on your record, which some of your...peers might say is a capital conviction and you..."

"And I should have been executed," I said, and watched, fascinated, as Nathaniel, while still talking to me, started patting himself down, as though he were trying to stop an invasive stream of ants that had climbed up his well-cut trousers.

"Oh, no. Well, maybe you would have been, if you were a commoner, but then commoners—" He reached into what appeared to be a hidden pocket behind his knee and extracted a square box of some sort. I watched carefully, in case it was a weapon, but he brought out a thin white cylinder and shook it. When the end glowed ember-red, I realized it was a cigarette. A few of my peers had smoked as an affectation.

He sucked on the unlit end as though that was the only way he could get oxygen and he'd spent the last three days without breathing, then expelled the smoke slowly. "Commoners can be executed because they looked at you wrong. Executing the...son of a Good Man was never going to happen."

"Even if the crime was killing a Good Man's heir?"

He gave me an odd lingering look, sucked on the cigarette again. "Not even then. He just had another heir." He put his hand under the growing ash of the cigarette and looked around frantically. Then he opened my desk drawer, rummaged around, brought out a little porcelain box used for gems, dumped the gems into the drawer, and shook the ash into the box. "But that's not the point. Your peers could still use it against you."

I frowned at him. "Would they want to? Good Man Rainer is dead." I hastened to add, "I didn't kill him. I found him—"

"I know," he said. "His son, Jan, kill— Oh, shit. Never mind. That is not for public consumption. But it's not Good Man Rainer you've got to worry about. It's..." He seemed to struggle with words, and I got the impression he was closing several avenues of explanation. I wonder how Nathaniel Remy had come by *that's not for public consumption* information. "It's anyone who could claim Olympus," he finally settled on.

"So?" I said, watching fascinated, as he stabbed his tiny stub of cigarette into the porcelain box to put it out, then lit another one so fast I could barely follow the movement. "You know, those things will kill you," I said. "I mean, they've removed most carcinogens from them, but they're still not meant to be used in great quantities."

"The— What? Oh, these. Nah, I'm not that lucky." He sucked in smoke. "So, you need to pardon yourself."

I blinked at him. "My crime prevents my becoming a Good Man, so I should pardon myself?"

He opened his mouth, then seemed to very carefully bite the tip of his tongue. He sighed. "Well, not . . . precisely. Your father needs to pardon you."

"Uh . . ." How crazy was Nathaniel Remy? Was I going to have to break it to Sam? "I'm sorry, but I'm fresh out of resurrection powers. And wouldn't resurrect him if I could."

Something very like a half-laugh caught in Nat's throat, causing him to cough puffs of smoke. He looked at me, really looked, as if evaluating me for the first time, as if he were trying to tell what sort of person I was. Then he looked as if trying to figure out what to tell me. "You know how the genlocks react to you," he said. "I mean, how all the men in your line can—"

"Open the same genlocks, yes, which is why my father always had additional security in things he didn't want me to see. And?"

"And, the judicial gen seals aren't any finer."

This didn't sound right. "Are you sure? I mean, they'd have to be—"

He shook his head. "Trust me," he said. "I'm a lawyer."

That seemed like a very odd claim to my trust, but I supposed a lot of them were trustworthy, popular image notwithstanding. "We have papers," he said, "From your father's time, so, you know, it's the right type of paper, and I've printed a letter of pardon. That ring," he said, and pointed at the signet ring, "has a sign function. Do you know how to set it?"

I must have looked helpless, because he set down his cigarette, inside the porcelain box, which he put on the desk. Then he held out his hand for the signet. I took it off, and put it on his palm, thinking that for some strange reason, Nathaniel Remy reminded me a lot of my nanny. Or at least, both of them could command obedience with a gesture and a look.

He held up the ring, and twisted one of the bands around the gem carefully, till a sequence of green lights came on, then told me, "Now put it on," as if I were about two years old. From inside his tunic somewhere, he pulled a sheet of paper that wasn't even creased. I suspected the man's clothes were sewn with multiple pockets, but did they also contain folders?

He set the paper on the desk, and told me where to press the ring, and how, so it left behind an imprint of my genetic code.

"Are you sure?" I asked. "They won't be able to tell it's mine and not my father's?"

"Positive," he said, as he made the paper disappear. Though he'd answered instantly, I had the impression of a hesitation. "I promise." He looked me over. "And now I will be gone and leave you to . . . to . . . whatever it was you were doing."

And like that, he slid out of the room and closed the door behind him as unobtrusively as his entrance had been explosive. And left me wondering what this creature was. If he was mad, he was the sanest madman I'd ever met. If he was sane . . . then he acted a lot like a madman. More importantly, what did he know that he wasn't telling me? It was obvious he knew something. Was it something that could hurt me? Had Max let this sort of thing go unexamined? Was that why he'd got killed?

Maxims my father had given me, about making sure you knew your servants and what they were up to, flitted through my head. I sighed.

Nathaniel had left his cigarette in the box. I put it out, carefully, then closed the box on the ashes, and set it back on the desk. I had the odd feeling he'd need it again and look for it there.

But why would he? And friends with Max or not, why did he know the room so well and act like it was his room? Had they been— No. Too much of a coincidence. I was projecting my own history onto Max.

My head hurt. What I really needed was a ride on my broom and to talk to some old friends.

Running Away

I STARED, FROWNING AT THE DOOR, AFTER NATHANIEL REMY left. All right, so this cell was much nicer than the last place where I'd been confined. But it was not much more free. And I'd known that. Of course I'd known that.

I rotated my shoulders as I thought. My entire childhood had been confined, hemmed in due to my peculiar position, my overprotective parents and the deference of those who were socially beneath me.

Of course the Good Man had more freedom. I could walk out of the house and go for a walk. I could tell them all to take a hike. I could have them put to death alphabetically, starting with A and ending with Z. And none of them could oppose me, at least legally.

Well, not if Nathaniel and Sam were right about confirming me.

But the truth was I couldn't execute them, of course. I was far too aware of their being real people. I wasn't sure I could ever execute anyone, though my father had seemed to do it almost whimsically at times. Perhaps that came with time. Or perhaps it was due to my father being a right bastard. I frowned at the closed door.

I could walk out of here, and go down to the city, and mingle with people. I could. Except that I could never walk out without

63

facing too many questions, too many looks. Sam would try to tell me there was too much to do—there probably was too much to do. Paperwork would have been neglected for at least three days and I remembered well the stack of papers my father signed every night, usually in breaks during the dinner, while mother and I tried to make conversation.

But I didn't want to sign papers. I didn't want to think. I wanted to be alone and have time to mourn Ben, and have time to think of what I was going to do in this house without Mother. Somehow I'd been counting on her to give me clues, to help me hide the fact that I'd forgotten the society of humans. To be one person who cared what happened to me, beyond my role as Good Man.

I ran my fingers over the scar on my face, which seemed, suddenly, to be itching and flaring with pain, even though at some level, I knew it was imaginary pain.

And then my body decided for me. I caught myself halfway to the door, to close it and lock it. My shoulders were flexing in the too-tight suit and what I wanted—what I needed—was to get out of here and to be in the air, on my broom. More than that, I wanted to visit my old friends. They would now be the Good Men, most of them. And most of them had known very well I hadn't done anything to deserve being slammed in jail. At least, I hadn't done what they said.

Most of them, in fact, had got the same call I had, and had only been saved from a like fate by getting there too late. I still didn't know what that was all about or why Hans had been killed, much less why I'd been blamed for it. I suspected if Ben and I hadn't got out of there fast enough, instead of being jailed, we'd have been killed like Hans, and someone else been blamed for the murder.

But no one who knew Hans and I could have thought I'd kill him. After Ben, Hans was my right hand in the Hellions, absolutely trusted and trusting. I don't think we'd ever even argued.

So . . . my old friends would know I was innocent. Whether they'd rejoice to see me was something else. It had been a long time, and I knew I looked quite different. But they wouldn't deny me or spurn me. Of that I was sure. So. I'd visit them. Javier, I thought, first. He'd been in the Hellions also, and as his father was close to eighty at the time, I couldn't imagine that he wouldn't have succeeded by now. And he had always been levelheaded. He could help me find my footing on the command. He could help me figure out how to be a Good Man.

And even if I was sure he'd never had any idea how things really were between Ben and me, he could talk about Ben as someone who had known him.

I had no idea if my broom and suit would still be where I'd left them, but it was worth a try. I went into the bathroom and opened both faucets over the basin, then opened the fresher door, then went back into the bathroom and turned the door knob on the closet to the left. Yes, it really was that complex. Mostly because I'd had it made when I was all of fifteen.

But it worked, too. When I turned around, a portion of the wall, one of the many panels, had popped out. And in the opening was what looked uncommonly like leathers and a broom.

I went to it and brought out a broomer suit and boots, a broom and oxygen tanks. And then I frowned at them. The black leather suit had red piping. I didn't remember red piping. The Hellions colors had been pure black, with a stylized drawing of flames on the back. Ben used to joke that it was very subtle and classy, our pattern of black on black.

Had I gone crazy? This one had no insignia on the back, but there was definitely red piping. But who could have cracked the complex—not to say insane—code to open the compartment? Impossible. And only Ben and I had known how to open it. Unless Ben had told Sam, though I had no idea why he would have, or why Sam would have told anyone.

Still, the suit smelled different. I can't explain it. But it did not smell like me. And putting it on I found that it fit me about as well as the clothes I was wearing. Better, since broomer suits are designed to accommodate a variety of clothing under them, so there was room for a formal suit. And there was no way my suit from when I'd been arrested would have fit me this way. I was—almost—sure that I could fit it, but it would have felt like a tourniquet.

I slipped the gloves on, and the boots. Those, at least, would be about the right size, but they still didn't feel like mine.

Perhaps fifteen years really had played havoc with my memory. Perhaps, just before I was arrested we'd decided to change the garbing of the lair, and I'd forgotten that in the rush of events afterwards. In the pocket of my suit were two of the disposable links I didn't remember buying, but which—button-sized and cheaply made—I might very well have.

The broom was right. I mean, it was my broom. Not only was it a polished silver Gryphon 500, but it had carved on it, painstakingly, the words I'd decided were my motto. *No One Can Jail a Free Man.*

I winced at them. Well. I'd found out better, hadn't I?

Fully attired, oxygen on my back, I went to the terrace, and took off from it. I went through the usual maneuvers I'd used when I was leaving the house, in case my father had set people to watch for my leaving, then laughed, hollowly, because if there were guards ready to prevent me from leaving, I could simply wave them away.

It wasn't until I was headed to Andalus Seacity that it occurred to me that I could simply have taken a flying car and perhaps a retinue, to visit Javier. This being a Good Man thing was going to take getting used to.

Andalus was relatively close to us, in a southwesterly direction. All of two hours away as the broom flew, which was one of the reasons that Javier and I had become friends when we'd both started using brooms, in defiance of our parents. We'd first met in Liberte, both of us trying to pose as commoners and failing miserably. I no longer remembered why, but, at all of fourteen, we'd got into some sort of disagreement that ended with both of us locked in a punching match. We'd been friends ever since.

While flying, I found myself once more admiring the landscape: the sea under me, the sky above me, the smoothness of the broom's flight.

The feeling that I would float up into the blue seemed to be gone, and this was good. It left me able to enjoy the freedom and to think. Not much seemed to have changed since I'd been arrested. No new seacities, and the coastal areas of the continents which I'd seen so far seemed about as populated as they'd ever been. Even the music I'd heard in the diner this morning was the same type of music, if not the same music, that had been played when I'd left.

Perhaps it is one of the illusions of youth that everything is new and constantly regenerating. Fifteen years seemed to have made almost no difference. Except for me.

Andalus looked as it had. I don't know if it's cultural—a part of the northern European culture, as opposed to the southern—to build in a more orderly form. Not that Andalus was exclusively Spanish or even Southern European. It was, in fact, one of the seacities where Glaish had evolved, first as a trade language and later as an official tongue. One of the seacities from where it had reached out to become the lingua franca of Earth.

If I remembered—and I barely did—it had started as a businessmen haven and attracted Spaniards and Mexicans, and people from all over South America, and refugees from the British Commonwealth diaspora, the speakers of English and Spanish being equally balanced.

But the building style was all Mediterranean, all Southern European. It looked like houses were built at every angle and in positions where no one sane would have built a house. The island was crowded and, in the light of day, presented a panorama of white and various Earth tones, slashed here and there by an unexpected green or vivid blue building.

The Good Man's residence was at the top and looked like late-stage obsession with Rome, as it tends to strike in civilizations as different as Renaissance old Europe, the classical US and twenty-second-century Syracuse Seacity.

There were columns. Columns and terraces, most of them not doing anything in particular except being columns and terraces, each gesturing at itself and screaming, look at me, I'm neo-Roman. Surely that means I'm the home of an enlightened ruler.

I frowned at the palace, remembering how to go around back, and duck beneath the columns on the left, and knock on Javier's window. But I couldn't remember if Javier's house, like mine, played musical rooms when a ruler died and the other succeeded. I might find Javier in that room. Or I might find an infant son of his, and what an alarm that would cause.

I remembered, vaguely, the plan of the house. His father's office had been at the back, facing the southeastern terraces. Which meant . . .

Well, like most Good Men, he had a private office and, in his case, a private terrace. That meant that I could accost him. Oh, he might have a secretary or two who went in and out of his office, but people in that kind of position weren't chatty and knew better than to spread rumors.

Not that my return was a rumor, or that it wouldn't be well known in no time, but I'd prefer if it didn't get divulged in this manner. And I'd prefer if it wasn't rumored I'd come to Javier for advice. Though arguably, that was exactly what I was doing. But Good Men are like wild animals: Any sign of weakness from one of them will cause the others to take immediate advantage.

Given my legal position, I could imagine what Nathaniel Remy would have to say to my displaying my metaphorical soft underbelly to another Good Man.

I landed on the terrace. I was fairly sure that Javier would be in his office at this time of day. And if he weren't, then he would come there soon.

His office had glass doors, though there were curtains on the inside that could be closed, they weren't. Through them, I could see Javier sitting at the desk, and I felt a sudden wave of relief. Something—I wasn't sure what—had made me feel as if all my friends had vanished, as though I were now a stranger to everyone, the only one of my crowd left.

But Javier looked much as he had. He was turned sideways to me, looking at a reader on his knees.

He was, as he had been, a small man and as slim as Nathaniel Remy, though of course on a much smaller scale. Olive-skinned with startlingly hazel eyes, he'd been a favorite with all the women in the hangouts my broomer lair had frequented. And he'd been surprisingly good in a fight. So good, in fact, that my larger size had given me very little advantage in our one and only dustup.

The rest of his office looked empty, and the door was locked. I knocked at the door.

He looked up, then jumped. I never saw him open the drawer, but there was a gun in his hand, and he was standing, facing me.

"Easy," I said. "It's me, Lucius."

He stared at me, the burner firmly pointed at my midsection. If he fired, it was going to make far more of a mess than that, because it would go straight at the glass, first. Depending on how that glass had been made, it could do anything from melt to burst outward and fly at me in shards. "Don't be stupid, Javier. It's Lucius Keeva."

His mouth opened, then closed. Then he frowned, and came to open the door for me. He pocketed the gun. He looked me up and down and frowned. "So, that's how it is, is it?" he said. "You escaped after all. We wondered at your being caught so easily."

"I didn't escape," I said, puzzled. Did he imagine I'd spent the last fifteen years living rough, like some sort of twenty-fifth-century Robin Hood? Maybe he did. Now that I thought of it. Never-Never was a secret prison for a reason. "Well, not until yesterday."

He frowned at me. Then shook his head, as though what I'd said was completely nonsensical. "Just as well," he said. "I don't mind telling you that the idea that the Sons of Liberty could penetrate into your house and kidnap you like that had me in a bit of a worry. Not to mention, of course, that I didn't want you dead." Those last words seemed weirdly perfunctory and caught my attention so much—did Javier want me dead? In the name of all that was holy, why?—that it took me a moment to realize the weirdness of what he'd said before.

Sons of Liberty? The same people who'd kidnaped Max and killed him? Was he confusing me with Max? Was something wrong with his mind?

No, wait, perhaps that was the cover story that people had been given. I'd always assumed my condemnation, and later Ben's death, had been public, the subject of holos and sensies. But perhaps not. Perhaps it had all be so fast and so odd because they couldn't risk making it public. And perhaps the cover story had involved the Sons of Liberty, though I didn't even remember hearing of them at the time.

Perhaps, I thought with sudden alarm, the Sons of Liberty were a made-up group, used to disguise executions the Good Men committed but couldn't admit to. It would certainly explain things better than the odd idea that they were the armed branch of the Usaians who had never before showed a tendency to do more than pray and hope for a Messiah to lead them to their long-destroyed continent.

I tried to formulate a response, cautious enough that Javier wouldn't think that I had lost my mind, but which would lay the groundwork to explaining the truth to him. Only I never got to, because he was looking at me, and grinning. "Some body you got yourself," he said. "Couldn't something have been done about that scar? You look scary enough. And I suppose none of the side effects have manifested, or has there not been time for it to show one way or the other? And how could you have got it done in two days? I thought the quickest time to do it we'd found so far was two weeks. What is it? New nanites? New drugs?

And how was it done? Why? Wasn't the last one just fine? You looked fine last month."

I felt like I had been caught in some sort of weird parallel universe where I couldn't understand what people said. Maybe it was true that I'd forgotten how conversations happened. Most of what Javier had said seemed like gibberish with no referent.

I looked around the office, which looked exactly like it had when Javier's father used it. I'd been there once or twice, with my father, for some sort of official, documented meeting.

Like my father, Javier's father liked heavy dark furniture, though I suspected his was antique furniture. I had a vague memory of his saying that his desk had belonged to the king of Spain. He hadn't said which, as though there had been only one. On a corner of that huge, dark desk, was a vast globe done in stone inlays. It didn't show the seacities, which meant it was very old.

On the wall was a portrait of a man who looked much like Javier, if Javier took to wearing a pointy beard and Renaissance garb. That man had a toy ship in his hands and his foot resting on a globe that looked uncommonly like that one.

I remembered when I'd been in that office before, I'd thought that a globe made for a damn silly foot rest, and wondered why someone who looked like a Renaissance nobleman couldn't have afforded something cushier. Now I knew better. Those gems, furnished to me over the fifteen years of my captivity, had done more than keep me sane. They'd taught me history and art and other things that were not really taught anymore, or not in any depth. That globe symbolized dominion over the world.

I turned back to Javier, who had sat back at his desk and was gazing at me with the sort of contemplative expression of a man looking at wild beast, fresh captured. "I am going to need your help, Javier. I'm going to need your help to figure out this thing."

"Eh?" He said, puzzled. "What thing?"

"How to . . . what to do as Good Man. How it all works. You must know my father gave me no instruction."

I saw his face change. I saw him open his drawer. Don't ask me how I knew what he was doing. I did. It made no sense but I did. Before he'd got the drawer open, I had his wrist in my hand, then his other wrist, as he tried to reach for what looked like a paperweight on the desk, and which was in fact either a paperweight or perhaps a call button for security.

And then I got the shock of my life. That up close, looking at Javier's face, I'd swear that those weren't his eyes. The color in them was the same. The shape was the same. I can't explain what I mean, but they weren't Javier's eyes, all the same. Whatever was looking at me through them wasn't Javier.

And whatever was looking at me through them was also making a determined effort to fight me, even with both his hands held in mine. He lifted his knee, and I sidestepped, and he kicked out at air, and he tried to bite my nose off.

"Damn you," he said. "Damn you. It's you, isn't it? What are you? Impossible to kill? We told Dante to finish you off. We told him."

I had no idea what he was talking about, but I didn't have time to argue it. I was in his office. That meant, by definition, we were surrounded by his men. And there was naked hatred in his eyes, and I didn't know who or what he was, but he wasn't my friend Javier. There was neither refuge nor protection here. There was neither advice nor affection, not even the consolation of talking to someone else who had been friends with Ben. What there was instead was danger.

The moment I let go of him, he would call his security, if he didn't just get a burner and try to kill me. The alternative was I killed him, but every sense rebelled at the idea. I couldn't kill Javier, even if he'd gone insane.

I transferred both his hands to one of mine. Easier said than done, while he squirmed and fought, but I was bigger, and I was much stronger than I'd been when I'd last seen him. With one hand, I unclipped my broom. There are ways to hit a man that won't kill him. I'd have to try really hard for one of those, as out of practice as I was.

As the broom hit him, I thought nothing had happened. He opened his mouth as though to scream, and I let go of his hands to clamp my hand over his mouth. But then he convulsed and went still. Was he dead? I couldn't stop to see. I was in danger. Someone could come in any minute, and how would I explain this?

I grabbed my broom, went to the terrace, and took off. I was well away from the island when I realized I should have called for help. After all, I was now a Good Man. Who would try to stop me, if I said Javier had had a stroke, or something.

But then, when Javier woke up he would accuse me of...what?

Being impossible to kill? Javier had tried to kill me? I felt like someone had pulled the rug out from under my feet. I might not have trusted him as implicitly and as wordlessly as I trusted Hans, but I had trusted him nonetheless.

What insane world had I escaped to? Perhaps it would have been better if I had drowned in my jail cell after all.

The World Turned Upside Down

SOME INSTINCT, SOME FEELING, PREVENTED ME GOING HOME AT once. No, I don't know what except thinking that Javier might have woken up, and if he woke up, he would try to send people to intercept me on the way to Olympus. He would assume I would return there, right?

So instead, I took a detour, and went to Liberte Seacity, where I landed on a deserted beach.

I'd had some time to think, and thought the best thing I could do was to talk to some of my other old friends. Perhaps they could explain what was happening, and perhaps they could tell me what had happened to Javier and why he spoke that way. Perhaps it was a stroke, I thought. In which case, my hitting him on the head could have done no good at all. But I didn't see how I could have got around it. I couldn't even find the stuff I needed to bind him, could I? There hadn't been anything I could use nearby. And to let go of him and go in search of it, I'd have needed to knock him out first, anyway.

No, I'd done the only thing I could, even if the violence of it bothered me. I didn't want to fight and I didn't want to hurt anyone. There had been enough of that, and anything that required me to do more of it, made me feel tired and old. Very old.

So I landed and took the portable links out. One of them had a series of programmed numbers, but I recognized none of them, so I took the other and dialed another of the Hellions—Josia Bruno, from New Verona Seacity. It took a while for him to answer because, I supposed that was his private number, and he was the Good Man, now. The face I got, floating midair, looked like Josia well enough. I'd chosen a deserted beach well, because landing in a broom was not strictly legal, but also so I could have sight as well as sound. But he didn't look like he recognized me at all. Which I couldn't blame him for, I supposed. I wouldn't have recognized myself either. "Jos?" I said. "It's Lucius."

"It's who?" he said.

"Lucius Keeva," I said.

He blinked. "You mean..." he said. And then frowned. "Dante?"

Don't ask me to explain it, please, but his expressions were all wrong. And what he said was all wrong. I pressed the phone off and took a deep breath.

Perhaps I was the one who had gone crazy. Perhaps I had gone completely around the bend and just hadn't realized it. Perhaps...

On a whim, on a desperate moment of insanity, I dialed Hans's number. It rang and I reached for the turn off button, because who would have it, except maybe someone new who had been assigned it? Or the person who had inherited from his father—his brother? I had a vague memory that he had one, the only other of my friends who had had a brother, though in his case we all thought it was double insurance because his father was so old. He wanted to make sure that the line didn't die out.

"Hello?" The face that appeared midair looked exactly like Hans, but there was no doubt it wasn't him. I'd seen Hans dead.

"Hans?" I said, anyway, for lack of anything else to call this face.

"What? Jan. Jan Rainer. And you are...?" His eyes widened suddenly. "It can't be!" he said.

"My name is Lucius Dante Maximilian Keeva, and I didn't kill your brother," I said. And in the annals of stupid things to say, that might take the cake.

The face hesitated, and I thought he was going to call me a murderer or threaten me with the law or something equally bombastic. But, proving once more that nothing would go as I expected today, instead he frowned, but in the way of a man who is thinking desperately through something. "Of course you didn't," he said. "Don't be ridiculous. But...how did you escape the execution? And where have you been these...fifteen years?"

"Never-Never," I said. It didn't even occur to me to lie. "Well, Never-Never for fourteen years, another jail for one."

He blinked. "Oh. And you escaped in the breakout?" he asked. "It's almost too...Have you gone home yet? To Olympus."

"Yes," I said. "But I...I got out and I tried to talk to Javier Nobles and I—"

"Javier?" he said. "How did you get away? Where are you now?"

I wasn't so completely off my balance that I would tell him the last, but I said, "I hit him on the head. He might need help."

Not-Hans shook his head. "Like hell. I hope the bastard dies."

"Beg your pardon?"

"You really don't know anything, do you?" Not-Hans said. "You were Hans's friend. I thought that you— Clearly they thought you— But..." He paused. "Have you talked to Nat?"

"Nathaniel Remy? Yes, he's arranging the papers for—"

Not-Hans looked exasperated, like someone dealing with a child or the mentally ill. "Go home," he told me. "Go home now. As fast as you can. You are not safe."

And with that Cassandra-like pronouncement, he turned off.

I could go home, of course. But I don't take orders well and it hasn't improved with time. So, instead, I pulled out the other link button and dialed the first pre-set at random. It rang for less than a second, and then a face that I couldn't immediately recognize appeared midair. It was a handsome face, or at least it would be if you looked really up close and personal. At the first casual glance it was an unexceptional face, topped with short brown hair.

The bit-off words as he looked at me sounded like French, and he frowned and said, "You are not Max."

"No," I said. At least this reaction made sense, though it didn't make sense that these buttons should be programmed to someone who expected to talk to Max, but perhaps the new possessor of the code was a friend of Max's. "I'm his older brother, Lucius."

"His older..." The man opened his mouth, closed it. "*Merde*," he said, very carefully. "This is an unexpected...uh. Will you pardon me, for just *un petit moment*? My other link is ringing. It seems like..."

I couldn't say why but I knew the other link was not-Hans

calling him. And the face I'd just seen was the face of Good Man St. Cyr of Liberte Seacity.

I took a deep breath. None of this made sense, and I would presently wake up, safe and snug in my cell.

At that moment, the link buzzed loudly. I thought it would be Good Man St. Cyr again, and I pushed the call receiving button. But the face that formed, midair, glaring at me, was Nathaniel Remy's. "You just couldn't wait to stir up trouble, could you? You couldn't even wait for the legal action to tell them there would be trouble on the horizon." He didn't look angry, though his words were forceful. He looked more exasperated and a little fearful. "Come home. I'll keep watch. And then we need to talk."

"I think I'm going insane," I said, in response, not the least because one of my own servants was ordering me to come home. No, not even ordering me to come home. Exhorting me to come home, with the sort of gentle authority a mother or a nanny might use.

"Going?" he asked, and snorted. "Come home. I'll . . . explain what I can." He frowned. "Seems like I'll have to, just to prevent you running your foolish head into trouble, won't I?"

Without waiting for an answer he disconnected.

I could ignore his summons and not-Hans's orders. Perhaps I should. I did not like the idea that they were telling me to go home. I did not like trusting in them. I was almost sure I didn't like Nathaniel, though I would do a lot to spare his father grief or trouble. On the other hand, I had the feeling that not-Hans and Nathaniel, at least, were genuinely worried for me. Not about me, not about what I might do—though perhaps that too—but for me, and about what might happen to me. And I shivered thinking of Javier and Josia.

And then I got on my broom and went home.

Hell on Broomback

I'D TAKEN PART IN MANY HIGH-AERIAL BROOM BATTLES. A FEW territorial disputes, a few fights over primacy. But those were never played for life or death. The stakes hinged on disabling brooms and, sometimes, on cutting off access to some place.

But the battle that raged just short of my rooms, in Olympus, was anything but for broom disabling.

From a distance I saw it, and wondered what my guards were doing. My guards. How odd to think of them that way. But then I had no reason to think that the men in black broomer suits with red piping, like the one I was wearing, weren't in fact my guards. It didn't explain how a guard suit had got in my secret storage, but it would make more sense than anything else.

This fight was for real, with burners blazing. As I watched, one of the probably-not-my-guards went plunging down, dead, his weight pulling his broom down.

I'd determined to go around and in through the front entrance, except as I got closer, I saw the people attacking the men who were probably my guards—or being attacked by them, it was hard to tell—were wearing the subtly better-tailored, distinctive non-reflective black broomer suits of Scrubbers.

I couldn't have stopped myself if I tried. There were three men against eight or so Scrubbers, probably ten originally—judging from two corpses down on the rocks near the ocean—and they were fighting like hell on broomback.

And anyone, anyone, including the devils of any mythology, who went against Scrubbers, were by definition friends of mine.

I jumped into the fray, burners blazing, wishing I'd brought the additional burners that I'd sequestered in my room. Fortunately I never, ever, ever leave home without at least two. And unless one of these burners failed, having more wouldn't have helped. It's not like I could also fire with my nose, or perhaps my elbow. In fact, given the need to maneuver quickly, I could only fire with one hand, the other being on the broom controls.

The moment I entered the battle, the Scrubbers converged on me. It was as well. I burned a swath towards my room, but even with my extraordinary speed, only managed to hit one of them—who fell towards the rocks—the others moved away too fast.

Not as fast as those people on my team did. Two of them, at least, seemed to be as fast as I was, and flanked me, aiming fire at people ahead of us.

A burner ray flew by my ear, and the man who had shot it screamed and fell. And I realized he'd been shot by the third man in the defenders group, who was not only as agile as the others, but who must be touched in the head because ... well, let's just say there are very good aerodynamic reasons why riding your broom upside down is near impossible. It is also one of the scariest things you can do. Relax the pressure of your thighs on the broom, and you'll fall to your death. It does, however, leave both hands free for firing and gives you an unusual angle to fire from.

One of the Scrubbers shot at him, and I cut the Scrubber down, while still in the act of firing. I thought that there was no way the poor guy could right himself or maneuver in time to avoid getting shot. It would have been hard enough, if he'd been firing with both hands while flying head-up. But at least I'd avenge him.

Then I concentrated on shooting two more of the Scrubbers while they were aiming for my friends. And I ducked barely in time before a burner ray got me through the heart.

The problem with this sort of fighting is that there is no way to think and no way to plan. You fight by the sense that someone somewhere might be about to shoot you, and you duck out of the way when your premonition tingles and says they're aiming for you. You don't pause, you don't think, you don't slow down. And you don't take time to breathe.

Until it's one Scrubber alone, and he's turning tail, and two of the not-guards are taking off in pursuit, but before you join them, there is the man who saved your life, and who should not have been able to right himself on his broom, or escape that burner ray, but who has, and is moving his fingers rapidly at you.

Broomers use sign language. You have to, when you're flying midair, and half the time wearing a mask and goggles, and have to communicate with team mates to coordinate actions.

I hadn't used broomer sign language in years, but this particular broomer was willing to repeat the same gestures over and over again until I got what he was saying. And what he was saying was: *To the terrace and inside now. Safer.*

Right. Very guard like of him. I landed on my terrace, then went through the door into my room. The guard landed right behind me, which I expected.

What I didn't expect was that as he pulled back the hood of his suit, he revealed the pale, precisely cut hair of Nathaniel Remy.

He pulled off his goggles and oxygen mask and threw them on the floor as though they annoyed him. "Order perimeter," he said, and his voice cracked with what had to be exhaustion.

"Beg pardon?"

"Perimeter alarms," he said. "And electromagnetic shield at least over the terrace. Too easy for them to come that way." He walked towards the door to the terrace and locked it, and much to my shock, because I couldn't imagine why he'd have the family codes, punched in the code to activate security on that door, so it wouldn't open under anything including an armed assault. It was, like the front door, dimatough, because my father had been a paranoid bastard.

I didn't move. I was too stunned. The last five hours had been insane, but this just might top it: Nathaniel Remy, trained lawyer and clerk of my house, wearing an illegal broomer's suit, and showing that he was no stranger to air battles, as well as hell on broomback. When in the name of all that was holy—or unholy—had he learned such a skill? What did he do with it? Highjack drug transports in the dark of night? What could he possibly mean to do? And how did he know the family codes? Who was he? What did he want?

He gave me a darkling look, as he undid his suit and pulled it off, to reveal the outfit he'd been wearing before, but which was now clinging to his body in sweaty patches. "Please, Patrician," he said, emphasizing my title with a near-ironic exasperation. "Would you call the front door and tell them to lock and to exert siege measures? They can very well rush through the front door, you know? And while committing suicide is your prerogative, I think you owe it to your retainers not to let them be cut to pieces and made to disappear just because you got the Scrubbers on your ass, sir." The last "sir" rang with ironic strength.

He was right. I went to the com panel on my desk, and punched through to my security and guards, and barked instructions for siege measures. They'd only been used, once, in my time before arrest, when my father was having a trade war with another Good Man, one he didn't trust not to attempt to kill him, but no one questioned or demurred in following them. Instead they jumped to it. I heard people running in the hallways, orders barked, and shortly the house announcement system crackled, informing everyone we were now under siege measures, no one would get into the house without being personally approved by myself or Samuel Remy, and that anyone who was out had to be approved and searched before being allowed in, similar measures would apply on supplies that might be incoming.

And Nathaniel Remy had dropped onto one of the spectacularly uncomfortable-looking ornate chairs and was shaking, his hands over his face. I wondered if he was wounded, then realized he was shaking with exhaustion. Berserkers don't feel it until they come down and then it hits them all at once. I wondered how long the battle had been going on, before I joined.

I stepped over to the bottles of liquor I'd seen earlier, uncorked the brandy that had been my father's favorite, poured one of my father's dainty crystal goblets full to the brim, and tapped Nathaniel on the shoulder. He removed his hands from his face and looked at me with a dull expression. I pushed the goblet at him, and for a moment I thought he would say he didn't drink, but instead he took it by the stem and drank it in one gulp, though he was still shaking so much that his teeth chattered against the crystal.

"Thank you," he said, at length, and took a deep breath, and seemed to shake less.

"How long have you been fighting?" I asked.

"I don't know," he said. "There was a while before Simon— I found them, in ambush. And we didn't have guards on duty, and besides, these are Scrubbers. If I lost that battle, they'd kill me. But they'd also kill anyone else who'd joined on my side. I couldn't involve the guards." He looked baleful. "They're not free to choose to join battle or not."

"I understand," I said, and filed for future reference the fact that Nathaniel not only knew what Scrubbers were but seemed to have an inflexible moral code that included keeping innocents out of the fray, even if the innocents were trained guards. Annoying though the man might be, that was one quality I couldn't help but find admirable.

He looked up at me and barked a half-laugh. "You do, don't you? Odd." His hands were patting at himself, the way they'd done before when he'd been looking for his cigarettes, but this time, perhaps not being in the grip of such a strong emotion, or perhaps being tired, he remembered himself and stopped. "I beg your pardon," he said. "I smoked this morning without asking you, didn't I?"

I shrugged. "Never mind. Smoke again, if you wish." I took the porcelain box from the drawer I'd hidden it in, and opened it, offering it to him as an ashtray.

He looked at it, then at me, brought out the cigarette case and extracted one, which he shook to light. "Thank you kindly, Patrician Keeva," he said. "I was dying for a smoke."

For some reason his using my title annoyed me. "Call me Lucius," I said. "I don't know how you kids consider these things, but when I was a broomer, if you'd fought beside each other, you were broomer-brothers, and there were no barriers and no titles between you."

He looked at me, and his eyebrows arched, and I got the odd impression that I was being measured very carefully. "Very well," he said. "Lucius. And you may call me Nat. Nathaniel is a mouthful and not even my mother uses it. And Remy is my father."

I got the odd impression I was being offered a high honor in his agreeing to call me by my name, instead of my granting him a boon by allowing the familiarity.

He took a deep lungful of tobacco smoke, then expelled it. "I suppose," he said, "we will need to talk."

"I believe so," I said. Unless I had become completely insane, I was facing something I simply didn't have the data to understand. And I wanted the data—I wanted to understand—now.

It wasn't amazing he'd shaken. It wasn't amazing he looked like someone had dropped a mountain on his back, or like he'd aged ten years since I'd last seen him. What was amazing was that he was alive and coherent.

"Can I have dinner for two delivered to the room?" I asked him. He blinked at me. "What?"

"Pardon me. Of course I can have dinner delivered. I am, after all, the Good Man. What I meant was, will you dine with me? If I have dinner brought in?"

He gave something that might be a laugh or a cough but which somehow sounded sad. "It's not necessary."

"Sure it is. You've been fighting for what? Half an hour at least. You need something."

He pinched the bridge of his nose between thumb and forefinger, and made little circles, as though massaging it. The sort of gesture someone made to get rid of an unbearable headache. Or to avoid crying, but I didn't think Nathaniel Remy was the type to burst into tears. "What I need," he said, flatly, "is a good dose of cyanide."

I had to assume he was joking. "No such luck," I said. "I wanted one of those for years. If I couldn't have it, you can't either."

He looked up, and again there was the shocked laugh-cough. "Do as you will, Patri—Lucius. I'm starting to believe you're the sort who will always pretty much do so, whether it is advisable or not."

I called down and ordered a dinner for two, confusing the kitchen by telling them I didn't care what was provided as long as it was fast, warm and had at least two courses. Just before I flicked the link off, Nat said, "Tell them to bring Goldie. I left him in the kitchen, in care of Mrs.—in care of the cook's adjutant because I was walking him when they—when I got the call about what you'd been up to."

I snapped, "And bring Mr. Remy's dog, which he says he left in the care of the cook's adjutant. Have someone walk Goldie up before the dinner is ready, please." I spoke more tersely than I meant to.

When I turned around, Nat was smoking as if it were the most important thing in the world and required his whole concentration.

"Keep that up," I said sharply. "And you won't need cyanide."

He laugh-coughed and looked at his cigarette as though he'd never seen one before. "What? These?" he said. "My dear Lucius! Have you not kept up with science? They're practically non-carcinogenic these days."

"I'm not your dear Lucius and you don't believe that any more than I do. If you smoke enough, even trace carcinogens will get to you."

"No," he said. I wasn't sure to what he was replying.

"Look," I said. "I know you don't like me. I don't know why but, of course, there is no reason you should like me. Plenty of people have not liked me in my life, starting with my father. But you saved my life today, and I appreciate that."

He gave me a half-smile. "Likewise. But don't feel exaggerated gratitude, please. I have three very good reasons to keep you alive. The first is that without you we'll be at the mercy of every Good Man who chooses to take us over. Mind you, please, you might just have involved us in a war, but—never mind. At least you present an appearance of legality to the world-at-large, who doesn't know what is really going on."

"I don't know what's really going on."

Cough laugh and a deep pull on his cigarette, and Nat shook his head. "Clearly. You shall be enlightened. Second, while you rub me wrong on the personal level, I don't think you've done anything to deserve the long shitstorm that's been unleashed on you, or the one that's still to come." He paused and sucked on that cigarette as though his life depended on it. His long, elegant fingers were nicotine-stained. His ornate silver ring glowed dully and I realized it encircled the finger normally used for a marriage ring. Was Nat married? If so, what was he doing involving himself in aerial battles? Didn't he have a responsibility to his family?

"And the third?"

"The third? Oh. Right, the third. My father likes you. My father and I have . . . our differences. But one thing he's very good at is telling the sheep from the goats, or in this case the sheep dogs from the wolves. He likes you. He says—" He shook his head. "Never mind. He likes you. And because he likes you, I assume you're a worthwhile human being."

"I'm glad—" I started intending to say that I was glad Sam Remy liked me, but I didn't think he knew the half of it. He might or might not know what his brother and I had been up to, but he wouldn't know, couldn't know how Ben had died. Not if he liked me still. And besides, Sam couldn't possibly know *me*. He'd known twenty-two-year-old me, but there had been so many years since. That pampered princeling was as dead as Ben.

But I didn't say anything because there was a knock on the door, and one of the younger servants that I didn't know came in with a curly-haired golden setter by his side. He looked so much like Bonnie, which my mother had got me, and which my father had got rid of when I was ten, that I couldn't help smiling. Seeing Nat, Goldie came into the room, tail wagging, and put his head on Nat's lap. Nat patted him and told him, "Sit. Sit, sir," while I nodded at the servant to leave.

I don't know how well-trained Goldie was. My own experience with setters tended to make me think they were the dumb blondes of the canine world, and all the training in the world might as well fly in and out through their ears. But he ignored Nat's order to sit, and instead turned towards me. The tail that had wagged madly went between the legs, and the ears went back. The defensive-aggressive posture of a dog facing someone he thinks is going to kick him. Great. Even dogs hated me.

But Nat scratched at the base of the dog's ears. "It's all right Goldie. He's ugly, but he doesn't bite." A quick glance at me and he started to rise. "I'll take Goldie to my father, shall I? One of my brothers can—"

I dropped into a squat, so I wasn't looming over the dog. I was still much larger than him, of course. "Come here, Goldie. Come here, boy."

Goldie hesitated half a second, then seemed to decide I was safe. His tail started again, and he rushed to me, ears flying. Moments later, I was fighting to make him stop licking my face, exerting pressure on his hindquarters to make him sit, and Nat had forgotten to smoke, and was holding his cigarette in what seemed to be nerveless fingers, while the ash grew long.

I managed to make Goldie sit, and stood up, leaning a little to scratch his ears. "There boy, I've already washed my face. Nat, I'd appreciate it if you shook that ash off before it falls and burns the carpet." And, as he obeyed, reflexively, I cast a disgusted look at the carpet. "Not that this is worth saving. I swear it looks like my father's stuff. If this was Max's taste I don't think highly of it. I wonder where my furniture is. You said they never throw anything away."

"It must be your voice," Nat said, looking at Goldie and me. Goldie was now leaning on my leg. "Or perhaps your smell. You are wearing Max's clothes."

"Uh?"

"Goldie," he said. "I'll explain. After...when they bring dinner."

Which they did immediately, wheeling in a table, with table-cloth and all, and a serving cart. It was a regular procession that came into my room. I'd had dinner brought to my room before, sometimes to share with Ben, but I'd never had this type of thing. Usually our dinners came on a large tray. I guessed it was different when you were the Good Man.

In the lead, two servants pushed a wheeled table, with white tablecloth. Following them were two servants, one carrying two branched candlesticks with candles—candles?—and the other carrying a tray with plates, glassware and silverware. Following them came two more servants wheeling a multi-tier serving cart, of the kind that has surfaces to keep food cold and surfaces to keep food hot, and which contained more covered trays, plat-ters of fruit and vegetables, tastefully arranged cheese plates and silver trays with dainties than would feed a family of ten for three days. And following those were other, uniformed servants carrying two chairs.

Before I could blink, the table was set by the window, the candles burning, the lights dimmed—did they think this was a romantic assignation? Had rumors of my misdeeds preceded me? No. It was just that my father probably only had dinner for two in this room when it was an assignation—plates and silverware in place, the serving cart disposed nearby, and a servant disposed behind each chair, waiting to serve us. That wouldn't do, not if I wanted Nat to talk. And Nat wanted to talk. I could see it in his eyes. And frankly, I needed him to talk, if I was going to stay alive in this brave new world.

I gestured for the servants to leave. They hesitated. "Do leave," I said. "We'll serve ourselves. We're competent enough for that."

They left, looking like I'd broken their toys. If I didn't need to talk privately with Nat I'd let them stay, just to avoid the whipped puppy look in their eyes. I locked the door behind them. When I turned back, Nat was sitting on a chair by the table, smoking.

He'd brought his improvised ashtray with him, and he was looking indefinably amused, in a way I couldn't pinpoint.

"Something funny, Nathaniel Remy?" I asked.

He shook his head, then looked like he was going to brave himself for a plunge. "Oh, hell, I doubt you'll believe it, but some of them are going to think—that is—"

I sighed. This would come up sooner of later. "I believe it. Some of the older ones know that your uncle Benjamin Remy and I were . . . more than friends, and they'll make a lot of very silly inferences, yes. Not our fault, and we can't help it. I'm sure they'll get over it."

He looked surprised. "Uncle Benjamin? Well, hell." And resumed smoking.

So, that wasn't what he'd meant. Which, I suppose, meant that he was amused that they thought we were conspiring. "Well, I suppose we are conspiring," I said. I got up and went over to the buffet and lifted the lids over several hot dishes. "Do you eat soup? Seems to be seafood soup, though of course it could be just algae and smell. But no, wait, I'm the Good Man and . . . yes, there is a shrimp in there. Presumably more too. It's good to see shrimp. It's been years."

"I'm not really hungry," he said. "I—"

I didn't really care what he felt. He might not feel hungry, but he'd need the calories and the warmth after that midair fight. I'd already filled two bowls, and before he could enlarge on how he didn't feel hungry at all, and could surely survive on air and nerves with the occasional lungful of nicotine, I'd set a bowl in front of him, and another at my place. I was back at the buffet, selecting one of the white wines offered and opening it, before he said, in a waspish tone, "You really are very determined."

"Yes," I said.

"And you don't listen well," he said.

"No," I agreed, affably, as I poured a glass of wine for him and one for me.

He quirked an eyebrow at me, but picked up his glass of wine and took a sip. Goldie was going between our chairs, thumping his tail with lethal force against our legs. "In fact, you're all-around a pain in the neck, aren't you?" he said.

"My father thought so," I said. "So much so he put me away for fifteen years. And Javier, today, said that I just wouldn't die. Which I suppose is true, but not for lack of trying."

The half-amused expression went from his gaze. He sat up straighter. He took a sip of his wine, looking at me the whole while with those cool, speculative eyes. It was odd enough for him to have dark-dark eyes, when he was that pale a blond. But his eyes, unlike Ben's which had been the same color, looked almost unreflective, swallowing the light and giving nothing back.

"None of it was your fault, you know?"

"Beg your pardon? What wasn't my fault? My not being able to kill myself?"

He shook his head, then took a spoonful of the soup, looked surprised and took another. "That too," he said, after that second spoonful, his spoon suspended between bowl and mouth. "I suppose that too, since being yourself, you probably put in a very good effort. But I didn't mean that. I meant everything that's happened to you." He set his spoon by the side of his bowl, on his plate. "I'll tell you what I know of your history—what my father told me—shall I? Then you fill in the blanks. I'm sure there are blanks since he never told me that you and my uncle were... involved. Though he did tell me that you... Well, I'd told him what was happening. He suspected it, already, and he told me why you'd been set aside from the... Why you had been sent out of the way and kept alive. Awkward too, since he was talking to me, of all people." He looked up and met what must be my baffled expression. "No, none of this will make sense, until I explain, but first of all—tell me why you were arrested, or at least how it happened."

I frowned at him. "I was in a broomer group—no surprise to you, I suppose?"

He shook his head. Of course, he'd seen me on broomback, just as I'd seen him.

"So," I said. "Javier and Josia Bruno, and Hans Rainer and... oh, a dozen or so of us, plus any number of children of our upper servants. We weren't very good broomers. I mean, not like the illegal broomers you read about. We didn't rob any drug transports but once, though we did our share of drugs. We tended to buy them. And we didn't get in many battles for territory because word had quietly got around about what we really were, and they were leaving us alone. But we had fun. We got away from the protocol and people watching us. I sold a lot of my jewelry to keep our lair in booze and narcs." I shrugged. "We started when we were about fourteen."

"Sounds familiar," Nat said, and there was a cigarette between his fingers. Before he could shake it to light, I said, "Eat."

His eyes widened, then the half smile came back. "Aye-aye, Patrician."

I glared. "Eat or I pour it over your head. I spent fifteen years eating mush. You're not going to let good food go to waste."

His gaze shifted from amused to serious, again, and I thought I detected a glimmer of compassion in them. I didn't want his pity. While he ate, I went on, "My friend Hans was odd, for about a year or so, before . . . and then he called me in the middle of the night. He said he was in trouble, and would Ben and I come out. He'd called other friends, too. He said he had to tell me something, but he could only tell me in person.

"When we got there, he was . . ." I shrugged. "He was too emotional to speak. And when he did speak, it didn't make any sense. He said we were all Mules, and I—" I shrugged. I remember we thought he was crazy, and we tried to calm him down. "We finally gave him a Morpheus injector to make him sleep. Without his expecting it, you know? We didn't know what he was saying, and he sounded hysterical." I paused. "And then we called his father."

"Oh my God," Nat said. It sounded like a straight-out invocation of the divinity.

"Quite," I said. "I've worked out that was the wrong thing to do. I've lived with the guilt of it, the knowledge I betrayed my friend. I've figured I as good as murdered Hans. It's been fifteen years, and I am not completely stupid. I can add ten and ten, if I remove my shoes and count carefully." I took a deep draught of the wine, because I didn't want to choke up as I told him about my downfall which was no more than deserved for what I'd done to Hans. I tried to keep it dry and short. "Next thing you knew, we were invaded by Scrubbers. Hans was shot through the heart immediately. The others . . . They died, one by one, and Scrubbers . . . You know what Scrubbers do to bodies to dispose of them?"

"Not exactly," he said, pushing his empty bowl of soup away. "And I suspect I don't want to, not over a meal."

"No," I said. "They tried to kill Ben too, but they'd have had to go through me for that. But then . . . But then Hans's father and my father—" I took a deep breath and said, my voice still echoing the surprise I'd felt that night. "My father! I mean, I knew he didn't like me, but— They came in, and they said that two perpetrators would do as well as one. And then...and then the seacities Peacekeepers came in, and they arrested Ben and me for Hans's murder. And then..." I choked and had to stop and breath. "And then they took us before a panel of five Good Men and they threw us in jail.

"And a year later they transferred me to Never-Never."

"Because you killed Uncle Benjamin," Nat said, flatly. "Which I must say proves that whoever is cranking men's fate up there has a hell of a sense of humor. Or was that also trumped up?"

I shook my head and wished, just wished, I could conjure Ben's ghost again as I had through my solitary days in the cell. "Not trumped up." I shrugged. "They tortured him. They took him to a special cell and they tortured him. He should have died. I don't know what they wanted to know. I broke into the cell to rescue him, but I couldn't...He wouldn't live. They were keeping him alive to torture him. I slit his throat."

"They didn't want to know anything," he said. "They were trying to get rid of him. I suspect he'd understood more of Hans's story than you had, just didn't know how to tell it to you. But he got some of it, at least, out through our network. And that—"

"Your network?"

Nat was rubbing the bridge of his nose again. "What do you think of subversive organizations?"

"What? I'm rather fond of broomers. And I helped a Usaian kid escape Never-Never," I said, half joking. "John Jefferson."

He looked, slowly, at me, with that kind of speculative look a mouse gives a defanged cat. "Let's just say my Uncle Benjamin belonged to a secret organization. As I do. And he got something out on our network, though it fell short of the whole truth. Something must have leaked, or the message was intercepted. Not unusual in prisons for wardens to know the channels for secret messages. It was intercepted and read, probably. And then they knew he was dangerously close to the truth."

"He didn't tell me anything," I said. I felt curiously betrayed. We hadn't had secrets from each other, had we?

"He wouldn't," Nat said. "He thought it was dangerous knowledge. He was right. And so they goaded you to kill him, and then they put you in Never-Never for it."

"Yes," I said, and felt tired and empty. There really was nothing more to say. They'd made me murder my best friend, the only person besides my mother and Max that I cared about at all in the whole world. "And they forced me to stay alive to feel the guilt."

He got up. "Eat your soup," he said, and went over to the sideboard, and poked around in it, lifting lids and looking. I finished my soup, and he removed the bowl and set it to one side of the serving tray. In its place, he set a plate with a chicken breast and something green and leafy. He'd made a similar plate for himself, and when I looked enquiringly at him, he gave me his half-amused look again. "The reverse of a suicide pact, shall we try that? You eat, I eat. I haven't eaten a full meal since—" He stopped as abruptly as if the words had been cut with a knife. "In the last two days. I haven't eaten much of anything, in fact. When I'm smoking, it doesn't seem to matter. And I was . . . Until you made me eat the stupid soup, I didn't realize I was hungry."

"I wasn't commenting on the food," I said. "Just on you serving."

"Ah. That is a plan of mine," he said. "I'm learning a second trade. In case, you know, they decide to kill all the lawyers." He smiled a little. "You don't have any idea, do you? Ah, well, the classics aren't taught."

"Shakespeare," I said.

He raised his eyebrows.

"When I was in Never-Never," I said, boldly. "Someone sent me a gem reader inside a food can. Nothing fancy, mind you. One of the cheap disposable ones. I made it last fourteen years. And they sent me gems. Mostly history. I bet you I know more about the non-mythical USA than anyone alive. Well, most people alive. Someone sent me caches of documents everyone else thinks are lost forever." I paused. "Weirdly, a lot of it has echoes of the myths of the Usaians, from what I can tell. Liberty and justice for all." I shook my head at the sheer unlikelihood of it. "And there was music and literature and art appreciation." I made a face at him. "I'm probably educated at dangerous levels."

He had narrowed his eyes. "I would bet you are," he said softly. He seemed to be making calculations in his head, and I was suddenly uncomfortable. "I think I know where those gems came from." I looked alarmed. "Please. Trust me that it would be the last thing I'd dream of, to turn the person in."

"The gems kept me sane," I said.

Again the quirked eyebrow, and I couldn't tell if he was baiting me. All he said was, "I'm glad." He cut a piece of his chicken with the kind of careless precision of someone who learned his table manners before he learned to walk. Ate it. Took a sip of his wine, and said, "Now eat. Let me tell you why you were framed for murder and put away, why my uncle Benjamin was killed, and why they forced your hand to kill him. Why they wouldn't let you kill yourself in Never-Never and why... And everything." He paused to eat some of the green vegetables. "Please, listen to what I tell you before you question it. I'm not insane, though sometimes I've wished I was. No, Goldie, down." He sighed as the dog put his paws on his knee to beg food.

"You talk," I said. "I'll make him a plate."

"It's not good for him to eat people food."

"Yeah, probably not, but can you blame him for being jealous we're eating and not giving him any?" I went to the serving cart and started making a plate with meats, trying to pick the ones with least spices.

Behind me, Nat said in a distant, cold voice, "For me it started when your father died."

Familiar Strangers

"OR RATHER," HE SAID. "WE THOUGHT HE HAD DIED. HE'D BEEN on a trip to Circum with your—with Max, and when the space cruiser, which they'd borrowed from Good Man Sinistra landed, we were told he had died en route, and that Max was in shock."

"So far it was believable," he said. "Max was my best friend, my closest friend. We'd been close since . . . well, I can't remember since when. You probably remember us playing together. I remember when he was smaller than I, but once he got bigger, I never caught up."

I filled the plate and put it on the floor for Goldie, who rushed to it. "Goldie! Manners," Nat said. "Don't act like you haven't eaten in days."

"I vaguely remember you," I said. "You're Max's age, just about, right?"

"Three years older, though I was always smaller after he hit four or so. Your mother thought you'd been raised too much in isolation, so from the time we could toddle, my father brought me over two or three times a week, to play. My siblings too, of course. We . . . Max and I, well, there's no guarantee of it, right? We might have grown up to hate each other, but we didn't. We grew up to be very close. So, when I thought he had ascended, I—" He shrugged. "I thought I could help him, and I came to talk to him." He frowned. "He treated me exactly as your father did.

93

No. More like, as your father would treat me if he were trying to impersonate Max. I . . . I don't care to relate that interview, but it was like, you know, of course he knew I was Max's friend, so he was trying to be friendly. But when you're . . . When you're close to someone, there's things you know. There's in jokes. There's references to things that you two have done and lived through. Like . . . like . . ." He seemed to be madly reaching, perhaps goaded by skepticism in my eyes. "Like, you know, we were broomers together, and there were . . . people from our broomers' lair." He sat back and twirled his silver ring on his finger. "Eat. You're not eating. Anyway, we'd kept our broomer stuff secret, and it was clear your . . . father knew nothing of it. Neither did what I'll call new-Max. New-Max didn't want his furniture, he wanted your father's things transferred here. New-Max didn't know about Goldie, who had spent most of his time at my house, though he was Max's dog." He gestured with his head towards the portrait on the wall. "And new-Max didn't know who had drawn that. He liked it, mind. And he wanted to pay the artist. Pay!"

"Who—"

Nat shrugged. "It doesn't matter. I thought I was going crazy. Or that Max had gone crazy. I thought he'd fallen and hit his head. I thought he'd had a stroke. I thought—"

"I thought all of that today, when I met with Javier."

"I figured. So maybe you won't think I'm completely insane. Though that's what it felt like to me. I didn't know what to do, or how to act. My friend was still here, but he was gone, and I didn't know why or if it was something I'd done, or if he'd ever return." He paused a long while. The cigarette appeared in his hands and I didn't dare chide him into putting it away and eating, because he was looking right through me and you'd think his memories were as horrible as mine. "And then there was a series of events I can't explain, because I don't think you know the participants, and some of them aren't mine to confide. But Good Man Sinistra's daughter disappeared, and when she came back, she had to rescue her husband from Never-Never. That's when we . . . That's when you were freed."

"Good Man Sinistra's *daughter*?" I said, shocked. It shouldn't be shocking, but Good Men had sons with such regularity, and usually no girls, that I'd long suspected some form of gene manipulation.

"Athena Hera Sinistra. About Max's age, so she was born when you— I don't suspect you cared much for birth announcements, though." Nat strained smoke through his teeth "Almost as scary as my sister Martha, but a good woman, all the same. Not that it matters. You're not likely to ever meet her. She's—elsewhere. With her husband." His pauses made me wonder if he resented that Athena Sinistra had married someone else. But that wasn't any of my business. "What matters is that she broke into her father's study and got some gems with information. What she discovered . . . What those gems revealed tallied with several other . . . other sources of information, including what we'd got from Uncle Benjamin. And what other people in the lair . . . There is this broomer who was severely disabled who, had that not happened, would probably have met the same fate you did. Or perhaps he would just have been killed."

He took a deep drag on his cigarette. "You must, you absolutely must believe that I'm sane as I tell you this, because you'll be tempted to think I'm insane. Because that would make everything so much easier."

"I don't think anything easy can explain what happened to me today. Or, in fact, what happened to me since I was twenty-two. So I'm prepared for the unbelievable."

He nodded. "First," he said. "Pardon me, it's none of my business, but it will help me understand some details. You said you and my uncle were . . . involved. This was . . . physical?"

I looked at my plate. Attitudes towards homosexuality have changed through the centuries. If those learning gems were right, in Greece it had been almost obligatory. Then, at various times it had been condoned or accepted. But even in eras when it was accepted, some people were violently repulsed by it, and not only for religious reasons. There seemed to be something built into the species that made some people loathe the very idea. Perhaps this was necessary for keeping the species alive.

I'd never talked about my love life. It didn't matter to anyone else, except Ben, really. My persona as the heir to the Good Man didn't have an official sex life. Oh, I had young women I took out to official occasions. I'd never had an interest in them, and most of them had never had an interest in me, though some would have thought it was grand for me to set them up and keep them as a fling on the side—but that would have been for the setting up, not for me.

It had never mattered. Ben and I had—I supposed it would be called fallen in love?—very young. And after that, it just hadn't mattered. He was safe and secure, in a world where anyone else might run screaming to the news holos. I didn't care to risk it, and he seemed fine with it. And besides, he was my main companion in everything else. He was mine.

I'd never told anyone else. Not even my mother. Never spoke of it. By the time I could have, I knew our particular society disapproved very strongly of it, at least for males. Oh, maybe not in some parts of the world. Since I didn't discuss it with anyone, I didn't know for sure. But in the places I knew, homosexuality was as disapproved of as any other unusual and possibly odd behavior. In many places, perhaps most, it was subjected to the death penalty. In Olympus it was at a minimum a matter for a jail sentence, though rarely enforced in the higher classes. "We were lovers," I said drily.

Nat Remy didn't seem shocked. He nodded. "None of my business, but...exclusive, or..."

I frowned at him.

"What I mean," he said, "is whether you also had an interest in women, or—"

"What? Some women make fine friends, but...not that way, no."

"May I ask if anyone knew about it?" he said. "And when it started?"

"I don't see why—"

"Because I think I need to, to explain things to you."

I bit my tongue, got up and went blindly to the buffet, where I slammed things around, pretending to look for something. I just didn't want to be looking at him. "I think we must have been around seventeen though we might have been sixteen when we started fooling around physically," I said. "And we were discovered shortly after. Someone—I don't remember who, one of the maids—opened the door on us, and screamed and..." I remembered the scene and part of me wanted to laugh at how ridiculous we must have looked. It had never occurred to us we were doing anything wrong. More importantly, it never occurred to us anyone would care. We'd been punctilious about hiding our escapades out of the compound, our souping up of stolen flyer-safety brooms, the first ones we'd tried out. But no one had ever talked to us about sex, and it never occurred to us what we did together was on the list of forbidden things. "There was a horrible scene. I think my father fired the maid or whatever, but everyone in the house knew, though most of them pretended not to. For about a year, I could only see Ben in secret. Then Max was born, and my parents got very involved with him and seemed to forget. And Ben and I took care to lock the door."

Nat nodded. He leaned back in his chair. Goldie, having finished his food, came over and put his head on Nat's knees. Nat lit another cigarette. "You say you've been studying history. What do you know about the Mules?"

"Eh? The Mules or the Mule Lords?" I asked, disoriented by the shift.

"Both."

"Ah." I had no idea what he wanted. But I ate a little of my chicken, reveling in the symphony of spices and seasonings, after fourteen years of eating salty mush and sweet mush and trying not to think of what Nathaniel was getting at. "Well, the Mules were first made to make up European populations that were falling precipitously. The first few . . . ah . . . batches were mental defectives, gestated by animals. But after a while, they perfected the process, had them carried by surrogates and started creating smart ones. Very smart indeed. They created them extraordinarily healthy too, and gave them various other enhancements for longevity, and they were used for everything from super-clerks to corporate couriers, to assassins. And then someone had the bright idea that if only we were governed by angels we wouldn't need to be wary of government. And government would be better than ever. They must have read, what was his name? James Madison. The man said government would be fine if we were administered by angels. I suppose it never occurred to him someone would try to create the equivalent. Anyway, they made the Mule Lords." I shook my head. "They were good as far as consolidating their power went. They took over territories that had initially been self-governing, like the seacities. And those who were made to be only sort of the masters of bureaucracy took over total control, anyway. And . . . things went very badly. In the beginning of the twenty-second century there was a revolution. And then there were turmoils. Most Mule Lords and their servants were killed. Perhaps all of them, though a legend persists that a number of them went off world in an interstellar ship they'd secretly built and which they ominously called the *Je Reviens*."

Nat leaned back further and absently patted at Goldie's head. Goldie must have been dissatisfied with the pets, because he walked over to me and put his head on my knees. I petted him, glad for his warmth. I had no idea where Nat was going with this, nor why he was giving me a history exam. "You're almost right," he said. "Almost. As far as we can tell, from documentary evidence, the *Je Reviens* was no myth. And a good number of Mule Lords went off on it. Most of the ones, in fact, who were designed to be rulers. The ones they left behind were, with one or two exceptions, the ones that they didn't want to trust in close confines. A few of them had been rulers, but most of them had been seconds in command, or ... or assassins. Or spies. Or," he smiled a little. "I have no evidence of this, but I suspect a few of them were created as honeypots."

"Mule honeypots?" The idea of bioimproved people being used to subvert by seduction was odd. What would the improvements have been?

"Never mind. There were twenty-five years of turmoil, when every civilized region burned, every archive was emptied, looted, destroyed, every building of note razed. The people who wrote at the time, whose writings we can still find, thought it was like the fall of Rome, or the fall of the USA all over again. They thought they were in for a period of barbarism, or at least privation. This time they thought it would last as long as the Middle Ages, and be everywhere, not just in North America. They thought things would be lost—" He took a pull of his cigarette. "This is when, of course, the Usaian religion was founded, when Bob Haute ... Never mind. Time enough for that later. But most people just huddled in place. And those with any hint of bioing or even who might be suspected of having such, because they were exceptionally bright or exceptionally beautiful or agile, hid and hoped no one noticed. Some of them were caught. Some of them were even really bioed, but most weren't. Envy had full rein. They were crucified and stoned and killed in inventive ways, in public, in major cities and rural byways. Until the storm passed." Another deep pull, and blue smoke twirled in the yellow candle light. "But some people were doing more than that. The Mules who had stayed behind were planning and ... arranging things. And making sure crucial, targeted knowledge was lost. A lot of them, after all, were created as spies, assassins and agents provocateur. It was their job."

"So you're saying some Mules survived," I said. Goldie was snoring with his head on my knees.

He nodded. "And then, when the turmoils passed, they took control. Slowly, they established themselves as genetically pure. The best humanity had spun off naturally. They gathered around them their bioengineered servants who had survived. Or other bioengineered people who had survived. People who were normal, except for having been genetically enhanced, usually for intelligence, and sometimes for looks—though most of those were killed off—and sometimes for other characteristics like vision, or hearing or... You get the point."

My mind has this very bad habit of getting ahead of me—of racing through, insanely—and adding ten plus ten while I'm back there, painstakingly counting two on my fingers. I looked at Nat. I remembered his fighting on broomback. I remembered the way Ben could move. "Were your ancestors bioed for speed?"

He gave me a tight smile. "Speed and coordination on one side of Dad's ancestry. Intelligence and memory on the other. Intelligence and organizational skills on Mom's. It doesn't always breed true, but mostly it does." He shook the ash of his cigarette into the ashtray. "The Mules reestablished themselves as rulers... as... Patricians."

I blinked at him. "It won't pass, Nat. Mules were sterile. And they were all male."

"Ah," he said. "There are other ways of reproducing."

"They were also keyed against cloning, and besides cloning is illegal."

"Um... Yes. But they were keyed against cloning in the twenty-first century, when it was practically in its infancy. And as for its being illegal... when did that ever stop those with power? Remember, you can open your father's genlocks. All Good Men of Olympus could."

"So..." I said, adding slowly, "You're saying my... ancestors were Mules. And yours were bioengineered, but still capable of reproducing normally."

"You're not running into the night," he said, vaguely complimentary.

I shrugged. "Hans said we were all Mules. It seemed insane, but..."

"But Scrubbers don't bother with the insane?" he asked, sharply, stubbing his cigarette, and starting another. He'd eaten less than half of his plate, and I got up, gently removing Goldie's head from my lap. The dog padded over to Nat and put his head on Nat's knees. I grabbed a platter full of fruit and cheese, and set it between us on the table, where both of us could reach it.

"I guess," I said. "I've had time to think about it."

"But you're still not quite correct," Nat said. "Oh, yes, of course, they reproduced by cloning." He plucked a grape from the platter and ate it. "That was why most of them had only sons. The wives were merely carriers, though I suspect none of them knew it."

"You mean, I was no relation to my mother?"

Nat looked at me. I sighed. "Never mind, go on."

"The few daughters recorded to Good Men were either . . . well . . . not all wives were faithful. Or they were the result of a long-term project to create a modified clone, a female Mule."

"Was—"

"We've reason to think Athena is one. There were others, but they were either severely handicapped or genetically flawed, or sterile. Or all of the above. Anyway . . . so, you see . . ."

"I don't feel as if I'm just like my father. We never agreed on most things. And he—" And he had been one of the most outraged at my relationship with Ben. "He thought Ben and I—"

"The human genome is a wondrous thing. They tried to build the Mules as cleanly as they could," he said. "Wysiwyg."

"Weezwhat?"

"Ancient Usaian word for 'what you see is what you get,'" he said. "But it's not like that. Some genes can't be separated. You can't take the good without the bad. And some of them seem to flip on or off randomly, in response to environmental pressures, both in gestation and after. You are not your father. But you are as close as an identical twin. Over the centuries, though, variations crept in."

"But that doesn't explain why Max changed when he—"

"No." He had picked up a piece of cheese, and now put it on the side of the plate and looked at me. "The thing is, the clones never inherited. You see, they . . . the Mules and their bioengineered servants, had access to all the biological science before the turmoils, and . . . and they developed a method for brain transplant. Yes, I know it's still risky in most cases, but not with their techniques, not to a clone."

Silence fell, except for Goldie's light snoring. I wanted to tell Nat he was wrong. But I was thinking of Javier asking me how I'd managed it in only a few days. I was thinking of a stranger looking out of his eyes. I was thinking of Josia. I heard something between a choked sob and a yell. And Nat's sympathy made me realize I'd made the sound. Goldie lifted his head and looked at me. "You mean they're all dead? All of them? All my friends? And do you mean Max..."

"Max was killed aboard that space cruiser, probably a few days out of Circum, and your father's brain inserted into his cranium," Nat said. "Max..." He shrugged. "I hope he didn't know what was happening. I hope he went to sleep and just never woke up. Sometimes I wake in the night. I hear him talking to me. Sometimes I pray he never knew. Pray!" He looked through me. "I think, you know, that I've gone quite insane, this last week, since I found out for sure. One thing is to suspect and the other to know. I think I went unhinged. Worry and pain turned to anger and...I've done things that I..." He looked at his hands, as if they were alien and strange.

"Yes," I said. It was choked. I wasn't going to cry in front of Nat Remy, whose eyes looked so much like Ben's, particularly when they filled with sympathy. I was not going to let him see me break down. I was not. I got up and stumbled to the drinks stand in the room. Not the brandy. I didn't even like brandy. I grabbed blindly, instead, for a bottle of unopened single malt, and tore at the seals and pulled the cork out. I drank from the bottle, feeling the burn in my throat, the warmth hit my nervous system almost immediately. It had been fifteen years. It hit me like a mule kick, but by that time I was back in the chair, still clutching the bottle. At least any moisture in my eyes would look like reaction to the alcohol.

Nat reached across and took the bottle from my hands, and I was about to protest when he wiped cursorily at the lips of the bottle and threw back a healthy swig, before handing it back. "I killed the bastard," he said, his voice oddly raspy. "God help me, I killed him slowly. I made him talk. Oh, God, I'd give a lot to forget."

I stared at him. "Max? You killed Max?" I almost dropped the bottle, but then I saw the horror in his eyes and realized this was a man two steps from the sort of abyss where all you do is scream and scream while life lasts. Out of pity, out of having lived there, on that cold ledge, I extended him a metaphorical hand. "I mean, you killed my father, in Max's body?"

He nodded. "I didn't believe it, not really, till I saw the sutures, and the replacement bone under the scalp." He shuddered, a body-long shudder. "And he talked. About you, among other things. But he talked about you as though you were dead. I thought the suicide attempt when you—when you crushed your nose had worked." He shrugged. "My father had talked. He'd said..." He shook his head. "It wasn't merciful, what they did to you."

"Why?" I said. "Why Max and not me? And why the elaborate setup to get me in Never-Never but not let me die? I suppose Hans discovered this? Why did Hans have a brother? For that matter, why did they have Max? Why—"

"I don't know about Hans. You know what I told you, about genetic characteristics that get flicked off or on due to environment or even gestation?"

I nodded.

"Well, either Hans had some genetic issue that limited his health, or he'd gone through some accident as a child that would also make it possible he'd die young. Whatever the reason, his father knew about it fairly early on, because he had Jan made when Hans was ten. But he might not have been able to wait for Jan. I think he planned to be transferred to Hans, then Jan, but... Hans found out. And he, poor bastard, confirmed it somehow. And then he called his friends. Only the Good Man found out he knew."

"I told them. I betrayed him. I made it possible for them to kill him. I am a monster."

He gave me a cool look. "You couldn't have known. How could you have imagined? And he made a bad job of explaining. Would you have done the same if you knew? No. Then you're not a monster. You made a mistake. We all make mistakes. Sometimes big ones." He made a face. "The fallibility of human beings is part of my religion, so please stop beating your chest. You're only human. Anyway, so his father sent Scrubbers. They could have faked an accident, of course. Or they could have made you all disappear, but you see, your father was informed and Max was only three. And your father wasn't that young. He was at the point where unforeseen disaster can strike the body, so..."

"So, he sent me to Never-Never but alive, as an insurance policy. But why was I discarded and Max...?"

"Well, you said you and my uncle, you were... non-platonic friends."

"How delicately put. Yes, very non-platonic." My voice was incredibly dry in my own ears. I took another swig of the whiskey, then passed it to his extended hand. He took a swig and passed it back.

He gave his cough-laugh, then shook his head. "It's one of those things no one knows where it comes from or if it is genetic or environmental. I mean, look, it could be either. And with draconian laws in place in most areas governed by Good Men, no one talks frankly enough about it to scientists, either. But if it's genetic it's a... a combination of factors no one has isolated. As such, it could be one of those things that could get flicked on in gestation. It seems to be hard to control for the person, but that doesn't mean... it's purely genetic. We just don't know. But there is a chance it is genetic or at least physical. And if it is..."

I remembered my father's reaction of disgust when he'd heard. I remembered his going to elaborate lengths to avoid being too close to me after that. As though I were carrying some virus. I blinked. "He was afraid of catching it from me? Like an illness?"

"Sort of. I suspect he wasn't sure whether the body or the brain had the most control in that. I suspect he was afraid he'd find himself trapped in a body that only rose to the wrong occasion. That's why I asked you if..."

"If I had any interest in women?" I remembered vaguely an interview with a psychologist shortly after the scene to end all scenes. "I see. But how did he know it wasn't a passing fixation? From what I've read in old literature, many young men—"

"He didn't. Of course. But he couldn't risk it. So he had Max made. Curiously with the same surrogate, who also helped raise him, presumably with the same diet, in the same environment." Nat shrugged. "Sometimes I wonder about people. I presume your mother was... comfortable. Maybe he even loved her, for given values... He only arranged her death—don't look shocked, of course he did—so she couldn't spot the switch of his brain to Max."

I wasn't shocked, though I'd have liked to be. I think I'd already understood it, somewhere along the line. A thought flickered through my mind, and I opened my mouth, but it was none of my business and I didn't care. I just didn't care. I changed what I was going to say. "You mean, the whole thing was scripted from the moment he found out I'd rather—"

"It's possible no," he said. "I mean, Max was created, sure. But it's possible that you'd simply have been disinherited on some other excuse, and Max would have become heir, and you'd have been allowed to live out your life...Until Hans. Then you had to be kept somewhere safe and where you couldn't talk. I think they first thought the regular jail was fine. You were by nature reserved, and if you had Ben, you would not get in more trouble than...But Uncle Benjamin wouldn't leave the matter alone even in jail, so they had to get you to kill him, so they had an excuse to say you were dangerous and slam you into Never-Never and into solitary. Then you could be kept alive, in the unlikely event something happened to Max and your father needed a transfer immediately."

"The interrogation sessions they gave me—surely they would have realized I didn't know anything."

He shook his head. "I suspect you knew most of it, at some level. You just hadn't added it up. You wouldn't accept this so easily now, otherwise. But you could have figured it out consciously at any time. Besides, some of the Good Men, maybe all of them, take a long time to break." He paused and blinked. "Trust me, I know that." He grabbed for the bottle and drank again. "Since they weren't willing to do radical damage to your body, they might have thought you were still faking it."

"Ah." I drank. "And that," I said, "is why my father had me put in solitary for fourteen years? He didn't care if I went completely insane?"

"Your mind was not their concern," he said. "As long as your body was healthy. And frankly, that only as a backup."

I lifted my left wrist and showed him the scar which included whorls where the muscle and tendons could not be knit together right, because the prison hospital had to patch it before my father had me flown to a regen center. "I tried to gnaw through my wrist. I got to the vein."

He looked disturbed. "I know. I know. He...told me. Not-Max."

"Yeah."

Nat took the bottle away from me, took it back to the liquor table and corked it forcefully. I'd have protested but I was afraid if I followed him, I'd fall on my face. He took a silvery contraption from the serving cart and pressed buttons. After a while, he put a beverage in front of me. It wasn't coffee. I've seen coffee. This looked and smelled like coffee's big brother, the one that beat up coffee and stole its lollipop. "Drink it," he said. "You're in a bind, and we can't discuss it while you're out-of-your-mind drunk."

"I'm not drunk," I said, and hiccupped. My voice resounded oddly in my head, as though it came from very far away. "It's just been too long since I drank any alcohol."

"Of course, and I should have stopped you. Drink the damn coffee."

You don't argue with crazy people and any servant of a Good Man who orders the Good Man around is by definition a crazy bastard—not that I had any reason to doubt Mrs. Remy's fidelity. I drank the bitter liquid, even though back when I was in this world, back when I thought I was human in the society of humans, I used to take sugar and milk in my coffee. Which was not as strong as that one. I felt it fight its way down, possibly with an armed force, and land on my stomach like a ton of concrete. Acid concrete.

"What do you mean, a bind?" I asked.

"Well, you...oh, hell, you probably couldn't have escaped it, anyway. The closest parallel is Simon. St. Cyr. And I think the only reason he is alive is that his father is not dead, but in a coma. He was in a flyer accident, and is comatose. There's the possibility, more remote every year, that he'll wake up and that those he had alliances with will have their old friend back. Because of that, they don't kill St. Cyr and take back Liberte Seacity. It's my fault. If I had thought there was the slightest chance you were alive and would claim your inheritance, I'd have put the bastard in a coma, not killed him."

I grinned at him. I don't know why, because I wasn't even vaguely happy. "Not your fault. This is a damned macabre comedy. It's no one's fault but the bastards—Mules. Good Men. Whatever you call them."

"Yes, but...now they're going to try to take you out. They will all turn their forces on this seacity and try to take it out. Mind you, you're not alone in that situation. Jan killed his father, in Never-Never when they broke in. I wasn't with them. I was...

busy. But Simon told me. I don't think Jan has let the news get out. But they will, sooner or later. He can't pretend to be his father, not forever."

"Two against fifty?" I said. "We're going to get destroyed. I'm sorry I... They're going to destroy the entire household, servants and retainers and all, aren't they? We're all dead men walking."

He grimaced. "Two against forty-eight. Possibly three against forty-seven. And this is no different than it would have been. Lucius, with not-Max's suspicious death, chances are that at least upper-level retainers would be killed, or at least extensively interrogated. I shouldn't have killed him, but...." He blinked. "I couldn't take extensive interrogation, and my father..." He paused. "We were considering how best to go to our people when you appeared."

I thought that was the most elegant euphemism for suicide I'd ever heard. The man had a turn for the memorable phrase. He should have been a storyteller.

"At any rate, when you showed up, I thought we'd file for legal recognition, and do it in such a way they wouldn't be sure you weren't Dante, while we marshaled a plan of campaign. But now our hand is forced, and of course, even if St. Cyr joins in—and I suspect... well, never mind. There's a chance he will. Possibly a good chance. And even if a couple more of the heirs of Good Men who have found out the truth, er... force succession and join in... well... I think, you know, that you're going to need other help. You're going to need a lot of help. I have an idea, but I can't reveal it to you until I talk to some other people. I've already talked to Martha and asked her to pass the question on. Upward to the organization my uncle Benjamin and I..."

"Martha?" I said, still troubled by the idea that Ben had had some great work he'd never told me about.

"My twin sister." He made a face. "Possibly my best friend, besides Max. Though I'm fairly close to Abigail, as well. The other four are all too young. Debra is just a baby. Though at thirteen, James is starting to understand things, but—"

"Seven?" I said. "There are seven of you?" The upper-class retainers tended to small families, though I suppose there wasn't a law against large ones. It was just that I'd grown up thinking of large families as something of lower classes and religious fanatics. "How Usaian-fertile of your family."

He looked startled, and I said "Beg your pardon," because one doesn't accuse a near stranger of belonging to a proscribed religion, and besides, Usaians lived in little, peculiar enclaves. Which I supposed explained nuttiness like the Sons of Liberty. Hothouse environments and all that.

"Quite," Nat said. He lit another cigarette and leaned on the table, very businesslike. "I don't think we can do much about it," he said, then, probably in answer to my expression, "I don't mean my family's fertility. That's my parents' business. Feel free to take it up with them if you feel the need."

"I don't have anything against or for it either way."

"Good, because we have far more important business. Tomorrow we'll go out, secretly, and meet with people. Martha, I suppose, but also Abigail and then, later St. Cyr and Rainer. We hadn't meant for this to start right now, but I think…" He narrowed his eyes and blew a perfect ring of smoke. "I think that it might be time to start the revolution."

Like a Thief in the Night

WE PUT GOLDIE IN A TERRIBLE SPOT. I UNLOCKED THE DOOR, and a procession of servants removed the meal.

Nathaniel got up and said, "I'll go back home."

"But you can't," I said. "We're on perimeter alarm."

"For the seacity," he said. "And electromagnetic shielding and missile shield and—"

"But my house is shut down."

"Of course," he said. "Your house will be the main target. But there is a tunnel between your house and mine. Please, tell me you and my uncle knew this?"

I shook my head. "Why would we?"

"Oh. Well. There's sentinels in it, so I suspect it would have done you no good for clandestine meetings. My father uses it sometimes, just to avoid the weather, and I suppose it never occurred to anyone to tell you about it. It connects near the offices. My house is included in the perimeter. Think about it, with my family generally being the main administrators to yours, of course we were set up to undergo a siege with you and still be able to come and go."

I thought that on my side that had been a single person, in new bodies. I suppose when you're over three hundred years old you get set in your ways. Trusting a Remy would make sense, and seeing your future general overseer grow up and vetting him before he ever came of age would be terribly cozy.

So I nodded to Nat. He said, "I'll arrange matters tomorrow, as we discussed. And meanwhile your guard probably knows what to do better than you do, but lock your door in either case. Come, Goldie."

Goldie took two steps with Nat towards the door, then turned back and walked all the way to me.

Nat sighed and smiled, and shook his head. "Come, Goldie."

Goldie took three steps towards him. Then he looked towards me. Then he sat down, exactly between us, and thumped his tail hard on the floor.

Nat looked at me in confusion. I cleared my throat. "He could stay with me."

Nat shook his head. "He needs his walk in the garden before going to bed, and I don't think you can do that. Or rather, I don't think you should. You are a particular target, I'm not."

I thought I'd be risking Goldie and I couldn't bear that. So I patted him and squatted to be level with his face. "Go with Nat," I said, pushing him in that direction. "I'll see you tomorrow. Go, boy."

He went reluctantly, looking back at me like we were being mean by forcing him to choose. Hadn't Max done this, too? Or perhaps Goldie had mostly slept with Max?

I waited till my room was clear, and then Sam Remy came in to report on supplies and provisions for siege, since this was siege. He looked grave but perfectly calm, and I started to think that Nat and I had exaggerated the whole danger. Surely this had happened before in the history of Good Men. Once they realized I knew nothing—or had known nothing—and made no move to attack them or their position, they would forget about me. I might never be very important in their councils. In fact now that I knew what they were, I didn't want to be very important in their councils. It was like being well received among the finest ghouls. But they'd forget me. Olympus was a small seacity and not particularly wealthy. It wasn't worth their trouble. A few days of siege and then this would revert to normal and I'd be the Good Man.

After Sam left, I ran a bath, because I could. I couldn't find anything to sleep in, which disturbed me more than it would have at one time. I used to sleep naked, when I was young. But in Never-Never, conscious that I was probably watched every minute, I'd got in the habit of sleeping in my suit. Now I felt like I couldn't sleep without it, and there was nothing like it in the wardrobe.

So I settled for shorts and a loose tunic, the kind of thing people wore around the house in summer. I made sure to choose from the drawers that Nat had said were Max's. Now I knew what my father—I still had no other name for him—had been, the idea of wearing his clothes had turned into a near-physical repulsion, a sense of the fabric itself being tainted. I would not touch them. Tomorrow I'd have them taken away and see if I could get new clothes. And I'd see if my furniture was stored somewhere in the house, too.

Meanwhile, I crawled into the big bed, wishing that I could have kept Goldie, wishing I didn't feel so alone. It had all seemed so simple, even if it had all seemed to be my fault. I still preferred simple to complex. And that guilt was like an old friend, like a blanket I'd held over myself for all these years. And now... Now I was truly alone, truly forsaken. And people wanted to kill me. People had wanted to kill me for a long time. My father, for one. Apparently since birth.

I stared at the ceiling, blankly, thinking this room was too big. I'd have a wall built around the bed. I'd have—

Now you're just being crazy, Ben said. *You know I always told you that you weren't guilty.*

"Ben?"

Right here. Always right here. I told you I wouldn't leave you alone.

I turned and fell asleep.

And woke with Goldie licking my face, ten seconds before the room exploded.

All right, in retrospect, the room didn't explode. But that is what it felt like to me. A blaze of light, the zing of a burner, a scream.

I yelled "Lights," and the light came on, and Nat stood at the side of my bed, a burner in each hand.

And I reached for the burner I'd slipped under my pillow—I told you I'm never without one, not by choice—and cut down the Scrubber who stood by my door and who was aiming at Nat, before he could fire. And then Nat cut his fellow down. Just to be sociable I shot the next. Nat held up the side by taking the remaining ones out. As he fell, I noted they were all Scrubbers.

And then we were both of us awake in a brightly illuminated room, with six corpses, and Goldie nowhere in sight.

"Goldie?" Nat called, as he holstered the burners, which is when I realized he was wearing only his underwear and two holsters. As a fashion choice went, it was odd enough, but what was more remarkable was that he seemed perfectly composed wearing it. "Goldie!"

A whine-bark came from under the bed, and Nat called him again. I could hear in Nat's voice fear that Goldie was hurt, but when Goldie came out, tail between his legs, it became obvious that he was just scared.

It was only when Nat had run his hands over Goldie and satisfied himself about this, that I realized the door to my room was open, blown up on its hinges. And Nat was on a com before I could think I should do it. "Father? Father? Dad?"

There was enough of a delay in answering that my heart started hammering in my chest with almost painful strength, and I realized I couldn't bear for Sam Remy to be dead. He'd been ... as close to a normal father to me as people who have real fathers have. Besides if he died, Nat would be in charge, and right then I didn't think that was a good idea. Nat looked over his shoulder at me, and I thought he was thinking the same thing I did. "Daddy?" Nat's voice was suddenly much, much younger.

Then Sam's voice came on, "Yes, son. You're in the Good Man's room. How is Luce—the Patrician?"

"He's well. Unscathed. But we have six bodies to dispose of."

"Ours?"

"Scrubbers."

"Ah."

"Are you—"

"I'm fine. I was just getting the resealing crews to start. I didn't realize any Scrubbers had got in. There must be a hole somewhere else in the house. I repelled them at the front door, though the door was damaged." There was some sudden talk, a couple of shouts in the background, and Sam's calm, very tired voice. Then Sam came back. "There was a breach at the kitchen door. A couple of people wounded. None dead. It seems the ...

ah...Scrubbers were too intent on making it to the Good Man to make sure that the victims were well and truly killed."

"If they'd killed him they'd then have made sure afterwards," Nat said, his voice flat.

"Likely. Son...uh...You..."

"I came in through the tunnel. From the...the secret tunnel." A hesitation and a sigh, as if he were confessing something terrible and his shoulders were thrown back, as though he anticipated and prepared for censure. "Max and I had a secret tunnel."

"Oh." Sam said and, unaccountably, he sounded both worried and relieved. I didn't think it was possible for someone to sound both. "Nat, it might be best if you stay..."

"I will sleep in front of my master's door," Nat said, an ironical note in his voice. "As soon as someone can get the corpses out of that spot. And, uh...cleans the carpet. Or takes it out. Or something. I refuse to sleep in a pool of blood." He looked at the door to my room, hanging on its hinges. They'd cut with burners on the hinge side, soundlessly. "It would also be a good idea if someone repaired this damn door. And if a guard were put outside all doors."

"How secure is your secret entrance?" his father asked.

"No one ever found it that Max and I didn't tell about it, and the two people in this world who know about it right now wouldn't talk. Possibly not even under torture."

"I see."

In moments, Sam and what looked like a battalion of helpers arrived. The corpses were carried out, the carpet, fortunately not attached to the floor, was taken out also. The marble floor beneath the carpet was scrubbed. It all took no more than minutes. The door was repaired.

Sam frowned and smiled at Nat at the same time, and told him he was a good boy, in the exact same absentminded tone that Nat used for Goldie, but I thought there was more emotion there, just not an absolute certainty on how to express it. Then he told me I was a good boy, too, which just goes to show you how tired and distracted the man was, because calling me a good boy was roughly like calling a mastiff a nice puppy.

One of the servants came back with a blue silk robe which Sam handed to Nat, saying, "You'd best put this on." I wasn't sure exactly what the robe did, except hide the holsters. I could see from Nat's look that he wasn't entirely sure either. Except perhaps he should be protected from my notorious self.

I'd like to say right now and for posterity that the thought of laying a hand on Nat Remy hadn't even crossed my mind. Certainly not while he was ably fighting off intruders, no matter what his state of undress. And not even afterwards. Laying hands on Nat Remy, I thought, would be much like laying hands on nitroglycerin: only to be attempted if one had tired of living.

In no time at all, the room was empty save for me, and Nat and Goldie. And the door was closed.

Nat opened the closet, got out a blanket, rolled himself in it, and laid down on the floor across the door. So that whole thing hadn't been figurative.

"Why...why did you come back?" I asked.

He sighed, as I turned the lights off, and his voice sounded much younger than he was, in the dark. "I went home, and then I thought this was possible. Though I never thought it was probable. But the fact that my father decided to sleep in his office, to supervise security...well. I thought I'd come through the tunnel and check on you. And Goldie and I had just come in, when the door came down. I'd come in the dark the whole way, so I saw them clearly. You know the rest."

"I know the rest," I said. "The tunnel. You'll have to show me where it is. It doesn't seem safe to me."

"It's very safe," he said, defiant. "I hadn't even told my father. He'd never even suspected it before. And no one ever found it. It's secure."

"But, for the love of...why the tunnel? Why in hell a tunnel to this room of all places?"

There was a long silence, a forceful exhalation. And then a defiant voice, in the dark, "Because I slept in this room almost every night."

And then Ben's voice, distinct, in my ears, *Stop being dense, Luce. And stop picking on the boy.*

"I wasn't picking on him," I said sullenly.

"What?" Nat said.

"Nothing," I said, with immense dignity. "I wasn't talking to you."

"But—"

"And it's none of my business, either," I said to both of them. "And I couldn't care less."

"Fine then," Nat said.

In my mind Ben chuckled. I punched my pillow and turned on my side, as I felt Goldie jump on the bed and climb in beside me. It really was none of my business. Sam Remy could take his suspicions and ... and do whatever with them. I wanted nothing to do with Nat. I wanted nothing to do with anyone, in fact.

Now that I knew that even if I married, I could never produce offspring, all I wanted was for people to stop trying to kill me. Then I could be the best Good Man possible for my city. And when I died, hopefully of old age, it could all do whatever it wanted. By then I would have—hopefully—arranged for safety for my retainers. No one could ask more of me.

I turned again and punched the pillow again.

The problem, Luce, and you know it all too well, is that it's highly unlikely they'll stop trying to kill you. Not when they just organized an expedition against your house. You're going to have to come up with a better plan.

I was going to have to come up with a plan. I was going to have to come up with a better defense. Much as I appreciated Nat's loyalty, how much did I want to trust him with my safety?

Goldie got really close to me and licked my face. I put an arm over his soft, warm body.

I don't remember falling asleep.

I knew I'd wake up to a world that would never be the same. Not for me.

LADIES AND GENTLEMEN,
WE DECLARE THE REVOLUTION

Lord and Master

I WOKE UP WITH MY CURTAINS BEING OPENED, THE LIGHT COM-ing in to shine against my closed eyelids.

Before my eyes opened, before my conscious mind connected this with the events of the previous night, my hand was under the pillow, grabbing the burner, and I'd brought it out, pointing it in the direction of the voice.

"Patrician!" the voice was outraged, rather than shocked, and there was a tinkle of glass, a noise of porcelain. I opened my eyes to see a man I only very vaguely recognized pouring out coffee into a cup—I knew it was coffee because I could smell it—and setting out toast and who knew what else.

Then I realized the room was full of people. And by that, I mean exactly what I said. Full of people. People swarmed in every possible corner, doing things I only half understood. A team of three people, for instance, seemed to be removing all the suits from the closet, and even the stuff that had been Max's from the drawers.

I turned my attention and—mindlessly—my burner on them. "What are you doing?"

The nearest man, holding an armful of suits, dropped them on the floor. He might also have pissed himself. I don't know. I didn't look. But his face had that mortified look, and his eyes crossed slightly as he looked at the burner. I turned the burner safety on, and put it back under my pillow, then crossed my arms. "I said, what are you doing?"

"T-t-t—" the man said.

"Taking your suits, Patrician," the man behind him said, looking somewhat doubtful. "I mean, your predecessor's suits. I mean, Mr. Remy said—"

"And where in hell is Nathaniel Remy?" I asked, because I hadn't seen him in the crowd, and realized only now that this seemed odd, since he'd fallen asleep in front of my door. I snorted. His master's door indeed.

"Nat-Nat-Nat—" the man who'd dropped my suits said.

"Do you wish to speak to Nathaniel, Patrician?" Sam's voice from near my bedside table. I turned to see him holding a bunch of those papers that could only be signed by the touch of the thumb with the right genetics, the kind of thing my father seemed to always be signing.

"I want to know why he's interfering with my clothes!" I said, and then realized that I was yelling at a man who was twice my age, who looked incredibly tired, who'd spent half the night up helping defend my house, whose underlings had got wounded and possibly killed, and who had always been kind to me. I said immediately, "I'm sorry, Sam. I'm not a morning person."

"Do you wish to keep those clothes?" he said. "Nathaniel didn't make those decisions. I did. I noticed that the clothes you were wearing don't fit you, and I presumed from the fact that you were wearing what the last Good Man wore before ascension that you didn't like the more . . . colorful suits he chose afterwards? We had some clothes made, though far from a complete wardrobe, and I thought—"

I waved my hand. "Sorry." I looked at the terrified man, and waved at him. "Carry on, never mind me." Then I turned back to Sam. "Who are all these people? Why are they in my room this early in the morning?"

Sam cleared his throat. "Those people"—he pointed—"are making sure that your windows are secured, and the balcony door, too. Last night, they used a disrupting device that unlocked the back door. We must make sure—"

"Fine, fine."

"Those people are making sure that any drinks on the drink

table are replenished. Those people"—he pointed to five people by the window—"are merchants of the seacity, whose business is disrupted by our present...situation, and they would like to talk to you. And those people," he said, pointing to four men by the entrance to the bathroom, "are waiting to help you bathe and dress."

I opened my mouth. Then I closed it. I'd read about rulers in the middle ages and shortly after. I'd read about rituals called the levee, in which everyone who had business with the king came to see him rise, and talk to him while he went about the necessary wakening routine. I remembered being highly amused by stories of how courtiers would loiter around while the king answered a call of nature, or turn a blind eye while the king's latest fling slipped out of the king's bed and through the door.

It wasn't so amusing to be in the position of those poor kings, though I supposed, now that I thought about it, that the government of the seacity and its territories was much like the government of one of the medieval countries. Certainly I was the ultimate and absolute ruler. I didn't know why I was surprised. But I knew why I was upset. I'd be damned if I'd wake to this every morning. Perhaps my fath—whatever the hell he'd been to me, had enjoyed it. Perhaps it made him feel how important he was. Maybe he liked that.

I wanted privacy to take a leak. I wanted a cup of coffee. And I'd be damned if I was going to have four men help me bathe.

I thought I heard Ben's voice in my mind say, *I'll have you know people pay very well indeed for that sort of thing.* It was exactly the kind of thing Ben would have said, with a quirk of a smile.

"Sam, get all these people out of here."

"Patrician?"

"Well, make sure the windows and door are secure first, then get everyone out of here. All of them."

He blinked at me, as if I'd spoken in ancient Aramaic. "Patrician?"

"Sam, you're neither deaf nor stupid. Get all these people out of here, now, or I'm going to. And I won't do it diplomatically."

He hesitated. "Even the merchants? I don't scruple to tell you, public relations—"

"Don't give them the right to watch me use the bathroom," I said. "Surely we have receiving rooms or parlors or something of the sort in this house where we can stow very important visitors while I wake up and make myself presentable? Serve them break-fast, or something? Surely they'll enjoy that more than taking a look at me in my birthday suit?"

He inclined his head. "And your bathers?"

"Sam! I've been bathing myself since I was three. You know that. Surely—"

"All right," he said. I had the impression there was something very like quiet satisfaction in his voice. He walked around the room, rapidly, talking to each group of people, including the men now hanging clothes in the closet. I don't know what he told them. They looked over their shoulders at me, as though he'd told them in another ten seconds, I'd cut loose with the burner. They hung up those clothes in record time and made for the door with almost comic haste. As did all the others. As Sam was heading for the door after all of them, I said, "Not you, Sam, stay."

He stopped, and turned around, as the door closed behind the last of my would-be bathers. "No offense meant, Patrician, but I also have not the slightest interest in seeing you without clothes."

"Was that a joke?" I said, and smiled at him. "Very creditable." Because it was either that, or take it as insubordination. My father would have. "Wait just a moment. I'll be right back. I just want to ask you a few things. I have no idea how to be Good Man."

I ran to the bathroom, relieved the pressure on my bladder, washed my hands, splashed cold water on my face, ran my fingers back through my hair, gave up on it, tied it back with an elastic band, made a face at my far more than five o'clock shadow and came back into the room.

Sam Remy was where I'd left him, still clutching his stack of papers. "Put the papers down on the bed, Sam. And help yourself to a cup of coffee." I noted there were five, as though my server had expected me to share my breakfast with the merchants. Per-haps he had. I couldn't tell. My cup, which he had poured, was lukewarm, but I downed it, realizing after swallowing, that it had been without sugar or milk. Maybe if I kept drinking it like this, it would put hair on my chest. Or maybe I already had enough.

Sam laid the papers down and came towards the table, but made no effort to help himself to the coffee. I looked at him, and realized his features were frozen, very much in something like... embarrassment? Anger? Confusion? I couldn't tell. And then I realized that he looked both relieved and offended. I wasn't sure about the relieved, but I thought I had a handle on the offended. I'd just told him I didn't like the way he had been doing his job. It occurred to me to wonder why he'd thought I liked it, then I rolled my eyes at myself.

Even if Sam Remy knew the truth about the Good Men—did he? Nat had been very careful to indicate that himself and Ben had been members of a secret and subversive organization, but he didn't say anything about his father or the rest of the family. Which, I suspected, was very much Nat and his way to protect them. Even if he were low man on a conspiracy and everyone else around him had more power and more decision-making ability, he wouldn't admit anyone but himself and a man who'd gone beyond the reach of the law, had been implicated.

But even if Sam Remy knew very well that the Good Men he'd served had both—all three?—been the same Good Man, he'd never have thought about it. His entire life, possibly since he was a little boy and his father the manager of the Keeva affairs, he would have seen the Good Man awaked like this.

"Sam," I said, "I'm very sorry if I embarrassed you. Truly, I don't do mornings well, and do try to think of my position. Not only have I wakened alone for the last fourteen years, I've been absolutely alone for the last fourteen years. Imagine what it's like to wake to that... circus."

He frowned a little, but a grin was trying to tug at his lips. It was an expression that reminded me too much of Ben for my mental well-being. He said, slowly, "Well, there is... I will admit that must have been disconcerting. Also, I am an idiot. I should have realized how that would have appeared to you." He straightened his shoulders. "I would like to tender my resignation effective today. I am clearly getting past my job, and my knowledge of past Good Men does not apply to—"

I poured a cup of coffee in a clean cup and looked up at him. "Do you take sugar and cream?"

"Patrician?"

"Luce," I said. "You always called me Luce. And please unbend. I remember the walloping you gave me when you caught Ben and me in the apple tree."

He looked briefly confused, then sighed. "I didn't have the authority. I shouldn't have touched you. But I was so scared you were both going to fall and break your heads. Dancing on the branches!"

"Yeah. As an adult, I imagine what I would have felt. It worked. We never did it again."

"No, and you never complained about me to your parents, either, which, trust me, didn't go unremarked."

"How could I? You were the closest thing Ben had to a father. And that I had to a father too, now that I think about it. Do you take sugar and cream?"

He came over. "I'll do it," he said, and reached for the creamer, poured a dollop in his coffee, while I poured myself a new cup of coffee. "Are you sure you wouldn't want my resignation?"

I didn't even look up. I poured myself cream and sugar and stirred. "You just want to punish me by making me work with Nat," I said. Then into the sudden silence. "That was a joke, by the way. You'll have to get used to my not-very-sparkling humor this early, I guess. I suspect eventually I can work just fine with Nat, but he's a little scary and, besides, he orders me around."

"If Nathaniel was improper in any—"

"Yeah, he very improperly saved my worthless life. No, he was not improper. He just told me things I needed to do and I needed to know, which, incidentally, are many, and he did it without ceremony, which I suspect I needed also. But he does scare me a little. So much intentness and competence."

Sam took a sip of his coffee and made a face. "Nat has always been driven," he said. "Sometimes I've thought . . . but you don't want to hear a father's worries. Am I to infer you don't want anyone in your room when you wake?"

"It's fine if you come in," I said. "Or the coffee, if we arrange it that way. I just need to know who it will be, and I need it to be the same every day. It takes me three cups of coffee to even function," I said. "You don't want to do that to me."

"No, Patri—"

"Luce."

"Luce."

"Right. Now, do those papers really need my signature or can you make do?"

"Unless I borrow your genetics," he said, "I really need your signature. They're mostly routine matters, and I'll explain each, but they're essential to keeping the seacity running."

"Other than that and meeting with the merchants—and what am I supposed to tell the merchants?"

"I'll be with you. I'll do most of the talking, but, yes, you'll need to be present. It's all a matter of public relations and ensuring that they realize you care about what you're putting them through. Mostly you're supposed to reassure them that they're important to you and to the seacity. It's very easy to start discontent that is very hard to put down."

I thought that last had come from a book of maxims, somewhere, possibly passed from Remy to Remy throughout the generations. But I didn't say it. I was learning. "What else do I need to do today?" I asked.

He hesitated. "There are supplies to arrange and siege logistics to finalize and—"

"Do I need to do those?" I asked. "Personally?"

"No, sir. I suspect you wouldn't know how to do most of them."

"At least that last is disarmingly frank. Now if we could stop with the 'sir,' I, for one, would greatly appreciate it. Now, be honest, by not taking a hand in that, am I adding to your burden of work?"

He shrugged. "I suspect mostly my daughter, Martha, will do it. I'll just have to sign it."

I looked at him. "You should take a break for a few hours and go home and rest."

"I intend to. I'm not as young as I used to be."

"None of us are."

He wrinkled his nose. "The only other thing on my agenda today is to . . . that is, Nathaniel told me that—"

"Yes, Nat said he was arranging a meeting of some sort."

Sam looked incredibly relieved, but only for a moment, because when I asked, "Where is Nat?" his face created tension lines, immediately relaxed as I said, "and Goldie, for that matter?"

"I've told Nat," he said, "that if you want Goldie—"

"No, no. More than glad to share him. Just wondered where he was."

"I suspect Nat has taken him for a run. He usually does around this time."

"All right," I said. "I just worried that . . ." I floundered. "That something had happened to him, since he was guarding me."

"Yes, Patrici— Luce," Sam said. "I understand." Which was

indeed very good, because I didn't understand at all. "Will there be anything else?"

"No," I said. "If I can have a few minutes, I'll bathe and dress, and then meet you wherever you tell me to."

He smiled, a faint, puzzled smile. "You seem to have the wrong idea about which of us tells the other what to do."

"I don't know what to do, you see," I said. "I'll come around soon enough and become a proper tyrant."

He raised his eyebrows at me, then decided I was joking and smiled and said, "I'll meet you in your father's . . . in the Good Man's office, then. And we'll meet with the merchants afterwards." He hesitated on the threshold. "You might need more than a few minutes."

But I didn't. To be honest, I don't think I knew how to take longer, anymore. I washed quickly, managed to tame my hair and tie it back, and slipped into one of the new suits—a slick black pants and jacket over a flowing white shirt affair. Then I stared at the mirror and frowned. And the person frowning back at me was someone yet totally different from the haunted prisoner I'd glimpsed when leaving my cell. I still had the same scar crossing my face. My hair was still long, though there's a lot to be said for proper moisturizing products, since it now shone a subdued gold and didn't look like an untidily piled hay stack. But the way the jacket and pants delineated my shoulders and muscles, I looked like what I was—a well-born man, not so old, who might know a little about how rough life can be but who has power and wealth, both, at his fingertips. The jacket was cinched around the waist, then had a sort of little ruffle at the bottom. The sleeves allowed the ruffled flaring cuffs of the shirt to show. It seemed to me fashion must have got a lot more frilly since I'd been away. Or perhaps I simply wasn't used to anything but a minimalist bodysuit. The dark color brought out the paleness of my skin and made it seem intentional, accentuated by the creamy, lacy white of the shirt. And the tailoring somehow made me look healthy and not intimidating. I slid on boots that came just above my calf, and which shone as discreetly as the—was it silk?—of the suit.

I slipped a burner into my boot and managed to strap another holster around my middle, in a way that wasn't immediately obvious. The problem with well-tailored clothes is that there was only one obvious place to hang that gun, and even that was all too obvious and would make people stare, or at least wonder what I'd padded with, or what had got me so happy. And I could live a long, long time without Nat Remy's sarcastic gaze that I was sure would rake over such an arrangement. And that was if he were discreet enough not to snort, something I wasn't about to bet.

So, instead, I managed to put the holsters in the small of my back. Not as reachable as I'd wish it, but hidden by the fall of the jacket's frill, which was of an ample cut back there.

Walking out of my room and encountering a sentinel who straightened and bowed slightly by way of salute, reminded me of other unfinished business. If I didn't want my father's clothes, I wanted my father's furniture even less. I walked back into the room, much to my guardian's surprise, and punched the link at my desk.

"Sam?"

The voice that answered me was several octaves higher than Sam's. "My father is down in the offices, Patrician Keeva. If you should need—"

"No." I fished from the torrent of names that Nat had poured in my direction last night. "Abigail Remy?"

"Martha, sir."

"Oh. I don't know how to put this order through or to whom, and you might not, also, but I'd like the furniture from my room removed, my old furniture restored if it's still available."

"Mmm," she said. "If it can't be restored would similar furniture be acceptable?"

"Definitely," I said. And then, because it occurred to me this would be a very busy day for everyone. "I'm sorry for adding to your work load."

"No problem at all," she said. "I'll just delegate. I believe my father is waiting for you in your office, Patrician."

"I do, too," I said. And refrained from adding *for my sins*.

Sam Remy was at his desk, in his portion of the office, which was the antechamber to my father's office proper. While my father's office, from what I remembered, was a vast room rejoicing in a desk set in solitary splendor, an armchair of the kind that could comfortably sit a person five times the size of normal men, this antechamber, as large, was crowded with desks, chairs, and people. It looked much like my room when I'd awakened, with people going here and there and in every possible direction, according to a choreography I was unlikely to understand, at least without spending a lifetime in study. In the middle of it, Sam looked perfectly in control, his desk piled with papers that he handed off at seeming random to various men and women who approached. He had his computer on too, with the hologram screen projected in front of him, and impossible to read from this side, the holograms casting shadows like stigmata on his tired face.

He shouldn't have been able to see me in the movement and crowd of the office, but his gaze fell on me almost immediately. A touch of buttons on the desk and the holograph screen vanished, as he stood up. "Patrician," he said, by way of both greeting and summoning me to his desk. I didn't protest. In public he'd call me Patrician Keeva or Good Man Keeva. I didn't mind that. It was only when he did it in private that I got the feeling I'd become someone else, someone I didn't recognize, if Ben's brother was treating me that way.

Sam didn't exactly order me into my office, but by standing back to let me pass into it, he herded me into it just as effectively as if he had, and I tried to obey. Only as I was about to enter it, a person came out, and I stopped.

Understand, Ben was never in any way effeminate. Not unless you count the slightness and the softness of being only barely past twenty. In his case it had not been pronounced. So the reaction of my mind was unreasonable and impossible. You see, it told me the person who'd come out of my father's office and now stood there, looking up at me with a poleaxed expression was Ben. And that was nonsense, because the person was, unavoidably, female. Though she was probably close to the same age Ben and I had been when we'd been arrested.

My mouth went dry, my brain stopped all rational processes. My lips opened to say "Ben," and I stopped them just in time. And into my complete confusion, Sam's voice came with the same affability and warmth as a sharpened blade, "Patrician Keeva, let me introduce you to my daughter, Abigail Remy. I don't think you'll remember her. She was barely four when you...ah...went away."

My head was doing quick calculations. She was just about the same age that Ben and I had been when Ben died. And she had Ben's dark hair, his slightly too sharp to be oval face, the somewhat aquiline nose, the mouth that reposed in a smile, and the eyes—those dark-haunted eyes that ran in the family. Her hair was pulled back at the base of the head, much like mine. She favored the same nondescript grey clothes her brother seemed to like, and she was looking at me with an expression bordering on alarm. Possibly because she was Ben's height, considerably shorter than Nat, and I loomed over her. Let alone that I was the Good Man and looked like I spent my free time engaging in street fights. "Pleased to meet you, Abigail," I said, in my very best company voice.

"Patrician," she said, and inclined her head. I noted she was holding a tray in her hand, as she squeezed past us.

And then I noted that Sam, as he gestured for me to precede him into the room, looked very worried indeed. I wanted to tell him I had no ill intent towards his daughter. Or his son for that matter. Then I realized that I really didn't. Well, I didn't think I could have intentions of any sort towards Abigail, other than a protective feeling, born of her resemblance to Ben. As for Nat...I had no intentions either. Not only did I feel anyone at all reaching for Nat was likely to withdraw a stump; not only was I sure that other than a feeling of...hereditary loyalty? Towards me, he didn't actually like me as such, but more than all that, I couldn't have any sort of intention of that sort towards someone whose livelihood was bound with me, and whose family had served my family for centuries.

I guess Ben and I had been too young and I, myself, too unconscious of my future destiny for the separation in our stations to intrude. I remembered envying him his family and his position in the world. I didn't know we might have grown up—at least had my situation been what it appeared—to have him envy my power. I had a moment of quasi-regret for the illusions of childhood, the short pang that comes with knowing even if nothing untoward, no nightmarish circumstances had intruded, it would not have ended well.

There was some old tale or other, which I barely remembered about the lion lying down with the sheep in some perfect paradise. But I couldn't understand how that would ever happen. The sheep would know—would always know—that his life was forfeit should the lion want to kill him. It didn't make for good relationships, be they friendships or love or anything in between.

I felt like I'd lost everything. I felt like the loneliest man on Earth. I stepped through the door, telling myself I'd have to dispel Sam's fears for his children at the first opportunity. Though, somehow, telling him that his children were safe because I had power of life or death over them seemed more like a threat than a calming remark. On the other hand, if I had it in my power, I would protect Nat and Abigail, and Martha, and even Sam and his dimly remembered wife, too. Because they were my responsibility, and I could hurt them without meaning to.

I hadn't asked for this responsibility. I didn't want it. But there was no one else around to take it and therefore it was mine.

I walked into my father's office. Like my bedroom, decorated for his use, it was all heavy wood, and dark leather and the sort of prints on the wall that spoke of vast estates and untrammeled territories. It occurred to me for the very first time to wonder how insecure my father had felt that he needed to surround himself with symbols of power.

However, the symbols of power worked. As in my room, the merchants looked out of place and conscious of it. I gathered that Abigail had just set the table with coffee and cups, with piles of fruit and little fussy pastries of the sort that yielded no more than a bite or two, most of it cream and froth. But none of them had sat down. Instead, they stood around the table, clutching cups and saucers and looking like they'd bolt if I said boo.

I didn't say boo. I'd been trained for this, and a voice at the back of my head told me it was because my father believed in physical habit as much as in mental habit. He'd wanted me to react before my brain could kick in. Or his brain, as the case might be.

And I did react appropriately without the slightest attempt at thought. My mouth shaped itself in a smile, and I walked forward and spoke in a calm, non-intimidating voice, about how chagrined I was that my small contretemps had inconvenienced them, about how badly I felt for it all. How I wanted, more than anyone else, to end this standoff as soon as possible.

I said nothing much other than that I regretted it, but my own voice falling on my ears sounded reassuring and vaguely paternal, and when I stopped, all of them were smiling, somewhat diffidently. I looked up and found Sam watching me with a speculative expression. And then he stepped in and I backed off, because there was precious little I could add.

While my conversation had been all polished phrases and zero substance, his was all matter of substance. Abatements and mitigations and who knew what. I hoped Sam was honest because if he weren't, I'd never know it. I realized, as I'd suspected in talking to his oldest son yesterday, that I had met someone far more intelligent than I.

It took him about two hours to talk to the traders, with my presence doing no more than gentling them.

When they bowed themselves out the door, consigned to the good offices of some sort of footman or doorman or something—someone young and very self-important in the dark green livery of the house, Sam Remy asked, "Will you be having lunch in the dining room?"

"What?" I said. "I just had breakfast."

He gave a tight smile. "Nat is likely to keep you most of the rest of the day," he said. "And it's not likely to be an easy..." He stopped himself and compressed his lips.

"Listen, Sam," I said, "I was never noted for my social graces in my private life, and being alone for fourteen years hasn't improved me."

His eyes widened in alarm, and I hastened to add, "So, I'll just say it. There are times...I mean, of course I get lonely like everyone else, but—" His eyes widened more. "BUT," I emphasized, "I want to make sure you understand that I have no intentions towards any of your family. No...I know you know...I mean...Ben and I..." I floundered. "But I have no intentions towards anyone in your household. Romantic or otherwise. I was very young, with Ben, see. I think it would have ended badly anyway. Not as badly as it did end, but our different positions—that is, I don't think—"

His mouth dropped open. He closed it with a snap. His fingers pinched and massaged the bridge of his nose on either side, the same gesture I'd seen Nat make. "Ah, hell," he said, softly. "Good Ma— Ah...Luce. I'm not ready to deal with what might have been. As for your assurance..." He seemed at a loss for words, then snapped his mouth shut again. "Go have lunch. Go down to the dining room. Give the cooks a reason for existing." He must have seen my intention of protesting, because he held up a hand. "No, listen. It's important that they see you're having lunch and...and following a routine. It will show them you're not scared and...and all that. Just do it, will you?"

I did it. Sometimes, there are things that are not worth arguing, and Sam's determination that I should eat was one of them.

So I sat in the vast, dimly lit dining room and ate my dinner
off fine porcelain plates, and tried to get at least three bites of
each of the dishes. At a guess there were fifteen of them, but who
was I to count? None of them was salty or sweet mush, it's all I
can tell you. And I knew for a fact that at the end of my meal,
all the leftovers were eaten in the servant lounge, so I didn't feel
I had to clean my plate. Which was good, because I didn't think
I could, short of exploding.

As soon as I could, I got up. I had to, because otherwise I felt
as though they'd keep feeding me. The service stopped when I
got up, but two of the servers were caught holding serving trays.
I bobbed my head at them and said, "Thank you." And beat a
hasty retreat.

I'd eaten in the dining room before, but only with my father,
and usually at a state dinner. I suspected there must be hand
signals or something to control the flow of the service. I'd have
to ask Sam Remy. I had a feeling before the week was over he'd
think me a complete fool.

Cloak and Dragged

I BEAT A RETREAT TO MY ROOM. IT HAD BEEN MIRACULOUSLY restored to my childhood retreat, even to the computer on the desk and the gems lying about it. On the bed, in the middle of the white bedspread was the stuffed giraffe that Ben had given me for my twenty-first birthday, as part of an elaborate joke involving my wish for a pet. It was four feet tall, with its legs folded under it, and it wore a collar with a tag that said *I Wanna Be Loved By You*. I blinked at it, and for a moment the world spun on its moorings and I was twenty-two again, and I wondered if it had all been a bad dream. But the voice that spoke from the vicinity of my closet, saying, "Is this all right? It was all packed together, so we assumed—" was definitely female.

I spun around. The young woman was older than Abigail, and shorter, and plumper, but had a definite air of family that identified her as belonging to Sam Remy. She also had the no-nonsense sort of look that made it seem like she'd be comfortable to be around, and a lot less high-strung than either of her siblings. Only her eyes reminded me of Ben—did the whole family have the same damn eyes?—even if hers crinkled at the corners and seemed disposed to look in amusement at the world.

At least I hadn't drawn a burner on her. "Martha?" I asked.

She smiled and extended a cool little hand that got lost in

mine when I shook it. A greeting of equals, nothing like the stiff head-bob I expected from a retainer. But I was starting to suspect the entire Remy family had very odd ideas when it came to equality and command. Except maybe Sam, who seemed to think I should be in full control of my domains.

"Lucius, right? Funny, you don't look a thing like Nat said."

"Uh?"

"Like an unredeemable bastard," She said, and grinned. "You don't look like one."

"I—uh—"

"If it helps, I think he meant it as a compliment."

"Thank you," I said. "I think."

She laughed at that—or perhaps it was something between a giggle and a laugh—and looked me up and down again, making me feel profoundly uncomfortable, for some reason I couldn't even understand. And then she lied. "You don't look a thing like your family. I think—" She looked at the watch-ring on the middle finger of her right hand. "Would you mind closing and locking the door? Nat will be here any minute."

I closed the door. Listen, at some point you do. If the entire world around you has gone crazy, it is considerably easier to fit in than to stick out like a sore thumb. Safer too.

I'd no more closed the door to my room, and slipped the lock to locked—even though I didn't even want to imagine what Sam would think if he realized I'd locked myself in a room with one of his daughters—than my wall opened up. Oh, I know it was a door. Of course it was a door. But even after it opened, I couldn't have distinguished it in the wall. I wondered who'd done the work, and how they'd managed to make the door meet the wall so flawlessly and how they'd dug a tunnel through dimatough.

Nat came in. He was wearing a broomer suit, with the broom clipped to his belt. Weirdly, since I knew how he'd spent the night, he looked more rested than he'd been before. I felt a brief pang of disappointment that he didn't have Goldie with him, as he came in and looked at me like I was completely out of script, then turned on his twin and frowned, then looked back at me and frowned harder.

"She told me to lock the door," I said, defensively.

He pulled the ashtray-box out of my desk drawer, pulled a cigarette from somewhere inside a broomer suit that didn't have any obvious pockets, lit it. "You're both supposed to be in suits. What *are* you doing?"

I was about to tell him I was in a suit, when I realized he meant a broomer suit. Martha made an exasperated sound, and dove for a bag near my closet. She was wearing the same sort of tunic and pants affair that Nat wore, in the same greyish black. In fact, were it not for their different sizes, I'd assume the three siblings shared clothes.

I wasn't even surprised—had lost my capacity for surprise, I guess—as Martha pulled a black, insulated broomer suit on, then clipped the broom to her belt. I decided that there could be no secrets here, so I went through the sequence to open my secret suit-storage place. And then I realized I really had no secrets, since the suit in there was new and, when I put it on, my size.

Either something in my expression gave my misgivings away or Martha was a mind reader. "Nat told me to put it in there. I'm sorry. Was I not supposed to know where that compartment was? Nat and Max and I discovered it, when we were little, playing around in the room. I put it there when no one else could see."

I clipped a broom to my belt. Nat finished his cigarette and started a new one. He finished that one, as I pulled the boots on over the suit—the proper way to do it while broom riding—and inspected my new goggles and oxygen equipment. Then I followed Nat and Martha into the tunnel open in my wall.

"Watch," Nat said. "You might need it." He showed me a point on the wall that looked like slightly scratched plaster, then where to touch to get the door to close. "Most of it is a natural bubble in the dimatough," Nat said. "Max and I found it beach-side due to an accident with a burner, and then we thought..."

We walked down what looked like an interior corridor in a house, and then dropped down an antigrav well, concealed in what looked like the ceiling of a natural cavern. Then along that to another antigrav well. The wells were of the sort you had to activate, and choose the direction on, and Nat showed me both points, one on each floor. Finally we walked through what looked like a very natural—and dank—cavern, to a door that closed and opened through as elaborate a sequence as the compartment in my ceiling, and then out a beach-side cavern onto the beach.

Yes, Olympus Seacity is a built seacity, made of shaped dimatough. But it was one of the first built, four hundred years ago.

Either the caverns had been built in, or they'd been worn into the side of the isle by tides and time. No. This cavern was made of stone, not dimatough. Perhaps the island had been poured on top of a set of islets. It wasn't an unusual anchoring method. And it meant some of the islets had become seaside beaches with natural caverns. And natural white sand, which crunched under my feet, as I followed Nat and Martha.

"Is it quite safe?" I asked. "We've been ambushed before."

Nat gave me a look. "Safe enough," he said. "We have patrols. I think they've decided on different tactics."

"Like?"

"Like home invasion. You know hand signals, right? Wait, of course you do," he added, clearly remembering the midair fight. He nodded. "Follow me. Martha can take the back."

"I can take the back," I said, and they both looked at me, twin frowns of disapproval and what I sensed was barely controlled eye rolling, like I was too dumb to live.

"No, see," Martha said, softly. "You're the target, not us."

"Yeah, if we were sane we wouldn't be taking you to this meeting personally. Mind you, sane is not something I've been accused of recently," Nat said.

Martha gave him the briefest concerned glance, then said, "No. See. We have to take him with us or they . . . the others won't—"

"Yeah, I know," Nat said. "So. Ready?"

I wondered about their organizational skills. I mean, if they were taking me to a meeting at a secret location, would they really want to take me this way? Where I could see where I was going? Maybe they thought that the years in captivity had dulled my sense of direction and that I didn't know we were headed for Syracuse Seacity.

No, wait. They couldn't think that. Nat, at least, knew that I was conversant enough with directions to go see my old friends.

It wasn't until we got close enough to our destination that I understood why they didn't care if I knew the direction I was going, or even that secret meetings were held there. Our destination was a secret in plain sight.

There is this part of Syracuse Seacity, once a thriving industrial neighborhood. It is called Deep Under because it is. If you remember that Syracuse has grown in levels, one new platform, on pillars, built on top of the others, blocking out at least partially both sunlight and fresh air, it won't surprise you that Deep Under is on the bottom level, so deeply ensconced in the shadow of the upper levels that it might as well be buried underground. Everyone knew it was there, of course, but, as with bad weather, no one did anything about it. And part of the reason for that was a huge, decaying multi-armed piece of machinery that blocked almost the entire entrance to Deep Under. At least, the best-known entrance.

It had, once upon a time, been a mechanical device that unloaded ships. I didn't know exactly when, though I'd assume it was in the twenty-first or twenty-second century, when the seacities were first built. It had the look and feel of that era, the flexible arms, metal combined with various ceramics, before ceramite and dimatough, both more durable, cheaper and more flexible than any previous materials. Modern machinery would not decay like this, with the ceramic coating falling off and the metal arms falling to pieces.

The cybernetic brain that had controlled the whole mess had decayed long before the arms, and when air transport had become so cheap that few ships plied trade anymore, the entire harbor had been abandoned. It would have been more expensive to dismantle the robot arms than to keep them in place.

The decaying robot allowed entry to broomers and to foot traffic, but none to the larger transports or law enforcement-type vehicles that could go in and "clean up the area" as the news called for with amazing regularity, since that pocket of lawlessness was said to be inhabited by every forbidden group from broomers to Usaians to prostitutes.

I think the first time I'd flown there, I'd been attracted by rumors of very specialized brothels. I'd never found them. Truth be told, I'd never looked very hard. It seemed to me an odd thing to pay for that sort of service, something I'd never quite considered a good use of money. Instead, I'd been distracted by cheap gadgets and a strangely free-flowing culture.

Flying past that obstacle was the very first test that any broomer had to face in Deep Under. First, because there were far more arms than eight. I'd guess more like eight hundred, perhaps more.

Some of the metal parts rusted and fell apart—and did so at unpredictable times, so that flying through it you could set off a storm of falling ceramic and metal pieces as the vibrations of your passing disintegrated the metal that linked them. Even when they didn't fall apart they had a tendency to move with the vibrations of anything near.

Was there a way to get through it? Well, yes. It involved flying with threading-the-needle accuracy through the open spaces between arms, while doing it at a controlled speed, so that it wouldn't set off too many vibrations. Even so, it was a chancy thing. Nine times out of ten, the arms would still move a little, and even the most careful of broomers could end up being unlucky.

I didn't mind that part. There is no life without risk, and we've all been dying from the moment we were born. Chances were getting one of those hunks of metal falling on you would kill you instantly. There were worse ways to die.

But I was out of practice, and I resented being made to fly in, when I knew there were other ways to get in—secret tunnels and passages people used every day. Then I realized that landing anywhere else in Syracuse was bound to attract attention and it would be easy enough for someone to follow us through one of the land passages.

Still, my body clenched in a tight knot, starting when Nat flew in between the arms, barely making the whole mess vibrate, and making it all look easy.

I followed at a different location. Look, no matter how much you tried, there would be some wind of your passage, and there was no reason at all to go through where someone had just gone through. That was just playing with fate. I aimed for and flew between the arms at the very top, taking a quick zigzag to the right then left again, as I realized there was a secondary arm back there, where I hadn't seen it before.

As I landed on the other side, Nat was waiting, standing in the middle of a street that led into what could only be called a permanent around-the-clock bazaar. He'd pulled back the hood of his broomer suit, and taken down goggles and mask. As I landed near him, he lifted his eyebrows and said the one word, "Show-off."

I realized he thought I'd gone through a difficult area to show my prowess on broomback, and that he didn't entirely disapprove. I could have enlightened him, but Martha landed with a sort of bounce, as though she had too much energy to be contained by suit and broom. She pulled back her hood, stowed goggles and mask in a pocket, and smiled at us. "Ready?"

Nat grunted something that might have been assent.

Deep Under is blocked at the other end by a water desalination plant. Two of the other ways to enter it are person-width openings between it and the columns that supported Syracuse's hanging gardens, a massive park directly above.

There were other entrances too, in the alleys between the buildings at the end of each block. But those alleys were really narrow and often blocked by loading docks. What was left, under there, were eight blocks of large buildings and one main street, most of it in complete darkness or as near it as could be, until someone turned on a lamp. All of it was protected by being inaccessible to most conventional peace keeping forces. Scrubbers could get in, I supposed, but I suspected they'd only be effective if they came in disguised.

Since this area supported illegal politics and illegal religion and illegal everything else, I suspected any Scrubbers coming in would be swallowed by the area itself. Most residents went armed and were fanatic about self-defense. And there were ways of making people disappear in Deep Under in ways they'd never be found.

So Deep Under was a secret everyone knew, but which no one official tried to investigate too closely.

There would be, I suspected, ways to deal with it. I'd heard, periodically, as my father's friends talked of blocking all entrances and pouring the whole area full of dimatough. But it never happened.

And part of this was that Deep Under carried on vital economic functions. More factories existed in this cramped little space than anywhere in the known seacities. Down here designer, and nominally illegal, drug compounds were created. Electronics were made cheaper and in greater quantities than anywhere else. And you could buy and sell anything—including, I'd heard, illegal bioengineering.

It was one of those areas even Good Men needed now and then. Enough to tolerate its existence, unless of course it became an open bed of sedition.

It was populous too, all out of proportion with other places. Kids played on the street in masses, most of them wearing headbands with lights on the forehead.

And all around there were tents and counters, bins and walking peddlers, carrying baskets and hawking their wares. Nor was there anything rational about their arrangement. Some of the vendors had fruits or produce, but the next one might have electronics, and others other things that I couldn't even identify.

Nat's bright blond hair helped, because since he was wearing all black, he'd otherwise be hard to see in the semipermanent twilight. He walked ahead, dodging carts and peddlers, playing children and the occasional dog. He seemed to know where he was going.

Martha folded her arm into mine. I felt her warm hand curve in. I didn't resist it, but neither did I make it easier for her. No use giving her ideas. Not that I thought she had ideas. The touch had a feeling of helpfulness, and after a moment I realized that three people walking single file following each other were far more noticeable than a man walking purposely ahead, who might or might not be followed by an ambling, strolling couple.

We weren't moving very purposefully, and eventually we lost sight of Nat in the crowd, but Martha seemed to know where we were going as well as he did. A toddler running full tilt hit up against my leg and looked up, with an arrested expression on his face. Martha laughed and patted his head. "He's ugly, but he doesn't bite," she said.

There were food shops under arcades, and broomers wearing various color markings. No one bothered us. We came to a narrow alleyway, to the left of which an even narrower doorway opened. Up from that doorway was a stairway, built with the sort of tall steps that weren't designed to be convenient to anyone's legs.

I heard Nat's voice somewhere, up there. The stairs were in complete darkness. Martha let go of my arm and—from the sound of her steps—fell back behind me. I couldn't tell, I had no reason to believe it, but I felt as though she were pointing a burner at the middle of my back.

My shoulder blades twitched, and I felt like shrugging convulsively. I didn't do it. It made no sense for Martha to be pointing a burner at me. And if she were I'd be damned if I let her see me sweat.

At the top of the stairs, the door was open into...

I couldn't see anything. There was a light pointing directly into my eyes. I closed them, reflexively, while I growled, "Shut the damn light off."

It was Nat's voice that answered me, "No."

In the Dark

"WHAT DO YOU MEAN NO?" I ASKED.

"No," he said.

"It's for your protection," Martha said.

"My what?"

There was a long, drawn-out sigh. I thought it was Martha, but it might have been Nat. It was Nat's voice that said, "If you see anyone in this room, you become a risk," he said. "If you decide to persecute us—"

"Which begs the question of why you brought him here, Nathaniel Greene Remy," a voice that felt older, and also angry, spoke from somewhere ahead and to my left.

"Because he needs our help," Nat said, his voice vibrating with an odd defensiveness.

"I wasn't aware we were a charitable organization," another voice said. This one sounded young and female.

"Don't be sarcastic," Nat said. "You know we take care of our own."

"He's one of our own?" another voice said.

"My father vouches for it that he has a claim on us through Benjamin Remy."

Hearing Ben's name pronounced aloud startled me. I sucked in breath, loudly and my face went tense and it must have shown because someone else, in the dark said, softly, "Oh hell." And then in a tone of deep disbelief. "You brought us the Good Man of Olympus, didn't you?"

Nat didn't speak. I didn't know if he'd made some sign, because I couldn't see him. Having to keep my eyes closed was making my skin crawl. I looked down and risked opening my eyes a little. I was standing on wooden floorboards that looked like they'd never been dusted, not once in the last three hundred years or so. Soft and grey with dust, they looked like they'd contracted, leaving spaces between them through which I could stuff my rather large fingers.

The room smelled of dust and disuse, but there were other smells, too. Soap and washed male and female bodies and something else which took me a while to identify, and when I did made my hair try to stand on end—it was the hot, scorched scent of a freshly discharged burner and of spilled blood.

I closed my eyes for a second, and when I opened them just a sliver again, I saw Nat Remy's boots, so close to me that he must be standing right by my side. "He's not what you think. Remember my last report. He's in peril for his life and he needs us."

There was a sound like huffing from the darkness. Then the same male voice who'd spoken first said something in a language I didn't understand but which sounded like old English, except it started with Nat's name and ended with Olympus and it sounded dirty. I heard a burner's safety slide off, and saw Nat's feet spread apart, as if he were bracing.

"Oh, for the love of the founders, John. Don't wind Remy. Or I won't be your second, this time."

Nat took a deep breath, as though to say something. I can't explain it, since I can't read minds, but I knew for a fact that whatever had been said in English was an insult, or at least an insulting joke. It had that feel. And I knew just as well that Nat had a cutting response on the tip of his tongue. But he let it go with a long exhalation. "I come," he said, "because I can't find any other way to protect him. The safety of the retainers and inhabitants of Olympus, many of whom are our people, depend on him and his life. They depend on us protecting him and keeping him alive and the Good Man of Olympus. The other Good Men want to eliminate him. And if he is eliminated, then my entire household dies. And all his other retainers."

"Dies?" someone asked. "Aren't we being a little melodramatic? Good Men have taken over other Good Men households with no major incidents before. Your family might be at risk, I concede that. But we've offered you—"

"Nat," the young female voice said. "Please repeat your report. I think George hasn't read it."

Nat swore softly, then recounted the gist of what he'd told me the night before. The incredible history about the Mules becoming Good Men. The brain transplants. It sounded insane, here, in the full light of . . . a lamp in my face. But no one else acted like it was impossible. Nat referred to reports turned in by Ben. Reports? Who were these people? And what did they have to do with Ben? I remembered what Nat had said about Ben sending out reports. Working for someone or something. Why had he never told me? His voice was suspiciously absent from my mind. Ghosts are never around when you want to interrogate them. One of the advantages of being imaginary, I suppose.

Nat ended with the description of the raid on my house the night before, then stopped.

Someone else swore. I didn't know who. The voice was too low and breathy to identify gender or age.

"So you bring him to us?" the voice they'd identified as John said. "Like that. What are we supposed to do about him? He's not one of us, and all of us risk our lives by revealing ourselves and what we are to him. You are the most at risk of all."

"Oh, please," Nat said, at his most bitterly sarcastic. "What's the worst that can happen? Yeah, I can get killed. Oh, I'm so scared."

He sounded like me, and I knew better. Suicide is only easy at times. At others, you have to work at convincing yourself you want it, no matter how miserable your circumstances. The body, the animal side, wants to live, no matter what the mind feels or thinks.

Then I thought of that tunnel through the side of the seacity, of Nat's admission to sleeping in Max's room most nights, of his knowing everything in that room, and of his flat description of torturing Max—no, my father in Max's body—and of what my father had confessed. But it had been Max's body. I suspected at an animal level it was also difficult for Nat to believe it wasn't Max he'd killed slowly. No matter what the brain knew. I shuddered.

"We can't protect him if he isn't ours," a voice said.

"We can," Martha said. "We've done it in the past for wives and husbands and daughters and sons."

"And whose husband—" John said.

There was a sliding ceramite noise from beside me.

"No, Nat," the young female voice said. "Easy. Burner safety back on, please. You don't want to do this."

It's amazing what you can get from a pair of spread-apart feet in dusty boots and the tautness you can guess in the calves and legs above them. I couldn't even see Nat's upper body, but I knew he was holding his burner in both hands and pointing it, somewhere into what was to me blinding whiteness. "Are we going to stand on points of law?" he said, and it sounded like he was speaking through clenched teeth. "Do you want me to walk out and never return?"

"You know you can't. No one walks out of the organization."

"Really? Try me. I know I'll have to kill all of you. See if I don't."

"Are you asking us to make an exception to bylaws?" the female voice asked again, softly, then added, in a familiar-command tone, "And please, do put the damn safety on. You're not going to kill me. You know that."

"I'm asking you to do whatever you have to do to keep him protected. I believe he is a strategic asset and a strategic advantage, but if the only way you can make this legal is to make him one of us, we can play that tune."

"We shall discuss this," another male voice said.

A door opened somewhere within the light. I heard steps walking away. Then Martha walked forward and turned off the light.

I blinked once, twice, and then I could see. We were in a large room, completely unfurnished save for two long benches against the wall in front of me, on either side of a firmly closed door. The one window to my right was crooked on the wall, implying significant age and settling. And the light that came through it was reflected shop light. I was effectively in the deepest dark for a few minutes, then my eyes adjusted and I blinked.

Nat got out his ubiquitous silver-metal cigarette case and pulled out a cigarette. He smoked in quick, short puffs, and paced, looking out the window now and then, as if he expected a flying ambush. He finished the cigarette and threw it on the floor, stomped on it, and started another. His burner remained in his hand, the safety off.

A glance at Martha showed me that she was looking at him and, unguarded, she wore an expression of the deepest concern. But when she saw me looking at her, she smiled. "Come sit," she said. "This is going to take some time. They call it a love of parliamentary procedure, but the truth is everyone who gets elected to the council is a windbag or becomes one."

Nat snorted. "You can say that again."

"Why, dear? I'm not a council member."

He snorted again, but his body remained tense, his shoulders taut across, his hand clenched on the grip with deadly force. I was relieved his finger was not on the trigger. Once more I had the impression that Nat Remy was waiting to explode and hoping someone would give him a reason.

Then I remembered something I'd read in history books of the twentieth century. Suicide by cop. That was when someone started a shoot-out with the police, or even just waved a gun-shaped toy at the police, to cause the police to shoot him down. I doubted any of those people behind the closed door were peacekeepers, but I'd bet that the violence Nat Remy wanted to commit was mostly against himself. However, if needed, he'd incite deadly violence, in the hope someone would kill him. One of the ways of overcoming the body's reluctance to die.

Voices came from behind the door for a long time. Nat smoked. Martha sat on one of the benches and I sat beside her. I inclined my head back, closed my eyes, lulled into a quasi-hypnotic state by the droning sound of voices behind the door, and by Nat's pacing and sharp inhaling of smoke. You could set your clock by the man's noises. Tick, tick, puff puff, breathe. Tick, tick, puff.

The door creaked open, not enough for anyone to look in, but enough for someone to speak through it. The young female voice. "Nat? We have some questions."

Nat stomped on his cigarette. The door opened for a moment on a glimpse of a grey suit, a well manicured female hand with perfectly oval, polished nails. And then Nat was in and the door closed.

And I knew who the young woman was. Abigail Remy. I was sure of it. Yes, a hand is very little to go on, but I'd seen her hand gripping that tray, and it now found a place with her voice, and between the two I was sure. Why the masquerade, when I knew of two of the siblings?

From the other side of the door, Nat's voice echoed, responding to their droning tones in a bellicose manner. I remembered he had taken his burner with him, and prepared to dive in and rescue him if shooting started. After all, he'd saved my life the night before. Besides, I was almost sure that Goldie wouldn't like it if Nat died.

After a while, the door opened a sliver, and Nat asked, "Lucius? Do you know the constitution?"

"What?" I asked. I was thinking I knew my constitution. I was built like a mountain with granite underpinnings. I'd not managed to die no matter what I did to myself. But what did that have to do with anything?

"The Usaian constitution!" Nat said, as if I were a particularly dumb student who'd just failed to spell his own name properly.

"The what?" Was this religion? I'd stayed away from religion most of my life. As far as I knew, my father didn't have any. I'd not been taught any. Now that I thought about it, if what Nat had said was true and we were made-beings, there was no religion on Earth that would accept us. After all, we didn't have souls. Which, now I thought about it, sounded about right.

I was sure my father didn't have a soul, at least. And if I had one, I'd never found it.

I didn't know if there was life after death. I was almost sure that Ben lived only in my own head. And though in moments of despair, I'd almost prayed, I didn't do it according to anyone's dictates. And besides, now I thought about it, I didn't think the Usaians even believed in a real God. Well, not as such. Something about the inherent goodness of mankind. Even if flawed goodness.

"Lucius!" Nat said, urgently, and I realized I'd snorted.

"I read it while in Never-Never, yes. I could recite some of it, if I tried."

"Okay, okay, basics. What about the Declaration of Independence, to begin with. Do you believe in natural, God-given rights to life, liberty and the pursuit of happiness?"

All right. Nathaniel Remy was insane. God-given rights. That sounded so nice. Where had God been when Ben had been killed miserably? Where had He been when I'd been thrown into a cell for fourteen years? And don't get me started on the pursuit of happiness.

And yet, I knew—I knew beyond all reason—that I was expected to say yes. Whatever these people were doing was supposed to make me and the city safe. Nat had said as much, if not directly clearly enough. And I knew he wanted me to say yes. So, what could I do?

But the thing is I didn't—couldn't—believe in God-given rights. Not really. I wasn't even sure I believed in God. "Uh," I said. I said it as though it meant something. "I don't know," I said. "I've never seen any God come out to defend those rights for anyone."

This time Nat snorted. He muttered something that sounded like "cork head" but which might have been ruder, then said, "No one believes God will defend them. We just believe they proceed from a source outside human granting. That they're inalienable and should be so. Mere law can't strip them away. Humans didn't give them and therefore can't abrogate them. You are supposed to defend them for yourself and others, because they're supposed to have them. Do you believe in that?"

I felt vaguely sick and couldn't think straight. Did I believe in those? I was supposed to defend their rights, was I? How well had I done at defending Ben's right to life? Or for that matter Hans's? They'd both died, rights or no rights. As for Liberty. "It's mumbo jumbo," I said. My voice came out as a growl.

Now Nat sounded almost pleading. "Lucius. Would you believe it if you . . . I mean, do you think it's something that society should strive for?"

"What? Nathaniel Remy." His full name, as they'd called it, with the middle name I'd never heard, pushed itself into my mind, and there was something associated with that name, something I'd read about. "Nathaniel Greene Remy. Are you an Usaian?"

Martha made a choked sound. Someone within the room shouted, though I couldn't tell what. Nat said, "Damn it." And then the door closed, and Nat was on this side, holstering his burner, grabbing my forearm in a death grip. My mind was still turning over, turning over things I'd half heard from my father and at my father's councils while I was growing up. Things I had read. Things I had thought.

Sam, Nat, Martha, Abigail. No. My house was shot through with Usaians. "Going to our people," Nat had said, and I'd thought he meant suicide. No. It meant taking refuge somewhere. Ben. Oh. Ben. It couldn't be. He'd have told me. Wouldn't he have told me? He'd kept secrets from me. Why had he? What had really been going on?

Nat had a grip on my arm and was dragging me across the room, to the corner most distant from the door. Martha started to rise, but Nat looked back over his shoulder at her, and his face must have told her something, because she sat down again, her eyes very wide.

And meanwhile my mind, my relentless mind, kept turning over the facts. The council of twelve. Tried by twelve. The thought came from somewhere and a saying about being tried by twelve, rather than carried by six. Protecting their own. Giving me protection. To protect me from the other Good Men, I'd need an army. Army. Most Usaians were peaceful in an almost dopey sort of way. Having lost their country and been sent into exile—those who escaped with their lives, about ten percent of them, if the books were right—through what seemed in retrospect an excess of holding back force and noblesse oblige, they kept mouthing about Manifest Destiny and other nonsense, and talking about the arrival of their prophet who was supposed to be the new George, in reference to Washington. And the new George would set everything right.

But there were the hotheads, the unrepentant bastards. There were those who said God helped those who helped themselves, and that nothing would happen without strife: the Sons and Daughters of Liberty. They could have been spun off into an independent sect, but Usaians would have to expel them and most of them—from what I'd read—seemed afraid to expel wind. So instead, the hotheads had been spun off or spun themselves off into an armed branch. The Sons of Liberty. It occurred to me I didn't know what they actually did. The Good Men tended to attribute any violent protest or act of rebellion to them. They tended to use it as an excuse to initiate massacres of hidden Usaians, or sweeps to destroy their information-dissemination branches. And to keep the hatred burning against the Usaians. And to keep the Usaians in fear so they didn't try anything.

But Nat had brought me here and submitted me to the judgment of the twelve. And he'd said they could protect me. And he was hell on a broom, good with a burner, and he'd killed Ma—my father.

Nat shoved me into the corner, put his hand on my chest, as though to hold me in place, glared at me. Before he could open his mouth, I said, "Benjamin Franklin Remy, right?"

It caught him off balance. His hand pulled back a little. "What?"

"His full name was Benjamin Franklin Remy, wasn't it? And he never told me. He never told me, not even as he was dying."

Nat blinked, his black eyes which normally showed nothing, looked momentarily stricken. "He couldn't tell you," he said. "He'd sworn an oath. The only way to leave is to die, and if he'd broken his oath, he'd have died anyway."

I swallowed hard. I felt as if I had a fever. It was like a headache without a headache, a pain I couldn't feel physically but felt nonetheless. "He died anyway," I said. As I clenched my fists. "He died anyway." I clutched onto anger. I wanted to be angry, because if I weren't I was going to start to cry, and I suspected if I started to cry, I'd never stop. "And he never told me." I swallowed hard. "He never told me he was in the Sons of Liberty."

Nat took a step back, and looked up at me, and for once his expression was readable. He looked confused, and also oddly guilty, and naked and vulnerable. He'd not have looked more vulnerable if I were holding a knife to his throat.

"And you're with the Sons of Liberty too," I said. I pointed at the door. "Your sister Abigail is in the council of the twelve. How can she be? How can you let her? She's what? Twenty? She's a child."

"We can swear oaths at sixteen," he said, and swallowed. "And Abigail was elected. Look, the Sons of Liberty are not what you think, we—"

"How do you know what I think?"

"We're not what the news say. No, we don't believe in taking everything lying down, but we have rules and councils and deci—"

"Don't care, Nathaniel Greene Remy. Don't give me soft talk. I've had enough of that and more. You're in an armed insurrection. Your whole family is part of it and—"

"Not my whole family," he said, hurriedly. "Not all of them. My parents, and my other siblings might believe in Usaian principles, but they—"

I snorted. "Don't care. Just tell me what you want of me. Why have you brought me here? What do you want of me?"

Nat brought out his cigarette case, took out a cigarette, shook it to start it, as he put the case back. His hand shook. "I want to protect you," he said, and sucked in smoke as if his life depended on it, while he stared up at me in a mixture of fear and something else I couldn't quite define. Why was he afraid of me? "I want to keep you alive," he said. "And there's only one way to do that and that's to call on the Sons of Liberty and their associated groups. The sans cou—other groups that get less press."

I shook my head. I shook it hard. "Honeypot" formed itself in my head. I'd read it in novels of the twentieth and twenty-first century. Honeypot was a seductive person, usually a female, of course, at least when approaching a male, who could convince people to act against their best principles—who could sometimes convince them to act against their best wishes. All to benefit some cause or conspiracy. I couldn't quite put things together. Not rationally. My throat had gone all tight, and I felt like I was going to throw up. "Not that," I told Nat's scared gaze. "Not now. I mean, what do you want of me? What did you people always want of me? Why did you... Why did Ben... Why was Ben thrown at me? Did he even want..." I couldn't breathe and my chest hurt. I felt like I was going to drop dead of a heart attack, right here, right now, after all my failed suicide attempts.

"What?" Nat asked, and seemed genuinely surprised, but the fear was still there, haunting and dark behind his eyes. "I just want to protect you. You were Uncle Benjamin's... You were Uncle Benjamin's. The only family he had beside us. He'd want you kept safe and alive."

"He was making reports from prison," I said, and my voice came out squeaky and raspy, both, as if the sound was having trouble making it past my throat. "To... to whom? How?"

"We had..." Nat licked his lips. "We have a network. It's not very good or very big. When we can, we'd like to... that is... When we can we save our own." He seemed to catch something in my eyes, some accusation I couldn't even make. "We were... they were, I was too young to know anything, of course, but I understand they'd organized a rescue, but it was all gone before... My uncle was dead."

Like that made things better. So, rescue had been on the way if I'd let Ben live a little longer. Suffer a little longer. If I could have endured his pain, he might be alive today. Life, liberty and the pursuit of happiness, my sore aching feet. If there was a God up there, any God, he was a stone cold bastard, much worse than I was, and I was a monster.

"Look," Nat said, he threw his cigarette at his feet and stomped on it. He opened his hands and showed me the palms, in a gesture of defenselessness. "Look, I want to save you. My family and I might escape if you fell, but I . . . But I don't think I could live with it. Not now." He looked up and said a word that I didn't think was in his vocabulary. "Please," he said. "Please." I had no idea what he was asking me for, though, and it didn't help. I backed up against the corner of the wall, glad for its coolness. I felt an odd longing for my cell, away from everyone.

"Listen," he reached forward and grabbed at my sleeve. "Listen, it's important, it's the only way I know to keep you safe. Please, please, please, listen to me. I . . ." He hesitated. He looked at me with Ben's dark haunted eyes. "I beg you to agree that you believe in the basic founding principles. I beg you to say you believe everyone is entitled to life, liberty and the pursuit of happiness. Then we can put you through the learning program, and while you're learning we can protect you." His hand clutched the ruffles on my sleeve hard, and his fingers bit at my wrist with something like desperation. "It's not just for you, though . . . though I want you to stay alive. It's for us, too. We've been unable to do anything for centuries. No one will pay any attention to rebels and our charter doesn't allow us to cause enough damage to civilians and innocents to intimidate the population. And even if it did, they would be more likely to turn on us. They view the Good Men as safety and sane government, and if we oppose them openly, we get painted as monsters. Even if the other Good Men are against us, if we have one on our side, we have a measure of respectability and we can get—"

And now I had it. The final piece in place. Ben had been a honeypot. And Nat had been one to Max. Pursuing the goal of subverting the Good Man's heir before he inherited. Intending to have a Good Man on their side. For the good of the cause.

They could join at sixteen. Ben and I . . . at sixteen. I felt as though I'd been beaten, every inch of my body pummeled. I was tired. I wanted to be back in my cell. I wanted to be dead. "Was that what you were trying to do with Max?" I said. "Corrupt him into your crazy religion? Did he know what you were? Did you tell him? Did you tell him why?"

"What?" He looked genuinely shocked, but of course he would. If they started training them at thirteen—"What? No. I couldn't tell Max. I didn't want to risk him." He looked very pale. "That has nothing to do with this. Please, just say you believe for now."

"No," I said.

"What?"

"No, I don't believe. I don't believe in any natural rights, and I'm not sure that your vision of paradise is good for anyone, much less for everyone. I've studied history, Nathaniel Greene Remy. I know what your beloved paradise was really like. The bickering. The wars. The bloody stupidity. And the lack of organization. The cross-purpose efforts. It didn't work then, and it won't work in our far more complex world."

But he was looking at me, so pale his hair looked dark by comparison. That and because it looked wet with sweat. Or at least I presumed with sweat, unless someone had upended a bucket of water on his head. "Oh, God," he said, looking up at me as if I'd grown a second head. "You can't mean—you can't believe—"

I didn't want to hear it. If I'd had the energy, I'd have punched him. But I didn't. Instead, I turned and stumbled out of there, at a half run. I was half-aware of his running behind me, and I don't know if he followed me all the way to the street. At least, he didn't catch up with me, because when I got to the end of the street and climbed on my broom to go through the mechanical spider, he didn't follow me.

Sturm Und Dragged

I HAD NO RECOLLECTION OF GETTING HOME, NO RECOLLECTION of going to bed, but when I next became aware of myself, I was in bed, in my room, completely naked and wrapped around a stuffed giraffe. I didn't remember sleeping. I didn't remember anything. Everything was dark. I got up and checked that my door was locked, then went back to bed, and wrapped myself around the giraffe again.

Oh, please. Stop the pity party already. It was Ben's voice in my head. He sounded furious. But I didn't want to hear it. I wasn't having a pity party. I'd realized what my life had been. It had all fallen in place.

I turned over and stared at the perfect darkness that obscured the ceiling. Ben had been thrown at me by his family, by his religion. I refused to believe he hadn't loved me. There were too many moments of shared humor, too many moments of delight in just being together. Those can't be faked or pretended. The friendship had been true and perhaps the love, but it remained that it had been an arranged relationship. He hadn't felt about me the way I'd felt about him.

But most painful, I'd killed Ben. I'd truly murdered him. I looked at my hands and remembered the homemade knife, and Ben's throat and the final flash of gratitude in his eyes. Rescue had been on the way. And I'd bet that the Remys could get access to the best regen. It could have saved—

It's a pity party with guilt streamers. Listen, knucklehead, my religion didn't throw me at you. We worried Sam half to death being involved because he was afraid I'd get hurt, while I...

"You?"

I was afraid you'd get hurt.

I turned over and buried my face in the giraffe. "You don't exist," I said. "You're a figment of my imagination. To all my other charming characteristics I will now add being completely crazy."

Now? He raised his non-existent eyebrow at me. *Luce!*

Could I smell a trace of his cologne, a hint of his shampoo in the giraffe? After fifteen years?

Only if they saved it in a sealed bag. Wait, they had to have, or it would be dusty.

I pressed my face into the giraffe and inhaled and tried to conjure Ben from non-existence. "I'm sorry. If I'd known—"

I didn't know; you didn't know. It might never have been true. Look, the SOL are not the most organized people in the world. They might have told Nat they were about to rescue me. They might even have believed that. But the chances are small to none. His memory in my mind waggled his hand in a dubious manner. *We used to joke by saying that the individualists had failed to organize.*

I didn't dignify that with an answer, though if I thought about it, I'd confess that they didn't seem the best organized group in the world.

Are you going to arrest them? Have them executed?

"What?"

Sam. Nat. My family. They are guilty of illegal beliefs.

They were. And I knew they were. And while I didn't know what the Sons of Liberty actually had done, as compared to what the media claimed they did, I knew it had to have involved some murders, some destruction of property, but how much, and in what circumstances?

And in my head, Ben set his jaw in the way I'd been familiar with, the way that meant he was about to stand his ground and hold it because he was sure he was right. *We look after our own,* he said.

"Nat killed my father."

I think that fell under private vendetta, Ben said. *You can't deny him the right of avenging Max. But I won't deny we'd kill Good Men if... Most of them do such things that...* He stopped and shrugged. *You'll figure it out. Most Good Men aren't good.*

If they were three-hundred-year-old Mules who murdered their own children to survive, I supposed they couldn't be, but I didn't say that. Instead I said, "I will presume that..." I couldn't believe that Ben would do anything bad. Illegal, perhaps, but not bad. And Ben had been one of them. "I'll presume that you wouldn't have joined if they committed evil acts."

Define evil.

"Things that hurt people."

Don't be an infant. Of course we hurt people. Even if they'd managed to rescue me from prison, guards would have died in the raid. I guarantee it. And property would get destroyed. By that definition I did commit evil more than a few times.

"You killed people?"

Only when it couldn't be avoided.

I wanted to ask him where and when it had happened, but reminded myself he wouldn't be able to tell me. One thing is to allow your subconscious to pretend to be the ghost of your long-lost friend. Another is to start believing he really is such. Instead I concentrated on the evil part. "You wouldn't hurt someone who either hadn't deserved it..." I paused. "You wouldn't kill someone unless doing so would prevent more deaths. Or if you had to kill in self-defense."

I wouldn't imprison them either, he said. *Or interfere with them. You could say I respected their rights to life, liberty and the pursuit of happiness.*

So. He'd won. He usually won our verbal sparring bouts. "It's not that simple," I said. "They can't make me change my religion to suit their needs. They can't ask me to sell my soul."

You aren't sure you have a soul, remember? I'll agree that Nat handled it badly, but—

"There was no way they could have handled it that I would have agreed. Your Usaian fanaticism is a pipe dream. If it was so wonderful, why did the original fall apart, amid external and internal strife? Why couldn't it even defend itself? The Regime of the Good Men has been stable for longer than it existed. And we've kept people happier."

Or so we'll think so long as news is censored.
I was quiet.
So, you're not going to denounce my family.
"Or harm them, no. How could you think I would?"
Then what are you going to do?
"I'm going to govern."

Riders on the Sturm

I WOULD ALSO HAVE TO FIND A WAY TO DEFEND MY HOUSE AND my seacity. I'd been holding on to a mythical hope, a child's game of pretending. I'd always known in the end it would come down to me, and just to me. It always had. And it should. My problem, my solution. Why should I have been counting on Nat Remy? As much as I'd failed in the past, everything that needed to be done to protect myself, or Ben, or anyone else for that matter, had been my business. My job.

I dressed and went to the office. My father's office. My office. No one stopped me. No one questioned me. I dreaded that Sam would ask me about where I'd gone with Nat, but he didn't. He took no more notice of me than if it had been my routine always to come and sit behind the desk and deal with accumulated paperwork.

The first day I did no more than sign piles and piles of paper with my signet ring. It was surprisingly tiring, the movement of pulling a paper from the pile and pressing my ring against it. I didn't read the paper. I couldn't read the paper. I couldn't concentrate enough to do it. But just signing them gave me something to do, and while the rest of the office moved around me, and Sam Remy now and then brought over new piles of paper, I found myself fitting in, acting as though it were all normal.

Routine. No more than routine. Someone brought me coffee. I drank it. Then I returned to my work.

After sundown, someone turned on the lights, and clerks started leaving. At last Sam Remy stood up. He looked hesitantly at me. "You should have dinner," he said. He didn't add "son" but I could hear it in the tone of his voice.

"I'm not hungry," I said. But I did get up and leave the office. There was no one else there, so my staying would serve no purpose.

Sam left before me. On my way to my room, I passed a room where the door was insufficiently latched, and voices came from it. I'd swear I recognized Sam's voice and Nat's voice.

"—an unconscionable risk," Sam said.

Then something muffled, and then Nat's—I was sure of it— voice, "He's not going to."

"How can you be sure? Nat, you should have asked before, you should have tried— You pushed him in a stupid way. What on Earth made you think it would work?"

"It would have worked with Max."

"He's *not* Max. "

"No." A pause. "No."

"Are you sure that..." Muffled.

"Out of time."

Muffled.

"Not if he dies. I couldn't stand it. I tell you I couldn't stand it."

I wondered if he were talking about me, but it seemed unlikely. Why wouldn't he be able to stand it if I died? Until a few days ago, he'd thought me dead. More likely that he couldn't stand the mess if I died. That made perfect sense. But I had no intention of dying.

I went to my room. I crawled into bed, fully dressed. Sometime in the night, I felt the impact of a body on my bed and a furry face pressed near mine. Goldie.

From the darkness came the sound of Nat settling down inside my door. So, he was still guarding me. Of course he was. He didn't want the seacity thrown into worse turmoil by my death.

In the morning when I woke up, he was gone. There was no one in the room, either, but a small table had been wheeled in with breakfast. Just looking at it turned my stomach, but I forced myself to have coffee and a slice of bread before cleaning—I used the fresher on vibro this time—and putting on clean clothes.

For three days I went to the office. For three days, I electroni-
cally signed papers I didn't read. For three nights, Goldie slept in
my bed, his warmth and company my only protection against the
terrible cold of knowing myself alone, the terrible fear of knowing
I couldn't do anything to protect those who depended on me.

For three nights, Nat slept across my door, on the inside. I
knew this, because I could hear him breathe, and because Goldie
wouldn't be there without him. But I didn't see him. And it
was better I didn't see him. After all, what good would it do to
dredge up old trouble? He had tried to railroad me into joining
a religion. I'd contravened his plans. He was still protecting me
for the sake of the rest of the people in the domain. But that was
it. It was not like there was any great affection or even respect
between us. I would say I felt sorry for him.

Except you're so busy feeling sorry for yourself, Ben said, and
I supposed he was right. And there was nothing I could answer
to this, so I didn't.

On the fourth day, I accidentally skimmed one of the papers
on my desk, and paused. The paper made no sense whatsoever.
"Sam," I said, puzzled at my voice wavering.

"Sir," he said and approached my desk. Did Sam look like he
was afraid I'd turn on him and have him arrested, or worse? Oh,
not outwardly. His external demeanor was the same as always—
responsible, respectful, perhaps paternal despite and behind all
this. But there was a hint of cringe in his gaze.

I suspected it wasn't even for him. Sam Remy had the sort of
mind that could face the noose or worse easily enough. But this,
if I were so disposed, would mean the death of his entire family. And I knew Sam much too well to think that didn't matter.

The worst was that part of me longed for him to treat me as
he had when I was a child—as though I were his brother or his
son. I longed to hear him call me Luce, or "son." But he just
stood there, very tense, staring at me.

"These papers," I put my hand on the pile I'd just skimmed.
"They direct farmers what to plant where, right?"

He inclined his head.

I frowned at him. "We don't have farms. There isn't enough
soil on the island to make for significant fields."

He shook his head. "No, but we do have territory in North
America that falls under our jurisdiction."

I frowned at the paper. "But . . . North America doesn't have two growing seasons. Not in the northern parts. Show me where this is." I stabbed my finger at the coordinates on the map.

Sam looked grave. "No. I know. But we always do it like that. We issue the seed to farmers and have them seed in November."

"Excuse me? Why?"

"Uh . . . it's always been policy."

It just wasn't good enough. I pulled another paper. "And this one?" I said.

Sam looked around at the office.

"Samuel Remy, answer me, is that also policy?" Was the man I had trusted since I could remember, a monster, as big a monster as my father, or worse?

He shook his head. "Not here, sir. Those documents are eyes only, and have always gone from the Good Man to me and from me to the Good Man. That's how it's always been. That's how it was under my father too. If you wish to discuss it, I think we should be in private."

"You can't mean we've been kill—"

"Not here, sir. I have your best interests at heart."

"My best—" but then I looked at the pile of papers and back at Sam Remy. My best interests might be right. If anything in these papers got out, I suspected that no Good Man would be left alive. At least I hoped not. And regardless of how bad my kind was, of this I was innocent. Other Good Men had sons who might be as guiltless. And I didn't want to reignite a new set of turmoils that would consume the innocent along with the guilty.

"Into my private office, Mr. Remy. Now." I picked up the pages that puzzled me and stalked out into the plush confines of the inner sanctum that could be locked and which I knew, from my father's use of it, was soundproof.

Sam Remy walked in after me, standing very tall in his plain dark suit. And it's no use at all telling me he was shorter than Nat and Nat was shorter than myself. I know all that. But in my mind, he was still a father figure. And I still believed he must have a moral reason for this, but I'd be damned if I could explain it.

As soon as he closed the door, I thrust the sheaf of papers at him. "Why are we creating famines? Why are we releasing targeted plagues among the people? Why are we killing inventors and curtailing inventions? Why—"

"We?"

The single word stopped me, and looking at Sam I could tell he looked grey and tired, exhausted, really. Like a man who's been carrying a heavy weight uphill for a long time, like a man who's lived divided, and who knows it, and on whom the pressure of a double life has been growing over the years, and who has been aged and sickened by it.

"You are...you were my father's right hand. You administered..."

He looked at me, serious, intent. "My son told me," he said.

And for a moment, scrambling, I wondered what his son had told him, and whether it was me he was angry at. But then he said. "He told me that there was only one man here before, his brain transplanted..." He took a deep breath. "I won't say I... my ancestors for that matter, hadn't suspected it, but it seemed so far-fetched and we had no proof. And besides, what could we do about it? And what could we do about those policies, which he enforced ruthlessly? What could we do? And don't tell me we could have fought back or died trying. Then he'd acquire other servants and I'd be executed, and nothing, nothing would change. It was all your...his decision. All his doing, Luce. And don't tell me we should have tried to murder him. There have been attempts. On him and on all the other Good Men, but the few times they succeeded, the uninstructed heir got killed and other Good Men took over. There used to be eighty, you know? No, we didn't know why. Of course, it makes sense now."

My mouth was wide open, and I snapped it closed. I backed up, blindly, to my desk chair and dropped into it, staring at him.

"I'm sorry you had to find out this way, Luce, but what could I do? For all I knew, you wanted to continue the policies. Besides, would you have believed me, if you hadn't seen those papers?"

I shook my head. I probably would have thought he was feeding me some crazy Usaian line. "But...if I'd signed..."

"Then everything would go on as it has."

"But...I signed some...I want them back. The ones I signed before..."

He shook his head. "Those are not...of this kind. And if..." He chewed his lip. "At the risk of your condemning me for treason, I thwarted a lot of those orders, even under your father. I changed them, or made it look like those executing them were incompetent. If you wish to fire me for—"

"No," I said. "No, Sam. But...why? It can't just be chaotic evil with no reason. Why was my father murdering thousands of people by means ranging from famine to denial of new medications? Why?"

"Three hundred years of stability."

"What?"

"Three hundred years of stability, sir. People say that the USA was an impractical dream, an impossible system because it collapsed, eventually, on its own, and because it was never stable. But the truth is, countries...or lands...or worlds with growing populations and vigorous innovation aren't stable as such. Too many young men will bring fast innovation and, with it, turmoil. You don't want that; you have to let war or plague kill it. Too much food and the middle class grows fat and sassy and is no longer contented with being the servants and henchmen of the nobility. What we have is a feudal system, and a feudal system necessitates closed population and technology, where things change very slowly, if at all." He paused for a moment, then went to the chair across the desk from me. He stood behind it, clasping the back hard. "Damn it, Luce, I sent you history gems."

"You..." I said, and then, out of my inadequate supply of words, I fished, "Thank you."

He shrugged. "It was all I could do. Like with this situation, all I could do was fake incompetence, but not so much incompetence I got dismissed." He paused and tightened his lips. His fingers drummed on the back of the chair. "My son told you that he and Martha and Abigail are the only Usaians in the family and that his mother and I are well out of it. That we might have sympathetic ideas but are not involved. I'm sure you were not fooled. Nat does almost everything well, except lie. He's a terrible liar. He can't possibly have fooled you. He and my other children didn't name themselves. And I didn't name myself. My name is Samuel Adams Remy. You know what we believe in. You know what Usaians believe in. You can't have believed I'd willingly do this or that I'd have done it at all had I any other choice."

"Because of life, liberty and the pursuit of happiness?" I asked. "But that's nonsense. I told Nat...I mean, those things don't exist. They have no independent existence outside human minds. They aren't natural laws. They aren't laws of any kind. And if one doesn't believe in God, one doesn't believe in them."

He stood up and grabbed my hands on the desk. "If one believes in humanity one has to believe in them," he said. "Because they have no independent existence outside humans, but humans don't have an existence outside them—not real humans; not the best in humans. Not..." He realized he was holding my hands, let go, and stepped back. "I'm sorry. Let's take this rationally. Why is that policy evil?" He waved at the nasty directives on the desk. "Why were you so shocked by them?"

"It kills people!"

"So does overpopulation," he said. "So do the wars that result from overpopulation. So does strife, and lack of stability. They also blight lives. So, why are those actions, which are designed to counter the evils that would result from their not being enforced, evil?"

"Because..." I struggled. "Because..." I felt like I was about ten years old. I wanted to run out of the office, slam the door, and go hide out in the garden until my anger and confusion passed.

But if I ran out of the office, Sam would...I didn't even know what he would do. I knew I wasn't ten. I knew I was the Good Man, and whether this policy went forward or not was my decision. And I couldn't let it go forward.

"It's wrong!" I said. "For one man...especially a Mule, one... individual to decide who lives and who dies, for...It's different if it just happens, if it comes from conditions. But for one individual to decide it for everyone else, to coldly murder others, to say it is for their own good...it's evil. I can't explain it. It's evil."

"It's only evil if you believe there's intrinsic value in each individual," Sam said, ruthless. "Only if you believe it matters that individuals are treated like objects. And you can only care, if each individual, in your mind, has the right to self-determination."

"Life, liberty and the pursuit of happiness," I said, my voice sounding very odd.

"Were you and Nat guilty of murder when you cut down the Scrubbers who tried to ambush you in front of your room?"

"What? No. They were trying to kill us."

"And what gave you the right to defend yourselves?"

"What? Of course we had the right—"

"Did you? The majority of the Good Men, the constituted authorities of this world, who have governed for three hundred years, think you should die. What right do you have to live?"

"I damn well have the right to live as long as I can stay alive," I said. "I— Oh." I scratched at my nose. "But Nature? And Nature's God?"

Sam shrugged. "I am a religious man. But some of my brethren aren't. Some of them simply believe in humans being humans and having the right to be human."

I took a deep breath. "I thought," I said, slowly, "that you weren't allowed to spank me, not even when I was little."

"What?" Sam said, genuinely surprised.

"That was a much worse spanking than when you caught Ben and me playing in the apple tree." I looked up and met his worried expression. "And perhaps even more effective." I raised my hand at him. "No. I'm not ready to make any profession of faith." I thrust the papers at him. "Burn those damn orders, then get me the gems of all the real history of this damned seacity. I want to know what's been going on. And don't tell me it doesn't exist. My fathe— I'm sure he had eyes-only history."

He quirked his mouth at me. "My ancestors have made... there is a record."

"Good. Bring it to me in my room."

When the Sturm Breaks

I DON'T KNOW HOW LONG I SPENT LOOKING AT GEMS, IN MY reader, in my room. I found the oldest one and looked at it, then read forward, slowly.

It wasn't just that the creature who had called himself my father had engineered famines and even engaged in wars with his fellow Good Men which were over nothing at all and simply designed to make sure the population of young men was kept down. Young men were troublesome, of course. Get enough of them in a population and you'd get war. Or innovation. Both of which could break the rule of Good Men.

All the way back, in the time of turmoils, there had been heavy suppression of information and of the network of computers that had allowed people to talk to each other, bypassing official channels, for much of the twenty-first century. Information was deemed special and important. After all, it could be misused and used to incite the wrong sort of opinions.

So, now, one needed a special license to connect to such a network, and only the right people were allowed to do so—the right people being those with a government purpose. Any media from news to porno holos had to go through the information council which was controlled by all the Good Men, in league. There was some sort of communication limiter in Circum. It prevented most peer-to-peer talk, beyond one-on-one. A private citizen couldn't even call five friends at the same time. Not without a license. And if you called too many of them serially, you'd find the authorities at your door, too.

And so no one knew how much of our daily life was controlled.

I don't know which shocked me more, the minute control of life, or the clumsiness of the control. By which I don't mean it was blunt—oh, sure it was, at the beginning. Famines and wars are large implements of killing, they take masses at a time. And they were still employed in my day, but only in rare emergencies.

Most of the time, what happened was that the troublesome elements were identified early on. Under the current regime, in all but the most backward domains, all young children were tested, exhaustively, and those that were too creative, too intelligent, too ... *different* could be either eliminated, destroyed or channeled into fields where they would do no harm.

As for an excess of young males, that could be curtailed by keeping food scarce and by managing the mass media and public opinion to make the idea of too many children repugnant.

When all that failed—and some of it had; I wonder how much through Sam's intervention, and how much because those people were cut off from the seacity proper and living in wilderness that had been almost depopulated since the time of the turmoils—there were famines and other more overtly evil tactics. Which was why I'd found those documents.

I didn't know what it said about me that it was the less overt tactics that revolted me more. My hackles rose, my teeth clenched, and I felt vaguely sick to my stomach. It was as though all these people, unknowing, were as imprisoned as I'd been in that cell. Only I'd known it and they didn't.

The touch on my shoulder made me jump half out of my skin and turn, away from the projected holograms.

Nat stood by the desk, smoking. He gestured at the gem reader. "Shut it off and unlock the door. You have the house in a flap. You've not shown up for any meals, and haven't answered the link when my father tried to call you. My father said you were just busy, but I think even he is afraid cunning assassins have got in."

I pulled back from the desk and blinked up at him, then rubbed my eyes, which felt like someone had poured sand on them. My voice wouldn't come out at first, and I realized my throat felt very dry, so I cleared it and said, "How...long have I been in here?"

"Twelve hours," he said. His smile was wry. "First you blew up at my father and dragged him to a private conference, then you locked yourself in here. Half the house thinks you've gone mad; the other, that you're writing Father's death sentence. I thought I'd better come in the secret way before he has to get honest at someone and tell them you've always been mad." He reached past me for the link button on the desk. "Do you mind?"

I didn't mind, so I let him and because the ash was growing long on his cigarette, I reached for the ashtray box, and held it out for him. He shook his ash into it and, as the link pinged said, "Dad. He's alive. Have them send up dinner, will you? He didn't realize how long it had been."

Sam sounded tired, as he answered. "I figured," he said. "Shall do."

Nat stepped back, picked up the porcelain box from my hand, looked around the room, as though seeing it for the first time. "Your furniture?"

"Yes. My childhood furniture. You saw it before when you... after Martha—" I didn't want to say just before we went to the horrible meeting. My thoughts about the meeting had shifted. Everything had shifted, and thinking about it made me feel vaguely sick.

It was still crazy and still religion, but much better than the alternative. If I were to join them... perhaps this could change. I could protect my people, I could protect myself and perhaps I could change things, too.

"Yeah. Wasn't paying attention. And the rest of the time it's been dark." His gaze was unreadable, as he looked around again. "I presume you like this better." And, without waiting an answer. "You and Max would have got along."

I didn't say anything. There wasn't much I could say. I noticed his gaze lingering on the stuffed giraffe, but he didn't make a comment about grown men sleeping with stuffed animals, and I didn't punch his lights out.

A noise outside the door caused him to cross the floor in long strides and unlock it. And if anyone looked at him funny for being presumably locked with me in the room, they didn't say anything. Once more, though, they set the table for two.

I turned the reader off completely, in such a way it would

need my genetics to unlock, by which time the servers had left the room. "The thing is," I told Nat, as though it was part of an interrupted conversation, "that I don't feel hungry."

"No." He lit a cigarette from the end of his almost finished one. "My father told me what you've been reading."

"You knew? You knew this was going on?"

"I knew some of it," he said. "I've guessed the rest. I've never exposed myself to the full torrent of it, no."

"I've only read about half," I said. My voice sounded aged. "I feel ill. I had hopes my father having me put away in solitary for fourteen years and murdering my little brother to steal his body was the worst he'd ever done."

"Yeah. You're an innocent sometimes, you know that?"

"It's the first time anyone called me that in at least fifteen years."

"Yes, but your society has been rather limited for fourteen years, so that's hardly a distinction." He looked grave. "Come, Patrician. Have some food. Do it not to upset my father."

"Will he be upset?" I asked, noting that Nat knew, at least, which levers to pull to get me to do something.

He shrugged and smoked intently, as if his life depended on it, before saying, "He's worried about you. Worried about what you'll think, after . . . worried about what you'll decide to do." Nat avoided my eyes very carefully, and I suddenly realized that he was worried too. And why shouldn't he be? Let me see—so far I'd called the attention of the other Good Men to the fact that I was not my father, in a way that Nat could not hide; I'd exploded out of a meeting of the twelve in a way that might very well have endangered his life; and I'd been rude, obnoxious and hard-headed in a way that could have set the entire house against me.

I'm not saying his management of me had been that good, either, but then I suspected after what had happened with Max and after what he'd had to do, Nat was not, yet, in his right mind. Besides, in many ways his hand had been forced all along the line. And now he'd turned his back on me, and was setting a bowl full of something on the table.

"Eat with me," I said. "And lock the door."

He gave me a theatrical look. "Two dinners together, Patrician? People will talk."

"Stop calling me Patrician. And the people who need to talk are the two of us."

He hesitated. I could feel the joke forming in his mind, but I didn't have the energy for this, not after what I'd just read. "I need someone to talk to about...what is in...what I've read. And...maybe I was an idiot to bolt out of the council—"

He crossed the room to lock the door.

"Have we been attacked again?" I asked. "The house, I mean. I've been so—"

"Buried in your own problems?" Nat said, charitably. "Go eat."

"Nat! Have we been attacked?"

He stopped by the desk, cigarette in hand, very tense. I had a feeling of words carefully weighed. He shrugged deliberately. "Nothing worth mentioning. Go eat."

I got up, feeling the aches of having sat far too long. The chair that had been set by the table was more straight-backed than my desk chair, but just sitting in a different position felt better. Turned out the bowl contained some broth. Nat didn't make me invite him twice this time. He helped himself to a bowl of the broth, and sat across from me. Setting the porcelain box next to the plate, he proceeded to smoke and eat in a way I was sure was banned by all right-thinking etiquette experts.

"Where is Goldie?"

"He was playing with the boys, so I decided not to bring him," he said, pushing the empty bowl away. "He needed the exercise."

"The boys?"

"My brothers."

"James?" I said, proud to remember.

He gave me an odd look, as though surprised I remembered. "James, Pat and Tom." He went over to the serving board and looked it over. "Do you eat fish?"

"I eat anything. Well, I'll balk at pink or green mush."

"I imagine," he said. Once more he filled a plate for me, as well as one for himself. I decided that there was really a lot of the nanny in Nathaniel Greene Remy.

"But you're the oldest of seven."

The briefest of smiles. "Debra is three. Are you really passionately curious about my family?"

"Is a large family a Usaian requirement?"

"I hope not," Nat said. "Of course, I'll probably die young. Now, what did I say. You've gone all white."

"Don't talk of dying young. Not...after what I read."

"Yeah, don't worry." He set a plate in front of me, took another one for himself. "I'm not the type that dies young, more's the pity. I'm the type they have to cut in half and bury each half at opposite ends of a river."

"Banks?"

"Ends. Banks would be way too easy." He ate and he started another cigarette. He smoked with the intentness other people reserved for things like making love or flying a broom through a narrow space, or avoiding a burner ray.

"Nat, what I've been reading, why?"

He looked up from his cigarette, at me, and didn't ask me the obvious question, nor mock me, instead he said, "You mean why it happened?"

I nodded. "I don't think..." I paused. "You'll probably tell me that it's epigenetic."

"What the fatal tendency to not finish your sentences? Must be, never noticed it in Max or the old bastard. Not that I talked much to the old bastard. Not normally."

"The...I'm supposedly his clone. If I...would I become like him?"

"What, trying to rule over twenty-five million people, Lucius? I expect you would, sooner or later."

"Is that the population? I thought we only had a million or so."

"Three million in the seacity proper, the rest in the...what do they call it? Aggregate territories. Your father...Your...whatever he was, claimed a lot of territory, as the blighted areas started getting colonized again."

"How much control did he have over it?" I asked. I had a vague idea of vast expanses of space. Continents seemed alien to me, seacity born and bred, but of course they weren't. Still, I had this vague idea that there was a lot of space to hide in a continent.

He shrugged. "For those people who live in the cities? Fairly tight. It's more or less like living in a seacity. Now, did he hunt over every rock and ledge for stragglers? I don't think so. I confess I didn't ask him. There were other things on my mind when I questioned him."

"I'm sorry. I didn't mean to bring it up."

"Don't apologize. Do you think I ever forget? Because it's not brought up? Do you think I forget it for a minute asleep or awake?" He looked up, then gave something that might have been a repressed laugh or a hiccup. "And I just lost my right to lecture you about drama, didn't I? Look at me calling attention to how special I am and how unbearable things have been for me. Never mind. My mom says she didn't drop me on the head as a baby, but she's probably forgotten. I did what I did because I thought I wanted revenge. I wanted revenge. But..." He shrugged. "Pardon me again. What you said, about what you'd do if you had that power? Probably. Look, the thing is, look at what I've done without that power."

"I don't know that you've done something wrong. I assume you needed to extract information, and he deserved to die."

"Oh, it's not what I did to him, Lucius. It's what I did to me. Don't you understand?" He looked up at me, and shook his head. "He deserved to die, I'll grant you, and I never understood opposition to killing those who are causing death or pain to others—if the guilt is incontrovertible, that is. As you've had occasion to witness—sorry about that—I also don't oppose killing in self-defense. But I should never have tortured him. No, wait. I should never have tortured him as I did, not in a way that..." He shook his head. "We needed the information, but there are drugs. And there's always virtus."

My face must have been a study in blankness.

"You can put someone in virtus and make them face their worst fears. I hear it's very effective. I should have tried it. We did need to know where he'd hid Athena's husband. But I went on, after that. And what I did...it diminished me. It might have killed part of me. And not just because he occupied Max's body." He looked at me intently, then sighed. "Look, I'm not a philosopher and I can't put it any better than this, but my idea of myself doesn't include torturing the helpless, and he was helpless at that point. Whatever else he might have been, he was helpless. Humans don't do that. Humans don't torture and kill helpless people."

"You haven't read what I've read. Humans do a lot of that, actually."

"No," he said, "you're talking about humans as they exist. But humans...look, we're not angels, we're not perfect. Any regime that puts too much power in the hands of a single human assumes we're perfect, flawless. We're not, and given absolute power, the flaws will show. But we're also better than the worst things we do. When you concentrate on...on the evil that men do, you miss

what humans can be. No. What humans should be. And then...
and then humans as such stop existing. Because we're not..." His
cigarette had burned down to his fingers, and he stubbed it, then
examined his fingers. "You're making me philosophize, but the
thing is, we're not, as humans, only what we do, but also what
we dream ourselves. A free society can't exist without humans
imagining themselves as ideal creatures better than they are."

I gave him a sidelong look. "Is this doctrine?"

"What? No. Just trying to explain why I feel as though I'm
exiled from humanity by what I've done."

"I think you're exiled from humanity due to rampant insanity."

"Ah, that wouldn't do it, Lucius. At least half the people are crazy.
What I meant to say, though, is that for a free society, we need some
sort of moral standards, and moral standards are, by definition, a
thing of the mind, not... not something you find in nature."

"Wait," I said. "Moral standards, like... who gets to sleep with
whom, that sort of thing, or—" I dug in my mind for other
things that had been considered morally iffy in the heyday of
moral preening before the rule of the Good Men. "Having too
many children, or too few?"

That time it was definitely a laugh. "Oh, sure. I am the one
to be talking about any of that. I meant real morals. Don't kill
others. Don't hurt others unless you have to do it to save yourself
or a lot of other people. Don't interfere with other people more
than you have to. Treat other humans as... as that ideal human
I was talking about, so you can treat yourself the same way."

"We're coming back around to life, liberty and the pursuit of
happiness," I said. "Tell me, Mr. Remy, are you a missionary?"

"Only if you preface it with world's worst," he said. He lit
another cigarette. "I'd give a go at being a honeypot, but I think
I'd be the world's worst at that too."

"Quite," I said, suddenly amused at his candor. Right now my
idea that Ben had been forced into a relationship with me, or that
Nat had been forced into a relationship with Max seemed odd.
I'd seen real pain in Nat's eyes when talking of Max. And as
for Ben— I cut the thought short, because I didn't need to think
of Ben now. "The better brand of honeypot don't leave cigarette
burn holes on the sheets. What you're telling me is, I suppose,
that one has to act as though everyone has a divine right to life,
liberty and the pursuit of happiness, so that the right will exist?"

He was nodding vigorously. "And so that...well...That it will exist for us too. Your father—I'm sorry, I don't know what else to call him—was only human in the purest sense in the end. No, I know he was a Mule, and that Mules are human. And that means he wasn't perfect. Given unlimited power...he became what all humans become in that situation: a monster. Because, you see, the other humans, the ones he ruled, weren't perfect either, so they didn't obey orders, and he kept trying to make them be perfect. To whittle them into people who would follow orders. And that's why you sense evil. He was denying other people the power he abrogated completely to himself. The power of self-determination."

"So you're telling me...That...?"

"That despotic government is evil. It has a long record. It always ends in blood."

"I thought that was what you believe because of your religion."

"It is. But it also happens to be true."

"I thought your religion promised you salvation from yourself, I mean, from..."

"All we've been promised is a land ruled by our principles, eventually."

"For which the Sons of Liberty don't intend to wait sitting?"

"God helps those who help themselves."

I stared at him a long time. He smoked impassively, not seeming discomfited by my unwavering gaze. "Why did you take me to the twelve?" I asked. "What did you expect, if I'd agreed to become a...whatever you called it, an initiate in your religion?"

He rolled the smoke in his mouth and expelled a neat ring which climbed out of the light of the candles and into the darkness above. "I expected to be able to call the resources of the Sons of Liberty."

"But you said they were not very organized. No, wait, Ben said that."

His eyebrows went up. "I thought Uncle Benjamin hadn't told you about the Sons of Liberty?"

"Well, not while alive."

The eyebrows climbed higher. "I am not analyzing that," he said. "Look, no, we're not the most organized people around. There's a joke. The individualists—"

"Failed to organize, yes."

The eyebrows didn't have any more to climb, so they just stayed pegged where they were. "Right. But in the end, some help is better than none, and we have some very experienced broomers in the ranks. And besides... Well, there are other organizations, in other seacities. We make a common front most of the time. There's the Sans Culottes, Guy Fawkes' Legion, Monster Hunters International, the Boys From Ipiranga, the Incarnate Legion and, oh, another dozen or so." He shrugged. "In the end, perhaps very little, but Jan Rainer will stand with us, and perhaps, just perhaps we can start something. Perhaps..." For just a moment I got the impression he was tamping down his enthusiasm, trying not to appear as hopeful as he really was. "Perhaps there can be hope for freedom after all this time."

It seemed like a forlorn hope. But then it all seemed like a forlorn hope. The question was did I want to go quietly into the good night, or did I want to go out as loudly as possible. I thought of those files I'd read, of the hundreds upon thousands of people the Good Men had killed over the centuries without anyone noticing. And that was without counting the people who had died because inventions that could have saved them were suppressed, because they or their inventors had been suppressed before they'd been disseminated. How do you measure a lost opportunity? How many drug-addicted broomers in the seedy parts of Liberte could have been space captains, had the present taken a different path—a path it could have taken but for intervention from above? How many people had died in engineered famines, who could have created an affordable space drive? How many of them could have birthed other geniuses that would grace us today?

All these people had died, all in mute reinforcement of the rule of Good Men. I looked up at Nat. "It would be better, would it not, to make a big splash, to ignite a fire, however brief?"

He smiled, this time a genuine smile without a hint of irony, and reached across the table and, putting his hand over mine, squeezed for just a second. His hand was hard, calloused and cold. Why did a lawyer have calloused hands? "Sorry, but I'm so glad you understand. I didn't know how to explain. If we can at least resist well enough that people hear of us, perhaps it will ignite a fire elsewhere, down the line, tomorrow or a hundred years from now. Otherwise... They'll eventually get us, openly or by stealth. And they will kill us. And no one will ever know. And no one will care."

"I want to join," I said. "A land ruled that way is worth it. Even if it doesn't last forever. Even if we don't live to see it."

Something seemed to have ignited Nat, even though he'd drunk neither serious alcohol nor the near-lethal coffee. He stood up, with a sense of irrepressible energy, and walked to the entrance of the secret door, then seemed to remember he hadn't explained what he was about to do, and he turned around and said, "Sorry. What I meant is, I'm going to go to the council and...And... I'm going to go. Don't wait up. The twelve love to jaw anything to death. But I'll be back as soon as I can."

Ladies and Gentlemen,
We Declare the Revolution

MY SOI-DISANT FATHER MUST HAVE BEEN VERY GOOD AT TRAIN-
ing servants, whatever else he might have been bad at. And
perhaps that was not a big surprise, since after all he meant to
make servants of every person under his rule.

What I mean is, they came in to clear the remains of dinner
and didn't seem even slightly discomfited that Nathaniel Remy
appeared to have dissolved into thin air. Perhaps they thought
I'd let him out without anyone noticing. At any rate, they were
the least inquisitive people imaginable.

I'd lingered over fruit and coffee, thinking I'd just made the
biggest mistake of my life, but unable to feel sorry for it. If I
held out, I'd be holding out in the name of what? Not being a
joiner? Being contrary to the end? There was nothing to gain by
that, and so much to lose. I looked at the pile of gems on my
desk, and thought that at the very least I owed it to all those
dead people, those destroyed people, not to go without a fight.

I locked the gems away on my desk drawer, I called the servants to clear the table, and I went to bed.

And woke up with Nat Remy calling out, "Lucius? Are you
decent?"

"What?" I was awake immediately, as I was whenever someone
came into the room, but this seemed rather early for a moral

177

enquiry. Goldie jumped on the bed, tried to lick my face and in the darkness, I patted him and pushed his hindquarters down.

"Are you dressed? Dressed enough to be seen by people?"

"Oh. Yes." I was in shorts and a light shirt, and though no one would call it a formal outfit, I'd need to go to the most distant and strange parts of the Earth to be arrested for indecency.

"Good," he said. And then "Light." Lights came on.

He stood in front of the secret door, which was closed. Martha stood on his right, and Abigail, blushing, on his left. Why was she blushing, I wondered? She was very young, and maybe she'd never been in a male's bedroom before. On the other hand, my bedroom was hardly indecent and I, sitting on the bed, patting the idiot dog, might be disheveled, but otherwise wasn't even mildly titillating. Then again perhaps she'd taken in the implications of Nat's secret passageway, in which case... it was none of my business. Surely she didn't think it had been built in a week. Martha just smiled at me in a matter-of-fact way, then walked across the room and opened the door. Sam came in. By this time, I was feeling seriously alarmed.

"Is anything wrong?" I asked.

Sam shook his head, and it was he who spoke, "It was judged easier to have Abigail and I carry proxies for the other members of the twelve than to have all of us get together here, or have you flown elsewhere. Our intelligence gathering tells us there's been a flurry of activity by Scrubbers. We're not sure what they're up to, and we are not about to take risks we don't need."

The other members of the twelve. The Sons of Liberty were all *young hotheads*. And Sam and his wife knew nothing of what their children were involved in. And I was innocent as a babe unborn. My house was not just filled with Usaians. It was filled with dangerous revolutionaries. And liars. And yet, I thought better of Sam for doing something about the injustices and crimes that crossed his desk every day, rather than sitting still and letting evil go on.

Sam had the grace to blush a little at my expression, then shrugged. "Sometimes, telling the truth will only endanger all those who depend on you, and to whom you swore to keep silent so they'd not be found out."

I inclined my head and didn't say anything. He cleared his throat. "Nat tells us... That is, he says you're willing to admit to believing everyone should be granted life, liberty and the pursuit of happiness as a fundamental right. Before he left the meeting, previously, he secured people's vote that you be allowed to join our organization on probation, if you professed such beliefs." Was his smile totally ironic? "Of course, I suspect two or three of them, at the time, thought it was more likely for them to get hit by a meteor that had lain in ambush in an alley, waiting for them to walk by. But we got them to agree to your full induction, and we'll do it before they can retract that. That way you'll be a full member. And we'll avoid another internal battle."

Nat cleared his throat and I thought he had suppressed laughter and it occurred to me that if any members of the council thought that they were too stupid to hold office and perhaps too stupid to live. Nat Remy was not a honeypot, and he might be the world's worst missionary. But he had inherited from Sam a kind of bullish gentleness that would keep bringing a point up, ever so gently but so continuously that the subject of their efforts couldn't help but surrender.

I didn't doubt that I'd been steered to this point. I'd need to be an idiot to not have noticed. But I was sure of one thing: Sam hadn't cooked those records. Contrary to popular belief, a complex narrative spanning centuries was hard to create without leaving huge holes. Heck, it was hard to create a simple lie spanning hours. Which was why most novels were enjoyed despite the holes in the narrative. And those records held. Which meant, whether he'd arranged for me to ask for them or not, the reasons I was doing this were real.

"So," Sam drew himself up straighter. "Lucius Dante Maximilian Keeva, do you believe in Life, Liberty and the Pursuit of Happiness as individual rights?"

"Yeah," I said and tried to avoid the three Remy siblings staring at me from my right side. They all looked rapt, as though they had no idea what came next.

"And have you read, and do you believe in, the Constitution of the United States of America, and believe, if followed, it would create a nation that would respect such rights?"

"Yeah," I said. Because it was easier than to explain I thought it had terrible loopholes and flaws, but would create a state superior to anything else before or since—at least as far as my reading of history went—and infinitely superior to the stability we'd endured for three hundred years.

"Do you realize the Usaian religion is proscribed in most of the Earth and that, if revealed as a member, you could be summarily or publicly and lengthily executed?"

"Yeah," I said, at which point it occurred to me that I was being asked life-changing questions, while I sat on the bed, with Goldie lying across my legs. It didn't seem right. It seemed like it should take place in an elaborately decorated hall, with flags flying and bands playing.

"And are you ready, nonetheless, to become a member, and to work towards the reestablishment of a republic under that constitution, even if it should mean the loss of—"

I fished the answer from what I remembered of my reading. "My life, my fortune and my sacred honor."

Someone sniffled. I thought it was Abigail. I hoped it was Abigail.

"And do you promise to keep secret and support your fellows in this fight to the limits of your ability, and not betray anything or anyone to the authorities no matter what persuasions are used?"

"Yes."

"Then Lucius Dante Maximilian Keeva, welcome to the brotherhood of free men." And then, to my profound and stunned shock, Sam Remy stepped close and kissed me on the cheek. And I'll be damned if his children didn't repeat the performance.

"And now," Sam said, "that you are one of us, do you agree to let us use the seacity as the basis for the start of our great work?"

I nodded. I had realized, sometime while reading those awful gems, that I wasn't going to be the Good Man by the end of this. Not if it worked. I'd be lucky if I still had my life at the end of this, particularly if we won. And yet it was worth it. If I had my life it would be enough, anyway. I'd never wanted to be the Good Man.

"Then, ladies and gentlemen, it gives me great joy to proclaim the revolution."

This is when all hell broke loose. Nat and Abigail hugged each other, Martha hugged Sam, then Abigail started crying, and wiping her tears to the back of her hands, and then two of them—I was too confused by then to tell which—hugged me.

And that should have been the end of it, or perhaps the beginning, but my life doesn't work that way. As things started to calm down, Sam said. "We'll leave now. You need to sleep. Tomorrow there's an awful lot of planning to do, and we need your permission for...everything, to begin with. And Nat?"

"I will arrange for Simon and Jan to come over. And also for military people to confer." He blinked. "Oh, and, Father, we forgot."

"We forgot? Wha—oh. Yes. Do you have it?"

Nat nodded. "Grabbed it at the house on my way over, when I got the girls," he said. He pulled a small box, maybe the size of my palm, from one of the pockets that he had to have sewn inside his tunic. It was one of those plain, ceramite boxes in which the cheaper type of jewelry is packaged. But the way he held it, as though it contained something immensely valuable and fragile made me wonder, as did the fact he had to take a deep breath before speaking, "I don't know if you know that each of us is supposed to own a piece of the true flag, identified as a flag that was flown in the US of A when it still existed as a sovereign republic. I know that people joke about being so many of them that they'd cover most of the world, but...a lot of flags were produced, and we still have a cache, kept in a climate-controlled room. There are also other forms of reinforcement of aged fabric. If your parents and your relatives were Usaians, you'd inherit one from one of your ancestors. Some pieces of the flag have been passed through family lines for centuries. They used to be worn on clothing, before we were proscribed, but now that would just condemn us and those close to us. So, we don't do that. But every one of us has a piece and knows where it is at all times. The idea is that when we start the revolution we'll bring it out and wear it, openly, on our clothing." He opened the box and extended it to me. It contained a scrap of blue cloth maybe three inches long and two wide.

As I took it from Nat's hands, I could tell that three white stars, grown grey with age and dirt, showed faintly against the blue.

"We debated giving you a new piece," Nat said. "But we thought you'd prefer this one. The stain on the top is blood of one of our martyrs who wore it sewn on his clothing at the time the religion was first proscribed. His fellow believers rescued his body and his flag." He hesitated. "There is no other blood on it, but it has belonged to many courageous and honorable men who paid the ultimate price for freedom." He had to swallow, before continuing. "The last one of those was Benjamin Franklin Remy."

And then I cried.

COME HELL

Nightmare

AFTER THEY'D LEFT, AND NAT HAD LAIN ON THE FLOOR, ACROSS my bedroom door, and the lights were out, I lay in the dark, with my hand on the box that contained the scrap of flag. I'd closed it again, because I didn't want to risk tearing the precious fragment. I couldn't hear Ben, but I could feel him all around, feel him closer than I ever had, as close as my hand on that box.

I thought if I opened my eyes, I would see him sitting on the bed, smiling at me, the same way Sam and Nat had when I had answered the questions. But I knew of course that I wouldn't see him, and so I kept my eyes closed and held on to the closeness, the sense of having him near.

I couldn't sleep, though there was nothing bothering me. Oh, a certain embarrassment over bawling like a baby in public, somewhat lessened by the fact that the girls—even Abigail, who couldn't have remembered her uncle very well—and then Nat had joined in. Though Nat had done a manful job of pretending not to feel his tears, till he turned away presumably to wipe them to the back of his hands. Sam hadn't cried, but looked like he really wanted to. And I'd stopped as soon as I could.

So, the embarrassment wasn't great, and the only strange feeling attending me was a sense of belonging, which struck me as very odd. I'd never belonged to anyone or anything before. Oh, my mother and Max, perhaps, but even there a certain constraint had remained, because first of all I, and them, belonged to my father, and only at a remove did we belong to each other. We weren't a group, but a few people over whom father held power of life and death. More so than I'd thought at the time.

Goldie had lain across my feet, and I could hear Nat turn by the door. "Nat," I said, low enough that he wouldn't wake if he were asleep.

"Yes?" he said, in the same sort of hushed voice, like he wasn't sure he'd heard me.

"This...revolution of ours," I said. "How likely is it we'll succeed?"

He made a sound that was part exhalation and part chuckle. "I'd give us a good ten percent chance," he said.

"Uh...that's not very good," I said.

"I should say," he said. "Our analysts, the ones who do these calculations, give us a ten percent chance." He paused. "And it is very good. The best it's ever been. Two Good Men in our ranks. And one who will cooperate, though his beliefs are different from ours."

"Two Good Men?" I had a vague idea of having heard this before. "Jan Rainer?"

"Yeah. He...he has just joined us. We...both of you need protection." He was silent a moment. "And I think in that case, Martha might have had some influence."

"Martha?" I said, and probably sounded more disbelieving than I should. Because when one thinks of dark and dangerous seductresses, Martha Remy, with the splash of freckles across her nose, and the sensible squarish face didn't fit. "I mean," I said, remembering I was speaking to her twin. "Not that she isn't a perfectly nice girl, but..."

"I know," he said. And there was amusement behind his voice. "But she has had a crush on Jan for the longest time, and I think they've finally come to some arrangement. I don't know for sure because she hasn't confided anything to me in those matters since at least twelve." Pause. "Don't tell my dad. He gets very odd about...that sort of thing."

I imagined. I suspected I'd seen some hints of that oddness.

"Speaking of not telling my father," he said, after a while. "If I don't shut up and let you sleep there will be hell to pay tomorrow, so good night."

"Nat?"

"Yes?"

"Doesn't the floor get awfully uncomfortable?" And because I could feel his mind scrambling in the dark and was not very interested in getting verbally—if not physically—punched, I added, "We could have a cot brought in or something."

A chuckle. "As much as it would provide an additional obstacle to someone breaking into your room, chances are I'd get tangled in it and not be very effective at defending you, if a force gets past all our other defenses. And that's the whole point of my being here."

"But it must be cold and—"

"Nah, much easier than the training weekends," he said.

"Training weekends?"

A long silence. "We...almost all our young men and some of the women are trained for war. Part of staying fit, should the revolution happen in our time. It's...religious practice. Usually we go into the continental protectorates, or at least the natural islands, because it's easier to hide. And we train in relatively small groups. But I've slept on a slab of rock, on a mountain, during winter. This is downright comfortable by comparison. Now, good night, Lucius Keeva. You do not want to get my father officially upset at us."

I tried, but it was a good long while before I was asleep, and I woke up with the door bursting open.

Before I was fully awake, I'd sat up, grabbed two burners from the bedside table, and was holding both of them trained steadily on the door. But the voice that spoke from the door was female, breathless, and said, "Where is Nat?"

I woke fully. The person in the doorway was Abigail Remy and though she was panting, as if she'd been running, she was pale as death. "Patr—Luci—sir! Where is Nat?"

I returned the burners to the bedside drawer. "I don't know. He was here when I fell asleep."

She made a peculiar huffing sound that managed to convey that sleeping was the stupidest thing anyone could do, and possibly—just possibly—a crime. Then she put her hand to her forehead, in a gesture that was so reminiscent of Ben it startled me.

Before I knew it, I was jumping out of bed, grabbing clothes from my wardrobe without paying the slightest attention to what they were. Something told me Abigail wouldn't get this upset over nothing. Not a young woman steady enough to be elected to the revolutionary council at twenty. From my encounter with that group, even though mostly I'd heard them and not seen them, they were middle-aged men of crusty demeanor. And Sam, their head, had patriarch written all over them. And yet Abigail had got elected. She was a young woman steady enough to have tried to hold the meeting of the twelve together in the face of Nat's rage and my obstinacy. "Where did you see him last?" I said, forcing my bare feet into boots. "What is your reason for being so worried? Did he say where he was going? He had told us he was going to contact Jan Rainer and Simon . . . I presume St. Cyr, since See-mon is the French pronunciation."

"I know," she said, and then in a tone of exasperation. "They haven't seen him, though he called them on a link to say he was coming."

"Perhaps there was an accident?" I said, doubtfully. But I had a growing, cold certainty that Nat Remy wasn't accident prone. Disaster, perhaps, but not accident. I slipped the box containing the fragment of flag into my pocket. I'd have to lock it in a drawer where the cleaning staff couldn't find it, both in case they realized what it was, and so they wouldn't throw it away by mistake.

She shook her head. "No. The thing is, I don't think he ever left." She looked up at me, and her eyes, so much like Ben's, were full of tears. "Goldie was alone, loose on the beach."

"On the beach?"

She nodded. "Nat wakes up early and goes running on the beach with Goldie every morning. Goldie came home alone. There is a scuffed place, and it looks like a flyer landed and like there was a fight. My father told me to stop worrying, we'll know in time. I can't stop worrying. What if Nat needs rescue?"

This was way too much like waking up in the morning, in the prison to which they'd sent Ben and me, and finding that Ben was gone, and having to figure out where they'd taken him when no one would tell me. I could read the same worry in her eyes. "Martha has gone to Jan, to see if they can find out anything."

"Right," I said. "Right." And because I had to do something, no matter how foolish, no matter how stupid, I said, "Show me. Show me the place on the beach that looks like it was trampled or scuffed or whatever. Show me."

She nodded, which goes to show you she was as out of her mind with worry as I was with confusion and the unpleasant memories of Ben's disappearance. We headed out of the room and down the hallway to the front door. Where guards barred my way. I didn't even react badly. I was just confused at finding my path blocked by my own guards.

One of them, almost my height, and probably close to Sam's age, spoke, looking embarrassed, "Sir, Mr. Remy said you were not to go out."

"What?" Was I under house arrest?

"Sir...there have been incidents. We cannot allow you to go out."

Abigail stopped short too, and suddenly looked like she would like to kick herself. "There have been battles," she said. "Around the house. Mostly broomer battles, but I suppose, if they see you...I mean, surely they have some way of seeing around the house, and if they see you...well..."

Well, it was different. I was a prisoner in my own house, for my own good. Not that it felt any better. I felt helpless, which was the last thing I wanted to feel. I had just started to feel that I had some control over my destiny and that my life was mine to spend or waste and now...And there was Nat. What had the idiot been doing, running alone with Goldie, if there had been incidents around the house? "What was he thinking?"

"He never thought he'd be a target. He's been doing this since he was twelve. You see, he was first turned down for the...for our...for training." She gave a dubious look at one of the guards, as though not sure he was one of the Usa—one of us. She walked away a bit, her hand on my upper arm, pulling me along. It was like a row boat pulling a cargo ship, but I let her, and I bent down so she could whisper to me without anyone overhearing, and she did whisper, urgently, "Because he was the...you know one of a pair of twins is always weaker? That was him, and he was seriously underweight and spent most of his childhood being ill. So they turned him down, and he started training up by himself till they took him. It's second nature to him, I think. I've never known him not to run on the beach every morning. And what would he think? Who would care about him and what he was doing?" Abigail said, understanding what I meant. "I mean, they're not going to arrest every person in the house, right? They'd have to bring a really big force to bear to do that, and then it would be really obvious and not something they could sweep under the rug with Scrubbers. I think they're still trying to keep any dissension secret, and they don't want a major battle. So they're sending small detachments, but we figured they would be intent on capturing or killing you. Oh, maybe Father if they suspected he had any say in your behavior. But... Nat? Who would care about Nat?"

I pulled her away from the door and down the hallway, to the door at the other end, next to my room, where the only rooms nearby were mine and those were empty now I was here. Better to be able to speak without constriction. I needed to know.

I had to force the words past my throat, which was trying to constrict. "What if he got in battle with them, and they killed him?"

"No. We'd have found his body. Why would they take the body? That makes no sense."

"The Scrubbers specialize in making bodies disappear," I said. The idea of Nat cut up into small, unidentifiable pieces and burned or dissolved made me ill. He'd been alive yesterday—a tight ball of enthusiasm and energy.

She shook her head. "Only in circumstances where it makes sense. This doesn't. They don't occupy the island, and arguably leaving Nat's corpse behind would scare us more than his disappearing."

"Perhaps they hope we'll go in search of him." I was thinking that they would undoubtedly know of my proclivities, and they would, undoubtedly, know of Nat's. Maybe they hadn't known Nat's before Max died, but surely they'd suspect, or know afterwards. And it was entirely possible they thought they knew more about the two of us than they could possibly know. Maybe they thought it was inevitable. And I'd spent a lot of time locked with Nat in my room, and he slept there. Surely the Good Men had spies in my house. I'd have them if it were reversed. And surely they knew Nat and I had spent a lot of time together. A lot of time together alone. Perhaps they thought I wouldn't stand to have him taken away from me. Perhaps this was a trap for me.

The problem was that though they were all wrong, I couldn't stand to have him taken away from me. I wasn't even sure that I considered him a friend. If I did, we had an odd sort of friendship that consisted of annoying each other into some sort of consensus. But he was Ben's nephew, and the more I thought of it, the more I realized he was not only an honorable man, but a loyal one. And I needed all the loyalty I could get.

She looked doubtfully at me. "I don't think they think the Sons of Liberty will go in search of him," she said. "I mean, we look after our own, but it takes a while to organize, and we'd never let someone who is a high-profile target go."

It hit me, perhaps belatedly, that I'd sacrificed some of my freedom in order to join the fight for freedom. Policy and organization. Not just Lucius striking out on his own. And part of me wanted to do just that. To take the secret tunnel to the beach and go in search of Nat. "I didn't mean the Sons of Liberty," I said, my voice catching. "And speaking of that, shouldn't you be in the Daughters of Liberty?"

She looked up at me. "Why? You mean you don't think I should be active?"

I blinked at her.

"The Daughters of Liberty," she said, "are support and propaganda. I'm not suited to that." She paused a moment. "You know Martha and Nat taught me broom riding and broom fighting, right?"

"You mean...but...you're a woman."

"What does that have to do with anything? The groups have that name because of their work in the Revolution in the USA. It has nothing to do with gender. And do you really want to argue this now? I thought we were going to find Nat."

I blinked again. "Find Nat? But you just said the Sons of Liberty don't do that."

"Did I say anything about the Sons of Liberty?" she said, and her eyes flashed up at me, just like Ben's did, when he thought I was being particularly dim.

"Us?" I said. "You and me?"

She nodded, intently, desperately, then hissed in annoyance, and made a head gesture that indicated that someone had approached. I looked in the direction her chin had tilted. That too was a Ben-gesture and I read it instinctively and without thinking. Steps from me stood one of my valets, seemingly dancing foot to foot, in the pose of someone who hopes to be noticed without actually interrupting anything. I wondered what in hell he thought he was interrupting. "Yes?" I said, turning to him.

"Patrician, if you would, that, is...Mr. Remy asks if you'd see him..."

I felt relief flood me for just a second, and was about to ask where Nat had been and where he was now, when I remembered. Mr. Remy was always, unless in very specialized circumstances, Sam. So, I straightened and said, "Where is Mr. Remy?"

"His office, sir."

"Father!" Abigail said, as though this comprised a comprehensive indictment of his manners, morals and possibly the fact he dared to be alive at all. And before I could ask what in heaven and hell she meant by that, she added in a rush. "It's just like him." She grabbed my upper arm again, and squeezed hard. "I'll see you af— I'll find you. Be ready."

And like that, she turned around and ran down the hallway, her childlike movements reminding me that she was indeed still a child in some ways. I had no idea what she meant by my being ready. I had no idea what she meant by finding me. For that matter, I had no idea what she meant by saying that she and I should go and find Nat. But the one thing I would need to make sure—very sure—I remembered was that she was the child, and I was the adult. No matter how capable, how daring, how brave she was, she was seventeen and I was almost twenty years older. Which meant it was part of my duty not to let her run her head into a noose or worse.

Which is exactly what I was thinking, as I walked back into the main offices, and by guess more than memory, identified the door to Sam's office right next to mine.

I don't know what I expected. But I didn't expect to slam the door open and find Sam sitting behind the desk, looking like this was a perfectly normal day.

My Son

AND THEN HE LOOKED UP, AND HE DIDN'T LOOK ANYTHING AT all like normal. He looked like a man who had lost his son.

There is no other way to say it, no other way to explain it. It sounds odd, but I didn't know there was a particular look that translated as that before, and if anyone had told me such a thing existed, I would not have believed it. And yet, that was the only thing that applied, when Sam looked up at me.

His features looked much the same as always; his expression was composed; his eyes looked perfectly normal. I don't mean to say that he looked like he'd been crying. He didn't even look as though he'd been worrying. But something—something behind his eyes, something behind the perfectly composed facade of his features— had collapsed. It was like a building that is wholly burned on the inside without the walls showing any damage from the outside.

In that look I realized two things: He was sure Nat was dead. And he would not let it stand in the way of the great cause that had already cost the Remy family two of their young men.

I wasn't so sure in either case. Oh, Nat might very well be dead. Who was I to say otherwise? I had no proof, nothing concrete I could oppose to the idea. On the other hand, I didn't think I could allow Nat to be dead. I didn't think I could take it. Not now, not yet, not like this.

"Sam," I said, my voice curter than I meant it to sound. "You wished to speak to me?"

His answer came quickly and in perfectly urbane tones. "Yes. You see, we're supposed to meet with Simon St. Cyr and Jan Rainer today, and before we do, we need to get some paperwork in order. I'm sorry to call you so early, but I haven't been to bed yet. I stayed up all night discussing things with the council of twelve, on how to steer this. It is obvious that they're going to launch a frontal assault as soon as they're sure that there is no way to get rid of you by stealth. Right now, the only reason they haven't attacked the island openly is that they have hopes the Scrubbers can do their job and take you out, and then they can deal with us as they would deal with any house that has lost its Good Man. Jan is going through the same. Believe it or not, this is both the best and the worst right now. Strategically, we shouldn't want the whole might of the Good Men to come to bear on two—or even three seacities—but on the other hand, this also doesn't allow us to defend ourselves, to get our own military force in place, or to request supplies and volunteers from the various secret organizations that have been fighting—" He stopped and stared at me, in shock.

Until he did so, I didn't realize I'd sworn, loud and profanely. Yeah, the sound of it still hung in midair. Yes, my mouth felt like it had just pronounced the words, the hard dental consonant pronounced hard enough to bruise my tongue against my lips. But I had no intention of doing it, and didn't realize I'd done it till Sam stared up at me.

"I beg your pardon?" he said, not so much in censure, but in total confusion, like a man who takes a step in the dark and finds nothing under his foot.

I took a deep breath, found my mind—or at least that part of it that had sworn loudly, rather than, say, punching a hole in the nearest wall at listening to strategy of revolution while Nat Remy was missing—while Nat Remy might, even now, be fighting for his life or worse. And I repeated the swearing, with careful and exact instructions of what we should do to the revolution, the Council, the Good Men, the army and the broom they rode in on.

For a moment Sam stared at me, speechless. I heard Ben, as clear as day, in his best, sarcastic tone say, mildly, *What? All of them, Luce? Even you don't have that much stamina.* And it occurred to me I'd never used that word in front of Sam, much less in that loud, decided and vulgar a manner. "I'm sorry, Sam, but—"

"Son," he said. His voice was at once commanding and hollow. The house might be burned to a husk, but its walls were stone, two foot thick and twice as hard to dismantle. "Son, do you think I don't know how you feel? Do you think I don't feel it too? Nathaniel was my son." He looked, of a sudden very tired. "My firstborn. Beyond that, he's been my closest helper. He's been my right hand for years. Do you think I'm not grieving?" He looked suddenly stern and angry, Zeus pater, or another of the old, unabashedly male divinities, in a raging fury. "Do you think I don't care? I will remind you that in many ways it is the second time I've lost my oldest son. I raised Benjamin from the time he was two. What do you want me to do? Scream and howl? Do you think I wouldn't do it if I thought it would bring them back? Or even bring one of them back? But that's not how life works. That's not how grown-ups act. We know that screaming and howling has no effect on the material world, and that dead is dead and nothing is bringing it back."

And now I was angry. In my mind, clear as day, was the certainty that this was how he'd taken Ben's arrest too—with grief, sure, with crushing grief, likely, but also with quiet and sure resignation, the kind that absorbed the body blow and lived to fight another day. If the Sons of Liberty, the organization he was working for, the organization he served to his last breath, had done anything, anything at all, there was a chance Ben would be alive today. That Ben would be alive right now.

I put my hand in my pocket, to take out the flag, to put it on the desk, to say that I didn't want any part of this organization that took its own members being destroyed and did nothing. But, though it sounds crazy, I felt a hand close around my wrist, and I heard Ben's voice, *Steady, Luce. You don't want to do that. And you know you don't. What else do you expect of them? They've been clandestine for two hundred years. Proscribed on penalty of death. What do you expect? Fighting spirit? They wouldn't have survived this long. They're the mouse that nibbles in the dark, not the cat who hunts in daylight.*

I took a deep breath. "I want you to not give up," I said. "I want the twelve to not give up. I want you to think where Nat can be. I want us to find him. He told me that the Sons of

Liberty take care of their own. He wanted me to join so I'd be protected. And now we're going to leave him alone to die? We're going to leave him for dead, when he might still be alive? You and the twelve can go to hell. I'm going to find him."

He looked up at me, startled, then asked a personal question.

"Not that I see where that's any of your business," I said harshly, and saw him flinch, which was good because if anyone else had asked that question in those circumstances, I'd have punched his lights out. To think that the only reason one could have for wanting to fight for Nat's life was physical intimacy was insulting and demeaning to both him and myself, and possibly to the whole human race. I expected better of Sam, and the only reasons I didn't get truly angry was that I knew the shock he'd just suffered, and that he had to be half out of his mind. I was half out of mine, too. But at least mine wanted to fight for what was worth it. "But no. I'm not even sure we're friends. But I'm sure he's a loyal and honorable man, and I'm sure he'd fight for me or for you. He doesn't deserve to be left alone to die in some ignominious way."

"Lucius, son," Sam said, very softly. "If I weren't sure he was dead—"

"How can you be sure? What sense does it make? Why would they kill him when they know how useful he is as bait?"

Sam stood up. His office had no windows, unlike mine. It was hardly larger than a quarter of my bathroom, about the same size as the cell in which I'd spent fourteen years. The desk was set halfway through it, halfway between the back wall and the door, facing the door. Now he started pacing between the wall and the door. "Why would they leave him alive, Lucius? Ask yourself that."

"I don't know," I said. "They left me alive, and more, they left Ben alive. I fully understand that I had to be kept alive, a way of storing the body in more or less working condition, but why keep Ben alive? Why not cut him down that first day? Was it just so they could force me to kill him, and have an excuse to put me away?"

"You don't know what strings I pulled, and how fast, to keep Ben alive," he said, looking up at me. He looked suddenly very tired. "You have no idea. They wanted to do just that. They wanted to kill him. Your...your father did. I convinced him that if he left Ben with you, you...your tendencies wouldn't be so obvious. No, I didn't know why at the time, but he clearly didn't want it to be known what...how you were. Now I understand, of course. He didn't want rumors of it to attach to him, if he ever had to ascend to power under your name. Not that it should matter to an absolute ruler, but clearly it mattered to him. And I convinced him there would be less scandal, and less trouble if he left Ben alive and with you, in jail. Only there wasn't less trouble."

"You have no idea what it was like," I said. "Or what would have happened to him, if I hadn't fought."

"Did I blame you? Did I ever say you were guilty in any way? I figured it out. And now that I know what your father really was, and what he wanted with you, I can see that his plan simply changed. It was still obvious, to everyone who knew you in jail, I'm sure, and to everyone who supervised it that you and Ben were involved. And it was obvious that there was talk and it would be remembered, so he thought the best thing was to get you put in solitary and give people time to forget. Plus, I suspect, Ben was caught passing out information. I know they tried to get information out of him before...I know part of the torture was for real information. I saw the files, though your father was cunning enough not to run those by me. But we didn't abandon him. We didn't abandon you." He sagged, suddenly, as though a weight had dropped on his shoulders. "You know we didn't. Even if all my cunning planning, my desperate pleading and maneuvering served was to make Ben's life last through one more hellish year, and to keep you distressingly aware and sane through your captivity."

Tell him it was all right, Ben said. *Tell him, damn you. Don't you dare pile guilt on him, on top of everything else.*

"It was all right, Sam," I said. Ben was irresistible in that mood, even if Ben was only a figment of my imagination. I knew as well as I knew anything else, that Ben would have said exactly that if he'd been here and present. "It was all right," I said. "You have nothing to blame yourself for. Don't you know I'd give years of my life and heart's blood, too, for another day with Ben? You gave us another year. Yes, it might have been hell, but not as much as even the best time without him has been. And as for my sanity, if it consoles you, I'm not even half sure that I'm still sane. But that's not the point. The point is that you have no proof that Nat is dead. You have no proof that nothing can be done. If I were the Good Men—and arguably I'm more like them than you are—I'd not give up such a strategic asset."

"It's Goldie," he said. And walked behind his desk, and sat down again.

"I beg your pardon?"

"Goldie had blood on him. Not his blood. Goldie isn't injured."

"But...did you analyze it? Do you know it was Nat's? I've seen your son fight, Sam. I doubt anyone could lay hands on him without there being casualties. In fact, if the sand all around the place where you think he was taken wasn't soaked in blood, I doubt he's dead. Because for someone to get to the point of killing him, he'd have killed ten of them first."

For the first time something like a glimmer of hope appeared in his eyes, but it was still too small, too frail, a mere candle against a sea of darkness. "But the thing is, Goldie escaped. And you know Nat. He would die to protect the idiot dog. And I think that's the only thing that can have happened, because they shoot animals without even thinking. They—"

"Muddled thinking," I said. "Not that I can blame you, since he is your son and I know you love him." And at his surprised look, I added, "It's quite obvious in the way you talk to him. But Sam, just because Nat would be willing to give his life for Goldie, doesn't mean he managed it. Just because one would be willing to jump off a cliff in order to fly, doesn't mean all the brooms get taken away from us."

He put his elbows on his desk, and, for a moment, hid his face in his hands. "What would you have us do?" he asked. "If they're using him to bait a trap, do you want to walk into that trap? Is that what you wish to do? What good will that serve? I won't have your blood on my hands, as well as his, Lucius. I won't have it. Personal isn't the same thing as important, and personally important is not the same thing as vital. Nat is important and personal to me, because he's my son. But I won't risk other people, nor the cause of the revolution, because of him."

I was about to tell him I was quite capable enough of getting my own blood on my own hands, and in fact had tried my best to do so, several times over the last few years. But I never got to open my mouth, because a fast rat-tat sounded on the office door.

Sam and I stared at the door, for a moment. It wasn't, I knew, policy to knock on my father's office. In fact, he could come and go as he pleased and not even Sam would intrude on his time. I didn't know if Sam had a similar policy for his underlings, but I suspected so, from his look of shock at the sound. Then he called out, "Yes?"

The door opened and Abigail's face showed in the opening, small and flushed with excitement. For a moment I thought Nat was back, but then I noticed her eyes were still frantic, as frantic as they'd been when she'd woken me in the morning.

She came into the room and slammed the door behind her.

"Abigail, for the love of God, we're talking about—"

"I know. But I just heard the holo cast and I thought you'd want to know—no, need to know—this."

"What?" he said.

But she had approached his desk and was fiddling the buttons on his link. Most desk links can serve as phones, intercoms and holo broadcasting receivers. She turned it on, so the holo formed in the middle of the room.

A smug man appeared in the middle of the room and said, "For the murder of Good Man Maximilian Dante Lucius Keeva. It is believed—" She hissed with frustration and pressed buttons very quickly. The smug man flickered and moved unnaturally, and I understood she was moving the cast backward to the beginning. In the beginning, the man looked very composed, staring at the camera with the sort of expression someone would have when announcing that a way to turn bird crap into chocolate had just become commercially viable. "Good news this morning," he said. "After days of intensive forensic investigation, the murderer of Good Man Maximilian Dante Lucius Keeva has been arrested. From what we understand, the forensic evidence is conclusive. The Good Man, a young man of whom most had the highest hopes, was tortured and killed by Nathaniel Remy, a lawyer in his house. Nathaniel Remy has been arrested for the murder of Good Man Maximilian Dante Lucius Keeva and is being questioned. It is believed that he murdered Maximilian at the bequest of Maximilian's so-called older brother, Lucius Dante Maximilian Keeva, who has claimed the position after Maximilian's death. The council of Good Men doubts this claim, and the claimant has refused to be examined, either genetically or psychologically, to determine his identity and his true motives.

Investigation continues as there are indications there might have been a sexual motive behind the elaborate and heartless killing." The man couldn't have sounded happier or more dirty-minded if he'd said he'd found dirty pictures of Max, Nat, myself and three sheep. "Execution is tentatively set for the tenth of this month and it has been petitioned to be held in public or through holo-vision."

Softly, What Light

THE TENTH. I HADN'T BEEN KEEPING UP WITH THE CALENDAR
as such, but I thought back to the day I'd escaped Never-Never,
then counted. Three days from now.

A silence stretched. The newsman was talking about something
else, I didn't know what. My mind hadn't moved on from those
last words, that set execution date. Public execution. Well, that
meant they had to keep him able to walk to the execution block,
didn't it? And in what way did they kill people these days, when
they did it in public? It had to be pretty spectacular, I'd guess.
After all, Nat had killed a Good Man. An example had to be made.

"Well," I said. "And *that* is not going to happen."

Abigail's mind must have been running on the same track as
mine, because she said, her voice wavering unsteadily, "That's
beheading, isn't it? When it is in public? At least they have to
keep him in good enough shape to walk to the block then, don't
they?"

"Not if it's a holo," Sam said, sounding very tired. "They can
pan in to him in position. No one will ever know what's not
shown."

His quiet certainty made me shudder. "He's not dead yet," I
said. "He's not dead yet, by damn, and we're not giving him up
while he's alive."

201

Sam looked up at me and swallowed hard, audible in the entire room. From the suspicious shine in his eyes, it was to control a desire to cry, and I wasn't even going to blame him for it, but I also wasn't going to let him tell me again that his son was personal but not important to the cause. And that was exactly what it sounded like he was pleading, when he said, "You were right and I was wrong. Both of you. He is alive. But this public execution on a set date...If ever there was a clearer trap laid. They know we know they'll keep him alive till then. And they know that if we can't find him before then, we'll make a push to save him from death. We can't do that. We can't play into their hands."

Abigail's lip curled, and she really was reading my mind as well as echoing exactly what Ben would have said. It was enough to make a man believe in reincarnation. "You know what? They might know that. Let them. Which is worse? For us to play into their expectations of us, or for us to blatantly abandon one of our own in public? When we're at the start of a good and hard fight, is it good to advertise to anyone in secret sympathy with us that we don't stand by our own, and that in fact, if they're caught, they can go hang for all we care? Is this what we want? Didn't you tell me about the fall and how it all started with infighting among the friends of freedom, while the enemies of it were always one steady and resolute block, no matter what their dissension?"

"No," Sam said. "But the thing is...I wonder why he didn't..." He looked at me. "You see, he was...We all are, at a certain level, outfitted with a last friend—a painless way to commit suicide. I was sure he was dead, because he knows the secrets he's possessed of, and what would happen to all of us if he betrayed us. He also knows that there is a level of torture no human can withstand without breaking and talking."

"Why not?" I said. "Ben did. Did Ben...also have a last friend?"

Sam shook his head. "No. That's when we started it, but..."

"But Ben surely didn't reveal all he knew. I can't believe my father would have kept you on staff if he'd known what you were. I can't believe any of your family would have stayed alive, either."

"No. But Ben had no other option, and Lucius, don't you for a moment believe we don't honor his sacrifice and his courage. He did give his life for freedom, even if his arrest and what happened after was not in the fight for the cause. He did keep quiet to his last breath. But this is a chancy thing. No one knows their pain threshold until it is brought to bear, and besides they use other things: hypnotics and virtus experiences, that can break the strongest man. It has nothing to do with physical endurance and all to do with mental stability."

"And you think Nat is mentally unstable?" It was another of those moments where anyone else but the father who clearly loved him saying it would have met with a physical answer from my fists. But I knew he loved Nat. I also remembered Nat saying something about his differences and I, who had never been part of a family, had a vague glimmer of the barrier that could form between a grown father and son. There were things neither of these two proud, reserved men would tell the other even under threat of death. I suspected Max had been one of those things on Nat's side, and clearly Ben's history had been one of them on Sam's side.

Did Sam think that by telling Nat about Ben's relationship with me, he'd have encouraged Nat in a path that Sam clearly thought dangerous? Or did he just feel too awkward of the subject? Did they both feel it wasn't the other's business? And Nat, whose whole family—unless his mother was the most oblivious woman in the world—was involved in conspiracy and proscribed religion to their hair roots, wouldn't share with his father the knowledge of a proscribed relationship, even though his father was quite aware of it.

The tangles of relationships between normal human males related to each other made me almost glad that I'd been born to the "father" I had, where there was no pretense of love or affection and no hope of acceptance, or even a modicum of caring between myself and my father. It would be worse, I thought, to care for people and not know how to tell them, or to care for them and fear as you see them careening down a dangerous path, and you're helpless to stop them.

Then again, that was the devil of it, because—through Ben, or because Sam obviously cared for me too, or because Nat was the only person, in this new life of mine, with whom I could talk with no barriers and holding nothing back, or because Abigail was as close to Ben come again, as a human being could be—I cared for the Remys and they were involved with me and I with them. And our relationships didn't bid to be any less tangled than any normal relationships just because I wasn't related to them.

"Damn it," I said. "Nat won't break, but I don't relish his being at their mercy a minute more than needed, and I don't see why he should be. We should—"

Which is when the incredible happened again. A knock sounded upon the door. Look, I'll be honest, in the circumstances I expected a buzz at Sam's desk. The knock was a measure of how out of their minds my household was this morning. And then I thought of course they were. By now the news would have spread that Nat had been arrested.

Everyone from Sam's secretary and my valet to the depths of the kitchen and the lowest potato peeler would know that Mr. Remy's oldest son had been arrested for Max's murder. They'd also have heard the story of how I was an impostor who had convinced Nat to do the murder. This made perfect sense for the other side to say, and it would make perfect sense to me if I were on the outside of our tight little cabal.

After all, what had I done the moment I got to the house? I'd spent a lot of time closeted with Nat Remy. What hadn't I done? I hadn't tried to go before the council of Good Men and make even a token effort to be examined as the Good Man. I assumed that papers had been filed with whatever legal mechanisms the council had at its disposal, demanding that they pardon me for Hans's and Ben's murders. But that would count for nothing if they could pin on me conspiracy for Max's murder. If this stuck—and I was at a loss for why it wouldn't—and if they did execute Nat three days from now, then I would follow him to that block as soon as they could capture me.

A wild bubble of laugh tried to break out through my lips, because the juxtaposition of their having kept me alive for so long when I would have gladly died, and now killing me when I wanted to live was so shocking. But though an inappropriate laugh tried to get through, I was strong enough to prevent it. I managed to do so, with only a hiccup, and, as I covered my mouth, I wondered how many of my household members were really Usaians. Because it was the only reason I could imagine for us to still be alive, still uncaptured. Anyone else would have believed what the news said and assumed that Sam must have rigged the genlock to react to me, and that I was an impostor.

As the cook had said on the day I came in, they did amazing things with plastic surgery these days.

Then the knock sounded again, and I thought perhaps it had just taken them this long to rig out an arrest party with the bravest housemaids, the trainee guards and the pastry chef. I let my right hand drop into my pocket, to hold the box with the fragment of the flag. I let my left hand dip into my other pocket for the burner I had in there.

And, as Sam called out, "Yes?" I removed the safety and pointed the gun straight at the door.

In the circumstances, with me ready to fire through my trouser's pocket at any intruder, the person who appeared as the door opened was a near anticlimactic shock, as she was Sam's secretary, looking first around the room in alarm, and then at the floor, as she said, "Mr. Remy, Good Man Rainer and Good Man St. Cyr are here to see you."

And it must have been that she was so overwhelmed by the visit of two Good Men that she didn't find the rest of the people who were there to see Sam worth mentioning, because behind her I could glimpse Martha as well as a few men, clustering.

Sam looked up, then squinted at the amorphous group. "Right, let them through, Mary."

She stepped aside, and the door was flung open, and suddenly the tiny office was much too full, and the door was shut, and everyone was speaking far, far too loudly.

I have never liked crowds, as my reaction to my first public birthday party should have proved. But there was more than that here. I'd been in solitary confinement for fourteen years. Solitary confinement is mainly known for its near-total absence of crowds. Which meant that there was nothing in my recent experience to prepare me to be pushed up against the wall of the room, while a bunch of angry men pushed in and up close to Sam.

I couldn't even follow what they were saying. Their voices were just sound, washing over me, while my heart thudded hard enough to sound deafening in my ears, and my breath came in short panting breaths. I knew I was ten seconds from a real, physical panic attack. There were too many people, too many bodies, too much noise. And while, unlike Ben and Nat, I'm not a berserker and was at no danger of flipping around on the hinge of panic and going after the assembled crowd with fists or furniture, I was on the edge of crouching in a ball on the floor, sucking my thumb and peeing my pants. And it seemed to what remained of my rationality that this was not likely to make the case to the council of twelve—I was sure that was who these were, judging from the way Abigail had elbowed her way into the middle of it and was speaking forcefully into the midst of the din—that we should risk even the smallest outermost part of the cause to defend me or help me rescue Nat.

Very censorious are people, Ben's amused voice echoed in my mind's ear. *Buck up, Luce. You have to keep your wits about you. Trust me, they're going to be needed. The twelve are ultimately a committee, and one of the great founders of our faith said a committee was a life form with no brain and three or more stomachs. You can't act the Hamlet now. Nat's life might depend on this.*

I took a deep breath and straightened. If it had been only my life, I'd have been tempted to let it go, and let it all slip free, and let it all go to hell at long last. But Nat deserved better from me. And besides, Ben would never let me live it down.

Look, it would be a fine thing for me if I were absolutely sure that there was no soul, no spirit, no life after death—just a random oscillation of electrical energies and biological whatch-macallits giving us all the impression that we had an individual consciousness and the ability to choose our own destiny and forge our own path. It would mean that I would never have to face Ben again, and his withering irony if I'd fallen even slightly short of his—exaggerated and impossible—vision of my goodness and my heroism. Yes, he had illusions about my looks and my strength too, but those I could do nothing about, and besides no one would hold it against me if I couldn't keep that up. But the goodness and heroism thing? He would require from me an explanation as to why I hadn't remained the hero he expected me to be. And what was I supposed to do? Spend eternity in a domestic squabble? I don't know about you, but that's not how I plan to spend even a weekend, much less forever.

So I took deep breaths to clear my head, and stood up straight, separating minimally from the wall. I became aware of Martha's shrewd gaze trained on me, informing me that she, at least, had a fairly clear idea of how close I'd come to assuming the fetal position. Behind her, an arm around her middle, was a tall, fair man whose features were familiar, and whose expression showed the personality of a stranger.

He looked like Hans, only much taller and healthier looking. I was going to assume that whatever had made Hans unsuitable for the succession had also stunted his growth, because if both he and this young man were clones of the same man, then something had gone horribly wrong with Hans's development. This man also looked like Good Man Rainer, of course. But his expression was like neither Hans's worried frown, nor like his "father's" smug and self-confident swagger. Instead, he had an open, direct gaze that reminded me of no one so much as Martha. I wondered if it was possible for people to come together out of a mutual attraction for reason and being too sensible for words. If it was possible, I didn't know of a single case, either in real life or fiction. Normally people were attracted by mutual impetuousness or strange quirks of personality, not by good solid reason.

Jan looked a little concerned, as he stared at me, but not as much as Martha. Perhaps, even if they hadn't really confided since twelve, Martha had heard more about the conditions of my captivity than Jan had.

A few steps from them, someone else was staring at me. He was, I gathered by dredging from my mind the memory of a similar but older face, the Good Man of Liberte Seacity. Small, dark, incredibly well-groomed, and wearing a ruffled shirt in tones of pale yellow, over form-fitting trousers of the darkest blue. I blinked and wondered if another Good Man's house had developed the same "epigenetic" issues ours seemed to have.

But then his eyes met mine, and I realized that the way this man dressed was part of a calculated effort to look gaudy and a bit silly. Because those eyes were at total variance with the clothes and the amiable expression on the rather regular features. They were all shrewd evaluation. I got the feeling he was evaluating my disposition to the last grain of sanity I could call upon and the extent of damage my captivity had done to me, to the last scar-whorl on my wrist.

And then I heard the sentence, "Once Lucius Keeva signs the papers to turn power over to the council."

And I was out of my corner, fists bunched.

A Free Man

I DIPPED MY HAND IN MY POCKET, AND TOOK HOLD OF THE FLAG in the box. Not to remove it. I had no intention of removing it this time, and I had no intention of leaving the organization. But, as my mind gathered the gist of what I'd only half-heard the last few minutes, I was ready to fight for it, and for me, and for the freedoms of the individual. And in that, I wanted as much of Ben's help as I could have.

Yes, I was aware that Ben was dead, and had been dead a long time. Yes, I was aware, even then, that the voice in my head was no more than a harmless illusion, a contrivance I'd managed to keep myself from becoming a gibbering mess, unable to make sense of the world or my own mind. Yes, I was aware that there was no power, no virtue in that scrap of flag that could carry me through what was going to be a damn difficult argument.

I can only point out that however much I might be the clone of a bioengineered freak, designed by researchers and built by scientists to have capabilities and abilities far beyond that of the normal human—as well as, it would seem, a moral deficit miles wide—I was still made from human materials and still human shaped and therefore subject to all the human foibles.

From time immemorial—judging by very primitive graves found so far back that our ancestors weren't even, themselves, quite human—humans have been holding on to objects and mementos of those who were in some measure heroes or revered. And from time immemorial, these relics were thought to confer some virtue upon those holding them. Does it matter if it was true or all a psychological effect? You leave me my psychological effects, and I'll leave you yours.

I waded into the fray, my hand clutched so tightly on the box that contained Ben's flag that it's a wonder it didn't shatter into a hundred pieces. I elbowed my way past sweaty, screaming men to the center of the roiling crowd, right beside Abigail. It wasn't that hard, once I'd overcome my fear of being surrounded by humans on all sides. After all, I was six seven, and that does have some advantages to compensate for the disadvantage of being the best target in any given crowd. "The Good Man," I shouted, as loudly as I could, "will do no such foolish thing."

A sudden and complete silence fell, and in the silence Sam gave the sort of hiccup that was, almost certainly, the result of suppressing sudden and inappropriate laughter. I gave him an indulgent look. "And I bet Sam would explain to you why if you'd just let him talk."

"Of course I can explain to them why," Sam said. "You must relinquish some of your power to delegates who can deal with the preparations for war and . . . other things, but you should never give full powers to the council to do as they will with the seacity."

And then there was a man, whose voice was distinctly familiar for having taunted Nat back when I'd been waiting in an antechamber with the light in my eyes. He advanced to the desk and pushed his face next to Sam's and asked Sam if he meant to be a dictator and the power behind my throne, which would have been merely annoying if he hadn't followed it up by muttering that Sam was as unstable as his damned son. Since I didn't think that it was likely that this man had developed a vendetta against the thirteen-year-old James, or either of the younger boys, I had to assume that he was talking about Nat, and apparently so did Sam, who pushed back on his chair and said, "John, as the head of the twelve, I will not overstep the bounds of my authority and punch your lights out, but you will consider yourself punched."

"I can punch him, Sam," I offered willingly. "I am not one of the twelve, let alone the head."

The man looked around, and stared at my fist, then looked back at Sam. "Oh, you're not going to deny that he's unstable, are you? Over the last year he's been riding to commit suicide and taking the organization to hell with it."

I believed it. I'd seen more than a bit of that wild despair. But I would not admit it. Not now. Not in front of Sam, and not while Nat was in need of the Sons of Liberty at his back. "Considering what has happened to him for the last year," I said, "Nat Remy has to be more stable than most people, or he'd have gone howling into the night. And I fail to see where Nat's stability or lack thereof has anything to do with why I should give dictatorial power to a council of ill-assorted persons of whose qualifications for the job I am wholly unaware."

"I thought you said he'd become one of us?" a voice said from the back.

"If by that you mean I swore sacred allegiance to your religion," I said, "I did. Which means all the powers of the government flows from the governed and that I will, in due course, relinquish any right to govern this seacity and its appertaining continental territories to an elected group whose election follows the rules they themselves set."

"We're elected," another man said.

Abigail snorted. "Elected by about two hundred people in a militant group devoted to destabilizing the current system of governance is not the same thing as elected by the governed."

"Precisely, Abigail," I said. "I am not elected, but there are mechanisms for governance in place, and I promise to doing the minimum possible to keep the seacity and territories running until the representatives of the people are in place. It is less disruptive to keep the power structure in place while we elect the new one. To the measure of the possible, of course."

"But we need to go through the seacity," John said. "And the other seacities."

"What? What do you mean?"

"There will be a lot of supporters of the Good Men in all three seacities," he said. "We can't afford to go into Liberte yet, of course, since St. Cyr"—he curled his lips disdainfully at the Good Man—"belongs to one of our allied groups, and they haven't agreed yet to come out in the open or to let him come out in the open as being in rebellion against the system. But even there we should be able to do discreet sweeps and remove the most stubborn of the ancient regime and neutralize them."

"John..." It was Sam and his voice sounded gentle and almost sweet. "John, what do you mean by neutralizing?"

"What? Kill them, of course. People's trials and all that."

"People's trials? Do you mean we'll kill them because they don't believe in our religion and in our ideals?"

"What? What else? Of course we will. We can't let the little power-mad weasels take over again; it will mean the republic will be built up only to fall again. You can't—"

"Do you really mean," Abigail said, "to have people killed for crimes of opinion?"

"You can't make an omelet without breaking a few eggs."

"I don't believe that's a quote from one of ours," Sam said.

"I'm sure it isn't," I said. "Though I fail to see how someone who has sworn to protect life, liberty and the pursuit of happiness of each individual can purport to be for summary executions of those who believe differently."

"But we have to," John said, and looked at me, with a slight frown, as though he thought I'd taken leave of my senses. "Surely you must see that. You can't build a republic if some people still believe the Good Men have special power to rule over all."

"What was the percentage of Americans who were patriots, or at least who fought for freedom, in the time of the American Revolution?" I asked the room at large.

"About a third," Abigail said. "But to be honest there were reprisals against the loyalists, in some regions strong enough to devolve into door-to-door fighting."

Yeah, she might very well be Ben's reincarnation, if I believed in such things. Ben, too, had always felt compelled to be intellectually honest, even when it damaged the point he was trying to make. "Yes," I said. "But it wasn't terror from above, at the orders of people with dictatorial powers. If it comes to war, we might have door-to-door fighting, too. We will not, while I have any power to say so, have summary and arbitrary executions, on the basis that someone holds the wrong opinions. If it comes to that, I will die by their side, and I will hold that I died in defense of the principles of y—my religion." Into the brief silence and while I could see John struggling to put a treasonous construction on my words, I said, "And what opinions would most of these people have? Even I, who had more reason to suspect the facade of stability, peace and order that the system has, had to be convinced by facts that the regime is infamous, and that a democratic republic, ordained by God or not, might be a horrible regime but it was the one that, in the full length of human experience, worked the best."

"But we can't have enemies in our midst, stabbing us in the back," John protested.

"So we should instead enshrine attitudes inimical to our very founding principles?" I said.

I looked over at Sam. "Sam, I do realize I will need to sign some orders to secure the island, and that we might have to curtail the movements of some people, eventually. I also do realize that I'll need to delegate some powers so we can get into a defensive state. But this is the governing council of the Sons of Liberty, not the governing council of the seacity, much less of the world. Right now, I'd think the Sons of Liberty would be more concerned with freeing the one of our own who is imprisoned. If not for his sake—and it should be for his sake—then for the sake of the secrets he might spill, which might endanger the rest of us."

"He's been outfitted with the means to seek quietus," someone said. "Before he spills any secrets."

"A fine thing, too," I said, "if it is known that the only thing the Sons of Liberty do for their own is allow them to commit suicide. Has it ever occurred to you that this will not inspire a lot of confidence in your commitment to individual right to life?"

"It would be his decision," someone else said.

"Yes," I said, my voice ironical, and I wasn't sure where these speeches were coming from—if from my panic in being in a crowded room, or from my idea of what Ben would say. "It would be the only decision we leave him. I'd like to point out, ladies and gentlemen, that if we go to war—and if you think the Good Men will cede power without war, you haven't lived in the same world I have and you're not part of the religion that believes it is one of the natural human flaws to crave more and more power—there will be a lot of us taken prisoner and tortured. Do you want people to think in that extremity death is their only friend? If not, I advise you to reconsider what you'd do to rescue Nathaniel Greene Remy, one of our own, taken because he is one of our own."

"It was no part of our directive for him to kill Maximilian Keeva."

"Really?" from Abigail. "Then what was the directive that we should kill all the Good Men we could if it would be beneficial to destabilization of the regime?" She seemed to remember belatedly that Jan and I were Good Men, and gave me a sideways look. "Except those of them who are with us, of course."

I let it pass, and managed even a slight smile at her. I was sure they knew as well as I did why the older Good Men had to be killed and why their heirs shouldn't.

"But we don't have the armies," a worried man, who had spoken very little said, from the back. "We simply don't have the force to break anyone out of a maximum security prison. Even if we knew where he is, which we don't. Even if we gathered every one of our trained men. We don't have the equipment, we don't have the numbers, we don't—"

"Adam," Sam said. "We do. We have enough for an operation of that kind, but, Lucius, we might not want to display it just yet, and bring this to a full-fledged civil war before we have time to turn public opinion at least somewhat in our favor. Part of the issue is that we don't control communications and, by now, half the people in the world believe the version of events given by the holo cast. And you have to realize that if they dig into your histo—"

"I know," I said. "I know. I'm sure if they actually believe I am who I say I am they'll come to far more dire conclusions than if they thought I was an impostor. I think that should be our first priority. Communications."

Sam chewed his lip. "It won't be easy," he said. "To do something about that. If, back in the twenty-second century they'd fought the oligopoly that banned expression and news reporting by average, unlicensed people, it was doable, but now... It's been three hundred years since it's been assumed that the government has a right to regulate speech and that something horrible, if unspecified, will happen should anyone try to allow everyone to access channels of mass communication. And the technology has developed to prevent it. Or not developed to allow it. Electronic communication is tightly controlled, dominated and supervised. You can't simply send a message to everyone you know at once, not unless you want some people to ask pretty sharp questions, and our links don't allow us to call more than one person at once, unless it's an emergency broadcast link in a flyer, and those are only activated under distress conditions. The penalty for using it und—"

"Father," Abigail said, sharply. "I think right now the penalty for being who we are is death. And I don't mean just because of our religion, but because we know we're in rebellion, or they will soon. And that means—"

"She's right," Martha said. "Right now we shouldn't mind about the penalties for doing anything."

"Eh, par dieu," Simon said. "We need to form a group to study this. It is as this creature, the Good Man Keeva, says." He gave me a look that a less careful observer would consider disturbing. "What we should be discussing right now is not how to alienate most of the people by punishing those who oppose us, but how to bring most of them to our side, because most of them have never heard of us. The purpose of the revolutionary groups, the Sons of Liberty and my own Sans Culottes should be to model good behavior and that . . . marvel of mutual care, civility and civic virtues that we think should be characteristic of a free society, no?" The name of his group caused me to do a triple-take on him, before dimly remembering it from the French Revolution in the nineteenth century—or was it the eighteenth? I had also a memory that they hadn't been exactly nice people, but how much of that was true, and how much the accumulated propaganda-patina of centuries? "We should care for our own, and fight for those who can't fight for themselves. And we should try to establish free communication, because without it, we do not reach the people. I'd say the fact that the flyers when they're falling can communicate in broad range to everyone around should give us a clue on how to overcome the silence. Yes, the other devices are hobbled so you can't communicate to more than one person. But those aren't. And how many of them are moldering in junkyards? I suggest we form groups to study what to do and establish a priority agenda. And that . . ." He bowed slightly to me, a strangely anachronistic gesture. I wondered whether it was part of the culture of Liberte, because I didn't remember his father ever doing anything like it, or if it was characteristic of his attempts to seem far more foolish than he was. "One of the principal points to discuss should be the rescue and freeing of Nathaniel . . . eh . . . Greene Remy."

Three or More
Incessantly Wagging Tongues

I WASN'T SURE IF COMMITTEES HAD NO BRAIN AND THREE OR more stomachs, but I was sure that committees had three or more voice boxes. What followed was, in a way, a foretaste of things to come, but it was also my first experience of why I didn't want to be involved in political life, even if the revolution should come off. Even should we win it. Even should the assembled masses of humanity come to me and ask me to be their ruler.

Arguably, this was only a problem in a division or country that followed any type of democracy. It would never be a problem with the type of government my father instituted, where he could, at will, order anyone elevated or destroyed and anything built or leveled. From my reading, I knew that there were Good Men who allowed a lot more dissension and discussion, and suddenly I wondered if it was because they were better at steering the actions of a crowd to where they wanted them, and if my father had chosen the far more dictatorial style because, like me, he hated days spent in subtle forensic maneuvering.

There is something to be said for the bastard, if that was the reason. At least he was sane enough not to want to be subject to insane arguments about nothing.

To me what followed through that day—given my temperament—was long periods of almost deadly boredom interspersed with panic at being in a room full of people, enclosed, unable to escape, and—what was far worse—have to steer them away from the most ridiculous ideas and the most precipitous mistakes.

It should be said that in this I had great help. The younger people in the room quietly took cues when I started to become agitated, and more often than not managed to anticipate what I was going to say. I slowly came to the conclusion that Martha was at least as sharp as Abigail, and both of them as sharp as Nat. Jan kept up with Martha, but he didn't speak much. And if they weren't involved, then I had truly lost my ability to connect with the human race and read feelings from looks and touches, because sometimes he would squeeze her hand, and she would launch into something that he clearly meant to say.

Once or twice, I noted Sam casting a worried glance at their clasped hands. He no longer looked like a burned out building, or a man who has lost his son, but he still looked like a middle-aged man riding too close to the edge of a heart attack, so I hoped he wasn't vehemently opposed to that match, though why he shouldn't be was beyond me.

Sam helped to keep the hotheads from the crazier—or more overbearing—ideas, too. He did it gently and with careful persuasion. I started to think he was just the sort of politician who would thrive in any form of democratic society.

And somehow the group moved en masse to the dining room, where three meals were served. Somewhere along the line the mystery of why my servants hadn't turned on me was solved. Even though not everyone in the house was a secret Usaian, the Remys had been shaping the hiring and keeping of retainers for hundreds of years, so the majority of the long-term, high-status servants were of ours.

The human animal is an amazing thing. When your perceived social superiors think that a theory or rumor is not only wrong but stupid, there is a tendency to fall in line. Even when those elites are far from unanimous. In this case they were. And it wasn't just the elites, but anyone with a record in the house. I presumed the lower-status employees—the pastry chef's third under-helper and the dishwasher—had simply surrendered to the argument that only fools would believe that Nat was guilty or that I was anything less than the legitimate Good Man. On second thought, the fact that we'd been under siege should have denied the idea that I was, stubbornly, refusing to submit to genetic examination. At least one would hope so.

In the end, our group—myself, Abigail, Martha, Jan and Simon— ended up being in charge of finding out where Nat was being held and forming a plan of rescue, with the rest of the group at large promising to give us what help and support they could.

And because finding Nat and rescuing him from what was sure to be torture and interrogation was, of course, of the essence, we were excused to go and discuss the matter in our own small group, while the big groups discussed the more burning issues of who should be allowed access to even limited means of communication, of who would be eligible for a constitutional assembly, and how many years they had to have served in the Sons of Liberty or the Daughters of Liberty or another of the more militant parts of the Usaian church, and whether they would have to be born to the religion or if converts would be acceptable.

What baffles me is that I'm sure they were glad to be rid of us and sent us out of the room with a light heart, because in their mind they were keeping us young hotheads from the really vital things that must be decided. All of them but Sam, who nodded slightly to us as we left the room.

We ended up in my room, of course. No, wait, perhaps it was not an of course. There were many other rooms in the house that we could have adjourned to, and my office or the dining room, or even one of the many meeting rooms in which my father discussed things with a never-ending succession of dignitaries, trade ambassadors and other very important people. But that was the operative thing. In my mind, all those rooms were my father's. I didn't know them as intimately, and I hadn't spent most of my childhood in them.

Even if my room had now been breached, its walls literally split to allow a secret tunnel, it felt like the safest room in the house, and only one my frazzled nerves could tolerate after the ten hours of insanity I'd endured.

I felt so safe in fact, that as soon as I entered my room, I realized I was in default of the Remy rules of civilization and civility, in that I was wearing no socks, and while I was wearing something under my clothes, they were my sleeping clothes. I had neither bathed nor removed my night clothes, after waking up. And I'd never had breakfast, and while we'd had meals served in the dining room, my stomach had been too tied in knots to eat much.

So as soon as the door was closed, I looked around, then waved them to the set of chairs between the desk and the place where they normally set the table when Nat and I ate in this room. And as I thought that it struck me that it had only happened twice, but it felt like a habit of long standing, and I hoped I'd get Nat back and be able to have dinner with him again.

"Please, find seats," I told them. "I won't be more than a moment. Martha or Abigail, would you order coffee and sandwiches?" Then, ignoring the fact that St. Cyr had raised his eyebrows at what I was quite sure was a tremendous breach of etiquette on my part, I grabbed a clean suit, underwear and socks from my wardrobe, went into the bathroom and briefly used the fresher. Briefly but with water. Of all of it, my lack of socks had been the most urgent thing to remedy, because I'd slipped on not my house slippers but my broomer boots, which had been chafing my feet—unused to shoes for fourteen years, and too tender to take the contact with bare, hard leather.

All the same, when I came out, feeling far more human—it's amazing the difference little things can make to one's comfort and sense of self—I was surprised that no one made a comment at my disappearance. And I presumed someone, possibly Martha, had explained the stuffed giraffe on my bed, because no one even gave it a look.

They'd left a chair for me, and I sat down, almost in front of one of two little, collapsible tables that had been brought in and were laden with trays of sandwiches and pots of coffee. I took a sandwich and Abigail poured me a cup of coffee, and I tried to count the sandwiches. I remember thinking that the kitchen staff had gone mad, because there was no possible way that five people, four of whom had partaken quite plentifully of the meals in the dining room, could eat all this, not unless we stayed in this room for the next eight hours with no other form of sustenance.

Chalk it up to the fact that I was fourteen years older than the oldest of them, and sixteen or seventeen years older than the rest of them. I was completely wrong. If we hadn't been so busy discussing what to do and how to find Nat, I'd have watched them in fascination while they ate sandwiches at a rate that seemed to exceed the chewing capacity of the human body.

As soon as I sat between Martha and Abigail—it had the feeling of being deliberate, as though the two of them had set to guard me—St. Cyr said, "Eh, we were just saying that if we hadn't blown up Never-Never at least we'd now know where to find Nat Remy."

"If you hadn't blown up Never-Never, and I assume you're a member of Nat's broomer lair, since he told me you were the ones to do so—then I wouldn't be here."

"We have to take the bitter with the sweet then, don't we?" St. Cyr said. "Now, this is what I was saying—there are several places they could be keeping Remy. My guess is that it's not one of the known high-security prisons. Jan was saying he still has access to a lot of information we cannot get otherwise, because his father was, after all, in charge of the Scrubbers and... other such things, for the Good Men. He says there are maybe three other facilities like Never-Never."

"See," Martha said. "Knowing us, and that we're likely to be looking for him, I think they'd be more likely to put him in a low-security prison, of the type they put broomers in, when broomers get in trouble."

"And I say that's nonsense," St. Cyr said. "They wouldn't want him in a minimal security prison. I don't know if they know or guess that the break into Never-Never was part of the operations of the Sons of Liberty, but they know it was the operation of someone associated with Nat." He held up a hand, in a request for silence. "Have to know, how else would they know that Nat was involved in killing Max? And so they will try to put him in a more secure facility."

Martha sighed. "Maybe. But it depends on whether they want to keep it secret, or to let us find out about it. If they want us to find out about it, and not be able to do anything, then they will put him in one of those six maximum-security prisons. But if they don't want us to find out at all, if they want us to make an attack in force to the place and time of the execution, then they will want him as secret as possible. And in that case, they'll put him in a low-security prison, reinforced for the occasion."

I sipped my coffee in silence, while St. Cyr told her she was out of her ever-loving mind, I finally interrupted by saying, "But what if she's right, St. Cyr? Here's the thing, if they can get us to make an attack in force, they can blame it on the three of us, and even if they lose—unlikely, since they have a lot more people, and a lot better weapons than we do—they can show us to be a threat to law and order, and perhaps a conspiracy that they can then accuse of anything that strikes them as convenient. Even if we acquire some control over communications by then, which you'll have to admit is unlikely—"

Abigail snorted in a most unladylike way and said, "If they've stopped arguing over who gets to write the long-form report on how many communicators must be salvaged from old flyers by then, I'll be shocked."

Martha gave her an indulgent look, and I continued, "Even if we have some control over communications, they will still be the voices people trust. Some name brands in news, some people, even, have been trusted for the last fifty years."

"Because they were never challenged," St. Cyr said. "I can honestly say that any time I was present at news-making events, and then read the report about it, I found hardly any resemblance."

"Perhaps," I said. "But people will still trust them. And we are, to an extent, a conspiracy. The fact that we're conspiring for freedom doesn't make us any less of a conspiracy. There are incidents and facts they could link to to prove that we are ogres, determined to bring down civil society. So for them, it is best that we show ourselves and our hand, by attacking in full view of holo-capture devices. Even if we manage to spirit Nat away, it just ensures that we become fugitives with everyone in the world against us."

"There are many places to hide," Jan said. "Some of our fugitives disappeared for years into the North American continent. From what we hear, a lot of those places are now fully livable, and the forest cover is back, and—"

"Yes, but as fugitives, we'd be effectively neutralized," I said. "And I bet you they'd have assassins able to track us down, because, well, you and I, Rainer, are not exactly low-profile escapees."

He inclined his head. "There is that," he said. "My gut tells me that you're right and that this would be the outcome they would try to get. But then we'll have no choice but to do what they want, because . . . how can we find the right prison amid hundreds of low-security ones?"

St. Cyr stood up, giving the impression of a jack in box, impelled to stand by some overpowering burst of energy. "Well, we could, all of us, disperse amid broomer bars and hangouts, and find out if there is a report of anything at all unusual. All of us are broomers, right? And each of us knows the codes, the behaviors, and each of us, even, has friends in other lairs. Well, probably not Lucius."

"I might still have *some* friends..." I said, thinking of friendly acquaintances and friends from lairs who had occasionally joined with ours for some party or some special event. It seemed to me that since the majority of those were working class and not Good Men, and since most of them had been in their twenties at the time, the chances of any of them having experienced considerable mortality—even given the fact that broomers, by definition, did stupid things at high speed—were relatively low.

"Well, yes, but your friends are probably fewer than the rest of us. I suggest that I, and—separately—Martha and Jan go and visit acquaintances in other lairs and see if there's gossip. Any strange behavior on the part of the law, like a sentence being vacated early, and the prisoner thrown out onto the big bad streets again, or even just a strange transport surrounded by armed men landing in the prison. And as for Lucius, I suggest he take Abigail as a blind and a reminder of current-day feuds and whatnot, should he need it, and go hit all the bigger broomer bars in the nearby seacities."

"They might have sent him to a seacity half across the globe," I said.

This time it was Martha who snorted, which goes to show that rude behavior ran in that family. It made me like them a terrible lot. "Like that bunch of paranoids would trust him too far from their reach. Let's face it: Nat—and you—are threats to the nearby Good Men and to the little alliance amid this group which are all within twelve hours—tops—broom flight of each other. Less than that in a flyer. Yes, all the Good Men will unite to punish the murder of one of them, but will they bestir themselves to do something about it, when their domains are half across the world? And will the local Good Men, who have no contact with them, trust them with a valued prisoner? I bet you not."

Jan sighed. "Then they are fools, because this will be the shot that was heard around the world."

Martha gave him a concerned look, then nodded. "We shall pray it is so."

Cloak and Skirt

FIRST I WANT TO REGISTER THE FACT THAT I'D NEVER BEFORE been prayed over or, for that matter, blessed. It was a very odd experience, particularly since—while I wouldn't be willing to bet that there was nothing after death—I was far from being convinced that there was an afterlife, or a God.

But before we left, Martha put her hands on my shoulder and Jan's and murmured something about God watching over us in our endeavor, and allowing us to find Nat and bring him home safe. And then she stood on tiptoes and kissed me on the cheek. Before that could register, Jan patted me awkwardly on the shoulder. They headed out towards the terrace, brooms in hand.

"Wait," I said. "It might not be safe."

"Safer than in recent days," Simon said. He looked at me, again, with those oddly shrewd eyes, above the wealth of improbably gaudy ruffles. "If you are right and they want us to run our heads into the noose, they're not going to try to capture us before, are they? That would stop them getting the big name. Besides, it's you they want to capture. And besides all, we're the Brooms of Doom, we know how to fight." He gave Abigail a lopsided smile. "Now, Angel, you bring him to the lair . . . oh, by midnight, and we'll discuss what we found if anything. I still say we'll find nothing

and will be left with looking at high-security facilities. I don't
know which one I hope for. They're both bad situations for us."

"Angel?" I said, feeling oddly protective and like this was
something that Sam should have been here to hear.

Abigail shrugged. "Sounds good, doesn't it? Means nothing.
See, I grew up with Nat and Max and Martha, and all of them,
and all their friends too treated me like a little sister. Martha
started calling me *Angel*, so then they all did. But they all treat
me like I'm a little kid and Simon is the worst of them. He keeps
warning me about boys, as if I were ten, instead of twenty."

"Would you be very upset with me if I also started warning
you about boys?" I asked. She wasn't exactly beautiful, but she
was striking and full of energy and fire, and I suspected like
most self-sufficient young women, she'd be curiously blind to the
workings of her own heart, much less to the possibly less than
honorable ideas of any young men approaching her.

She gave me a side long glance. "Not at this point. I expect
everyone I meet will become as bad as Nat."

"Is Nat bad? That way?"

Her eyelids came down halfway and she sighed. "We'd better
go out through the tunnel," she said, stepping to the door and
locking it. "We'd better make it as stealthy as possible. I'll go
out first. Despite what Simon says, there's just the bare possibility they'll be scanning for you specifically. I still feel you're a
high-value target. If I were the Good Men, I'd still try to capture
you, anyway."

While she was talking, I'd opened my secret compartment and
was dressing in broomer leathers and—because I wasn't sure where
exactly our search would take us, in a pair of longer, just-below-
the-knee boots with a serious look of utility-wear about them.
It was the type of boots that were worn by workers who had to
wade through low-flowing rivers or step into flooded basements
to repair pipes. Though they were leather, they were made in such
a way as to be impermeable. I had no idea who had thought to
furnish me with a pair of those, but whoever it was I loved him
or her. These would keep my feet warm should there be a long
flight ahead, and they would keep them dry and clean, should
we need to wade through one of the piles of refuse quite normal
in certain areas of town.

When I was done, a look in the mirror told me I looked like

a dangerous broomer indeed. Good, since I was going to go into those certain—by which one should read dangerous—areas of town accompanied by Abigail. I figured I needed all the intimidation I could muster. Sam would expect it of me, and perhaps Nat too.

I asked her again, when we were in the tunnel. "Do you feel that Nat is overprotective?"

She gave me one of her sidelong glances. "That would be an understatement," she said, at last. "You have to understand that Father is always very busy. The Keeva—your property is extensive and hard to manage, particularly since—"

"He circumvents some of the more outrageous orders, yes," I said.

"Yeah. And Mother is big in the Daughters of Liberty. Her training is in communications and propaganda and..." Abigail shrugged. "For some reason, this got Nat thinking that he was as good as a surrogate father to all of us. All of us, even Martha. And me. I mean, I don't mind his acting like that towards the younger kids, because someone has to look after them and James is too much like Nat and inclined to take the bit between his teeth, but by the founders, Martha is his exact age, and I'm almost their age, and what business does he have treating us like we're young innocents in need of sheltering? It's like something doesn't fit together in his head and he... Well, he has this compulsion to... When we trained in the countryside, one time, I saw this chicken. She had a clutch of chicks, you know, but she didn't seem to be satisfied with them, and she kept trying to shove the cat's three kittens under her wings, too, to protect them. And I looked at her and thought that was Nat to the life."

I couldn't help a chuckle, though it hit me, immediately afterwards, and with sobering certainty that this explained why Nat had devoted so much time to explaining things to me and trying to help me. It wasn't that he liked me. He'd said, many times, that he didn't, or at least that he wasn't sure if he did. But he still tried to protect me—even though I was fourteen years older than he.

"Oh, don't get me wrong," she said. "It's endearing in a way, and I realize he takes on a great burden, trying to make sure we're okay, and also that he has saved all of us—except perhaps Martha—from problems. But he tends to manage and... parent everyone. He even did to Max, which..." The sidelong glance again, and I realized she had no idea what I knew.

"I know how it was between them," I said, though I suddenly

wondered if I did. I'd assumed the horrible torture that Max's seeming rejection had been to Nat for a year had come from Nat's being the dependent member of the relationship. But if he weren't, what had been working on him? Guilt? Guilt that something had happened to Max and Nat couldn't save him? That was bad. If it had been just moving his dependence away from a partner who made the decisions and extended him protection—as their relative social positions would indicate—then when he found out that Max was in fact dead; when he executed the body that had been Max's, he would have been free. But if he felt guilty on the possibility of Max having been brain washed, then finding out Max had been killed, and having to destroy the body to kill the murderer would have increased that guilt to an unbearable amount. Perhaps taking me, metaphorically, under his grubby wing was a psychological attempt to compensate.

"Which was vaguely creepy," Abigail completed. She pressed her lips together and looked stern. "I feel very strongly one shouldn't parent one's lover." And to the chuckle this surprised out of me. "You might think I'm silly, but I would hate it horribly, on either of end of that. I don't want someone I love—when I love someone, that is—to parent me, and I'd hate to do it to them." She was quiet a moment, while we dropped to a lower level of the tunnel. "Though to be honest, Max didn't seem to mind. I never knew if he minded it, but put up with it because of Nat, or if he really found it convenient to have Nat tell him when it was time to eat and ask him if he'd remembered to brush his teeth."

"No, really," I said. "He didn't—"

"Ask him about brushing his teeth? No. Not since Max was about ten, at least, but he did buy most of Max's clothes, and told him what to wear when, and Max just...let him."

"I take it you don't let him do that? To that extent?" I was thinking of the grey suits all the siblings wore.

"I hope not," she said. "But it is awfully convenient, and awfully comfortable, to let other people take care of all your small problems, you know? Before you know it, you're relying on them, and even when you don't, it's like...It's like having a boulder at your back, you know? No one can sneak up behind, and if you're tired, you can lean back against it. That's...that's why it's so odd not to have Nat, not to know if he's alive or dead. It's...it's like not knowing if the sun will come out tomorrow."

She turned back to look at me. "Lucius, we must bring Nat back. And he must be alive. He must."

I told her what she wanted to hear. Look, I'm as rational as the next man, and as willing to face the truth, but what good would it do to shatter her hope, or even to seed doubt? Would it make it any easier for her to accept Nat's death, if he was dead? I didn't think so. If we found Nat dead, it was going to be a reverberating blow anyway, one that would shake her to the core, and possibly me too. All that telling her this was the overwhelming possibility now would do was to make her worry more from the beginning, and perhaps make it harder for her to be effective in rescue, which in turn might assure that even if Nat were alive, he would die when we got him.

I don't know about you, but moral purity must always take second place to saving a man's life, in my consideration. So, I lied. "We will find him, Abigail. And we'll bring him back alive. I promise you."

She rubbed the back of her fingers across her eyes and turned around. "What a fool I'm being. As though you had any choice over whether he's alive or dead right now, or even if we can get him back alive, even if he is. I shouldn't ask you stupid questions."

"We will bring him back alive, if I have to move heaven and earth and time to do it," I said, and was shocked to hear the earnestness in my voice which came out somewhere between a whisper and a growl. "If it's something I can do, I will do it, Abigail."

She didn't turn back, which was a little disappointing after such a dramatic statement on my part. Instead, she nodded. "Yes, let's get on with it and make haste." And then added, with disarming frankness, "You see, I'd never realized how important Nat was to me. He'd just...He was just always there. I didn't think about it. I thought...I thought he'd always be there. I'm not prepared for the alternative. I've already lost Max, who was like a brother to me."

Making Haste Strangely

WE WERE IN THE FIFTH BROOMER BAR OF THE NIGHT. WHICH IS to say that all the broomer bars we'd been in so far were starting to run together in my mind.

It wasn't that difficult. Broomer bars are, if not all alike, all of a type. They tend to be in the lower economic areas of seacities, and sometimes of natural islands. For all I know there are several on continents too—brooms would seem to be a damn good idea when getting over vast, sparsely populated regions. But my area, the area I'd spent my broomer years in, and the area I was interested in right now, was not near a continent, so I didn't know.

Broomer bars were always in the lower class area, often in the parts that had been roofed over by the construction of platforms for new development. They tended to be sparsely decorated—though one or two of them, perhaps being owned by people with aspirations to ambience, had pictures of brooms on the walls. Or pictures of bosomy girls riding brooms in the type of outfit that was guaranteed to give them frostbite within two seconds, even at lower altitudes and lower speeds. Perhaps my lack of appreciation for the art had to do with the fact that it did nothing for me. Or perhaps I had the type of mind that would analyze the incongruence of such pictures even if they depicted male broomers in next to nothing. I rather suspected that. It was a handicap.

231

But I wasn't going to be able to test the theory in this particular bar, oh, so not originally called Brooming It and located
in the lowest reaches of Syracuse Seacity, probably not more
than a few meters of dimatough up from whatever remained of
Never-Never. I might have been able to, if the owners had been
inclined to art, because it took me about five seconds—I'm slow
that way—after we went in, to realize that the clientele was almost
exclusively male, that the broomer suits, even if not necessarily
expensive, were better tailored than the ones we'd been seeing,
suggesting used suits got fixed to fit the new owners, and that
Abigail was not getting the normal-wide eyed wolfish looks, but
rather puzzled stares.

Abigail must have realized the nature of the place at about
the same time, because she looked back at me, a startled expression in her eyes. I grinned back at her, reassuringly. "You might
have to protect me," I said. And someone—Nat, when we got
him back—would have to cure the girl of that unladylike snort.

I leaned down, to speak in her ear. "We won't stay long," I
said. "Since it's unlikely you'll know anyone here, right?" I knew
there were exclusively male, exclusively homosexual broomers'
lairs. The best known was perhaps the Lavender Buzzers, which
had approached Ben and me to join, way back when. They were,
however, big time serious broomers, with the sort of connections
that allowed them to get squeeze from drug transports in order
not to get robbed. Though they knew us only by our first names, if
we joined, they would sooner or later attract attention they didn't
need. It was a bad combination all around. Neither Ben or I needed
the money or had the drive—at least I didn't—that impelled the
rest of them. And having us aboard would call attention to them.
Which considering in how many places in the world attraction for
a member of the same sex fell under capital crimes or just short of
it, would be unfair to them. And to us. But I'd had friends in the
Buzzers and a half dozen other lairs. I just hadn't socialized much
outside my own lair so I hadn't frequented the watering places.

She nodded tightly, but whispered back, "But you never know,
so let's get a drink?"

I nodded, and we started elbowing our way to the counter
at the other end of the bar. This meant cutting in the middle
of several conversations and squeezing gingerly past people in a
clinch. I wondered how carefully raised Abigail had been and

if I was giving her the shock of her life, but to be honest, she didn't seem to be even surprised or curious. Though perhaps that was the unflappable quality Ben used to have, where you'd never know you'd caught him off guard until days, or sometimes months after, when he chose to talk about it.

I put my arm over her shoulders, nonetheless, to pull her past the tighter knots of people.

We'd just made it to the counter, and I'd ordered single malt, straight up, not bothering to give a brand, because they were not likely to have more than one brand handy. Abigail was ordering something that required explaining what a Pink Upright was—what did she think she was doing, exactly?—and I was about to cut her off and point out that perhaps she should go with a glass of wine, when a voice called behind me, "Luce? Ben?"

I turned around. Coming towards us, elbowing his way, was a somewhat modified version of what used to be a familiar face. What surprised me was not that he'd got a few pounds stouter, or that his hair had receded to the point that the pony tail that gathered it in the back looked like an afterthought. No, what puzzled me was that I immediately retrieved a name to go with the face. Not his last name, of course. If I'd ever known that, and I doubted it, because it wasn't how broomers worked, it'd never got used and I'd since forgotten it. But he'd been known, in broomer circles as Birt the Bat, for reasons known only to himself and possibly his mental med tech, if he had one. Most of these names were self-bestowed, and there was nothing even vaguely batlike about Birt. Mouse maybe.

He'd been, when I'd last seen him, a cute young man, with emphasis on young, perhaps all of eighteen, but looking younger, with light brown hair, an oval face, and the sort of slim build that suggests growth will still happen. Growth hadn't happened. Not upwards.

Strangely his cheeks filling in hadn't made him less mouselike, either. He just looked like a contented middle-aged mouse who didn't spend too much time running on his wheel, because that was for the young.

His expression flickered minimally as I turned around, as though for just a moment he weren't sure who I really was. But then he nodded, as though to reassure himself, and said, "I knew it. Lucky Luce. Where have you been hiding yourself. And . . . Ben?"

But Abigail turned around and Birt gave me an uncertain look. I didn't know if, in this light, and with Abigail in broomer suit he'd spotted the crucial difference between her and Ben, but her age was obvious. I cleared my throat. "Birt, this is Abigail, she's Ben's...uh..." I cast about madly, and decided it wasn't any use complicating matters with mention of Ben's brother. We tried to keep mention of family to a minimum in broomer circles, even back then when there was less cause to obscure our identity. Besides, Ben supplied in my mind *sister. Just say it. Easier to make a joke out of it. You don't want seventy questions about my family. Even if it were safe. You want to stir the conversation.* "This is Ben's sister," I said, firmly.

Birt jumped a little. "Oh, then...oh, then...And Ben? You two are still together?"

"As together as ever," I said, and my hand went into my pocket for the flag in its box.

Birt grinned. "Oh. Well. And you, that is..."

"Abby's just starting out on the brooms, and I'm showing her the ropes," I said. And I really, really, really needed to get her snort under control. She smothered it in whatever pink concoction she was drinking, but even Birt might notice it at some point.

A few minutes later, we were sitting at one of the tables, on the outskirts of the crowd, drinking and talking. Making up a history and a vague, general reason why Ben and I hadn't been around wasn't that hard. I told him we'd had to raise Abigail. I made some comment about needing dough and having taken—I dug in my mind for the most dangerous and out of the way jobs I could think of—mineral scouting jobs in the middle of old Europe, jobs that were done mostly on foot or broom, living in tents.

"Man, that must have been rough," Birt said. "No wonder you look like you've had a fight with steamroller and the steamroller won."

Like he looks much better, Ben said, in my mind, his voice sounding stung at the implication that my looks were less than wonderful. *Exactly how many people did he eat to get to be that size?*

I ignored Ben, because even in a broomer bar, people get worried when you talk to someone no one else can see, and instead said mildly, "Yes, but much easier to explain two men raising a young girl without getting too many questions asked, right." Abigail, thank heavens, didn't feel a need to either help or hinder with my invention. Her gaze, across the table, showed a vague kind of admiration for my imagination. Or perhaps alarm at the past I'd just given her. As for me, I wished it could have been true. I had a feeling roaming around alone with Ben would have been fun, even when it got rough. And raising Abigail would have been fun too. And, undoubtedly, rough.

Birt believed it. Well, what reason did he have not to?

Then came the obligatory catching up with what had happened to various people I could no longer even remember, and Birt telling me about some guy or other he was apparently living with.

It was Abigail in the end who stirred the conversation towards arrests and prison breaks, by talking about the Brooms of Doom and the break into Never-Never.

"You're with the Doomers, now?" Birt said, looking over our suits with their red piping. "Good outfit. Not very active usually, you know, and people have sometimes accused them of being lightweights, but that break into Never-Never was a thing of beauty. Man, we didn't even know it existed, and I guess it was mostly political stuff," he pronounced political with all syllables distinctly separated as though it were an alien word and a strange concept. "But a few people I know were sprung, and, man, do they tell rough tales. Good thing for the Doomers to have broken them out."

From there it was a hop, a skip and a jump, to talk about people who had been arrested recently and any weird events they'd witnessed, and I shocked myself by managing it as adroitly as Sam might have. Abigail helped. The pink whatevers didn't seem to have muddled her wits, though she ordered a second one, and she was showing a marked tendency to snort and giggle more. I noted that Birt seemed to give her way too appreciative looks, which just shows you never know, and put it in reserve at the back of my head, in case at some point I had to give him the punch that Sam and Nat would have wished me to. But he never overstepped the line, and he might not even have been aware of the interest in his gaze.

Encouraged, he told us several long, pointless tales about the very best prisons to end up in, and the very worst ones—for a highly subjective idea of best and worst, considering the main attraction in one of the prisons seemed to be a really hot guard.

And then we hit pay dirt, with a suddenness that left me breathless. "Only Sanders the Snake, remember him, with the Buzzers?

No. Wait, he was after your time. He's a righteous flyer, nonetheless, never at a loss, and good in a pinch, you know." And again, I wished that Abigail would control her snort, particularly her snort-giggle. "Anyway, he was arrested. Minor matter, nothing to jump about, just you know, a few kilos of oblivium in possession."

If possession of oblivium, particularly in the kilo range, was a minor matter, then things had got far more interesting in the years I'd been away. Because when it came to illegal drugs, oblivium had been in a special category by itself. Most drugs were forbidden. Tons of things were forbidden in the seacities. It gave the Good Men a reason to arrest you if they wanted to for whatever purpose. But most of the drug consumption and possession was ignored most of the time. It was rumored, and I now knew it was true, that the Good Men owned most of the drug creation facilities and farms and controlled what got into the market.

I'd got to know this was true because the introduction of oblivium had been one of the *stabilizing* measures engineered by my father. Population stabilizing for one, because oblivium use came not only with a sky-high mortality rate—the fun and the lethal dose were that close together—but with more regularity than would be considered good by anyone but my father, it induced homicidal fits, which had the advantage of taking out vast swaths of other people who didn't use the drug. In fact, at our trial and possibly in the media, Ben and I had been portrayed as under oblivium influence while committing the murders.

"So, he was taken to this prison, in Shangri-la. But he didn't stay more than a few hours, even though they'd given him, like… two years. So, you know, I was surprised to see him back on the streets this afternoon, and he told me these guards came in and cleared the prison and turned everyone loose, and there was this high-security transport. He thought they were transferring the prisoners from Never-Never there, which would make sense, except he says it was a small transport, and he wondered if they only managed to keep like less than ten prisoners in. But then it was really small and he says maybe one. Anyway, it's weird."

Abigail and I traded a look. We let the talk stray to weird things in general for a while, not wanting to call attention to our interest in the prison, because Birt might be three fourths air head, but he might not. I was never sure how much of it was an act.

Then Abigail came back to it, by a circuitous route, talking about things that were named weirdly, and got to "That prison, isn't it named something like Coconuts? The one that, ah, Snake escaped from?"

"He didn't escape," Birt said. By then we'd bought him maybe five drinks, and his speech was starting to get a little slurred. "At least he says it's no trouble at all escaping from it, you know, because in some cells over time they've loosened the fresher assembly so it can be pulled over, and then you can go out through the drains to the sea, but the thing is, this time he didn't have to, which he was glad about, because he had new, fancy boots, and he didn't need to destroy them in the muck, you know."

"Yeah," Abigail said, and went back to her point. "Isn't that Coconut Guard, or something like that?"

He gave her an odd look, then said, "No. Coconut Heights is the overnight lockup in Olympus, and no one has any idea why it was named that. This one is out on Shangri-la. I think it's called something like Correctional Facility for the Rehabilitation of something or other, but everyone calls it Coffers."

And then we had to continue the conversation for a while longer. Had to. Again, Birt might not be the smoothest pebble in the brook, but I doubted he was a complete simpleton either. In fact, before we acted on anything he said, I was going to have to double-check it. Because now I was completely aware of how shot through with my father's spies and informants every place and every group was.

But Birt seemed inoffensive enough as he took leave of us on the street outside the bar. "Give my best to Ben," he shouted out, as we walked down the street to the place where the roof wasn't directly overhead and we could actually take off on the broom. Birt, himself, went the other way down the street, probably looking for another bar.

Ben snorted in my mind, with a sound like Abigail's and I would have told him he was a bad influence on her, except she couldn't hear him.

We took off and Abigail signaled for me to follow her and told me we were going back to the lair with finger movements so rapid it betrayed she spent a lot more time than I'd have thought on broomback. And there didn't seem to be any way to argue with her. Nor did I know where we could go to confirm the stuff about Coffers.

Consensus

THE BROOMS OF DOOM HAD A MUCH BIGGER AND BETTER APPOINTED lair than we'd ever had. It took up most of a warehouse in the Deep Under region of Syracuse Seacity, so that Abigail and I just had to fly around a few minutes, then fly through the disabled robotic arms, before we landed and walked to the lair. To be honest, I wasn't even sure that this was not on the bottom floor of the building where the Twelve had first gathered to meet me.

The lair must at one time have housed flyers ready for resale, one of those places that have niches on the wall, each large enough to accommodate a family flyer, with open space in the middle for special show-pieces and for the salesmen to walk around and meet customers. It was that big, and some structures in the corner looked like what would remain after those niches were removed.

Most of the space was open and shadowy, but there was an entire area partitioned with boxes, pallets, pieces of ceramite or dimatough, and the occasional blanket. Our lair had never got that sophisticated. We all slept in the same communal space, and if you wanted privacy you had to look for it in the shadows or around the edges, or, if you were lucky, behind a pile of something or other, usually debris from wrecked brooms and parts for broom repair.

Abigail led me to an open area, past some of the sleeping cubes. It was clear it had been set up as an eating area in that it was marginally cleaner than what you found in this sort of place, and that there were various seating arrangements. By which I mean that no chair, stool or pillowlike object was the same height, color or rough size. They'd either been scavenged from discards or bought from some tenth-hand store one by one. It could be either or both.

The funny thing is that the moment we entered the area, Abigail became the perfect hostess, asking me to sit down and if I wanted to eat something. As it happened I did. I was no longer twenty. She might have drunk five or six pink whatsits and look no worse for the wear, but after what must have been all of three single malts—I'd ordered more than that, because we'd been to five bars, but I'd nursed them parsimoniously, and when we'd left had left more than half in the glass at each bar—if that many, I felt like I needed something to soak up the alcohol. Besides, I was sure this would be another late night or early morning or whatever. It better be. I grudged every minute that Nat was in enemy hands and at their mercy.

I was eating a sandwich—a surprisingly good one too—when the others straggled in. First Simon, who still managed to look as if he dressed to attract attention in a line of costumed dancers and who, somehow, had managed to go through the lowest dives around and emerge without a wrinkle on his ruffles. He'd grunted something that might have been *allo* or *allors*. I'd noticed his tendency to lapse into ancient French, which was nonsense. Liberte Seacity had, it is true, Gallic origins, but those had been from Francophone Swiss, and at any rate, the patois they spoke was no closer to real French than Glaish was to ancient English. The seacities were such a melting pot of languages and peoples who fled the catastrophic if slow-motion collapse of old Europe that hardly a single tongue escaped unchanged. I'd decided that for whatever reason Simon thought that French helped with his non-threatening image. And perhaps it did, a little, as he spoke it, since it was pantomime French or stage French—French as spoken in period dramas in which the French character was often either the evil seducer or the comic relief.

Martha and Jan stumbled in shortly after.

And then we talked. And it soon became obvious that we had all heard the same story. We'd had different sources, mind you, but the story was always roughly the same.

The problem became how much of it to trust.

"It's not that it's implausible, *allors*," Simon said, leaning forward on a thin, tall stool that caused him to look much taller than Jan or Martha and about my height. "When you think about it, the sort of prison they use for the sort of petty drug infraction that gets most broomers arrested would be packed on any given day. So, if all the prisoners were sent out at once, the story would be everywhere. Particularly after the break into Never-Never got into the rumor mill, sparking a bunch of conversations about prisons and detention."

"But would they just kick all the prisoners out?" Abigail said. "What we have to ask ourselves is, wouldn't they consider it likely that knowledge of this event would be indeed everywhere at once, and that we'd come to know it? They know we have broomer connections."

"Not the way I see it," Martha said. "They're laying a trap for Lucius, mostly. They don't even know about the rest of us. And if the trap they're laying is for Lucius, how are they to know he'd go bar crawling and gathering information? Hell, we'd not even thought of that till a few hours ago."

"Okay, so maybe it almost makes sense," Jan said. "But it's the almost that bothers me. Wouldn't they have seen the potential for us discovering where Nat was and finding a way in? If there is a way in."

That part at least was different, as in, no one had told them about the way to escape Coffers, which of course, happened to make an excellent way in. That is, if we could figure out which freshers had been loosened so the bases could be pushed, and if we had any idea at all where the drains for the sewers ended.

We didn't. But that wasn't the hold up. The hold up was that none of us—not one—could be satisfied that this was real and not a trap. And walking into a trap tonight was on no one's plans.

After a good two hours pointless discussion, Simon, who for some reason seemed to hold authority in this lair, broke up the discussion and told us to go to bed. I hesitated. "If I go back home," I said. "There is a chance of being ambushed. Not high perhaps, but—"

"Oh, not home to bed," Simon said. "To bed here."

"He doesn't have a bed here," Martha pointed out.

"Surely we have accommodations for guests, *enfin*?"

"Well," Abigail said. She seemed to hesitate minimally, then took heart, as if daring herself to do something. "Perhaps . . . I mean, if you don't mind, Lucius, you can stay in Nat's space. I'm sure he wouldn't mind, and it saves us having to figure out a place where you're not likely to be walked in on by a drunken broomer or an amorous couple."

I nodded. Nat's space, whatever that was, would do fine. "I don't like this," I said, as Abigail drew me into the partitioned area. "I don't like waiting. You don't know what every hour in the sort of situation he might very well be in, can do to a man. You don't—"

"I do," she said. "And I don't like it either. Except that of course you can't expect us to go charging in to what might be a trap, either."

"No," I said, and was about to add that I could always do it alone, when a head popped out the blanket-hung door of the partition we were passing. He looked remarkably like the unlikely angel who'd freed me, and he said, "Ab'ga'l, wanna see a boom?"

Was that a flash of panic in Abigail's face? She put a hand out and grabbed the other broomer's arm, and said, "No, Fuse, you can't make a boom in here. You know what Ma—what Simon would say to that, don't you? It's not safe, and he doesn't like it when people get hurt."

The creature addressed as Fuse blinked. "I wasn't going to set off a boom," he said, with the supercilious exactness of an aggrieved six-year-old. "Just to show it to you and tell you what it does."

Abigail sighed and gestured for me to follow her. Inside was a small compartment, with a vast working table, covered in materials I couldn't identify. Some of them smelled chemical, and some looked like they were made of strange, sparkly materials. When Fuse turned away, Abigail told me over her shoulder, in a loud whisper, "Don't touch anything. Most of it will explode on contact."

Now Fuse was turning back from the bench with a radiant smile, the sort of sweet smile he'd had when he broke me out of jail. "No, no," he said. "It's not like that. Not this new one." He picked up what looked like a glass globe only slightly larger than a marble. "This one you can carry in your pocket for months. It won't explode until you throw it with force, like this," He lifted his hand, holding the marble, and Abigail was on her tiptoes, grabbing his hand with both of hers, so he couldn't throw anything out of it. "No, no, Fuse. Not in here. You promised, remember?"

"Uh. Yeah," Fuse said, and then started talking about chemicals and how he'd put a shell with a cushioned something or other on the globe, and how this meant it needed an impact above...

I zoned out, my mind spinning over the problem of how to figure out if the setup with Coffers was a trap or not. Again and again I wondered how we could know. And again and again I got that we couldn't. Which didn't make it any easier to accept. Nat still needed rescuing, but could I allow all these people to risk their lives in what might be an enterprise that would never succeed?

I had something like the glimmer of an idea, the sort of feeling one gets when there's a solution to a problem, but it's not appeared in words in your mind, yet, so all you have is a feeling. And then Abigail smiled at Fuse and said, "It is all very interesting Fuse. It is quite a lesson, isn't it? And now, you know, we'll have to go, but I'll be back later to talk some more to you, okay?" To my surprise, she kissed him on the cheek. To my greater surprise, he made no movement to follow us.

Still, it wasn't until we were a long way away that she said, "He's perfectly good with explosives, you know? They work the way he says they work. He made the shaped charge that got us into Never-Never. The material shattered a little wrong, because he couldn't be expected to know twenty-second century dimatough, but the rest, he got quite right."

"But...he's mentally deficient. Who taught him to work with explosives? Wouldn't that be dangerous?"

She gave me a very serious look. "He is the son of Good Man Mason, and he—" She sighed. "He had an accident going through the spider at the entrance, you know? He was running from his father's guards because he...he had discovered something terrible."

"I'll hazard I know what was so terrible," I said.

She nodded. "I thought you might, but I didn't know what Nat or Dad had told you, and I certainly didn't want to be the one to break the news to you."

"I understand," I said, as she pulled up a corner of a blanket separating a cube delimited by boxes and pieces of ceramite.

"This is Nat's place, and I'm sure he wouldn't mind if you sleep in it for a few hours. Maybe with a clear head we can figure out what is best to be done about breaking him out?"

"I hope so," I said. If my mind had been machinery, it would have had glue poured on its gears. That's what it felt like, slow and submerged in something that kept pulling me in irrelevant directions, or stopping my thought completely.

"Me too," she said. She went into the cubicle, and held the curtain up, so that I ducked in after her. "Light," she said, and the lights in the area came on.

I was so surprised to find myself in what looked like a regular room in a well-to-do house, that I stopped cold.

Abigail let the curtain fall. "We have to find him, Lucius. We have to bring him back."

And then she was gone.

The Man, Alone

THE CUBICLE SMELLED LIKE NAT. I HADN'T REALIZED BEFORE that he even had a distinctive smell, but he clearly did, and it was all over this area: a hint of aftershave, a remainder of cigarette smoke, and something else, indefinable, and vaguely reminiscent of cinnamon.

There was a carpet on the floor. The bed—a double bed—had been carefully made and sported a heavy, embroidered bed cover, not the sort of scraps of blankets and worn-through wrappings you found around the lair. There was a trunk in a corner, a desk in the other, and there were pictures on the wall.

My wandering eyes stopped on the framed picture over the bed. It was in the same style as the picture of Max and Goldie, but the subject was quite different. I found myself staring at it, as I slowly absorbed the fact that the nude man depicted was not me, not even me at twenty. For one thing, back then, I'd never let my hair grow that long, so that it formed an almost leonine mane. When I was twenty, I wore my hair pretty much like Nat wore his, well cut and shaped to the head. The other thing is that the expression wasn't mine. I didn't think even in my youngest days I'd ever looked that . . . well . . . innocent. The other discrepancy I took to be artistic license, because after all, what artist wouldn't increase a man's endowment, even if both himself and his patron knew it was wrong. *Nonsense,* Ben said in my mind. *Looks accurate to me.* Which meant the part of my mind that played at being Ben had some . . . inflated ideas as well.

I was still looking at the picture, when I realized this one was signed, in the corner, and that the name on it was, unmistakably Nat Remy. I blinked. Nat. But he was a lawyer. It was like opening a door and finding a garden where you expected an office. Suddenly I had a glimpse of Nat, the older brother who had assumed the parenthood of his siblings, and yes, anyone who came in contact with his family, while his parents devoted themselves to his great cause.

I looked at the drawing, and it wasn't simply that it was good. There are any number of good pieces of art that are mechanical, contrived and not alive. Nat was a good stylist, but that wasn't just it, nor was it his trick of returning to an almost minimalist style at a time when holos could improve on and add visual richness to mere nature. That was also a trick of learning and of habit. Craft. Any reasonably good craftsman who was intelligent enough could have come up with that. No. What I was looking at here was of a different order. The drawing, sketchy though it was, showed in every line Nat's feelings for Max, from the admiration of his physique to a protective tenderness. Someone who drew like that was someone for whom art was a passion, an overmastering drive that forced him to create, even if the drawing in public areas had to remain unsigned, because he wouldn't want his father to suspect that Nat had any other interest but in working for the family's cause and in helping his father with the management of the Keeva estates.

It made me want to laugh, then cry. The crying part came when I imagined how it must have felt when Not-Max, whom, at the time, Nat didn't know wasn't in fact Max, had asked him who had painted the portrait now in my room. And also because I wondered what else Nat didn't bother talking to anyone about, and how much of himself he hid. I would guess a great deal.

I'd assumed his reserve and oddness was from having lost Max so recently, and from the circumstances of it. But now I wasn't sure. Now I wondered if they were simply part of being Nat Remy, who always did what was expected of him, even if the doing almost broke him in two.

I turned the light off. I lay on the bed and tried to sleep. The bed smelled like Nat, too, though I'd only lain down atop the covers. By which I don't mean that it smelled like it wasn't washed, but more like a faint scent of Nat's aftershave, and his cigarettes, and the undefinable smell that was him had stayed behind on the bedspread, from his spending so much time here.

I wondered why he would spend time here. For Nat to be a broomer at all seemed an odd thing. It was hardly the behavior of a dutiful son, the scion of a respectable family.

But then I suspected it had all started just like Ben and I had started at our lair. It was a place where you could go and be yourselves. Oh, not a place to have sex. That could be managed at home, or not too far, and in ultimate instance, a place could have been bought or procured. No, it was a place where other people knew of our relationship and accepted us as a couple. Broomers were many things, but it had never occurred to any broomer—not even the contrived upper-class broomers our friends were likely to be—to have any taboos on sex.

It occurred to me that it was funny. Most of the others viewed the lair as a place to go and have all the offbeat sex you chose to have, while people like myself and Ben, and I suspected Nat and Max, went to the lair to be monogamous and in all but our genders conventional.

What we cherished wasn't the fact that no one would burst in on us while making love—which at any rate wasn't true, since at least in our lair the sense of private space was a bit lacking and some people would not just approach but try to hold a conversation—but the fact that we could hold hands, or lean on each other. What was to other people a normal part of normal, public life, to us was the most rare of clandestine pleasures, and could only be purchased at the cost of becoming broomers.

So, I understood Nat's initial involvement with the lair. What I didn't understand was why he'd continued coming here and practically living here when Not-Max held tenure. And then I got that too. When he was here, he could pretend everything was well at home and that Max was himself.

I felt a great wave of sadness for those games of pretending, which I could completely understand. I had pretended for fourteen years that Ben was still alive and could still talk to me.

Closing my eyes, I lay immobile on Nat's bed, trying to sleep. I could do this. I had managed sleep, successfully, on many past occasions.

My mind tried to spin on the problem of Coffers. Was it a trap? Or had these people failed to realize that I would still have acquaintances in the world of broomers? I hadn't realized, until I thought about it hard, that I still had acquaintances in the world of broomers, so I could hardly blame them for not realizing it as well. But that meant— No, wait, what if they thought I wouldn't dare approach any broomers anyway, not after they poisoned the well with their theory of my having had Max killed? Surely they would think that anyone meeting me would turn me in.

They would never understand the webs, in layers, of deception and protection that were part of any broomers identity and particularly of the identity of any broomer who was up to something pleasantly—or for that matter unpleasantly—illegal.

Half of the people we'd seen at the bars might have seen my picture on the holos and heard me referenced as Good Man Keeva or, what was the quaint phrase they were using? The Pretender to being Good Man Keeva. But it didn't matter. Most of them simply wouldn't associate a face seen outside a broomer context with a face seen inside it. Beyond that, even if they had figured out who I was, most of them would never tell. The brotherhood of broomers might rest on the fact that we all knew some appalling or illegal fact about the other, but it held nonetheless. To reveal a fellow broomer was to reveal yourself.

But anyone who hadn't been a broomer would never have found that out, and I suspected most Scrubbers and most people who worked for the Good Men had never been broomers. There were two very different mind sets there.

Of course most children of Good Men were broomers. I stopped and frowned. But most children of Good Men died before they ever came to adulthood, and they weren't the ones making the decisions. No, the ones hunting me and setting traps for me were Mules, those ancient horrors who had managed the Earth into destruction, and who hadn't been young at any time when there were broomer lairs. Most of them hadn't been young when there were brooms. And they were raised apart from the human race, as biological artifacts, not considered quite sentient. Their experience of life would be very different. They would certainly not know the codes that went with belonging to a lair.

So . . . I thought, as I turned and tried to get comfortable on this bed that wasn't mine, on the bed of a man who might even now be at the tender mercies of the best torturers that could be deployed by the council of Good Men, they might not have realized we could figure out their ruse. And if we hadn't figured out their ruse—in fact, if we hadn't come up with this possibility—the likelihood was that even now we'd be looking for maximum security or secret prisons in the stamp of Never-Never and trying to figure out how to get Nat out of one of them. We'd certainly never have stumbled onto Coffers as even a possibility.

The idea that they'd set it up for us to hear of Coffers in broomer bars started to seem far-fetched. When I was very little, I thought that my father was this omnipotent being who saw and knew everything I did and that he could guess all my secrets and see everything I'd been doing. Then, as I got older, I realized that he didn't know a quarter of what I was doing. Some of it he stumbled upon, but that part was only because I was so very bad at hiding.

And I suspected the government of the Good Men was like that. It could stay powerful and in control simply because it was so large and it had so many and varied resources at its disposal. But it wasn't supernatural. It couldn't guess every unlikely turn our minds would take. And if they'd come up with the idea of hiding Nat in a lower security prison, they'd think they had done well enough, and they weren't about to complicate it all by also adding a layer of disinformation.

Or were they? The one thing you could say about the Good Men was that, having lived very long, they managed to grow crazier, more eccentric and certainly more paranoid as time went on. Perhaps this type of mind game was what they did for fun, in their spare time.

I turned again. Then I sat up and realized my body had made a decision, even if my mind hadn't. Sleep was not going to happen tonight. I'd just turn, and toss and turn again, and I'd not be able to sleep. Not while I knew what Nat was going through and could imagine in exquisite detail what he must be suffering and how hard it must be for him to keep from denouncing all his friends and his family too.

I didn't think he would denounce them. I suspected there were very few things in the world or out of it, for that matter, that could out-stubborn Nat Remy. But I knew he would have to suffer not to. And as someone who had undergone the best tortures of the best torturers, I could imagine what they were doing to him in vivid and unwholesome detail.

Then I thought that at least with myself they had been restricted in their tender mercies by the fact that they could not damage me without regening me, because anything beyond minor scars would eliminate my body as an emergency host for my father, should he need it before Max was ready.

No such restrictions hampered them with Nat. Not really. The normal execution for his type of crime was beheading and even if it was broadcast, they could tune in to his being positioned on the block. Hell, he wouldn't even need to be alive for that.

The idea caused a clenching of all my muscles, an instinctive protest in the pit of my stomach, and a rising rebellion along every fiber of my body.

Like hell, I thought, *Like hell they will do that.* And it seemed to me that Ben's voice echoed me.

And then I was putting my boots back on, and moving rapidly out of the lair. I was halfway past the private cubicles area before it occurred to me that if someone—Simon, Jan, Martha and particularly Abigail—saw me, he or she would try to stop me. Which meant, I'd best be stealthy.

I managed to slink, close to the shadows or the improvised interior walls. Well, as close to slinking as someone my size could do, which wasn't terribly stealthy but was better than swaggering in full light, in the middle of the open space.

At the door I faced a problem, because there was a guard. Okay, he was a young broomer, who—though the light didn't allow me to verify that detail—probably still had more spots than beard, and whose posture and general look announced late teens or early twenties and diffident. But he had a burner in his hand, and in my experience it was just good policy not to crowd the man with the weapon. Particularly when he wasn't quite a man yet. And particularly when he looked uncertain.

On the other hand, he wasn't supposed to keep people inside, was he? At least I doubted. Broomer lairs weren't known for keeping their members prisoners inside, and a guard was there, usually, to give the alarm if someone tried to come in. On yet the other hand—what, you're counting?—he might do no more than nod and shrug as I walked out, but he would be able to tell the others I had gone out. I doubted there were many people of my build and general looks around here.

And if someone chanced to ask, or even the kid felt insecure enough to go and ask someone about my leaving the lair—since I was a stranger to him—he would probably get the others to come after me.

While I'd come to the conclusion that I must try to save Nat right now, and that it was worth it to risk my life going to Coffers, where he might or might not be kept, I wasn't willing to risk anyone else's life on this.

I could go back to the room where I'd eaten and where I'd met with the others. If I remembered, no one had bothered to clear the plates and glass. And one or two of those, lobbed far enough above the kid's head, would rivet his attention on some place outside. And then I could run fast, behind him, the way he wasn't looking.

But just as I turned, to go look for something to throw, the kid shifted his position. The movement brought his face into light.

It was a face I knew. It took me a moment to remember from where, because the last time I'd seen him, he was pale as death and streaming water. And telling me he couldn't ride brooms. Apparently he could, however, lie. Well.

But once I recognized him, I immediately experienced relief that John Jefferson had made it to a safe place and, presumably, to his daily life, and an immense relief, because I wouldn't have to try stupid tricks from old holos. I could just talk to the boy and get him to let me go out, right? After all, he owed me his life.

For I Was Lost

I WALKED SLOWLY INTO FULL LIGHT, AND THE KID SPUN AROUND to look at me. For just a second there was a confused look on his face, as if he couldn't quite place me, then recognition with just a hint of fear. I couldn't blame him for the fear, either. When he'd last seen me, I'd been mowing down men like grass. But though his eyes remained apprehensive, he gave me a smile. "Hi," he said, and then, as though at a loss for words, again, "Hi."

I smiled at him, trying to make my smile reassuring. I wasn't absolutely sure I succeeded. Look, it's been a long time since reassuring has been part of my repertoire. At least, I presume it failed, because he took a step back. But I suppose he remembered I saved his life, because he didn't train that burner on me.

Still, I could hear his breathing, shallow and fast, and his eyes were wide with panic. I said, keeping my voice low, "It's okay. I'm here with friends. I'm not a member of the Doomers, but I'm visiting. Now, I want to go out for... for something. I'll be back. If anyone asks if you saw me or anyone go out, would you mind horribly denying everything?"

He blinked at me, as, I suppose, knowledge that I wanted to leave the lair warred with the memory of watching me kill several people and show very little emotion. He didn't step away from the wall, but he lowered his head to me, not quite a bow, and not quite a nod, but something in between.

253

I told him, "Thanks," as I stepped gingerly past him into the darkness outside. I did think that perhaps the knowledge that I was now of his religion would reassure him, so I turned around and gave him the thumb-forefinger salute. By then, I couldn't see his expression and perhaps it was a step too far.

I stood in the middle of the street, thinking which way to go. I'd need a decent flyer. There were two options for this. One was to leave down-under, hit the stairs or the grav wells to upper levels, and look for flyers parked outside the nicer places. The problem with that, of course, is that everyone had seen broadcasts mentioning my presumed guilt in Max's murder, and while that particular broadcast hadn't shown my picture, I was sure others had. I figured I was somewhat safe in outlaw areas and areas where people had an arm's-length relationship with law-enforcement. Beyond that... Beyond that, I'd have to look for another solution.

Well, no large flyers could come through the spider. It was what made this area safe, that no police raids, no peacekeeper enforcement could get in here. But the place was filled with shops and factories, and even in the middle of the night, there were people everywhere and kids running around with miner's lamps on their heads, playing games of the sort that kids have played since humans lived in caves.

I put my hand in my pocket, to touch the box with the flag fragment, and tried to think things through. There were transports that brought stuff in. They were built peculiarly, narrow and long. Not unique. They were used for other sorts of applications, too, including transport for people who lived in the old streets, the ones where the houses dated back five hundred years and had been encased in clear dimatough inside and out to stay standing. Narrow flyers kept accidents there to a minimum.

Of course, those narrow flyers accommodated only a couple of people and usually enough cargo space for, say, a dozen bags of groceries, or three smallish kids. By definition not enough for a peacekeeper force. Of course, I didn't need a peacekeeper force. What I needed was a flyer I could fit in, and in which I could carry Nat. If he needed to be stretched out—I really didn't want to think of what they might have done to him—he'd fit on the floor behind those front seats. And I'd seen those cars—whole fleets of them—in this area before, bringing supplies to factories, or stuff to sell, I presumed.

The problem, though, was that most places down here worked around the clock. Which meant their cars would be in operation round the clock. And if things still worked down here like they used to work when I was young, then they would establish high justice with a flicker of the burner and very little thought. Not that it was a crime-ridden area. Even broomers with lairs here did their outlawing elsewhere. But any type of property or person crime was summarily punished. Which was probably why kids could play on the street, unsupervised, at all hours.

I walked towards the end opposite the spider as I thought, and looked into every alleyway and corridor. The two were virtually indistinguishable down here, where the whole place was roofed over, and where building was totally unregulated. You could walk down a street, and suddenly find yourself in the middle of someone's dining room—or restaurant, nor was the distinction between those two often blindingly clear—and then all you could do was apologize and back out.

I passed some places like that, and I passed others that were clearly alleyways, outside factories or homes. But those factories were noisy and animated, and the homes had people flitting in and out. I walked on. Then it occurred to me that the place had a vertical dimension. It was a good seventy-five feet to the terrace that roofed it over. And in that space there were not only multistory buildings, but people had created multistory alleyways in between. They were accessible by broom and by rickety ladders affixed to the side of the buildings. In this case I took the ladder, because, like an idiot, I'd left my broom back in the lair. So I climbed the ladder up, one level, two, three. And then I realized that finally, here, I'd discovered Deep Under's equivalent of residential streets. There were flyers—and brooms—parked outside silent, sleeping houses.

I'm paranoid, right? It's a perfectly logical outcome of my upbringing. So I went all the way to the topmost level, then shimmied along the wall, in the deepest shadow, to the backmost parked flyer. And then I got out my burner, and was just pointing it carefully at the gen lock—no that won't cause the flyer to spring open, but it allows you to get your fingers in there and jiggle it open, when the most imperious whisper this side of a Good Man's council room sounded.

"Stop."

I stopped. Not because the whisper was that commanding—all right, maybe that, a little—but because down here if I didn't stop, I might well be stopped with a shot through the head.

Then I spun around, quickly, using my fast-movement ability, and pointed the burner.

"Oh, for the love of heaven, Lucius. Stop that, too." Abigail was on broomback, about ten feet from me, and looking—somehow, despite goggles and hood—furious. She hadn't put on her oxygen mask. But even so, how someone can look furious, when all you can see of her is a bit of pointed nose, a little pointed chin and a slightly too pressed together mouth, all of this ten feet away and in semidark, I don't know. Then again, she did look like Ben, and I used to read Ben pretty well.

As I clumsily lowered the burner, she flew nearer, dismounted, clipped the broom to her belt, and glared up at me in a way that, had she been taller than I, would have had me cowering and covering my head. "Stupid," she said.

It was a final pronouncement, and yet it had a sort of indulgent tone, like an adult's comment on a toddler's embarrassing and endearing mistake. "You can't burn the genlock without killing the alarm first," she said. "You'd have had the whole street on us in another minute."

"These things are alarmed?" I said.

"How can you not know that?" She sounded exasperated.

"Uh. I've been away for fifteen years," I said. Pointing out that even before that my flyer theft experience was somewhat limited seemed rather beside the point and also, in this particular circumstance, I suspected it would diminish me in her eyes. I mean, what was I supposed to say, *I used to pawn jewelry so I could buy stuff instead of stealing it?* It seemed downright paltry and cowardly of me, in retrospect.

I didn't even want to imagine in what circumstances Sam Remy's second oldest Daughter, brought up in a mansion, belonging to the upper crust of the seacities—even if her brother and sister had introduced her to their broomer lair—had stolen flyers. *Training, I imagine,* Ben said in my mind. *The Sons of Liberty are always prepared for a fast getaway, even if it involves a little violation of someone's right to property. Well, stands to reason, when it's a matter of life.*

"Were you trained in flyer theft?" I asked.

Abigail gave me an odd look over her shoulder. Then nodded, and I didn't seem to have the heart to tell her I wasn't talking to her. Ben smirked in my mind, and I didn't want to know. Between training weekends in the wilds of the continents and training in stealing flyers—and what more, targeted assassination?—it was no wonder he'd had so many *family weekends*. Or that he arrived back from them so exhausted. Had I been blind? The odd thing was that I'd never even suspected he was playing me false with another man, much less with a whole organization.

Abigail brought something out of her pocket that she touched to a very precise point outside the flyer. "Electronic disruptor," she said. Then she pointed a burner at the lock and burned it, but instead of putting her finger in and tweaking the opening mechanism, she pulled some other gadget out. I didn't dare assume that she was just afraid of putting her finger in there. I assumed she knew something I didn't know—that perhaps the locks had changed markedly since the last time I'd had occasion to do this.

In fact, I waited till the door had been opened, and until she went in, before I tried to follow. Only to get unceremoniously pushed aside, as she carried out something that looked like a white ceramite box and set it on the ground as though it were fragile. Then she jumped into the flyer, and I just managed to jump in after her, before she sat behind the controls and pushed the door closing button.

"What makes you think you're coming along?" she asked, glaring at me, as I squeezed myself into the too-small navigator seat and shut my seatbelt.

"What makes you think I'm not?" I said calmly.

"Because there isn't evidence that Nat is at Coffers," she said, as she took the flyer out, manually, on a perfectly smooth course out of the tunnel/alley and into the greater space, tilting slightly to aim at the space between the arms of the spider, and talking all the while, "and even if he is, we don't know that they haven't set a trap for us. And if they've set a trap for us, there is no reason for you to risk yourself."

"There is every reason," I said.

She took us through the spider, and I realized I'd been holding my breath, when I started breathing on the other side. And then *she* asked me the same personal question her father had asked me.

"You're not too old to have your mouth washed with soap."

She gave me a sideways look with lowered lashes. "That," she said, "is hardly an answer."

"That," I answered in the same tone, "is none of your business, and besides it's seriously unflattering to your brother. Is that the only reason anyone would want to rescue him?"

"No." She seemed to think about it. "I have reasons to rescue him. There's any number of people who have reason to rescue him. I just don't see any reason why you'd be willing to risk yourself, unless—"

"No," I said. "If you must have a plain answer, we're not. I don't even think he likes me. But then you're being unflattering to me, if not to Nat. Why shouldn't I want to rescue him? He's saved my life at least twice, and probably more, at serious risk to himself. And he's your father's son, and I would prefer not to distress your father. And a million other reasons."

"I see," she said, and frowned as she turned forward. "So you're saying it's considerably more serious than that."

I refused to rise to the bait, not least because I had not the slightest idea what she meant. If she meant my feelings for Nat were serious, then she'd missed the part where I didn't even know if he liked me, and I sure as shooting didn't know if I liked him. But if she meant my rescuing him was a serious endeavor, based on deep thought and moral beliefs, then she was right. Instead I said, "Do you even know where Coffers is? Do you have directions? And you're missing the entire reason I wanted to come in alone. It was so that you and other people who have lives worth living wouldn't get hurt or killed."

"Oh, yes," she said. "The horrible heartbreak of being healthy, wealthy and one of most powerful men in the world. Sure, you have nothing to look forward to. And of course I have directions. I'm young. I'm not mentally damaged."

Which was a severe misestimation, if she thought she could lecture me in the way she had been without suffering any reprisal. But I didn't know how to answer her. I couldn't explain that I'd felt like I had nothing to live for, and that, in fact, I had deserved death for fifteen years. And I surely could not tell her that I didn't expect to be wealthy or powerful by the end of this war we were about to start. Not if we won. And I hoped we won anyway.

Instead I stayed quiet, trying to think of a way to get rid of her, but I also couldn't think of a way to do that safely. Oh, sure, I could highjack the flyer by main force, make her land and push her from it. But first subduing her would be nearly impossible without permanent damage. And second, if—as I suspected—Nat had been captured more because of his nearness to me than for his guilt in Max's supposed death, then Abigail was at equal risk, wandering around the streets of some other seacity. And third, because the damn woman would probably steal a flyer, come after me, and probably get to Coffers before me and alone, when I couldn't protect her.

After a while of flying, tensely, her hands clenched on the steering stick, her fingers hovering on the keyboard, she sighed and relaxed. "I'm sorry," she said. "It was a pretty rude question, though you know, all the servants think—" She gave every impression of biting her tongue. "And it was none of my business, but I was trying to . . . If you got mad at me, maybe you'd ask me to let you out and maybe . . ."

"And maybe you could go to the jail and get yourself killed alone?"

"This would be different from what you're trying to do?"

I shook my head. "I'm bigger. I'm older, and I have more experience of prisons."

She giggled. It was sudden, and I think like my impulses to laugh out of turn, completely unexpected. Then she shook her head. "Being locked in a cell for fourteen years doesn't show you how to escape." Then she looked contrite, almost immediately. "I'm sorry. But, I had training and weekends of exercising for war and experience of live fire."

"Live fire?"

"Exercises, mostly. Our young people—"

"Your brother said young men."

"All our young people, though it's gender segregated," she said. "We train for war. We always knew war would come." She paused, and added, "If we were lucky."

So, Ben had been going away for weekends to sleep on frozen ground and be burner-shot at and all the while I had no idea. I must have been the most oblivious young man in the world.

"But this is not war," I said. "Not a frontal attack. I mean— what we're about to do."

"You do know," she said, "that the Sons of Liberty . . . that is, you do know that we have engaged in these before, right? And that I have taken part in this kind of raid before?"

I didn't. But I could believe her, watching her fly. "I take it you disabled the tracking mechanism on this and we're not transmitting our location to every traffic control tower we pass?"

"Part of the reason to steal the flyer in Deep Under is that they don't have those mechanisms in them. Think about it, stands to reason. They're almost as illegal as illegal broomers. They don't want their purchases or their errands traced."

"And the ceramite box you took out?"

"Oh, that? Remote bomb. They could have blown us up once they'd figured out the flyer was missing."

I started to think I wasn't prepared for this. Or at least that she was more prepared than I was. But I'd be damned if I admitted it.

"I know where the entrance to the sewer is," she said. "On the side scarp of the island. But we'll have to park the flyer on the beach, and it might be discovered. In which case we'll need other plans for escape."

I grunted. There really wasn't much else I could do. This woman had all the plans and everything under control, and all I could do was let her take charge. Fortunately I didn't have to like it. Even more fortunately I was sure my meager talents would be requited somewhere along the line in some humble capacity.

Into Hell

JUST BEFORE SHE HID THE FLYER BEHIND AN EMPTY WAREHOUSE on the shores in Shangri-la, I asked her, "Did you follow me? Out of the lair?" Because even if we'd had the same idea at the same time it would take a marked coincidence for us to take the same direction out of the lair, let alone for us to end up on the same level and trying to steal the same flyer.

She nodded. "I was right behind you, though I was coming out on my own. But I saw you talk to John. He told us which way you'd gone. I only delayed to go back in and get your broom. Otherwise I'd have overtaken you earlier."

Which was the first time I realized she had two brooms clipped to her belt. It just goes to show you how confused I'd been back in Deep Under, with her staring at me like that, and ordering me around.

Now, she stood up, unclipped my broom, handed it to me. "You're going to need it," she said. "The entrance to the sewer is not even underwater at high tide. The rest of the time it's up there. And at any rate it's on a sheer wall that ends in the sea."

She pointed around from where we were.

The only way I can describe Shangri-la is as a ramshackle type of seacity. Most of the other seacities had been started as high-tech havens—places where the skilled and the productive went to hide from increasingly more dysfunctional states, which made skill and productivity impossible. For those who've read twentieth-century literature and happen to have the same tastes as Sam who sent me books in prison, they were all sort of a sea-based Galt's Gulch. In fact, the Rainers' city was called Galt, and I suspected it came from that.

But of course that wouldn't be all. Tax laws weren't the only laws to be evaded. A number of seacities had sprung up that specialized in less savory forms of freedom—those where all forms of prostitution or flesh trade were permitted, including those that would result in the death of one partner; those in which drugs even more dangerous than oblivium were made and consumed as a matter of course; those in which gambling and shady money operations were based; and those like Shangri-la, which provided all three in one big mess of lawlessness.

These seacities were mobile, propelled by motors beneath the waterline. Their erratic course would make it difficult for them to be tracked and caught when their activities became too obnoxious. And for almost a century they'd been the scourge of the seas, eventually becoming too obnoxious even for their laissez-faire sister seacities, which had joined in a league to take them down.

Most of those seacities had been destroyed, bombed into oblivion, their assets and their human population dispersed or obliterated. But not Shangri-la. It had somehow been claimed wholesale by Liberte, and it had been anchored permanently.

The prostitution business and the money laundering had been stopped, or at least sent underground, but the drug manufacturing continued at a blistering pace, under the aegis of St. Cyr. And it was distributed through Good Men channels throughout the other islands. Nominally illegal, the laws against drug production were enforced so erratically that drugs were everywhere and, of course, it allowed for population control and for discouraging or diverting the less conforming members of society. I suspected in a healthy society drug use would be less destructive, but in a society that destroyed its young, drugs of the more extreme kind became a way out of life.

I wrenched my mind away from that forcibly and into the way that Shangri-la had been anchored. Once the seacity was completely built, anchoring it had been a difficult matter of pouring new dimatough that extended it, and bound to the dimatough already in place. This was easier said than done because Shangri-la, as well as being mobile, had been designed to be inaccessible, so that on all sides, it had all sheer, tall dimatough cliffs, and the city itself was perched atop, as well as drilled down into, the dimatough—casinos and factories and everything drilled into tunnels all the way to the base. When binding it in place, and making sure it wouldn't drift, no matter how violent the tides and how hard the storm, it had been poured down and extended over a small set of rocky islands, to which it had been bound as a way of keeping it from moving.

The result was an odd topography for anyone who had been raised in a seacity. We were used to flat surfaces, often built up in terraces and platforms, but having started out flat on their own.

Most of Shangri-la was like that, if at a height much higher than sea level, consisting of a very thick base and a flat surface above. But the part where we had landed was an odd tongue of dimatough covered, imperfectly, with dirt, on which a few straggly trees were trying to grow without success. That dimatough portion extended in a rather steep ramp from the top of the rest of the island, down to the area where we were, a few feet from the ocean, and then around, to surround portions of the island that were still sheer cliffs. You could stand on a strip of dimatough just large enough for a couple of warehouses and look up at the sheer cliffs above.

There were sewers there, it goes without saying. There had been before the city was anchored. Holes bored into the rock, but too far away from each other to provide a foothold for anyone trying to climb the wall. And I had a vague idea—I'd read a lot, and one of the things I'd read had been a novel from the twenty-first in which the plot consisted of trying to get into Shangri-la, to steal jewels or something—and so I thought that there were traps at the entrance of those sewers, anyway. Whether that was real, though, or the imagination of the writer, it's hard to say.

Anyway, the sewers had been left up there, all a hundred feet up, punctuated by oozing holes in the dimatough. To keep it semisanitary in the warehouse area beneath, some genius had carved a vast gutter and a channel system that diverted the effluvia to the sea. That channel passed right of where we'd hid the flyer, between a warehouse that looked abandoned and another one whose door opened the other way.

"It's risky, of course," Abigail said. "Since we can't lock it. But we'll have to risk it."

I nodded, not saying anything. The way she'd pointed was not to this wall, which was probably good since some of the warehouses were clearly busy and these people would get curious—wouldn't they?—if we were to fly up on brooms and go in through the sewer like that in full view of them.

Not that I was sure the way she pointed, to a part of the wall that was over the sea, was out of sight, but I could pray. I walked with her along the gritty little shore of dimatough, which seemed to be covered in more broken glass and discarded bits of ceramite than the sand and dirt that had doubtless been dug up from the seabed to cover it, as it had in more prosperous seacities.

On the extreme-most tip of it, she started to unclip her broom, and I put my hand on her arm and held. "Abigail," I said. "You know which entrance is to the right sewer, right? You researched it?"

She nodded once, her features tense. She'd got the oxygen mask out and put it on, though she hadn't brought oxygen bottles for either of us. We'd have to rely on the concentrator in the broom itself. That was fine, provided we weren't going really far up or really long distance. I'd still have felt safer with bottles, but I understood the principle of not having them: moving faster and more easily. Also that just quite possibly Abigail had never thought to get them, for which I couldn't blame her. Without her we'd be on one broom and given my size I suspected her little, ladylike broom would never have got more than five feet off the ground.

I held onto her arm again, as she tried to move away. "No, Abigail, listen. You show me which tunnel to enter, but I go in first."

She gave me the eyebrows-lifted look that in Ben would have meant *the hell you say, buddy.* I sighed. "Look, I read a novel, and it might be ad-libbing on the novelist's part, but I read a novel about trying to break into one of these tunnels in the twenty-first, and they had all sorts of cunning tricks and traps." She made an impatient exhalation and I said, "Yes, Abigail, I do know that in the twenty-first this place was an illegal seacity and would have to defend itself, while right now it is under the protection of the Good Men, but bear with me, will you? Wouldn't they have some alarms in the prison sewer? To prevent people coming in."

And now she rolled her eyes, and that too was a Ben expression. "Why would they prevent people coming into the prison?"

She said, sounding testy. "It is not the normal thing, you know? Most people try to break out of prison, not into it. And besides, Lucius"—she didn't add *knucklehead*, but it was implied in her tone—"this route is often used by escaping broomers, and it wouldn't be if it had all sorts of cunning traps and devices."

"Fine," I said. "But then you have to ask yourself, if it is a normal way for broomers to escape jail, why has it been left without traps?"

Again, the escape of air in a hissing sound between her teeth reminded me that she was very young and had a distinct lack of patience for those older and slower than her. "Look, it's a minimal security prison. I think the longest sentence given here is about six months. It's a revolving door. The same broomers come in over and over again. If they escape, it's less time that they have to be fed. And if you tell me that then they should abolish it, you're missing the entire point. The point is to keep up the appearance of a lawful system, with minimal involvement and expense. Let's face it, particularly in drug distro, most broomers are indirectly working for the regime. Are we going to continue the debate society, or are we going to rescue my brother? Because if you just want to stand here and talk, I'll go, and you can wait."

I almost laughed. Yes, I knew she was furious at me. And yes, I knew to her mind it would seem like I was debating small and pointless bits of the plan ahead. In that, she was much like Ben, too. Or perhaps it was that Ben had died very young, and therefore had never lost this trait. But instead of being stung I was charmed because I remembered my own youth, my own rashness. It was like looking onto a summer's day from the middle of cold, bitter winter, with nothing but more winter in store. Amusement must have danced in my gaze, because she looked bewildered for just a moment, which gave me time to say, "Never mind that. Yes, you're probably right, but on the off-chance you're not, or that they've put something in since they brought Nat here, let me go ahead, will you?"

She shrugged. "Whatever makes you happy. Now, you brought burners, right?"

I supposed after leaving my own broom behind, I deserved that, but I just answered with, "I always have burners."

And then we were airborne. She really must have investigated—I supposed by filtering the accounts of the various broomers who had escaped this way—because she didn't even hesitate about which tunnel to stop in.

The tunnel itself surprised me. I'd expected it to be narrow enough that we'd need to crawl along its length on hands and knees, but instead—and much more pleasant when you considered the sludge along the bottom and trickling from the tunnel opening even if I couldn't smell it through the oxygen mask which I'd kept on, since I suspected the air here might be less than wholesome—it was large enough for us to fly into and for me to not even have to bend much—just inclining my head allowed me to fit.

If I could read Abigail's eyes through the goggles, what they were saying was that I was an idiot for going ahead of her, when I looked like some kind of giant, and she could slip quietly along in the shadows. All very well, but I still felt I couldn't risk her. What would I tell Sam if I let her get killed? What would I tell Nat? Because—I told myself, taking a deep breath—Nat was going to be alive, and I was going to rescue him.

The sludge came to almost the top of my boots, and I tried not to think what it was, because it would only activate my gag reflex, and I sloshed along in it, forward, while I heard Abigail slosh behind me. So much for making a stealthy appearance. We would have to count indeed on the fact that no one would expect sane people to break into a jail. Perhaps.

It got colder as we continued inside the tunnels. I don't know why, except that we were going farther away from where the sun warmed the sheer surface of the cliff onto which the sewers opened. Colder, and darker. And yet, other senses kicked in. I can't explain it, except by saying that perhaps I'd developed more awareness of other people by being in solitary for so long. But no, that wouldn't apply. After all, I'd completely failed to recognize Abigail's nearness in Deep Under. But then again, in Deep Under, there were too many people all around, and perhaps I simply couldn't be aware of a single signal.

I don't know. What I know is that in that dark and probably smelly—thank all the gods for the mask that didn't let me know that for sure—tunnel, I was very aware of all sounds, of all movements, and particularly of sounds and movements that were or might be human.

And that's what saved our lives.

We'd just got to a point where the main tunnel broke up into several branching-out tunnels, something like an intersection in a highway system, and I stopped, to allow Abigail to indicate which one to take.

She had touched my arm, and extended a hand into my field of vision to point, when I became aware of sounds and movement at the entrance to one of the tunnels. Nothing was visible yet, but I could hear sounds that were more than the random sloshing and dripping of the liquid around us and underfoot. The sounds were much, in fact, like the ones that Abigail was making behind me.

I went into fast mode, shoved Abigail between me and the wall so that even if I were cut down it was unlikely the burner would get to her. The burners I had in hand got shoved into "slice" instead of burn by a flicker of the thumb. No, I didn't think about it till afterwards. Not consciously. But afterwards I reasoned it had been the right thought, because in this dark space, light was very visible and far more obvious than mere noise. Light would announce to anyone else along the tunnel that there was someone breaking in.

So I didn't use it. Instead, as two men emerged from the tunnel—darker silhouettes in the dark space—I hit them fast with the cutting ray. They fell gurgling, before they could fire and—I hoped—before they could give the alarm to anyone else. From behind me, Abigail gasped. I gave her more room, afraid I'd crushed her too hard, but she made no move to escape the space, and when I looked back at her, she just nodded, the bits of her skin that showed having gone very pale. But she nodded and hand-signaled, "that tunnel."

I nodded to let her know I'd figured that much out, and proceeded ahead of her, this time slower and trying to move with more stealth. Stopping by the corpses, I bent down and got their burners. Yes, I was wearing broomer gloves, which is good, because they were not only half submerged, but they were adding to the flow with blood and guts. But they had good burners, and, even in the dark, I could tell they were the flat, black burners that were assigned to most of the Good Men forces and which were never traded in the market unless they had been stolen.

Not Scrubber weapons, mind, and these men were not Scrubbers. But they were wearing some sort of uniform, and this made me feel both an infinitesimal amount of relief—I hadn't killed innocent broomers trying to escape the prison—and tense up, because unless I were wrong, these were Liberte prison guards. Which meant...there would be more ahead.

And no, I didn't expend much thought on the idea that St. Cyr's own guards might be cooperating in keeping Nat hidden, or in imprisoning him. Look, I'd seen enough of those papers to know that a Good Man's control of his territory is at best nominal. No one man can control so many operations at so many different levels. It is one of the downfalls of all dictatorial regimes that are larger than a small village, that the dictates of the one true ruler end up being enforced, ignored, distorted and sometimes created by a vast bureaucracy. Depending on what that bureaucracy, or parts of it want to do, the result will be varying shades of evil. It is never good. I'd read enough of those papers to realize that even with Sam in control, even with the bureaucracy being, obviously, shot through with Usaians, most of the results were at best erratic and at worst evil. Even well-intentioned people in a bureaucracy end up having to defend themselves from encroachment by other people trying to acquire more power, and end up having to do things for how they look, instead of their results. That meant no order went undistorted. The big lie of the various isms of the twentieth century, from fascism to communism, was not that they'd bring paradise on Earth. Every tin pot dictator had been promising that, presumably since we'd first crawled out of caves. No, their lie was the assertion that this time—each time and each iteration—was different, because this time was scientific. In fact, no dictatorship could ever have science on its side. Insofar as science could be applied to social behavior, the only sound science on governance shown through multiple experiments was that the more concentrated the power, the worse the results.

And from the fact that St. Cyr was still a part of a secret organization and hadn't called it up into the light of day and told it to take its place in governing, I suspected most of the organization beneath St. Cyr and working around him were not believers in whatever it was the Sans Culottes believed in. So I doubted St. Cyr was double-crossing us, or had feigned lack of knowledge about Nat.

On the other hand, I suspected the Council of Good Men had

picked exactly this place because they knew that we wouldn't think of it, even if we thought of lower-security prisons as a possibility. I also assumed there was a plan in place and ready to kick in, should Simon decide to "officially" inspect the prison. It could be anything from razzle-dazzle, to Nat being kept in a secret and easy-to-hide portion of the place.

So, I continued very carefully indeed, down the somewhat less wide tunnel, where I had to bend down a little further. I also tried to slosh less. I'd like to say that helped, but I'm not sure. I'm almost sure the only thing that helped was my super-fast mode, my being attuned to noises that might be human, and my frankly disturbing—even to myself—tendency to shoot before thinking.

We met three more two-guard teams along the way. None of them took much effort to dispose of, and I got all of their burners, though I gave three of those to Abigail because my pockets couldn't hold any more. And if she thought my habit of letting no burner go to waste was odd, she didn't say anything. Her posture had lost that odd dragging-sullen-teenager look it had shown at first, and she was walking as stealthily as she could, too.

The tunnel bifurcated again, after we killed the last team of two, and Abigail signaled, her hands only visible because she was wearing grey, instead of black gloves, to the third tunnel on the left. "It's a dead end. The fresher at the end is the one that opens."

I nodded, and hoped she could see it. If she could it was only because I was light-haired.

But she followed me quietly. There were no guards there. Which could be good or bad. On the good side, it could mean that there were more guards along the corridor, which continued on. On the bad side, it could mean that they too knew exactly which fresher slid off its moorings and allowed people out. And in our case, in. Or maybe there were more than one, and they weren't sure, but what kind of prison didn't have cameras? I balked, and stood, breathing hard, while Abigail bumped into me from behind.

Her fingers moved in the dark, signing, "Are you okay? Heart attack?"

I shook my head, and I signaled back "Trap. Sure of it. Trap."

Then I realized she couldn't see my fingers, which were in black gloves, and I repeated the signaling against her arm. Her hands flashed fast. "You're crazy."

It was hard thinking through how to explain things in sign language, and clearly enough that she could get it by touch, but I did my best. "No. Cameras. Prison. Know which. Will watch that."

She tilted her head, and shrugged her shoulders in an eloquent show of "What then?"

I had no idea, but my body did. I grabbed her arm, went back, and took a random tunnel. She made a sound of protest, which I ignored completely. I walked on and, after a moment, she followed. I thought that for better effect I should go all the way back to the beginning and take completely different tunnels, but that was never going to happen. If I did, I would end up completely lost. I had to assume in her study of the prison, Abigail had figured out what the areas of higher security were, the areas in which Nat was most likely to be. I didn't want to disorient her further.

I had the growing feeling at the back of my head that this was a quixotic enterprise and more than a little crazy; that I would never have engaged in it if I'd been in my right mind; that Abigail and I were going to die here. It didn't matter. Sometimes, when you've already made the mistake, it was just as good to keep forward as to back out. As Shakespeare said, if you're in the middle of the river, it's just as good to wade forward as back. At a guess, if we left now, they'd find the dead guards and they'd move Nat. Or reinforce security. Right now we had a shot at freeing him. It wouldn't last forever.

I waded down the tunnel, relieved to find no one there, but still a little wary. Hopefully we hadn't managed, by sheer coincidence, to find ourselves in the one tunnel where there was another loose fresher. The tunnel dead ended, and Abigail pointed upwards. "That's a drain valve," she gestured, "now what?"

Now, I took one of my plentiful borrowed burners and put them on cut. The good ones, the police issue ones, were a marvel of the art, and could cut through anything, even ceramite. They had a little trouble with dimatough, though held in place long enough and hard enough, they would shatter it. But the valve above us was mounted on ceramite. I cut it off by cutting a neat circle around it.

Don't ask me how prison freshers work or what the valve contained. All I knew is that it was round, and massive, about the same general mass and bulk as my trunk. I pushed Abigail against the wall, to be out of the way of it when it fell. Unlike household freshers, which are a distinct unit, mostly meaning a shower and a vibro-cleaner, prison cell freshers were an integrated all-in-one vibro and toilet and several other functions, including a unit that pared your nails when you put hand or foot in. This one seemed to be arranged for water also, because there was a lot of clean water released when the valve fell into the sewer. Presumably, I'd somehow cut a water pipe. I didn't mind it, since it felt and looked, in the light from above, as clean water. I crawled right into the opening, with the water sloshing around me, grateful the valve was large enough to give me a way to crawl through.

The cell was empty and the lights were off, though the filtered light that came from the hallway through the open door was enough to seem dazzling after the darkness. It's possible the camera was off. I don't know. I know alarm wasn't given immediately. Still I located where the camera was on the wall—it was visible, unlike whatever had watched my prison cell, even if far enough above that floor and the cot and table, and anything that could be climbed, that it would be unreachable. It was not unreachable to a burner and the burner took care of it, just as Abigail came in behind me.

She was a sensible girl, and no more had she climbed up, than she took a burner in each hand. Then she seemed to realize I'd have no idea where I was going. Again, presumably she knew, because after a quick look around, she returned a burner to her pocket, and gesture-spoke, rapidly, "To the right out of here. End of corridor. Take grav well down. Then down again. Then corridor. May God be with us."

I can honestly say that in my entire life with the broomers, I'd never found a need to do the sign for God, but I somehow knew it and recognized it when it was made.

We followed her plan, and there was no problem until we got to the last corridor, by which point alarms had started sounding, loud and clear.

We should have been dead. We would have been dead. Guards poured ahead and behind us, burners drawn. We had only two advantages. One was my odd speed trick. The other was Abigail's ability to know exactly what part of the hallway I couldn't see or hadn't covered. No, I don't understand it, and I wouldn't know how to do it myself.

We went two steps, three. I burned and she burned. Ahead and behind. And behind and ahead, we proceeded, back to back, killing numbers of enemies that should have overwhelmed us.

And then suddenly Abigail whimpered and fell. I thought she had stumbled. I reached for her. I didn't know what to do. "Abigail," I said, even as I burned in a circle, to left and right and in front, to keep the enemy at bay. "Abigail, for the love of God, stop fooling around."

I don't know when I realized she was dead. I should have realized it earlier. The corridor was well lit, and there was a hole the size of my fist between and below her breasts, where her heart should be. Someone had used the cutting function of the burner, on wide dispersion.

I burned around me with blind abandon, setting both burners to flame and setting fire to the bastards. If it started an inferno in the prison, I no longer cared. I was a dead man walking, and Nat would die with me, which would undoubtedly be a better fate than whatever they'd planned for him.

And Death is at My Side

STEADY, LUCE, STEADY, BEN'S VOICE, CLEAR AS DAY, AND FOR THE first time in all the time I'd been alone and desperate, in all the time I'd dreamed of just a glimpse of him, I could see him. Not just in my mind's eye, but in reality with my eyes. He looked a little odd in a way I can't describe, besides the fact that he was obviously still twenty-one, as he'd been when he'd died, and that, well, he was there, while he was dead. But other than that, he looked much like he'd looked before they'd arrested him. He stepped through the attackers—most of whom were on fire, and bumping into each other, and came to me. *Steady, Luce, steady,* he said again, his voice sounding in my ears and in my head, all at once. *Don't you dare waste her sacrifice or let the boy die. Take the burners. Take her burners from her pocket. Throw out the one you expended cutting the valve. Take the rest of them. All of them. Put them in your waistband. There.*

I obeyed, blindly, even while burning with my free hand. At the bottom of Abigail's pocket was a small round, marble-like thing. I realized it was Fuse's bomb, and I took it. I wondered how it could be used, but it didn't matter. If all else failed, I could use it to blow myself and everyone around me to the kingdom that would never come for the likes of us. Then I remembered something else, and on impulse, looked inside her tunic, and

273

found a pocket, and in it a box much like the one they'd given me with the fragment of flag. I took that, and slipped it into my pocket. Then I took the other gadgets in the pocket, too, two of them being the ones that she'd used to break into the flyer. No, I didn't expect to need them, but how was I to know what I'd need? Truth was I *expected* to be dead in minutes.

All this was done at fast, very fast mode, and I burned around me every few seconds. I'd like to say my attackers were getting fewer, but they weren't.

That's it. Good boy. Now, burn your way that way. Yeah, watch your back too, but burn forward in that direction, as fast you can. That's where the boy is.

I did as he told me. No, I don't believe in ghosts. Don't ask me how he knew which way to go. Perhaps I did. Perhaps my subconscious guessed that the path more carefully defended was the one I should take. Who knows? Stranger things, Heaven and Earth and all that. I was not in shape to think. I was barely in shape to breathe.

All I could think was that I'd let Abigail die, and I'd have to answer to Sam for it. Losing his son had almost killed him. I knew the horror behind his stern facade. Losing his daughter—

Steady, Luce. Burn. Faster.

It was easy for him to say. He was just floating along with me. He didn't even seem to walk, and he could go through guards, and the least he could do was lend a hand and burn some of them.

I would if I could, Luce, come on. And he was beside me, and he was . . . There was a feeling he was pulling me along. No, I couldn't feel anything. There was no physical sensation of any kind, but it felt like he was willing me to move forward. Which was good, because I felt exhausted, suddenly, and that was weird, since I hadn't been all that tired till Abigail fell. Of course, the fast mode takes it out of you.

Eventually there were no more guards ahead, but there was a secure door, and Ben told me to blast it and I did, giving it both burners set on cut, at high speed, till it fell. It fell outward, because in this prison, I guess, they didn't want the prisoners to burn in case of a fire, unlike in Never-Never. This was normally a minimal security prison. I jumped out of the way, then into the opening.

And the cell we entered was normally a minimal security prison cell. Now it was—

I surprised myself by vomiting, suddenly and violently. Nat

was strapped to one of those tables they use in hospitals. He was naked. There were implements...

I'm not going to describe what they'd done to him. Suffice it to say it seemed they were going a long way to replicate what he'd done to Max's body as he killed the bastard who'd called himself my father.

For a moment, for a heart-stopping minute that felt like forever, I thought he was dead, and I felt that I would just collapse on top of him. Beyond the nausea, something must be very wrong with me, because my vision was swimming in and out of focus and I just wanted to sleep.

Behind you, Luce, burn. I turned and I burned, without thinking. Three guards fell.

Now, get the boy out of here, Ben said. *Out, both of you.*

I obeyed. Even though I thought Nat was dead, I obeyed. I set one of the burners on low range and cut through the straps that held him to the table, careful not to cut into Nat. Part of me wanted to cry and part of me wanted to vomit, and though the entire memory is hazy and confused, I think I did quite a bit of both before I had him free. And then he opened his eyes—those dark, brooding eyes—and looked at me. For just a moment, he looked terrified—a look I'd never thought to see in Nat's eyes—and then he smiled, a big smile with just a hint of tiredness. "Max," he said. His voice was the sort of croak people get when they can't scream anymore. "I knew you'd come for me." Then a flicker of regret crossed his face and he said, "I'm sorry. They took your ring." I looked, instinctively, to his ring finger. The ring was indeed gone. So was his finger. All of his fingers.

I choked, and wasn't sure if it was tears or vomit, or just the extreme tiredness I had to ignore.

Yes, you do have to ignore it. Forget it. Get the boy out. Now. You're at a lull while they get more guards in, but there will be more guards.

I tried to pick Nat up in a way that wouldn't hurt him further, decided there was no way to do that and threw him over my shoulder, in a fireman's carry. I'd like to say he weighed almost nothing, but that wasn't true. Instead, it felt like I was carrying all the sins of humanity, all the unredeemed evil of the world on my shoulder.

But Ben was calling me, and I had to run back, after him, keep up with him. Use all my speed, use all my strength.

Only it was hard. The floor was slick with blood. There was

blood all over me. My clothes were soaked in blood, and I didn't know whose—Nat's or that of the people I'd killed. I kept stumbling because I was so tired, and having to drag myself up, and stumbling again, and sliding, and managing to just keep from falling with Nat on me, and Nat was heavy and felt cold and I was afraid he was dead. And I had to keep going. I had to.

And Ben had started cursing, in a way he rarely did, unless he was really upset or scared, and he was calling me names which he'd never, ever done before.

I stumbled and held onto the wall, and wished I could die right then, and Ben came back and called me. *Come on you bastard, come on, you pampered princeling, show me you're a man for a change,* he said. *Show me you have a right to call yourself a man.*

And I pulled away, and I stumbled after his retreating form, and I cried because now even Ben had turned against me, I didn't have enough breath to protest.

I tried to run out the way I'd come, but Ben said no, and he led me another path, and I don't remember any of it, except I had to burn some people, and they looked really surprised. I took three grav wells. I ran down a hallway. There was what seemed to be a side door ahead of me, and it had a sign on it that said "Alarm will sound if opened." Alarms were ringing deafeningly already, so who cared? Ben told me to burn through the genlock holding it closed. I did. And then I stumbled against it, and it opened. And I was in a yard filled with flyers, the sort of flyers used for transport of clean linen and such for the prison.

I don't remember using Abigail's gadget, but I must have. I remember getting into the flyer, pulling my oxygen mask down, and still not being able to smell anything but shit and blood. I remember laying Nat down, on a pile of clean sheets and pulling a sheet over him, but I didn't cover his face, though I was sure he was dead. I remember locking the flyer door from inside, and bashing with the butt of my burner the "brains" of the machine, that allowed it to be remotely controlled.

I remember Ben driving me, pushing me, with words like whips, *That's right. Show me there is more in you than self-pity and selfishness. Show me you're good for something. Do it. No one cares if you hurt. No one cares. Get this thing in the air. Now, Luce. Stop whimpering like a little girl. They're coming for you. You must get it up now. Now.*

And then, as he was giving me coordinates to set, he yelled for me to hurry. He told me no one cared if I died, but I must get the boy somewhere where they could take care of him. I must save Nat, even if I died doing it. Then, as the flyer took off with a jolt, and pinned me against the seat, he said, *Take the link from your pocket. Now, Luce.*

Blindly, I did. Blindly I dialed the code he told me, though it made no sense. It was not a code I knew and it seemed to be an invalid code. The link rang for a long, long time, and then Sam's face appeared midair. His eyes widened.

Before he could talk, I said, in a thread of voice, "I think Nat is dead. Abigail—" but Ben was screaming, *No, no, no, tell him you'll be on the beach, in Liberte. Give him these coordinates*—Ben rattled off numbers—*Tell him you're landing there in . . . twenty minutes, according to programming. Tell him. Tell him he must have people to protect your landing. You'll be pursued. Tell him to have emergency vehicles and regen available. Tell him you have Nat with you. Tell him he's alive. I don't care what you think. Tell him. Tell him both the boy and you will need immediate first aid and regen. Yes, you too. TELL him, you useless bastard.*

I told him, because Ben was very loud and I wanted to sleep, and I couldn't go to sleep with him yelling like that. And then, with a vague idea that Sam too was yelling questions at me, but it all seemed very distant, I closed my eyes.

And I felt a touch of cool fingers on my forehead, a hand smoothing back my hair, which had come loose and was everywhere around my face—and I knew they were Ben's fingers, Ben's hand, Ben's touch. And I couldn't open my eyes, and I couldn't talk, but I thought at him that I was sorry to have disappointed him, sorry to have made him lose patience with me. Sorry to be what I was and no more. Never quite good enough.

His response, more in the mind than in the ears was very faint, fainter than a whisper, fainter than his touch, but it was completely different from what he'd said before, it was like what Ben would have said while he was alive, and it fell like distilled sweetness upon my bruised soul, *You didn't disappoint me, Luce. You never disappoint me. You did well. You were always the best of men. They'll take over now. Tell Sam I'll look after the girl.*

And then there was nothing.

When Angels Die

I DON'T KNOW HOW LONG I WAS OUT. I CAME AWAKE BECAUSE someone was pushing and pulling at me. No, several people. And it hurt like hell. And it wasn't even that it hurt and then it was gone, no. It was a series of repeated hurts, so that I would just be recovering from one, when the other would hit, sharp and sudden. And the lingering pain mounted too, in a crescendo.

I wanted to go back to where I'd been. It was dark and calm and cold, and there was the vague impression that Ben had been there too.

I tried to curse my tormentors, but all that came out was a childish whine. I remembered Ben telling me not to whine like a little girl and I bit my lower lip, hard.

Sam's voice spoke out of nowhere, "It's okay, Lucius. You'll just need some regen."

I wanted to tell him it was Nat that needed regen, if he wasn't dead, while poor little Abigail was beyond all regen, and it was all my fault, but I couldn't get the strength to speak, and my eyes were streaming tears and I couldn't stop them. Then someone else above me, a voice that seemed familiar but I didn't know from where said, "I'm going to give him Morpheus. There's no reason for him to be awake."

"Do it," Sam said, sounding very tired. "Now, what do we do about Nat?"

And I realized he didn't yet know his son was dead, and I took the miserable, unending certainty I'd failed all of them and caused Nat's and Abigail's death, with me into an awful sort of cloying darkness that clung to me on all sides.

After a long time, I realized there was something else. A ray of light, a distant feeling of warmth. I went towards it, though it was hard to say how, since I didn't seem to have a body. And Max was there and a shaggy golden dog. At the first sight, I thought it was Goldie, then I realized it was bigger. And then I recognized Bonnie, my dog, that I was sure my father had killed when I was ten, because it had growled at him. Max, who was all grown up and looked like the picture in Nat's cubicle in the lair, was throwing a stick. The dog was retrieving it. Neither of them paid any attention to me.

And then I remembered Nat didn't have any fingers, and wouldn't be able to draw or paint, and I'd have cried, only I didn't have any eyes, either.

Other dreams came. I'm sure they were dreams. My mother was holding me, and I wanted to tell her she wasn't really my mother, then I didn't, and she was laughing at me and telling me I was as much hers as I could be. And then there was my broomers' lair, all of them, even Hans, and we were setting off on our brooms, but then Javier told me I couldn't come because I'd forgotten to bring my body with me.

Dreams flickered into dreams, all with a feeling of loss, a feeling of something missing. Almost everyone in them was dead, and they couldn't seem to reach me, and I couldn't reach them. I couldn't go with them. And I didn't have any body.

And then there was Abigail, sitting right next to me. We were in the prison corridor, where she'd died, only there were only the two of us there, sitting side by side, with our backs to the wall, and she still had the hole on her chest, but it didn't seem to bother her, and she wasn't bleeding, though there was blood down her suit. There was blood all down my right arm, too, and most of my shoulder appeared to be just the bone, glaring white amid bits of fabric. And the rest of my body was covered in blood which soaked the fibers of the suit, and I realized, in shock, the blood was mine. I'd been hit, many times. Funny, I hadn't noticed. It hadn't hurt. Perhaps things never hurt when you're dead.

"When you promised your life, your fortune and your sacred

honor, what did you think it meant?" she said. "Did you think it was a game?"

And then I woke up. Only it was not immediately obvious.

I woke up to a sudden feeling that I had a body, and my body was lying on something soft, and covered by something soft, and I was looking up at something gold and warm and solid. And then the something resolved itself into wood planks, and I thought it was odd. It had been many years since anyone in my line had been buried. Or anyone in most of the world. Usually the dead were cremated. And what whim had caused them to bury me in a pine coffin?

Then I became aware it couldn't be a coffin. Or if it were, it was the world's largest coffin, because Nat was standing a few steps away from me where the wood formed a peak, so that he could stand straight, even though it was only a palm or so above my head while I was lying down. It was, I thought, a peaked roof, and I was lying right next to where it ended, against a short wall, also made of wood planks. And Nat looked fine—of course, all the dead in my dream looked fine, too—and he was smoking.

And then Goldie came out of nowhere and jumped on me.

"Goldie, stop that," Nat said, just as the dog started to lick my face. I managed to push Goldie away and said, "I didn't know Goldie was dead."

Nat lifted an eyebrow at me. "I don't think he is," he said. "Mind you, I'm not an expert on dead dogs, but I don't think they eat as much as this one does. Not to mention the other end of the business. Dead dogs don't do that either."

I looked him over. "But you're dead," I said. "And I'm dead."

He walked over and sat on the bed, still smoking, and looked intently at me, as though trying to determine how far I had taken leave of my senses. "Sorry to disappoint you, but I'm very much alive. You were a matter of more debate for a while. Something in your cells. I'd guess the stops they put in to prevent cloning. We don't have any techs in the small and exclusive group that caters to the Good Men. We can't recruit them for obvious reasons. So, our medtechs had no idea what to do with your gencode. It gave them a hell of a time with regen. That's why it took so long. They finally had to get hold of some notes or something that Simon St. Cyr had. Otherwise you'd be gone."

"So long?"

"Five months," he said. "I've been out here for almost six months."

"Out here?" I asked.

"A safe place. I'll explain later. We couldn't be where they might do a sweep and apprehend us. Well, it was fine while we were sealed in the regen tanks. A regen tank is much like the other, it's all in the ID tag you fake. But for recovery, we were sent away. My father has quite outrageously got your gen-signature on all sorts of contingency documents and has been doing what he pleases in your name. I'm very afraid you'll have to get rid of him when you go back, for abuse of power, you know..." It was clear he was trying to joke, but the joke didn't quite take off, probably because I'd started crying. I didn't realize I'd started, until I saw his expression crumple into a look of chagrin and concern. "Now, Luce, what the hell?"

"Abigail is dead."

"I know," he said, and his face was still grave but less panicky. He fished in one of his tunic pockets, then mopped at my face with a handkerchief that felt scratchy. "Before I was sent out, we had a ceremony in the family to lay her spirit to rest. We... sent her off in style. Thank you for bringing her flag, by the way. It meant the world to my mother."

"It was my fault," I said. "I should never have let her go."

"It was not your fault. They actually got the whole story out of you—everything that happened. Part of it was you kept talking—while you were out of your mind and they were trying to operate on you and pump enough blood into you that the small part you retained after leaking from all the wounds was enough to keep you alive—part that they gave you babble juice, so they had a report in case you died. And you probably prevented her being killed in the entry tunnel. Besides pulling a minor miracle in getting me out of there, when you were bleeding to death."

"Bleeding?"

"You really need to learn to speak in longer sentences, Luce." He expelled smoke, and smiled at me, a smile that was more willingness to smile, than the real thing. "People will think it was your brain that got blown away, instead of your shoulder."

"My shoulder..." I remembered the dream. "To the bone?"

"Yeah." He stubbed his cigarette out on a little round ashtray, then lit another. "Well, you managed to lose some of the bone, too, and a great part of your forearm. Let's say your arm was only attached to you by the force of your will power, a bit of skin and a shred of bone. You're a wonder for the ages. How did you manage to lift me at all? It would take two arms. And how did you manage to fire two burners and for that matter to break into a flyer and program it, with me over the good shoulder, with the other shoulder incapacitated?"

"I used my tentacles," I said, and closed my eyes, just in time to hear his sudden laughter, which made me feel inexplicably better. I lay there, not asleep, but with my eyes closed, listening to him draw in smoke and exhale it in measured cadences. Goldie nuzzled next to my neck. And I was warm, and nothing hurt, and I definitely had a body. I felt tired, but it was a pleasant tired, like one feels at the end of a long day of hard but enjoyable work.

And then Nat spoke, "Did you really..." He paused. "That is, what you kept telling Dad, when you were delirious, not to worry because Uncle Benjamin was looking after Abigail. And then when you... when they gave you stuff to make you talk, you seemed convinced that he'd been with you the whole time, and that in fact he directed the entire operation to get us out of there, after Abigail died."

I opened my eyes. He probably thought I was completely insane. I thought I was completely insane, but what else could I do? My nanny, long ago, used the quaintest phrase when getting me to confess something. She told me to tell the truth and shame the devil. I have no idea why the truth would shame the devil, but I also had no idea what else to say right then. So I said, "I saw him. I...I hallucinated his voice while I was in jail, but not like that. I mean, I sort of saw him, but in my head, you know? Not with my eyes. And I didn't hear him with ears, only with my mind." I shrugged. "I always thought it was just a coping mechanism, one of the reasons I'm only somewhat insane and not a raving lunatic." I paused. "But there, in the prison, I saw him. With my eyes. And heard him... And he was... very commanding."

"Yes," Nat said. He inhaled and exhaled, and it occurred to me that perhaps I was really dead, and perhaps I'd gotten better than I deserved, because I could imagine paradise like this, in this pine-roofed room that sloped in both directions from the center, lying on a soft bed, with Goldie by my side, watching Nat smoke.

Then I remembered I didn't want Goldie to be dead, and Nat said, "I saw the holo. I even understand all the justifications you gave and, by the way, you're the only man I know who, delirious, wounded and with babble juice, paused to give explanations and figure out rationalizations, while telling the events he's been asked to tell. Abigail was right. You're a one-man debate society." He smiled, which took the sting off the pronouncement, then he said, "It's just that none of that explains why my father is sure that Uncle Benjamin took over for you, when you passed out aboard that flyer. He says you told him I was dead and Abigail was dead, and then he heard my uncle, and my uncle told him to... well, all the things you said my uncle told you to say. My father swears it wasn't you. He swears it was Ben's voice, and that the last thing he said was that same message you were desperate to deliver to us—that he'd look after Abigail." He frowned a little. "I hope it is right. I mean, if there is life after death, and I'm not sure either way, but the chances are good that girl will need minding. She was very young and had a talent for getting in trouble."

I heard the grief in his voice, and all I could do was reach over and touch the hand that didn't hold the cigarette. His skin felt soft and was no longer nicotine stained. New fingers. He wasn't wearing his ring. I remembered he'd said they'd taken it. "I'm sorry I didn't recover Max's rin—your ring. You told me it was missing."

He gave me a fleeting smile. "I remember. I thought you were Max, you know? I had the foolish notion he'd come for me when I died, and I hoped that was it. And I was missing quite a lot more than my ring."

"Yes."

"I don't seem to have compromised much though. Oh, I don't have the resistance you Good Men have, apparently," he said. "But it didn't take much more than a few reshufflings of meeting places and operations to keep everyone safe. And I never told them about Dad or the others in your household." He made a face. "I might have told them you'd converted."

"That figures," I said. "But that's fine. Even if I can't ever go back to my position. When I said life, fortune and sacred honor, I meant it."

He nodded. "Oh, you'll go back. You need to. But for now, we're on the North American continent, at the edge of the repopulated areas. We're staying with a family of our people, and we are on special assignment while we recover and stay out of the way of the big boys and their planning."

I don't know how long I took to ask more. I think I fell asleep momentarily, but maybe I just rested and got my wind back. I felt incredibly tired, which made perfect sense in my mind, because in my mind it had only been minutes since I'd driven that flyer out of Coffers, with Nat lying on a pile of sheets, and—to my mind—as good as dead, while Ben called the shots. It was so vivid and so recent that it was a relief to open my eyes and see Nat sitting there, perfectly alive, and whole and hale, smoking his cigarette. Later, a medtech explained to me that the type of tiredness I felt the first week or so after I woke up was an effect of the regen itself. He threw in a lot of strange words, and I can't swear to you what it was all about, though I'm almost sure he mentioned prions. To this day I don't know if that was related or a side excursion of the type learned men throw in to remind us—or perhaps themselves—that they know what they're talking about. Whatever it was, the liver apparently has trouble process-ing the . . . by-products of regen. And in my case the whole thing was complicated by having to have special adjustments made to the regen. In any case, for a week and a bit I got a good idea of what it would be to be a hundred or so and senile, unable to hold a thought in my head for more than a few seconds and not having the wind to carry on a coherent conversation.

Nat was awfully patient with me. When I opened my eyes again, he was petting Goldie who, still cuddled next to me, had turned around to put his head on Nat's lap. He grinned at me and narrowed his eyes, causing wrinkles to form in the corners. "The special assignment, before you ask, is for us to canvass the farms and settlers around here and sound them out. Well, not really around here, because around here the Longs know every-thing there is to know and they can very well tell us how their neighbors lean, though we probably still should talk to them ourselves. People like to be asked, and not have their contribu-tion taken for granted."

I raised my eyebrows, but he must have known how low on breath I was because he didn't give me time to ask, and said, "War supplies. Well . . . food and clothing. And young people who want to volunteer, of course. We might even get some of those, though at a guess they'll want to form their own band. They're stubborn bastards out here. Have cut ties with most administrative structures and grow most of their raw materials and buy what they need to process them. You'd be amazed how independent one can be when one is willing to use suppressed inventions. Not that anyone is looking this far out, of course. They're also oddly tolerant." His eyes got a faraway look, as if he were thinking something through. "You can be and do whatever you want, provided you hold to decency in treatment of others."

"We're supposed to ask them for food and clothing?" I asked. It seemed daft. I remembered my own stores at the house, filled to bursting with so much stuff that even when we were under siege I could have a whole wardrobe made. And then, if it were needed we would have the stuff that never got thrown away in that house. Food, I supposed could be harder, but the three sea-cities in rebellion had plenty of ocean floor space. And while the improved algae which could give us everything a man needed to survive, and took a lot of processing before being palatable, they were edible and they were easy to grow.

Nat looked incredibly amused. I can't explain it, but he had a way of laughing at me when I said or showed I thought something foolish that should have rubbed me wrong, but didn't. It wasn't so much like he was laughing at me, but like he was laughing at my idea, with the complete understanding that he, too, might think the same thing if he had followed the same course of gathering knowledge. What I mean is that he didn't find my ideas stupid, and he didn't think I was deficient in understanding, that much was clear. What he thought was that it was very amusing how a rational person could be so wrong. "How big do you think this war will be, Luce?" he asked.

I said, "Well, three seacities against the rest. We don't have a chance, do we?"

He grinned. "It's not that bad. Yeah, three seacities, as far as territorial areas go, and we're sure now that Simon will throw in with us. It was touch and go for a while. Simon is . . . slippery. He can't help it. It has saved his life for too long." He stubbed his cigarette and lit another. "The Sans Culottes have a different program, you know. Different beliefs. And I suspect eventually, after the revolution and the war, there will be a fight between our two sides. Maybe not in our lifetime, but it's inevitable. It's happened in the past, many times, under many different names." He stubbed his cigarette and lit another one. At least he wasn't lighting them one from the end of the other, although I wasn't sure it was that much different. "But the thing is that the administrative areas aren't all that important. This will be a war not over territory but over ideas. There are many factions that have been against the rule of the Good Men for a long time. There are... Well, people like us and the Sans Culottes, and then are more... traditional religions. We're not a traditional religion, you know that, right?"

I blinked at him. "I wasn't raised with much of any religion, so— All you asked me as if I believed in the... principles, and that I can believe in. I always felt as though there was... someone, but I won't guess who or what."

He grinned. "Well, we're not. We don't even require that you believe in God, just that you believe in the principles we hold holy. And you can believe in another religion at the same time. Within our ranks there are people like myself and my parents who believe in God and are almost absolutely convinced there is a life after death. There are people who not only believe in life after death, but who think they can describe to you the color shoes you'll need to walk on the clouds. Those are the ones that tend to believe in the prophecy that George Washington will come back, the chosen one, in some manifestation which will precipitate the revolution and lead us all back to the land of plenty. And there's a lot of people who don't believe in God but believe in the principles, and believe, once the principles are set in motion the outcome is as inevitable as if God had preordained it. We rub along together very tolerably, as we did, if you believe the texts, in the old USA before it fell. We hold strong opinions on freedom of belief, freedom of expression, the right to self-defense, right to private property and others. All coming from the first principles we swear to. If you consider that we have a concept of sin, a sin is to violate one of those, unless of course it is absolutely needed for survival. But other than that, we really don't have an idea of sin. And we withhold opinions on matters such as who should sleep with whom, what type of underwear one should wear, how many children are a proper number, the use of intoxicating substances, the use of money and most dietary rules."

"Most?"

He nodded. "I think so. Never asked, but I'm fairly sure cannibalism is frowned upon. It's not good for you, and it would upset my mother, which is as close to a concept of sin as I was raised with."

It occurred to me I was being amused. Or that he was trying to amuse me. "But Nat, will it be war? Will it be war for sure?"

"Oh, yes. Inevitable. There have already been a few...dustups, but for now things are very tightly balanced and our people are trying to hold the lid on it. Not too much provocation, not too much push. We're letting them think there are very few of us, perhaps just a bunch of broomers—the dustups have all been with broomers so far—and that we'll be easy to put down and they don't need to be in a hurry to do it. It might be the only thing keeping the full war from erupting. And meanwhile we're stocking madly and making an inventory of everything and everyone we can count on. Because as soon as the war starts, there will be revolutions in some seacities. Other places, like most of the administrative territories, will go into full rebellion. Or declare themselves independent. Part of it is to give the Good Men so many places to scratch that they won't have hands to cover them all."

I looked balefully at him. "I suppose I'm no longer a Good Man?" I wasn't sure if this was good or bad. Ben's dig about pampered princelings still hurt. Even if Ben had been no more than a figment of my imagination. Or had he been more? Look, I don't claim to know what Man is made of. I don't claim to know what comes next. I just found no Ben where Ben used to be, and figment of my mind or not, I was going to miss his accustomed presence. Perhaps I didn't need him anymore—whether I'd created him or not, to begin with.

He shrugged. "I think you are. I think technically the seacity is still yours. I confess I only know what's happening there when I come across a holo report, and in this area that's nowhere near every day. But I assume if there is something important, Mom or one of the others will tell me. Last I heard, the entire family was trying to convince James he's too young to join officially. I believe Mom has him analyzing semantic data or other make-work, just to keep him quiet." He frowned at his cigarette as if it had offended him personally. "I think once it comes to shooting we're going to have a heck of a time holding the line at sixteen years of age. It seems to be part of the species that very young men want to fight, and I don't know how to prevent them. I don't think anyone does. I've told my father to start teaching the brat, or he'll go in half-prepared and get himself killed." He must have read my expression because he sighed. "I'm sorry. I forgot it is still very recent to you. I miss Abigail. I probably will always miss her and I will probably always mourn her, but it's been four months and the wound is no longer raw. I . . . None of us holds it against you, in any way. We all knew her all too well.

"Look, Luce, they didn't send us out just on rest and recreation. Yes, I'm sure my father pulled some strings to get us sent here, instead of a lot less comfortable places. It's a place we often send our wounded, and the Longs have their lives so arranged they'll never be suspected or looked at askance, so we're safe here. For one, they have a hundred and fifty acres and are in the middle of it, where they can control who even comes near. And don't be deceived by the log cabin and the quilt. Yeah, they're real, and they were made of local materials, but the trees were cut down by robots, and the cotton on the quilt is spun by robots too. They're an odd mix of ancient and ultra modern, more modern than the Good Men have allowed us to have. And they are very kind to us, and they gave the two of us the entire attic," He pointed with a cigarette. "My bed is on the other side, the bathroom, with fresher and water is there, desks over there, with readers and writers and probably holo viewers, though I haven't looked for those. There is a curtain in between our sides of the room, and if you need help getting up even when it is closed feel free to holler. I don't think you'll be much use to anyone, including yourself, for about a week or two. Don't look outraged. I went through the same when I first came here, and let me tell you, having a motherly stranger—because Mrs. Long is motherly and she was then a complete stranger to me—help you to the bathroom is something else again.

"Anyway, after you're better I'd like you to join me in my sweeps, which I'll be doing and will resume when you can come with me. I've been doing them alone, on my broom, flying out to the newly resettled areas, in the middle of the forest, talking to the people I find, sounding them out, then back a few days later, and my dad hates it like poison, because anything could happen to me. Most of the people out here are good people and most of them are decent, but remember when I told you my religion didn't believe in human perfection? Yeah, not even here. So there have been a couple of sticky situations. And that's not counting what nature can throw at you out here. So...You're needed and we'll put you to work as soon as you're able. For now your job is to rest, eat—please, they feed me about ten times what I can eat, and I could use someone to take some of the load off me; I'll never lose the weight I'm putting on—and become yourself again. As soon as you can, we have work to do."

TO WAR, TO WAR

Paradise Regained

FOR THE NEXT WEEK AND A HALF I CAME AS CLOSE TO MY IDEA
of paradise as I'm ever likely to be. I don't know about you or
anyone else, but when I die I'm going to a farm in a space cut
out of a pine forest. There will be chickens and pigs and cows,
unruly kids and, I'm afraid, Nat and Goldie too.

There will be Mrs. Mary Long too, as sweet a woman as I'd
ever met. Perhaps not sweeter than my mother, but less reserved.
Where my mother could and did withdraw into her grand dame
persona and put even me at a distance, Mrs. Long never did. And
her husband, and her whole warm, tolerant family.

I first met her that day when Nat was done telling me how
important our mission was, because she came up the stairs. Nat
shut up when he heard her steps on the stairs, but stubbed his
cigarette and jumped up from the bed, when she said "knock
knock" from the door, which was open. At first I had the impression he'd got up so she didn't find him sitting on my bed, because
perhaps she'd find it improper.

Then I realized he'd got up to help her, because I heard her
say, "Why, thank you, Nat."

Nat came into the room carrying a tray, which he set on a
small table that seemed to be just behind my bed. I could see
it by turning.

"It's good to see you awake," the lady said. She was plump, though not markedly overweight, probably a head and a half shorter than Nat, probably on the low side of fifty, with reddish hair, a lot of freckles and a ready smile. "I heard talking and since Nat doesn't usually talk to himself I thought you might be awake and thought I'd bring you something light. The med tech said we were supposed to feed you as much as you'll eat, so I'll bring food up a lot. Don't worry if you don't feel like eating it all, we have pigs." Then she seemed to realize we'd never even been introduced and extended her hand to me. "I'm Mary Long, by the way, and of course I know you're Patrician Keeva."

This was not something I was about to let go. "Not in the least," I said. "I'm Lucius. I mean, you can call me *Mr. Keeva* if you insist, I don't think I'll keep the title much longer, but if you call Nat *Nat* and me *Mr. Keeva* I'm going to feel hurt and left out."

She smiled and a dimple appeared. "Well, then. We can't have that. Would probably delay your recovery. My husband will come up sometime to introduce himself." She fussed with my bed clothes and adjusted my pillow. "If you want to sit up to eat, there are more pillows there, inside the window seat. Nat can fetch them."

I wanted to say I wasn't exactly an invalid but I suspected if I tried to sit on my own I'd do something humiliating like pass out, so I just smiled and thanked her. Nat must have suspected my embarrassment because he said, "Well, now, he can't very well sit up as such. He'd ding his head on the ceiling."

She smiled. "He probably would. We're terrible hosts, aren't we? But this was the only quiet guest room we had. The others are near the kids' rooms. Mind you, I'm not saying you won't get them all up here, sooner than later. Well, all except Jane, who is sixteen and thinks she's too big for hero worship. But the others have heard. And . . . well . . ." She blushed. "They're boys, now. And we've all seen the holo, of course. And the boys especially . . . Well, you know what boys are like with heroes. So, if they get too bothersome, just have Nat swat them and send them back down the stairs where they belong. But here is the only place away enough they won't be on you all day long."

Nat got the pillows and they arranged me half-sitting, and really, I thought Mrs. Long was going to kiss me on the forehead. The pillows smelled of herbs. Weirdly, as embarrassed as I was, I didn't feel uncomfortable, not as such. Of course, I did have a few questions, but I was reserving those for when I was alone with Nat.

Mrs. Long's idea of a light snack consisted of a good half loaf of bread, butter and something that Nat said was apple butter—it did taste like apples, at any rate—a pear sliced in neat quarters, as though she were afraid I'd not have the strength to bite into the whole thing, and a glass of milk. Fortunately I discovered I was ravenously hungry just smelling it, hungry enough to fight tiredness, and was trying to spread the apple butter stuff on a slice of bread, with marked lack of success due to my half-reclined posture, until Nat came over. "Here's an idea," he said. "Assembly line. I assemble the food, you convey it to face."

Mrs. Long smiled and said, "I'll leave you gentlemen then. If you need anything, don't forget to holler. Dinner will be ready in an hour and a bit. Will you be coming down, Nat, or should I send up a tray for two?"

I opened my mouth to tell them I could eat alone, but Nat didn't have his mouth full of bread and apple butter, and said, "A tray for two would be nice, Mrs. Long. I have to make sure he doesn't fall asleep and drown in the soup or something."

She was gone before I could protest. And when I managed, "Drown in the soup, really!" after she'd left, Nat just smiled and said, "You probably would, you know? You keep nodding off. I don't think you're even aware of it. And she'll bring you enough soup to drown in."

He'd buttered or apple-buttered all the slices of bread and now stepped away and lit a cigarette. I talked to his back, "Holo? What holo did they see?"

He turned around and did his best to show me two empty hands, in a gesture of non-aggression. It wasn't quite right because a hand was holding a cigarette, but I'd give him A for effort. "Not my fault," he said. "Security holo. I told them you wouldn't like it, but Mother said..." He trailed off. "Well, never mind, but the thing is, she thought it would be good... well... for your image, and so she passed off copies into the auxiliary core with you know, do not for the love of heaven copy and distribute. I don't think there's a single Usaian household that doesn't have at least a copy by now, and I'm sure a lot of other people do too."

"Mother said?"

"I knew you wouldn't let that go. You really have a rare ability to fasten on the one thing of all I most don't want you to pay attention to." He looked suddenly grave. "Look, you're not a child, and you're not stupid. You know that part of our work is turning people against the Good Men. We just don't want you to get swallowed up in it, should...well, when things get ugly, all right? We want people to know you're not like them and you've fought against them. Sorry if that meant violating your privacy a little, but we want it imprinted on the public consciousness, that all the bastards might deserve to die, except Lucius Keeva. Do you understand?"

I sighed. "I understand. I don't have to like it, do I?"

He gave one of his cough-chuckles. "I don't particularly like it. Remember, in this hero-holo, I got to play a slab of meat thrown over your shoulder, and the parts of me that were recognizably human aren't parts I normally wish to flash in front of all the Daughters of the Revolution. But I do see the need for it."

I was mulling over everything he said, while I ate and drank my milk. I didn't remember drinking milk straight since I was about five, but this tasted good. All of it tasted good, making me feel, once more, I'd got somewhere beyond my normal state of life. "Are you afraid of new turmoils?" I said.

He shrugged. "Luce, I'm not a strategist. I'm barely a good underling with enough executive capacity to know how to minimally improve on or change orders. My father is the genius. But I think that it's quite possible we're trying to create turmoils. There is a great deal of fear of biogen and of the Mules. Strangely, the Good Men have used that fear to keep themselves in power. I think it might be related to their real loathing for their congeners who— Never mind. You don't want my own explanations and rationalizations. Suffice it to say that it's much easier to manipulate people based on their fears and their hatreds than on their reason and their desire for liberty. The Good Men have kept the Earth in miserable subjugation, but it's been a predictable subjugation, where nothing much changes and where there's a path to doing pretty well for yourself and your children, given a willingness to jump through hoops and some conformism. But for most people—unless they were at the wrong end of one of the engineered plagues or famines—it's been a pretty comfortable life. Comfortable people don't rebel."

He got up, lit a cigarette and started pacing. I'd come to

know Nat well enough to realize when he paced he was trying to reach some conclusion in his mind, trying to make sense of something. I started nibbling on the pear while he spoke. "It's always been more uncomfortable for people like us, of course," and then making it clear he wasn't talking about just Usaians. "But then it's always been more uncomfortable for people like us, except maybe in ancient Greece and places like that, though even there I wonder." He paused. "And not just people like us in the sense that..." He floundered. I realized that Nat simply didn't like to speak of private matters, not even to people he trusted. I also realized he trusted me, and felt a sudden warm glow about it. "In the sense that we are attracted to the same gender, and most people aren't. I mean the regime of the Good Men, like most dictatorial regimes that rely—they have to—on controlled scarcity and controlled conformity, are hell for all the outliers the...the people who don't quite fit in: eccentrics, oddities, people who think differently, people who are smarter or dumber than the rest.

"What has always puzzled me about history is that all those people, yeah, and people like us too, seem to support the tyrannies. Every tyranny that comes along.

"I think it's because, at heart, we want to belong. All humans, I mean. And we oddlings think that in a dictatorship we'll have to belong. People will be forced to accept us. But the thing is that any regime where power is centralized is a regime where conformity is enforced, any dictatorship, any government strong enough to enforce anything is a disaster for us. For all the odd people. We can be silenced, put out of the way, killed. That is always there, hanging over us. On the other hand, I think it is part of the attraction of dictatorships for...well...for people who are normal enough to fit into the designation of average."

I almost choked on my bit of pear. I've said I am by nature paranoid, right? Not that paranoid. "Nat! That's not true. Your father...I'm sure your father...I mean, he knew about Ben and me, and I don't think he ever felt we should be put to death. And as for—"

"Oh, please. My father is no more average than we are, though his oddity is of a different kind. But I didn't mean that average people want to kill those people they personally know who are... a little different. No. Most people will have some exception of the sort that goes *he's a little funny, but he's one of ours.* But that's the thing, see, humans are by nature tribal. Blame what we come from, apes who, like you, had a tendency to overthink everything—" He gave me a challenging look, but I let it pass and he went on. "Awful materials to make us out of, and one wonders what God was thinking, only of course, perhaps it was the best choice, awful though it was. These are tribal creatures, creatures of the band. And we are too. And that means that anyone who sticks out too far hurts tribe cohesion and, unless linked to us pretty closely, arouses the need to stop them. I think the Good Men, not just by killing people like us and... other eccentrics, because they don't kill enough of us to make a difference, but by forcing us to go underground and not show our strangeness, contribute to most people feeling safer, feeling better. That's not the way to get a revolution going. But showing the Good Men are the very thing they taught everyone to hate will get the revol— Luce, for the love of heaven!"

I thought he'd gone crazy, then I realized, somehow, I had milk all over my face and he was wiping at it with a napkin that had been in the tray. I'd fallen against the milk, knocking the glass over, then landing my face in it. Without waking.

"Not drown in the soup," he said. "You were about to drown in the milk." Then, more contritely. "I'm sorry. I've been boring you into sleep."

"No, no," I said. "I'm just exhausted."

"I know you are," he said, still sounding guilty. He took the tray from my lap. "I'll take this down, you rest."

I think over the next week and a half that command was the thing I most heard from Nat, from Mrs. Long and from Mr. Long. I didn't hear it from the kids, but that was only because none of the boys seemed to be able to speak in front of me. I'd wake up and they'd be gathered in a semicircle, staring at me as though I were a strange and wondrous object, and when I talked to them, I got open mouthed blank-eyed stares. Jane on the other hand, a more redheaded version of her mother and very pretty, would blush redder than her hair and more often than not hand me a cookie or a slice of cake—at a guess to keep me from talking to her.

But most of the time Nat and I were left to our own devices. Even Goldie deserted us, disappearing in the morning, and coming back at sunset, streaming mud or soaked in water or, on one occasion, covered in leaves and dirt. Nat would send him back down the stairs with "Not in that state, sir" then yell for one of the boys to wash him and dry him. Once, he'd explained to me, "He goes with the boys. Fishing or hunting or whatever they're doing in late summer. He probably plays a hound of great valor or something like that in the kids' games. And probably a pony for the younger ones." And to what must have been my alarmed expression at the idea that the kids might abuse Goldie, he'd smiled. "Oh, I've never seen him this happy. I think we've been boring that dog, Luce."

I don't exactly know what Nat did during that time. I knew he was afraid to leave me alone, and much as I'd have liked to tell him he was wrong, the few times I'd tried to get up on my own in the first few days didn't end well. Sometimes when I woke up from dozing, I found him using a reader. And one time, when he sat on my bed, smoking, his fingers were streaked with red and dark brown and green. In the confusion of trailing sleep, I'd reached for his fingers and made some sound of dismay, because I think I imagined he'd hurt himself. How that explained the green, I don't know.

But he'd pulled his fingers out of my reach, looked at them and laughed. "Pastel, Lucius. Not some weird kind of green, alien blood. I was by the window, trying to get the landscape. A forlorn task. Strangely, the new fingers have to learn from scratch. Odd, isn't it? The mind knows, but the body has to learn."

That too was the theme of my second week in paradise. As I started being able to get on my feet without passing out from tiredness, I found that my left arm needed to be taught every-thing that it had known before. It did not move as precisely as it had. It was like my arm and my fingers had minds of their own. And yet, Nat remained incredibly patient. Even when I was fully walking and went downstairs, and strolled—slowly and in a measured way—around the farmyard, he accompanied me, like a shadow.

Towards the end of the second week, stung by my continued weakness, my inability to do the simplest things, annoyed at him for seeing it when I didn't want to be a pampered princeling and I wanted to stand on my own two feet, I turned on him and told him a lot of foolish things, including, "You don't have to shadow me. You're not my nanny. And, damn you, I don't want your gratitude."

He'd looked shocked for a moment, I think not so much by what I'd said as by my rudeness. Nat was one of those people whom rudeness would always shock. He could understand violence and hatred, but not wanton nastiness in social intercourse. But once the shock passed, amusement lit up his dark eyes, and his lips tilted upward the slightest bit. "I'm not doing anything out of gratitude, Luce. If I were, I'd be kicking you in the shins when no one was looking. I don't like being beholden. I don't like doing things because I have to. I'm doing what I am because, annoying though you are, I'd feel bad if you fell and broke your head. I have a strong feeling that I'd feel saddened by it, and I hate to feel sad." And thus, leaving me without any retort, he'd continued shadowing me.

By the third week I was fine, but he postponed our starting our work amid the locals with some mumbled excuse. In time I came to understand it was because he too needed some time to take a deep, relieved breath, in this case his relief coming from the fact that I was finally recovered and would not be impaired my whole life—something he didn't tell me he and the medtechs feared but apparently they had.

That week was spent by him—in cabal with the Longs' irredeemable offspring—in teaching me to fish, making me help to feed the chickens and muck out the pigs, picking of wild berries for preserving, and finally, taking me hunting.

"It's a favor we do them," Nat explained of the hunting. "And not just because it gets more meat in storage for the winter, but because deer run rampant around here and are a problem with the crops. Deer and wild pigs. Bear and wolves haven't made it back, nearly as much. There were fewer of them, and they were more affected by the scarcity and the plagues-gone-wrong unleashed at the end of the twenty-first. So the pigs are the biggest predators—descended from what used to be farm pigs, but you'd never know it. And the deer are everywhere and by themselves are holding back the regreening of the continent."

The regreening didn't even surprise me or arouse my curiosity, until Nat and I did start on our mission for the cause, flying through primeval-looking forests, to find isolated farm families and sound them out on their opinions. Turned out we were a perfect team. Nat, carefully raised by a good and pious family, could put on his expression of concern, his best manners, and somehow look five inches shorter and five years younger and thoroughly inoffensive, even when asking people the most outrageously personal questions about their beliefs. And I could loom beside him, silent and vaguely threatening by reason of bulk alone, reminding them that anything they attempted against him wouldn't end well.

I'd like to say my services in protecting him were needed very often, but the fact was that most of people we met were decent and kind and, even if most were not quite as materially well off as the Longs, they were good people. They received us with open arms, and talked with the free flowing talk of people who hadn't seen strangers in a good long while and were starving for news of the outside world. And if some of them suspected we were a couple—some seemed to in the way they linked our destinies, by asking if we meant to clear a farm, the implication being we'd do it together—very few even raised eyebrows, much less saying anything ruder. And we met a few of our kind, too, none of whom seemed more or less accepted than anyone else around them. Or better or worse. In fact, the two times we got in serious trouble, one was when some older farmer took it into his head we were a danger to his daughter, and another when one of two men, more or less clearly a couple— Never mind. The situations never went beyond what could be managed by my pulling a burner and covering our retreat. There was never fire actually exchanged, and we stayed away from those two farms in the future.

More often, we came home with jars of jam and invitations to us and the Longs to come to the next... whatever the popular local entertainment was, most of it self-staged, the Fall Dance, the Theater Performance, the Philosophical Debate. Yes, those were all more or less at the same level of providing amusement for the masses, which probably is a good snapshot of how isolated and bored these people were, even with holo recordings and other modern facilities. Because of the controls put on long distance communications, all the holo and general broadcast stations were where the transmission could be controlled by censors. There were none close enough to echo out here. Most broadcast didn't reach this far, and most of them were starving for novelty. I attributed their strange hospitality to that.

"Partly," Nat said. "But partly because the distance between farms encourages minding your own business, and the type of people who do well out here are...remember the outliers I talked about? People who don't feel quite at home in society. Stands to reason. People don't go out and start life again in what could be a dangerous environment unless they are truly unhappy where they are. So they tend to leave each other alone. But we are social animals, and so they have to socialize. The result is strict rules about hospitality and, well, a broad tolerance for those who are different, even the very different. Before you came, I met this old guy who lives with three pigs. All the pigs were a feral liter, raised from piglets. The weird thing was not that he didn't eat them, or that he talked to them. No, the weird thing is that he thought they talked back. Worse, he seemed convinced they were related to him. One of the shoats wore an apron...But all his neighbors treated him and spoke of him as if he were only a little funny."

As for the mission, it prospered. Most of the people this far out were either Usaians or readily willing to sympathize with the cause of getting rid of the Good Men. Most of them were willing to pledge entire cellar-fulls of preserved berries and bushels of dried deer meat to providing for the eventual troops. Not that this was universal. What Nat had said about oddities living around here, and the oddest ones were the ones who were vehement supporters of the Good Men and of genetic purity—whatever that might mean—and of order and stability.

This was why Nat was always the one to talk first. He'd sound people out by degrees, always taking the next conversational step in a way that he could backtrack from and deny everything. I can honestly say not a single person of those who disagreed with us had any idea that he didn't agree with them as well.

"This is all going to erupt, too, isn't it? When the fight becomes open?" I said.

"I think so," he said. "Tolerance and laissez-faire have limits and people tend to get swept up in larger movements, and I think our war will set fire to the entire world. There will be war in these woods, in these farms. There will be people hanged and farms set ablaze. There was in the first revolution and there will be again. Human nature doesn't change that much."

And when I looked as I felt—like I was bringing death to

paradise—he said, "Don't worry, Luce. It will be better when it's done. Not perfect, but for most people it will be better."

And on the way back home, sitting in a grove of some tree that was not pine—the only tree I knew on sight—sharing a lunch of cheese and walnuts, I'd asked him, "How come these massive trees? If history is right, even three hundred years ago nothing grew here, because of the biophage bacteria. But these look like they've been here for millennia. Does history lie or—"

"Nah," he cut off a piece of cheese with his knife. He didn't smoke when we were in the middle of the forest, probably afraid of what a careless ash-flick might do, but he always looked like he wanted to, like his hands were restless and he didn't know what to do with them. "It's just that in the USA, before the fall, they'd developed faster-growing trees: for paper, for furniture, even for landscaping. For some reason those seeds proved hardier than the natural ones. When the bacteria consumed themselves and vegetation could return, it came back very fast. I suspect in twenty years the problem will not be allowing the regreening to occur, but keeping the trees in check enough for fields to be planted and for humans to establish some sort of traffic between populated areas." Then he'd laughed. "But I suspect the seacities can use the wood, and making wood furniture a fad beyond the richest households shouldn't be all that difficult either."

I often remember that lunch—just the two of us under the trees, hours of broom-flight in each direction from any human—as one of the more perfect moments of my life. And even though the world was going to hell in our absence, for the three months I helped Nat scout resources in the northern North American continent I was happy as I'd never been before, not even when I was young and thought I lived a charmed life.

It couldn't last. I think I knew it even then. I knew that the world would intrude, probably in painful ways, soon enough. Knowing it put an extra golden glow on those days. We weren't together all the time. For one, young volunteers poured into the farm, camping at the edge, and Nat often spent mornings trying to teach them the arts of war, whatever those were. But most afternoons we were together and when we were "home," as we'd taken to referring to the Longs' place, we helped with farm chores, and I think one of the proudest moments of my life was when Mr. Long looked up, seeing me help load one of the servo-wagons to take corn back to the barn for storage for winter, and said, "You'd not make a half-bad farmer, son." Weird to be so proud of that praise. And odd to be so stung by the rumination that followed, "Of course, even with robots, farming is not something you want to do alone. Else you become like that good old boy Rogers, him who talks to his pigs."

But the sense that the golden time was coming to an end rushed in on me with greater speed the closer we got to winter. Perhaps it was the chill in the air, the fact that most of the trees-that-weren't-pines were standing naked, looking vaguely forlorn and like they were holding their arms up for mercy to the sky. Or perhaps it was the sense that something this good couldn't last.

Before I knew anything was wrong, or precisely what might be wrong, I noticed that Nat sometimes looked worried when he read something in his portable holo reader. Since this usually happened after a trip to a relatively large settlement, I asked him if those were news gems, and he'd tell me no. But he never told me what they were. It was weeks before I found out that they were news gems of a sort, but the kind that was passed amid Usaians and which had internal news of our organization, which is to say news of my seacity which was now, openly, under our control.

But Nat didn't tell me, and those last two weeks, the most exciting thing going on in my life—despite all my misgivings—was our preparation of the Fall Festival, the big self-made entertainment in our area, hosted by the Longs in one of their outlying barns. This year, possibly at the suggestion of Nat, who knew how much I'd enjoyed reading the plays, it was to be a staging of *Midsummer Night's Dream* by the ancient Shakespeare, adapted and changed to Glaish, of course, but still much the same play, and not a bad one to welcome the shorter days and colder nights we knew were coming, nor the storm of blood and pain most people didn't know yet loomed over them.

Nat's and my part in the entertainment consisted of—helped by the Longs' brood, who were to be rewarded by being allowed to pad the numbers of forest fairies in the play—helping to clean the cavernous empty barn, setting out the stored benches for people to sit in and devising the decoration and lighting of the stage. Nat painted scenery too, for the first time giving me a glimpse of his ability to suggest an entire forest, or a brilliant night sky with a few old boards, a few dabs of paint and a few lines drawn just right. Goldie, of course, helped both our efforts and the play, the night it was staged, by getting in everyone's way, licking faces at the most inopportune moment, and, once, getting tangled in an array of lights we'd just put up by chasing some small creature—a rat or a squirrel—behind the stage. It had all ended with Goldie covered in lights and looking offended in his dignity because we couldn't stop laughing at him.

Then, on the night, everything went well until the last act. Then, as Hippolyta and Theseus wed in brilliant if makeshift grandeur upon the stage, and Nat and I sat side by side on a bench, trying to ignore that the old man and his pigs were sitting behind us and keeping up a lively conversation, even if we could only hear one side of it, someone came into the auditorium.

I wasn't aware of it. We were laughing at the fact that the players—Jane being Hippolyta—were doing their best to ignore Goldie even while he put his paws on their shoulders and tried to lick their faces. Someone leaned over Nat and said something.

His laughter stopped abruptly, and he turned. The person leaning over him was in full broomer attire and the first thing I thought was that she looked too old to be a broomer. Not that she looked... Well, she was slim, and clearly in good shape, but that close it was impossible not to notice that her face looked weathered and bore upon it the marks of living far more than twenty-some years, or even thirty. Her hair might have had some white in it, but that was impossible to tell, because it was the exact same color as Nat's. And that was the second thing that hit me—how much she looked like Nat.

Even before Nat turned and said, "Now? Mother, what is so urgent?"

Revolution

WE'D FOUND OUT WHAT WAS SO URGENT MOMENTS LATER, AROUND
the Longs' table. And none of us were laughing. Though Nat was
smoking for the first time outside our bedroom upstairs. And
even his mother's reproaching look as he lit a cigarette from the
end of the other didn't make him slow down. Instead he smoked
nonstop and paused only to ask questions, "What do you mean
the twelve have taken charge and Father is in jail? Father is one
of the twelve."

It is not right to say that Nat's mother was a lot like him only
a lot more polite and calmer. Nat himself was almost always polite
and, I'd found in these months, infinitely calm and patient, even
in the face of that tantrum I threw over my own weakness but
aimed at him as though it were his fault.

It is right to say though that Nat could lose his calm suddenly
and startlingly and that his mother seemed to become calmer
and more patient as he did. Perhaps because she knew her son
and acted as a counterweight to him.

"Yes, but, Nat, you see, since your sister . . . That is, there have
always been two factions in the twelve. Those who believe that
the principles must be applied even when they work against us,
and those who feel we must ignore the principles until . . . until we
restore our country, and only then applied, and that the principles

307

won't come into being unless they're imposed . . . dictatorially from above. And when Abigail . . . Well . . . Mark Mirable was elected in her place and—"

She paused while Nat gave vent to his feelings about this person, in language I'd never heard him use. Like Ben, he wasn't usually even insulting unless the circumstances were intense, and I'd never heard him be profane. Mrs. Long, who'd come in with us, insisting it was her duty as hostess to forego the post-entertainment party for the sake of making us coffee and serving us cookies while we talked, had looked at Nat openmouthed, proving it wasn't just my personal knowledge of him that was insufficient. Betsy Remy though, didn't turn a hair, just waited till he slowed down and started repeating himself and said, "Just so, Nat. And you see, he thinks that with the war started, it's important to make sure the loyalty of everyone in Olympus is to the right people."

"That again?" I said, and was rewarded with an even look from Nat's mom and the slightest of smiles. Unlike Nat, who inherited his dark eyes from his father's side, she had blue-grey eyes which gave an impression of immense calm. "Quite so, Lucius," she said. And the way she pronounced my name and looked at me made me feel like she'd been in my life since I was very small. Which I suppose she had been. At least, I had vague memories of her in the background of my life since I'd known Ben or maybe before. But she made me feel as if I'd never been sent away, as if the years in prison had never happened. "And I find it just as tiresome as you two do— No, Nat, don't tell me how much more than tiresome you find it. I've been telling you since you were two that swear words are not an extension of your vocabulary but a show that you've run out of vocabulary, and while in some circumstances one can't help it, really, enough is enough." Nat shut up, looking like a little boy put in his place. In any other circumstances it would have made me laugh. "But your father opposed this nonsense. He would. He said we'd start witch hunts and run people out of the island or confiscate their property and destroy their livelihood over their private opinions when hell froze over. And so they put him in jail, accused of sympathizing with the dissenters, and there will be a People's Trial in two days, and I must tell you that People's Trials were never anything our people did, but I didn't tell them so, or they'd put me in alongside him, and I couldn't let that happen because I had to come and tell you. You must come back and you must stop all that nonsense."

"Mother," Nat said. "Other than springing Father out of jail and bringing him here, I don't see what you think we could do."

"Your father and James," she said, and looked flustered. "Well, you know your brother, Nat. We couldn't stop him. Not—"

"I know," Nat said, looking worried. "I know. But what do you expect us to do, other than springing them out? Damn it, Mother, we're not magicians."

She looked pained at his swearing and folded her hands on the table in front of her. "I have a plan," she said. "But it will require the Good Man— That is, Lucius, if you—"

"Anything I can do, of course," I said. "Though I have no idea what that would be."

"No. But I will explain. And at any rate, I've been telling Sam for a month it's time you boys came back. We need you, no matter how much wonderful work you're doing out here. And I know it's wonderful. I've read the reports. But we need you at home, now. Nat, your regiment is fully in the war. And Lucius, we need your authority in place."

Impossible not to say yes. Impossible not to go along with her plan, even when it turned out we needed to get some of our young volunteers, registered and trained in the last few weeks, a raw body of teenage boys with more willingness than ability to fight to come with us, to face down the *revolutionary guard* who had taken over my palace and was running roughshod over the rights of those people whom I couldn't help but feel were mine to defend.

"Jan and Martha and some of Jan's guard will help too, but you'll need the numbers," she said. "And, I'm afraid there will be…well, you can't help unpleasantness in this situation, can you?"

We'd assembled the volunteers hastily. We'd packed our belongings. Just before we left, in flyers, not caring to keep our journey as quiet as Betsy had kept hers, Nat had pulled me aside. "I'm leaving Goldie here," he said. "We'll pick him up after the war."

I said, "He's your dog. Why are you telling me this?" because I couldn't ask him what he meant by *we*, much less by *after the war*.

He shrugged. "I know we'll miss him," he said, as if I hadn't spoken. "But I really think he'll be safer here. Yes, there will be skirmishes here too, but the Longs will look after him and he'll have freedom to roam around. Back home, I'm afraid that someone will avenge himself on him while our backs are turned. If I were Mother, I'd send the little kids out here too, but I guess that's more complex. But it's not likely that Goldie will forget us, or pick up bad manners, or eat poisoned berries, or whatever mother would worry about with the little ones. Anyway, I thought you'd want to come say goodbye to him for now."

I wanted to come and see Goldie for what I was afraid might be the last time. I didn't know if I had any right to feel like that, but for the last three months, he'd been our constant companion every evening, always at our heels when he wasn't terrorizing the neighborhood with the Long boys. And over the time since I'd gotten out of Never-Never, he'd slept on me at least half the night, since he was a fair dog and insisted on dividing his attentions equally between Nat and me.

Though I knew Nat was right, it was tough saying goodbye to the hound of valor. And if I hid my face in his fur, and if it was a little moist afterwards, well, we all know Goldie liked to lick faces, and anyway, I wasn't young enough or stupid enough to cry over losing the company of a dog that wasn't even, really, mine. Even if I mourned the passing of the golden summer and the happiest—perhaps the only unadulteratedly happy—months I'd known.

More Than One Way to Win

I DON'T KNOW AT WHAT POINT IN OUR JOURNEY BACK NAT AND
I got separated and set on radically different paths. Not physically. At least not until we landed. There were five flyers brought
back, most of them filled with young volunteers with two months
or so of training at most. On the other hand, they were young
volunteers who'd handled a hunting burner—and on occasion
bow, since they were often used near human habitation, in the
territories—from the age of five or six and they were young
volunteers who'd helped fill the larder and keep their home safe
from man and beast their whole lives. On the whole, I'd take
them over any number of trained but less hardened troops.

Nat and Betsy and I were on the same flyer. And this was
when I first became aware that Nat's preoccupations, his abilities
and his focus were somewhat different than mine.

Not that this had been completely obscured from me during
the last three months. For one, while I'd been helping with farm
chores, Nat only occasionally joined in them. Instead, he'd spent
a lot of time at home training the young volunteers we'd gathered
from the various outlying farms and who'd made their way to
one of the Longs' fields, where they'd camped in large tents. I
had a vague impression he was training them, but I never went
to see what was going on. I, myself, had never been trained in

311

the formal art of war, and it seemed more useful for me to muck out the pigsty or milk the cows, or even to fetch and carry for the Longs.

And Nat was always at all the meals, sitting by my side, keeping up a barrage of often inane conversation with Mrs. Long, Jane, and occasionally even me. And he always went to bed when I did, lying across the attic from me, past that mostly closed curtain, in the warm summer air that flowed between the two open windows at each end, more often than not plunging into some philosophical discussion with me, one of those conversations for which there is no beginning and no end and which I understood belonged to the adolescence of normal human beings. Having never had a proper adolescence, I enjoyed that bantering of ideas, that examination of the universe, of good, of evil, and of the possibilities of humanity that I'd never gotten to experience before. And, of course, Nat and I had flown off together to scout more farmsteads. And we'd spent time together in projects like setting up for the Fall Festival.

With so much time together, it was easy for me to discount the time we spent apart and to assume he was just doing *Nat things*, things in which I had no interest.

Not that I mean he was doing anything secretive or shameful, or that he wasn't perfectly open about it, or even that I should have felt stung when I realized how different his preoccupations were from mine. And yet, I did feel stung when on the way back he spent the entire time on two links, talking to people I didn't know or barely knew.

After a while, listening, I realized one of the people was someone in his "regiment." I assumed it was the training unit of the Usaian youth that he'd practiced with. Someone he addressed as "sir" and of whom he asked respectful questions and to whom he listened with rapt attention. Later on and over time, I'd find that someone was a gentleman by the name of George Herrera, who would go on to become a famous general. At the time, all I could do was look at Nat, who took terse notes in one of those little disposable electronic pads used for memos and who spoke what was, to me, a foreign language. When he was not talking to Herrera—I don't know if the man was a general at the time—he was on the link with one of the young men we'd recruited, a twenty-year-old by the name of Liam Chen, from a

farm on the far reaches of the repopulated area. I remembered
Liam because his parents weren't even Usaians, and yet he had
instinctively agreed with all of our principles, and two days after
our visit had arrived at the Longs' farm, on a broom, with all
his possessions in a backpack.

To him, too, Nat spoke a foreign language. Timing and units, and
the charge rate of burners—all right, I suppose I understood that
last one, but not in the context. At least Nat didn't call him "Sir."

And Betsy was talking to the young man who was piloting
the flyer, telling him where to approach and where to land, so
we wouldn't be detected.

I shouldn't have felt stung, but I did. Part of it, I think, is
that over the last few months Nat and I had been practically
inseparable and, probably because of my initial, greatly weakened
condition, I'd felt as if I had if not all at least a great deal of his
attention. And the other part was that I'd been very badly trained
not to be the center of attention. Think about it. I'd been born
as the son of the Good Man, the future heir. Even if things had,
in fact, been quite different, and my chances of inheriting were
zero, I didn't know that, and neither did any of the people who
interacted with me. Sam might have suspected that something
was badly wrong, but he had no idea what. What that meant was
that from the time I could toddle, every servant, every functionary, every cog in the machinery of the ultimately corrupt and
dictatorial regime into which I'd been born, had been bent on
ingratiating themselves on the person on whom, they thought,
all their future chances depended.

I'd never sought to be the center of attention, mind you, but
I'd never thought to avoid it either. In that, Max might have
been more self-aware, or at least more aware that his entire life
shouldn't be lived in the glare of the public eye. That this should
have been the cause of his untimely death was a cosmic joke I
wasn't ready to unravel yet. As for me, even prison hadn't brought
home to me that the universe didn't revolve around my grubby
belly button. After all, in the jail to which Ben and I had been
consigned, we'd been the most prominent prisoners—which was
part of the reason he'd been the center of so much ill will. And
I'd known, even then, that they attacked him because I was a
little too prominent to be safe. And in solitary, I'd been the
center of my own universe.

Do me the justice of understanding I realized all this while sitting on the floor of that flyer, while Betsy sat next to the pilot, discussed landing plans, and occasionally calling someone on the link for the local conditions; and while Nat called two people, one of whom was totally unknown to me and discussed things that were utterly unintelligible to me. I realized it and accepted it, and it's not as though I threw a big temper tantrum to pull the center of attention back to me. But Ben's ghost—or my subconscious—had been correct. I was a pampered, self-centered princeling, and the awful recognition of this fact made me feel very small and insignificant and more than a little forlorn, as I sat there, quietly, while the people on whom this operation depended organized things.

In the event I was about to discover I was not insignificant enough.

We landed in the middle of the night, and I'm not precisely sure why. History books give several places, and when I asked Nat which one was the true one, he gave me one of his rare impatient answers, something about having been too worried about what they were about to do, too on edge, to pay any attention to that stuff, and now he couldn't remember, and I should ask Betsy if it was all that important. But Betsy had also told me she couldn't remember, so I have to assume that for whatever reason those two prefer to keep the place of our landing that night a secret. Don't ask me whatever the reason. Perhaps they thought we might need a secret landing place again on the seacity of Olympus.

At any rate, we landed in the dark, even our own lights out, and by instruments. As soon as we landed and the door flew open, three women and one man came in, all about Betsy's age. At the same time, Nat was barking commands I couldn't understand and sending the young men in the flyer out into the night in groups of six, while he stood by the door and gave them instructions in a clipped, fast tone that was impossible for me to follow, even had I the slightest idea what he was talking about. It was much like hearing a coach giving instructions to a team by referring to a play book. It was all about going to coordinates so and so and executing contingency *xyl*, unless the other side did *vhx*, in which case they were to default to *mzy*.

He wasn't smoking. It was the longest I'd seen him not smoke. He had a burner in each hand and two more burners shoved in holsters on a belt. He was wearing the same clothes he'd worn all day out at the Longs', a slightly more fitted grey tunic than it was his wont to wear, and a pair of perhaps much too fitted black pants with work boots that ended just below his knee. Somehow he made it look like a uniform. His features were disciplined, and I couldn't imagine him displaying any emotion or giving one of his disconcerting bark-laughs.

Well, I might be nearly useless, but there was one thing I could do. Given my fast-moving trick, and my ability to shoot fast and accurately, I could join one of those teams going out into the night. All right, so I had no idea what those oddly named plans were, but I was almost sure, given a little effort, I could follow and imitate the movements of some raw twenty-year-old who'd never seen combat except the play-fighting in the Longs farm.

I got up, and as Nat called the last six young men, I joined them. Nat went into his rapid-fire instructions, then, suddenly, his gaze fell on me. You'd think it would have happened earlier, considering I towered over everyone else in the group. But he'd been looking from face to face, and suddenly his gaze hit my chest, and he tilted back his head to look me in the eye. You'd think I was a coiled rattler ready to strike. His brows rose, then came down, his eyes narrowed, and, suddenly, and to my complete surprise, all the weariness of the world fell on his features—like he'd been dealing with all the idiots of the world for all of eternity and now, at this moment, I was the embodiment of all of them. He told the boys to "Scram," and then he looked up at me, as they jumped off the flyer and ran out into the night. "Lucius," he said. "What in the name of the founders do you want?"

"I can shoot," I said. "I can join in. I can be useful."

His eyes widened. He said again, "Lucius," in that tone that implied *you subnormal twit, and this is an insult to subnormal twits everywhere.* "My mother told you how you can be useful. They need you to address people. They need your voice and your image if possible to reach as many of those people as possible. You'll be very useful. Without you none of this would work."

I shrugged impatiently. Yes, I had listened to the harebrained idea that because of that damn holo which the security cameras had taken from the prison, and the notoriety it had achieved amid our people I was a great propaganda weapon, and my opinions and my ideas could sway a majority of the seacity to our side.

I thought Betsy's idea of my influence were greatly exaggerated, if not completely wrong. But it was not something I was going to ask her about.

"But I still see no reason I can't take an active part first, before it is time to make the address, or whatever it is."

He shook his head, and managed to look as if I were even more subnormal than the subnormal twit he'd taken me for. "Look," he said, "I don't have time to explain things in words of more than one syllable, so I'm going to give you orders, and you are going to forgive me, Patrician. I'm going to tell you that, on penalty of losing not just my good opinion, but possibly my father's life, you are to do absolutely what my mother tells you to do. You are not, under any circumstances, to expose yourself to danger. You are to behave like a mature adult on whom several lives depend, and not like a rash teenage boy out on a lark. Do you understand me?"

I had it on the tip of my tongue to tell him exactly what I understood and what I thought of his high-handed approach besides. But just as I opened my mouth to speak, something in his eyes caught my gaze, and I realized I'd never seen Nat worried before. Not worried like this. And I couldn't speak, beyond saying "yes."

I will still confess that if he had said "Yes, what?" and waited for me to call him "sir" or to speak in a more military manner, I would probably have decked him and ruined all our chances of winning that night. Fortunately, he didn't. He just raised his eyebrows at me, and sighed, then opened his mouth. Then closed it so suddenly the snap was audible, then looked... unreadable, and said, "Goodbye, Lucius. Stay safe." And jumped off into the night.

Leaving me in the hands of the Daughters of Liberty.

Daughters of Liberty

I DIDN'T LEAVE THE TRANSPORT. WELL, NOT TILL MUCH LATER that night. Instead, more people came in, men and women, all in their middle years. Most of them ignored me, going to Betsy and getting instructions, then setting about inexplicable tasks. They brought in furniture, and curtains and things I had no idea of a use for, like an antique folding table, the top in polished walnut, which they sat in front of the curtains and a heavy, rather patriarchal-looking chair, much like the ones in my father's office. Then, on the desk, they set a pile of gems, a gem reader of considerably better make than the one that had kept me sane in prison, and a signet ring. Make that my signet ring.

After a while, when they started hooking up equipment around it, it occurred to me that they were setting up a makeshift broadcast studio. What was more, in accordance with Betsy's idea that I should address the public, they'd set up the studio to look like a portion of my office at home, or at least what someone who had never been there might think was my office: nice furniture, symbols of power and all. I supposed the gem and the gem reader were supposed to look like I'd been hard at work ... doing what? I presumed not reading novels. Perhaps reading reports of the situation.

When a total stranger—male, as it happened—started removing my shirt, I balked, and I balked loudly enough that Betsy looked away from the three conversations she was carrying on and at me. I knew when she looked at me that she was going to take much the same attitude as Nat and tell me to stop making a fuss and allow myself to be dressed or undressed or made up like the puppet I was meant to be.

To my surprise, she snapped out, "Royce, are you out of your mind? The Patrician can dress himself. Just give him the clothes you want him to wear."

Royce looked surprised. To be honest, he'd looked surprised at the idea that I could speak. It took me some weeks after that to realize that the holo of my exploits in freeing Nat had given everyone the idea that I was a big and inarticulate brute not at home in the world of ideas and speech.

No. It wasn't my exploits. It was my exploits combined with something long built into the human psyche, who knows why, that those who are big and strong and capable of feats of daring and strength must of necessity be stupid and slow of mind. How that myth had persisted in the face of all the brilliant giants and dim-witted small people who had graced the pages of history was inexplicable. The idea must serve some evolutionary purpose, so firmly was it planted in the minds of otherwise rational people.

After the surprise passed, Royce handed me a black shirt and pants, in a material that felt like silk but was probably one of the more expensive synthetics. It looked, in fact, much like a few of the suits I'd left behind in my closet at home, and might be one of them. That he tried to explain to me how to put it on is something I will leave for a clinical psychologist to understand. I suspect if it weren't for Betsy's eyes on him, looking just faintly disapproving, he'd have followed me into the fresher to make sure I changed my clothes properly and didn't, out of naivete or high spirits, put the pants on my head and the shirt on my legs.

When I emerged, dressed, I had to balk again, this time at a relatively young woman—for this crowd; she must have been about thirty-five—who instructed me to sit down, not in the carefully set up studio, but in one of the other chairs, and then took my ponytail in her hand and said, "Royce? Do you know if we have a good barber among our people?"

Betsy intervened on that too, not saying it, but making me feel like I was pulling her away from more important matters, by saying, "No. You can't cut his hair. Yes, I know it would make him look more respectable, but you must leave him as looking as close as possible to how he did in the holo. Yes, I know he has been in the sun and looks far healthier, but that's good. No one expects him to look as pale and ill as he did in that video, but you must, must leave him recognizable. Cut his hair and half the people are going to say he is a body-double, a lookalike pulled in for this stunt. And then all his value will be gone."

For a moment I felt as though Betsy felt that without my propaganda value I would mean nothing to her or her family, but then when Royce presumed to explain to me that we'd be using for the transmission an array of communication devices pulled from junked flyers, because "It doesn't suit us, not yet at any rate, to have external enemies know there's any dissension in the ranks, and if we broadcast in the normal way, we give them two advantages. First, they can interfere with it through the controls put into mass communications worldwide. And second, they will hear your transmission, which will have two down sides. The first is that it will let them know that we are fighting against ourselves, which of course will cause them to attack and obliterate us before we can collect ourselves. Second, it will make them realize you have strategic importance to us and increase the risk of a hit on you. Now, these broadcasting apparatus we're using will transmit in all frequencies, because they were designed as emergency communication in case of a fly accident, so they will interrupt every link talk, break in on every broadcast. And we have enough of them set up in a relay that the effect will cover all of the seacity and a little of the sea area around, but not beyond. I don't know if you understand—"

"He understands, Royce, the idea came from a meeting with my son and the Patrician and their friends," Betsy said, and looked at me, from across the room, giving me a sudden, warm feeling that I hadn't fallen into some strange reality in which I wasn't actually capable of thinking.

Royce backtracked rapidly, apologizing if he'd offended me, and explaining he didn't know I was an electronic communications expert. He looked, in fact, like I was a zoo animal, who all the keepers had thought was some form of bear, but who had suddenly grown a magnificent pair of antlers. Which, now that I thought of it, might be much more apt than I wanted to think about.

Before the communication session started, and while the young

woman who'd wanted to cut my hair put a reader with the speech
I was supposed to give in front of me, so I could prepare myself
in advance, Betsy leaned in to me and whispered, so only I could
hear, "You don't have to play the fool, Luce. They assume anyone
who is new to the organization needs training wheels and knows
nothing, not just of conspiracy but of the world. Feel free to put
them in their place. It will do them good."

Then there was a lot of sitting around. Obviously we were waiting for a signal, and I tried not to think of Nat and those young
men, out there, in the night, being shot at. I tried to remember
that despite the fact that Nat had gotten caught by the enemy
while out jogging—and, while I didn't do him the injustice of
thinking he'd been unarmed, probably under-armed—he was a
capable man, and an able fighter. I'd seen him on broomback
and had no reason to suspect he'd run screaming in the face of
fire. On the contrary.

But civil wars are always uncertain, and this was more than a
civil war, a family squabble, amid members of a secretive organization that were, if not all related, at least all people who had
lived for a long time in each other's pockets and whose ancestors
had lived in each other's pockets. Such wars could quickly turn
very uncertain indeed, like family squabbles in which sides change
overnight, on the whim of a personal like or dislike.

In my mind, I was minding the backs of each of those young
men, worrying that our effort would fail, and worrying about Sam
and James in their jail cell, hoping that they would be restored
to freedom, hoping it would all work out, without even knowing
the full details of the plan I wanted to work out.

And then the signal came. Betsy's link rang, and she answered,
and Nat's face appeared midair, in front of her, visible to me
because she was standing by my side. "It's ready, Mother," he
said. "Let her rip." And then he'd hesitated for just a moment
and added, "Father and James are fine." Then he vanished, and
we were on.

It shall count against me, if there ever is a final judgment in
which hearts are weighed that I had a moment of dismay that Nat
hadn't said so much as "Good luck, Lucius." Why he should say
that, when all I had to do was make a speech was beyond me,
but I still felt vaguely regretful he hadn't done it. No. Vaguely
slighted. Pampered princeling indeed.

So instead of repining, I'd faced the pickup of the mechanism that had been rigged so you didn't need to hold the button down and scream into it, as you normally had to do with an emergency broadcasting mechanism. And I'd spoken in the measured accents, the cultured tones I'd been taught to use. In that speech, I used the training my father had—often quite literally—drummed into me on how to behave like a model Good Man.

Nat had told me, sometime while I was fighting my left arm and learning to have full control of it again, that my father's training me to be a Good Man in demeanor, posture, speech and attitude was not an act of pointless cruelty. Like the training of my arm to function properly even though my mind remembered its functioning just fine, my father had meant to train me to behave like a Good Man, so that the muscles would remember; so that my face would hold the proper expression by training, so that my mouth would produce the proper sounds; so that my body would hold the proper posture.

The idea that these characteristics would outlive me, and continue in my body memory, even if someone else's brain occupied my cranium made me shiver, but I had no reason to doubt it, not after my experience with my arm. And Nat had said that though he'd noticed a lot of things wrong with Not-Max, it had all been cast into doubt because so many of the movements and gestures remained so characteristic of Max, even if others weren't. It was that which had kept him in a despair of doubt until he'd found physical proof of the transplant.

Whatever reason those things had been drummed into me, they served me well that night. I might in fact be a self-centered pampered princeling who felt stung that the play-friend of his makeshift recapturing of youth over summer had more important things to do than cater to his pride; the self-involved Patrician— but it didn't show. I saw that broadcast a few weeks later. In addition to the broadcast, someone rigged a camera for pickup and recording of the holo. And I looked good and calm and responsible—in fact better, calmer and more respectable than I had looked at any time in the past fifteen years.

I was not aware, at the time, of how my appearance had changed again. The Longs didn't have anything against mirrors. At least I don't believe so. They probably had them in their freshers, and possibly even in Mrs. Long's bedroom and almost certainly in

Jane's. I'm sure if I'd asked to use a mirror, they would have let me, of course. And if I'd had any reason to do so, I'd have done it. But since beard-growth inhibitor came into common use, men have lost all need for a mirror in their freshers. Unless a fashion comes in for men to wear makeup as it did in the seventeenth and again in the late twenty-second centuries, the only freshers and bathrooms with built-in mirrors will be the ones that have female users.

Nat's and my bedroom in the farmhouse didn't have a mirror, nor did the bathroom—little more than a fresher unit—next to it. I didn't mind, as I'd combed and tied my hair by touch for years. And it never occurred to me to find a mirror.

Which was why my first view of the recorded holo of that broadcast was such a shock. I looked...well. I hadn't looked well when I'd first seen myself in the mirror of that flophouse on Liberte. I'd looked grown-up, sure, and muscular. But I'd been much, much paler than anyone who hadn't spent fifteen years indoors would be. Which made sense, since I had in fact spent fifteen years indoors. And I looked...not exactly gaunt, but haunted. Which also made sense, I supposed, since Ben had been my constant companion for those fifteen years, dead as much as alive.

On the broadcast, I looked tanned, with the reddish-gold tan of a fair man who spends a lot of time outside. The sun that had beat down on us while helping with the harvest or taking long broom rides into the outskirts of populated territories had left not-unbecoming lighter streaks in my hair. I'd put on weight, too, though I was a long way from being fat, partly because I'd spent most of the time away involved in activities that demanded physical effort. But my face, while not as broad as Max's in his grown-up portraits, had filled in a bit with flesh, making my prominent cheekbones less skeletal-looking, and giving the whole the look of a man in his thirties who might not have had a precisely easy life—my scars were still visible even if less livid in the tanned face—but who also hasn't slept out in the elements and been chased down the street by beggars afraid he'll make the neighborhood look bad.

The address I read can be watched. It can also be read, but if you read it be aware it is the version first put in front me, and not what I actually said. Why both versions persist is one of those things I can't explain except by saying that the Daughters of Liberty were planning ahead. They knew history is not in fact written by the victors, and history is not even a coherent compilation of the facts that someone thought made a better story. History is, instead, a hodgepodge of the various stuttering versions of what someone thought happened, as full of holes as witness accounts of any accident are, as my account of my small role in the beginning of the revolution that ignited the Earth is. In fact, in the rare occasions when a coherent narrative emerges, it is almost always wrong. And when a convenient and easily believable narrative emerges, told by someone who tries to tell you that he or his ancestors were always and without fail on the right side of history, someone is trying to sell you something, and chances are the price is more than you're willing to pay.

The speech was this, the bits about my past and the hints about possible Mule origins of the Good Men removed by yours truly while reading. I didn't judge it to be a good time to create that kind of doubt. I didn't know who had written the speech, or what they meant by those hints—perhaps no more than to create the seeds for an eventual revelation. But I remembered what Nat had said about its being much easier to get people to revolt if one pushed their loathing or their fears. And I didn't particularly want their loathing or their fears activated against me. Not then. So I elided them, and instead said this: "People of Olympus, I am, as most of you know or will have heard, the Good Man Lucius Dante Maximilian Keeva. I come before you tonight to explain that though my people have ruled the island for generations, I have in recent months become a Usaian. I know most of you have been taught to fear and hate my religion, but there are any number of you who don't, because you are in fact also secret devotees of it. To those who have never heard of us, or our beliefs, or who have heard only accounts that distort and debase our principles, let me assure you we are guided by three major rules: that the individual has a right—or should have a right—to life, liberty and the pursuit of happiness. From these descend several other rights, including the right of self-determination; the right of creating and owning what you create; the right to self-defense, even if the state determines you should die; the intrinsic value of the individual, even the individual who for whatever reason doesn't quite fit into the mold of the community in which he resides." I paused to let that sink in, then allowed a little levity to show in my eyes, and allowed my mouth to form a quasi-smile. "You will notice that nowhere there does it say that we sacrifice babies, nor that we believe our war goddess can curse you. That is because those and various other fables are myths and do not apply to anyone I know, in my religion or out of it. In fact, to my knowledge, we do not have a war goddess. We simply believe humanity's destiny is freedom and prosperity, and that the two go hand in hand." Another pause. "I know in recent weeks you've been introduced to my people as an occupying force. I was away, unavoidably detained by other business, and not aware of what was happening at home. Let me assure you what happened—what has now stopped—was an aberration. Over the centuries of secrecy and proscription some of our members got so . . . zealous, that they were willing to impose freedom by force, from above. Most of us know that this is not possible. And while it is true that our seacity is or soon will be facing a concerted attack from forces that oppose us, I refuse to treat every Olympian who disagrees with me as an enemy. Unless you actively work against us, we shall leave you alone, to pursue your own happiness. We might have to temporarily curtail some of your activities, like your ability to communicate with people outside the isle, and your ability to visit friends and relatives in other seacities. These will be temporary hobbles on your freedom, which we hope to lift as soon as your activities can no longer be a danger to our cause. Until then, allow your Usaian neighbors to talk to you. No one will force you to believe anything, and no one will treat you differently if you don't, save for those minor hobbles mentioned above. But perhaps if you know who we are and what we are trying to do, you will feel less apprehensive about the future. After all, in the future we wish to construct, every Olympian will have a right to his opinion, and a right to vote for and pursue the form of governance he thinks best." I'd given them the kind of warm smile I'd been trained to give, the kind that let them know that while I was above them by birth and raised as such, and though my responsibilities were far above them, I considered them my family and my bosom buddy, each and every grubby one, down to the last broomer hopped up on oblivium, and the last whore on her back in the cheapest flophouse in the seacity.

And then the transmission ended and I slumped in nerveless relief on the chair, only to be called back by Royce, gingerly handing me a link. When I pressed Accept Call, I found myself—in blinking disbelief—facing my butler. "Sir," he said, "we need another half hour to finish cleaning your room and changing the sheets. Will sir want it before that?"

I laughingly assured him I didn't. For one, it took me longer than that to get home, because first a small flyer had to come pick me up, and then we had to fly blind, in the dark, so that I would never, ever, ever know where the larger flyer had landed or where I'd given my speech.

When I finally made it home, I noticed no signs of vandalism, and nothing broken or dirtied by the People's Committee, or whatever it was they called themselves, occupying my home for the last three weeks. At the time I thought perhaps their depredations would be more visible in the full light of day.

But it turned out that they weren't. They weren't because there weren't any. Other than sleeping in my—and several other—beds, using my chairs and desk, and stealing a few—very few—of the showiest artifacts, they'd left the house alone. They were not vandals, after all, but idealists. Idealists convinced of all the wrong ideals, but idealists nonetheless.

Once the sheets had been changed, and my room had been cleaned, the home was, in fact, as far as I cared—I had never really noticed, much less cared for my father's collection of twentieth century paintings—back to being my home.

I fell asleep as soon as my head touched the pillow, feeling only the lack of Goldie who, for the last few months, had slept with his muzzle resting somewhere between my shoulder and neck. And I woke up with a footstep in the room, and a burner in my hand and pointed at the person.

The end of a cigarette glowed in the night. "Peace, Luce, it's me."

I pushed the safety on the burner and threw it under my pillow again. "Why?"

"Why what?"

"Why are you here?"

"What? Come to sleep across your door, of course."

"You know that's not needed. Now I'm not the most important target. And besides, you have other duties. You're in charge of the strike force, or whatever they are."

"Whatever they are, they are quartered in the merchant guild for the night, pending someone more intelligent than me figuring out where to park them permanently, come morning. Probably in another seacity, at that."

"And Liam Chen?" I said.

"Liam Chen what?"

"Did he survive the fighting?"

"All of them survived the fighting, Lucius. We had no casualties. Well, a few burns, but nothing serious. And I don't know about Liam particularly, didn't see him, as he was in another part of the city. Why? Do you have a particular interest? I can call someone and ask."

Was that a dangerous tone in Nat's voice? Poor Liam. I realized that if the Usaians had a hell, I was going to burn in it forever because the suspicion in his voice was balm to my soul. "Not really," I said. "I just knew he had taken on as your second-in-command and feared he was peculiarly exposed. I . . . we recruited him, so I felt responsible, but I don't really care."

"You're a strange man, Lucius Keeva," Nat said, and I heard him spread his blanket and lie down across the door.

When I woke up he was gone. I wouldn't see him again for three months.

The Wheel

WHEN MY DOG WAS TAKEN AWAY WHEN I WAS TEN, MY MOTHER consoled me by getting me a hamster. It didn't live very long, and I never got very attached to it. I mean, I had nothing against it. I like almost all animals. But I never felt for him—or her. I never figured it out—as I would have for a cat, a dog, or another creature who could join in the games Ben and I played as children.

The hamster never did much but run on a little wheel in its cage. Sometimes I'd wake up in the night and hear it running madly and feel very sorry for it, running, running and never getting anywhere.

For the next few months, I was that hamster. My days were insanely busy, but not driven by any purpose I could understand. Betsy set my schedule. I'd become...a project, I think. It might have started as a way to make sure I wasn't engulfed in whatever firestorm was to come, but it had become something else. I'd read, in one of those books that Sam had sent me in jail, that pilots, in one of the USA's fights in the twentieth century, used to paint bosomy women on the nose of their planes to remind themselves what men fought for.

If I'd been bosomy and female, I'd have felt like one of those. As it was, I was not sure what I was, except that there were speeches to deliver, statements to sign, and people needed to see

327

me on the holo transmitter to feel reassured. Now, I don't know about you, precisely, but when I want to be reassured, the thing that comes to mind is not seeing some oversized bastard with a cut across his face and the expression of a bull terrier that's been baited beyond his endurance. It probably proves I'm not a normal man, who knows?

Between that and the fact that Sam had me going through my patrimony, to decide what was mine and what belonged to the people of Olympus, I barely had time to eat and drink, much less to sleep. Mind you, for my part I'd told Sam my possessions were the stuffed giraffe and my bit of flag, but he'd looked at me as though I were out of my mind and told me you don't right an injustice by starting another injustice and that there is no such thing as collective guilt or collective innocence—not that I remembered ever telling him there was—and that they wouldn't strip me of all my possessions as the start of an era that granted people their property. They were not Sans Culottes, he said.

Which was just as well, because if I remembered my old French that meant without pants, and if people started running about my house without pants that would get around and give a very odd impression of me and my retainers. Probably destroy my usefulness as a propaganda weapon. And no, I was not sighing and wishing someone would do just that. Well, not in front of Sam or Betsy, anyway.

Apparently anything that had been brought into the family by one of the women my "father" had married and used as incubators was, of course, inherited by me. Which meant I still had considerably more money, jewels and propriety than I knew what to do with, and Sam was not about to let me donate any of it to the cause until "you understand more about money." And when I'd bridled at that, I'd tamped it down quickly, because I realized he was right. My entire experience of life was based on being a child, who, by definition, used money but didn't fully understand it, then being a prisoner whose most prized possession was a near-disposable reader. I didn't understand money, didn't know how to earn it, or what to do with it. Though in the back of my mind a vague project was forming of trading all of those trinkets, jewelry I never wore and property I'd never set foot in, for a few hundred acres in the North American backwoods, equipped with all the most sophisticated work robots money could buy. Maybe

I'd even get three pigs and one would wear an apron. Or maybe Nat would let me have Goldie.

But the important part of that work, and of going through centuries of snarled accounts and determining which of that property was still extant and could be claimed and liquidated, was to get money to finance the revolution.

It's something the history books rarely mention, among all the pomp, the blood and the glory, but revolutions and wars, like all human endeavors, run on money. There were troops that needed to be paid, however irregularly. They had to be fed too, and it turned out Nat was right, all our efforts for that had come to almost nothing. As our forces in the field grew, two seacities had experienced revolutions, the Good Men and, alas, their heirs having disappeared in mysterious circumstances and the seacities taken over by revolutionary committees.

I didn't like that above half, since the revolutionaries sounded much like the people that had been ousted in Olympus, but Sam told me we couldn't make sure the entire world was on the right path. Yes, we could look after Olympus and its territories. We could make sure here, at least, the principles were kept. But not all our allies in the fight were Usaians, and we needed them all. We couldn't engage in internal squabbling while we took down the most dictatorial regime the world had ever known. He called them *fellow travelers*, a term I knew from reading about the beginnings of the communist religion, and told me that they would be welcome until the current enemy was put down. For now we needed as many allies as possible, to help liberate the Earth from the grip of the Good Men, and, more important, to help free people's minds from the grasp of indoctrination.

The fighting had started in earnest, though one of the things I rarely had time to do was look through the news holos. I read about the action in Syracuse, one of our major losses. They were all losses, followed by a huge list of casualties, and after them I'd be required to give a speech to the people of Olympus because Sam was always afraid they'd rebel. Our grip on their loyalty was, to put it mildly, unsteady. So I'd have to get in front of the broadcasters and say empty, ridiculous things like that we'd killed more of them than they'd killed of us and that I wished we could sell them a victory at such a price again.

At that time, normally, we didn't even have casualty lists, and in my mind were all the young men Nat and I had recruited to the fight, and their sisters, not a few of whom had streamed in after them. How many of them were dead by then? Was Nat even alive? I had no way of knowing.

A day or two after these engagements, I'd finally get to peruse the casualty lists, and read name on name in mute horror at the number of them, in mute relief when I didn't find any name I knew well enough to feel it. When I didn't find Nat's name.

If the summer spent in the North American woods—I'd since found out it was not in the old USA territory, but near it, at the edge of what had once been the country of Canada—had been my golden summer, this was winter, in metaphor as well as reality. Life was hemmed-in with duty, places I had to be and things I had to do, most of them mechanical and uninteresting, and yet all of them tiring.

I think I'd have given up eating altogether—not difficult as my house was being run on a skeleton crew, and eventually by no one, almost every able-bodied person having joined the war effort. If I didn't ask for food, I didn't get it—but I was not allowed to starve. When Betsy had found out my idea of dinner was a sandwich I made myself and choked down with a glass of milk if there was any or water if there wasn't, before collapsing on my bed at the end of the day, she'd let me know I had not just a standing invitation, but a standing order to join her family for dinner every night. They'd retained the nannies who looked after the children and who had now taken on the additional duty of cooking and cleaning. And Martha helped, though she rarely stayed for dinner. On those rare occasions, though, we talked, and I came to prize her company and her good sense.

And that, that hour or two a day spent in the company of the children—Betsy and Sam were more often than not absent and eating at their desks—might have been all that saved me from becoming... I don't know what, but not good. An automaton going about tasks someone else set for him. But the children, even if they were much like Goldie—creatures that didn't understand what was happening or what we were engaged in—came to look forward to having me at the table, the one adult they saw all day other than their nannies. I'd more often than not read them to sleep at night. The nannies thought it was very good of me and very patient. I found out that this was something Nat usually did, because Sam and Betsy had never been very good at making the time. And so, to me this duty became a rope to salvation, taking me out of my new cell and into a light of freedom of sorts. Because, see, though I was theoretically free, I had become an asset of the revolution and jealously guarded, and it seemed like my day was as sterile and hard-bound as my time in that cell. I did things because it was time to do them, and I couldn't just leave and do something else. And I had nothing but the children to remind me of what this was all about.

The kids reminded me. I could imagine that what I was enduring was for them, so they would grow up free; so they wouldn't ever have to spend decades in a cell for things they didn't know they'd done wrong. So they'd live under the rule of law.

Besides, they seemed to like me, which, like Goldie's affection for me, was reassurance that I'd not been born some sort of freak, some unlovable, terrible monster, cut off from humanity.

"Don't be absurd," Martha told me, one of the few nights when she'd come in for dinner and helped me put the children to bed, after watching in open-mouthed disbelief as I read to them and helped with their prayers—they being Sam's and Betsy's children, their nightly prayers were of course for the restoration of the republic, to which I'd added a prayer for the safe return of our soldiers, which might not be canonical, if we even had a canon, but which was my own plea for shorter casualty lists. And for Nat's life.

Without the kids, I'd have been lost in the darkness I'd lived in for fourteen years and started thinking lovingly of cots dropping on my face, and of chewing through my own wrist. Though at least my new confinement had better opportunities for suicide. I could always have opened my veins in a warm bath. Only I couldn't, because the children needed someone more than their distracted nannies, more than parents too busy with the revolution to be parents.

"Don't be absurd. Of course you're human. And I never saw anything more monstrous about you than about anyone else." Then she'd looked at me, straight on, and said, "What have you been doing to yourself, Luce? What is chasing you down the dark corridors of your mind?"

I had no idea what she meant, feeling like she'd just used some line of poetry. Had to be. Only lines of poetry were that strange. Or perhaps the woman had an inconsequential mind, at odds with her solid and sensible exterior. Must have, because her next question was just as absurd. "Has Nat sent you a letter? They don't let them call, did you know? Too easy for the communication to be traced and troops to be found."

I shook my head and had the impression she was surprised, which was silly. Everyone seemed to imagine some kind of grand relationship between Nat and I, because we'd both lost lovers, and because, I suppose, we were the only ones of our inclinations most people knew. That wasn't true, either. I'd found quite a few more among our people, amid my household, amid Betsy's secretaries, for that matter. Like Royce, who improved on acquaintance though he'd never be one of my favorite people. But it was none of my business to expose other people's secrets. And in a way they were right. Nat was the closest thing I had to a friend. The closest thing I'd had to a friend since Ben died, because Ben had been that too. I'd lost both, my best friend and my lover, when he'd died. And then I'd lost the illusion of his ghost in Coffers. I'd not seen him, not even in my mind, since then. When I tried to pin down his image in my memory, it shifted and changed, and I couldn't remember his features exactly anymore.

"Well, mind you," Martha said. "That man is the worst correspondent in the world, and the two letters he's sent me were nothing but veiled instructions for me to be a good girl, make sure I eat and brush my teeth at bedtime. No, not that blatant, but that's what it amounted to. But he did ask me to check on you."

I knew as she said it that she was lying, and a little more ice accumulated over my life. She tried to explain to me why I was so important for the cause, why I was chained to transmitters of various kinds, sending transmissions to keep people in Olympus quiet, recording transmissions for our North American protectorates, recording messages for the troops in the field. "People are making a huge change, and even for those of us, and I'd say we're no more than maybe a tenth of the population—Usaians I mean. There are more than that who want this change, but we're the only ones who have looked forward to this day for centuries... anyway, even for us, it is difficult. It's like... in the twenty-first century, when technology was changing the way people lived at such a fundamental level that people weren't sure of anything. You can get irrational decisions and a sort of madness of the crowds then.

We don't need that, not while we're engaged in the larger battle. So, we need to give them a minimum of security. They and their ancestors have been conditioned to look to the Good Men as being something special. And you're one of them, but you're one of us, too. You believe that it's worth it, and that there's something wonderful on the other end of this war. And they have seen that holo of you rescuing Nat—most of them have by now, even outside our ranks—and they know just how extraordinary you are and yet that you care enough for one of us, for someone who is just average, to go into a jail and bring him out, almost dying in the process. You're a walking propaganda coup, Luce, and it's no wonder Mother is working you into the ground. But I'll have to talk to her, or she'll work you under the ground."

I told her not to. A pampered princeling I might be, but the last thing I needed was to have a woman more than a decade younger than me take up my defense as though I were a poor, lost creature. I'd be a man, I'd endure this. I'd prove Ben wasn't wrong in his trust in me. And Nat too, if he trusted in me.

Coincidences are an odd thing. That night when I got to my room there were two folded sheets of paper on my bed. They were folded on themselves and wrapped with bands of the sort of ceramite that can be encoded with an address and a destination and be delivered by robots. It was one of the many things that had never been allowed into production by the old Good Men, perhaps because of the ability they allowed people to communicate without supervision. We'd put them in production, I'd found through Martha, to allow fighting men to communicate with people back home without risking the communications system which was still in the grip of the Good Men. Not that this was without supervision. Clearly these sheets had been clumsily removed from their address bands, read, censored and put back into the bands. I'd later on find out this was procedure. Sam had gone into a lecture about how this sort of temporary violation of the rights of expression was acceptable in the cause of greater freedom. I didn't care. I cared slightly more for a very official-looking note folded into each of them, apologizing for the delay, because these two notes had been sealed into another band and gone to the family of another fighting man, and only directed to me by the correspondence office when that family pointed out their mistake.

How they'd found out who it had come from, much less whom it was supposed to go to was beyond me, unless it all hinged on a pattern of otherwise random seeming dots along the top of the sheet, because the notes—both of them—were short on anything personal or even full names.

The first one read in its entirety. "Dear Luce, I hope you're well and they're not working you too hard. They're working us into premature old age here, but it's good to be doing something, at last. Heard from the (censored band of liquid ink) and the idiot dog is doing well. Make sure (censored band) doesn't enlist. (Long censored band) much too young. I hope you're taking care of yourself. NGR."

The second one said, "Dear Luce, Mother tells me you (long censored band) and that's good. Thanks for looking after the littles. Mom and Dad mean well, but (long censored band). (Short censored band) Goldie (censored band) but they got the antivenom in time and he's doing fine. Syracuse (censored band) not something I want to live through again. But at least wartime is good for (censored band) promotions. Stay well and safe. (Short censored band) NGR."

I didn't know whether to laugh or cry and I have no idea what the censors were thinking. For instance, what could there be in the fact that Goldie had got bit by a snake to make them carefully censor it? Not that Nat's letters would have been much better without those. I had occasion to find out, he truly was the most dreadful correspondent, or, for that matter caller. When away from the person he was trying to talk to, he seemed to forget the human touch and yet feel he should have it, so his messages were an odd mix of straightforward information and attempts at showing some sort of emotion, which did not translate well in straightforward information mode.

Not that I was much better, as I found out when I tried to write to him, realizing that this was even possible and that I had, possibly, been remiss. As remiss as I thought he'd been.

My note to him, conscious that he probably had next to no privacy in whatever lodgings he had, and that this would be read by censors and by who knew who else, was "Dear Nat, Keeping busy. Much too busy, but never mind that. Didn't realize I could write till Martha told me. Having dinner with your family every night, and reading to little ones." Realized he must have known that from his last letter, but still felt I should reassure him. "Glad Goldie is all right. I miss him. I pray a lot before reading casualty lists. Don't be on one of them." I hesitated a long time over the closing, before writing, all in a rush and feeling terribly brave, "Yours, LDMK."

I found out later that most of it, including my moment of foolhardy and rather timid daring had been carefully covered in censorship ink.

But the letters showed that, while under fire and under peril of death, Nat had thought of me as much as he thought of Martha. It gave me heart.

Perhaps I'd come across as truly pathetic, because Martha, Jan and Simon started including me in their war councils, which I suppose is what passed for parties these days. Their councils were about as boring as Sam's and Betsy's talks, but sometimes there was wine to go with the boredom. And I wasn't sure what was going on with Jan and Martha. Martha said it was all very complicated because Jan felt he couldn't marry her, because he could never give her children and also because he didn't know what was going on with his position nor how it would end up.

This conversation was on my terrace, outside my room, over-looking the ocean. Part of the good side of being at war is that the seacity was no longer under particular attack. The battle lines had moved a little far off and we weren't nearly as affected, so the terrace was safe. We'd come back from one of our meetings—the problem we were trying to get around being how Simon could declare the revolution in his own island without bringing retribution on himself. Right now, he was useful to us, since he could get us news from inside the Good Men councils, and provide us with advance knowledge. Not that he was fully trusted. In fact the only reason he was still alive was that his father was technically still alive and I guessed the old guard hoped their friend would come back. Which was part of the reason that Simon acted like an idiot—so he could look inoffensive enough that they didn't try to kill him, as they'd tried to kill me even before I was in open rebellion. He too improved on acquaintance, which didn't help us decide what the right moment was for him to pivot between playing the fool to being truly the man in charge there and declaring *la revolution*, which is how he referred to it, for *Liberte, Egalite, Fraternite*.

I'd tried to argue the last two had no business being imposed from above, but Martha had made frantic shushing motions, and I'd shushed. And now, she was sitting on the terrace wall, and talking about her relationship with Jan, and revealing far more feeling than I'd ever seen her even allude to. "Maybe I should take up smoking like Nat," she said. Then gave me an odd smile. "Or maybe Nat and I will eventually lose patience and drown you and Jan, like a litter of misbegotten kittens." She'd grinned. "You should see your face, Luce. I'm joking."

Still I cared enough to reel back on my heels when the next battle report came in. Maybe it was to be expected. So far our people had escaped, had survived in some number to fight another day because the other seacities had failed to organize enough to come down on them like a united force. This was partly because Good Men were no better at working together than any other wild and solitary animal. They had their small groups, their alliances. But uniting the whole might of the forty-five or forty or however many of them were left was an impossible task.

Or had been, until a couple more seacities turned and killed their Good Men. And then they, or most of them, had brought... not armies... strike forces. Exterminators, as it were, falling upon each infected place, each focus of infection, and cleaning out our grand army in the same way as they'd once exterminated rogue broomers. And seemingly with no more effort.

The casualty lists went for days, and you could read them, pages and pages and pages of them. I read them till my eyes ached, till they felt dry and gritty and hot. It was difficult because many of them weren't even in alphabetical order. Through them I found out about Liam's death and Tommy Long, the Long's oldest son, and of Jane Long, too. Through them I found out that there had been attacks on areas of North America thought to be hotbeds of rebellion.

Nat's name I didn't find at all. But I couldn't be sure I hadn't just accidentally skipped it, so I kept reading again and again to verify.

A Grand Expedition

I WOKE UP WITH THE DOOR TO THE TUNNEL OPENING, AND I was sure I was dreaming. I sat up and said, "Light," and caught Nat in the glare of it, dazed, blinking, looking at me as if he didn't recognize me.

He was wearing a uniform. We'd started having those, partly to give the units cohesion, partly because there were so many seacities fighting and it helped to know which seacity you were with. Olympus had—I had very little to say to this, and I suspect, honestly, it was Royce's idea—a sky-blue uniform, with a mountain peak for a patch, shown at sleeve and chest. It clearly came in the two army sizes I'd read joked about since the twentieth century: too large and too small. Tradition, I suppose, since there was no reason for this at a time when we could have printed the uniform to the measures of each soldier.

Nat's uniform managed to be both, hanging off him in folds and leaving his ankles and wrists uncovered. Though part of the reason for the folds was revealed in those ankles and wrists, both looking like there wasn't a spare ounce of meat, let alone fat on them. His face too had gone much as it had looked when I'd first met him, under the grief of Max's discovered death and the horror of what he'd done to Max's body: all harsh planes and sharp, pointy angles, and circles under his eyes that made them look even darker and for

337

once completely opaque. I have no idea what he'd done for haircuts. I was fairly sure he hadn't taken garden pruning shears to his own head, and yet that's what it looked like with long swipes of hair cut almost to the scalp, and long strands that overhung one ear and fell into his eyes. Beard inhibitor cream must be one of the things that they were running low on, because the light glinted on blond hair all over his face. His lips looked chapped. There was a patch of something dark and greasy across his forehead, and he appeared to be dead on his feet. I could smell him from where I was: sweat and something that stank chemical and burnt.

But he was alive and that was better than I'd ever expected. I was off the bed before he'd stopped blinking at me. I unbuckled the holster slung across his middle. He was not, I think, fully rational, because he tried to hold on to it, before I pulled it off and said, "No, Nat. You're home. If someone comes in, it's my job to shoot them."

He didn't smile, but he nodded, and he let me take the holster and the other holster from around his waist. I wanted to drag him into the fresher. I wanted to get him food. I wanted to have him home, to look after him, but I guessed what he needed the most was bed. And as short on personnel as my house was, and as much as there might be no one to wash those sheets in the next month, I dragged him to the bed and told him to lie down. I only had to say it once. I think he was asleep before he was fully horizontal. Screw the sheets. I'd burn them.

He slept for almost forty-eight hours, playing havoc with my schedule, though my schedule was in a shambles too, since Betsy didn't know what I should tell people. Or to whom I was telling it. Our news was patchy because the Good Men had at last cut us out of the broadcasting network, so that we weren't even getting their propaganda. Simon told me at least one of the cities that had rebelled had fallen and the Good Men had put everyone, man, woman, child to death. Whether true or not, rumor of it spreading to the other cities was solidifying Good Men rule. The two broadcasts I made were meant to keep the people in Olympus from rushing my house and killing us all. Not that I even knew if there had been any rebellion. Because other than those two broadcasts, I spent the time in my quarters, keeping an eye on Nat. I wasn't sure how much he was like himself. I wasn't sure who would wake up when his long sleep was over.

These things are always timed precisely to be their most inconvenient, and of course Nat woke up while I was away, recording the second broadcast. I came back to my room to find he'd got up and changed the bed and made it. The contaminated sheets were in a pile by the window, because he clearly had no idea what to do with them.

As I opened my door, he came out of the fresher, in a cloud of steam, wearing my robe. It was big, and fluffy and white, and it made Nat look even paler and more washed out. Also, he'd used the beard remover. His hair still looked frightful, I supposed, but it was soaking wet and he had combed it back.

And after two days of sleeping, the smile he gave me was still exhausted, as though he'd been running and running for days, and had just managed to stop. "Sorry, Luce," he said. "I have no idea why I came here instead of my house. But when I woke, I couldn't stand my own smell, so I figured I'd wash before going home to change. Sorry about the sheets and I'm afraid I made a total mess of your fresher, cleaning up. I have no idea how to clean it either."

"Nonsense," I told him. "You are home. And you're welcome to dirty my fresher or burn my sheets any time you want to," and before he could look at me like I was nuts, I added, "Let me make you something to eat." I started towards the door, and he followed me, barefoot and wrapped in that ridiculously large robe.

The one thing the kitchens at Keeva House weren't meant to be was cozy or family like. They also hadn't been designed to be easy to use. The room itself was cavernous and probably could have housed ten families, just by itself. It was also full of specialized appliances and complex machines designed to extrude pasta or make pastry or other things I had never learned to do. Frankly, the machines scared me a little. I'd never even learned to use an automated cooker. Instead, I'd defaulted to cooking as I'd seen Mrs. Long do it. I'd asked her for recipes and she'd sent me a gem by courier, with news of Goldie, too.

Most of the time what I made myself consisted of either sandwiches or bits of cow imperfectly seared. But I'd tried a few of the recipes, nothing too complex. And since Nat had just woken up, I figured breakfast—which I was quite capable of having for every meal I wasn't dragged to Remy house to eat—would do. So I broke eggs into a bowl, scrambled them and started frying them, at the same time as I brought out a pile of bacon to cook over a griddle, leaving a corner of it for pancakes, which were close to the top of the achievements of my culinary art.

While I was turning the last pancake, I found Nat at my elbow, looking at me with an unholy sort of amusement shining through the horror and the tiredness in his eyes.

But he said nothing, and I put the eggs and bacon in one platter, the pancakes in another, set them on the little table nearby, that I think had been a work table for the pastry cook, got a clean plate and silverware and ducked into the even more cavernous pantry for a bottle of syrup. When I emerged, Nat had set another plate, across from his.

I said, "I'm not really hungry. I had dinner at your parents' house."

He said, "Don't make me eat alone." The words crossed in the air, and he won. I got a spoonful of eggs and two strips of bacon. Truth was I had eaten. But the last two days were the first I remembered eating in weeks, because before that when I tried to eat I kept thinking of everyone who would never eat again. And, if I must admit it, worrying about Nat and whether he was dead or alive.

Then I realized I hadn't given him anything to drink, and got up and made coffee, which, in my gleaming kitchen, designed to cook and serve banquets for hundreds of people, I made by straining boiling water through a—clean, thank you—sock, filled with coffee grounds. As I put the cup in front of him, he was looking up, and the unholy amusement was back in his eyes.

"I never learned to use the implements," I said. "I don't even know what makes coffee, and I'm afraid if I turn it on, robots will come out of the wall, grab me and roast me with an apple in my mouth." I was rewarded with a shadow of a smile and continued, but couldn't help getting more serious. "And I don't want to use the energy. We're being strangled on powerpods."

"Yeah," he said. "Yeah. It was a problem for us too, though..." He shook his head. He ate. I ate, and looked at him. He was still fourteen years younger than I, but no one would believe it. I wanted to ask him if he'd given up and if we must now prepare for an onslaught on the seacity, and how we could prepare. I wanted to ask him what had happened, and what had sent him back home, dirty, tired, starved and half dead. I wanted to ask him a thousand questions, and I could ask none of them. So I sat and nibbled at my food and watched him eat quantities that would scare a large contingent of teenagers.

After he was done, he nursed the coffee, looking at me. I pretended to be very busy with my quarter strip of bacon, trying not to ask questions.

"It's not bad coffee," he told me at last. "Quite passable. But the unit for the coffee maker is tiny and probably still has enough charge. Remind me to teach you to use it later. It's the same we used at home."

He drank his coffee and I gave him more coffee. "I know how to make biscuits," I said.

The unholy amusement again, this time with a little smile. "Impressive," he said. Then there was a long silence. "We were asleep," he said, at last. "We were asleep, but of course...there were sentinels. We didn't know. We were...where I was, we were the first to be attacked. They blocked the entrances. They threw exploding canisters and gas canisters inside. They...People were burning in the room, the first room they...and people wanted to go in and help, and I had them seal the exit, so they...I always have to tamp down the berserker. Berserking is lousy for a soldier, and this time...I was scared and shocked and shaking so much I almost couldn't walk. But I had to. And I led them...I led all five thousand of us...I. There was a tunnel and I thought we'd be trapped like rats. And I—" He covered his face with his hands, and he shook. And I thought he was crying, or maybe he wasn't, but in either case I didn't have a right to violate his privacy by looking, and I didn't have the right to touch him, and any comfort I could offer would fall so short of the mark as to make it worse.

And I thought the problem is that they had trained and they had gone on trips and they'd had live-fire exercises, but in the end we didn't have soldiers. We had boys who had been trained for war, like their fathers and grandfathers, but who'd never thought it would come in their day. Not even Nat.

I got up. I got the plates. I dropped them into the cleaner. I came back. I sat down. I stretched out my hand and clasped his shoulder. He leaned almost imperceptibly into my grasp and shook.

After a while Nat stopped shaking, and removed his hands from his face. He didn't look like he'd been crying. He took a deep breath and said, in a perfectly normal voice, "We lost about thirty percent of our people, but seventy percent of us got out. Not just where I was. Everywhere. We were sent back to our sea-cities of origin if... if they're at risk of attack. I should be down at quarters, but... I don't know why I'm here. It was odd to wake up in your bed." And then after a pause. "And you'd better burn those sheets. There's been an outbreak of lice."

That's all I ever got out of him about the incident where he was one of the principals, indeed the one without whom no one else would have escaped. Within days, our people started calling it the Broken River Massacre. It didn't take me long to learn that Nat's part in it was far more heroic and far less casual than he made it sound. Not that I learned much more. Nat never mentioned it again and, save for a burn scar up the side of his left thigh which he refuses to have regened away, there is nothing else I can add.

Nat went somewhere to report mid-afternoon, but they told him to quarter wherever he was and to stay on call. He came back to my house, after stopping by his parents' house to get his civilian clothes. He didn't have another uniform and there was no point wearing it around the seacity anyway. That night, when I came back from my duties, such as they were, I found he had set up the small dining table in my bedroom, and he had managed to turn on enough of the machines in my kitchen to have a decent dinner made, if not in the style I used to be served.

"The children will be counting on me for dinner," I said.

"Nah. I went over. I told them I was going to steal you tonight. They were happy to see me, so they're willing to let me keep you away. Mind you—for one meal only, Tom said." He turned serious. "We need to talk. There are things that need to be done if we're going to turn this and I can't get my parents to understand. I can't get anyone to understand. I think it might be time for us to take the matter in our own hands and the bit between our teeth, so to speak, and do a little unapproved action. And I've been talking to Simon and..." He looked at me, puzzled. "What are you laughing at?"

"Not laughing," I said. "Smiling. You told me to remember I wasn't a teenage boy on a lark."

His features relaxed and he even smiled a little. "I was so worried that night," he said. "With my dad and James in jeopardy. I was worried you'd get in the middle of it too." He paused. "But sometimes, Luce, one does need to do things that people back home don't get. We've been fighting this war on their terms, and on their terms, Luce, they win and we all die. I'm not willing to let that happen. I'm not going to say on my terms we win and they all die, but there is at least a chance."

"All right," I said. "We eat. You talk."

The gist of it was that we were being strangled by energy dependence—the powerpods came through Circum Terra, a scientific and energy processing station in Earth orbit, which we didn't control. And we were being killed on communications, the second tying up with the fact we were so badly outnumbered. "There are a lot of people who would come to our side immediately, and a lot of others, probably half or more than half—the Good Men have got that intrusive and people, at least see the waste and the fraud—who'd come to our side with a little persuasion, a little appeal to their prejudices, their inborn hatreds," Nat said. He was smoking again, having procured cigarettes during the day. "But they won't because we can't communicate with them. And the knot to this communications problem is in Circum Terra too. That's where the dampening mechanisms are that keep the communications of Earth locked down, so that only the transmitters the Good Men have built with the bypasses they enforce can broadcast to the entire Earth."

"It's very easy, then," I told him. "We'll go to Circum Terra and rearrange things, so the energy gets sent to our own receiver—we have a receiver, right, or we can build one? And so that the communications will be freed. Problem solved."

He was looking at me, his eyes dark and serious. "You know, I'm approached by a lot of people who think I'm a legend, simply because you rescued me."

I blinked at him. "All I do is make these stupid little broadcasts, just for Olympus."

"Um." He nodded. "Perhaps. Mother and Father— Luce, what in the name of the founders are you doing making lists of your property that's to go back to the seacity?"

"Yeah, I know, waste of time. I told your father I'd be happy with a stuffed giraffe and a piece of flag, and they could have all the rest. I meant, it was all, ultimately stolen from the people."

Nat made a rude noise, then proceed to tell me the people didn't own anything, not as such, that you can't steal from a collective but only from individuals and that whatever my father had stolen was from individuals long dead. And most of it had probably come from governments, not individuals, when the Mule Lords had taken over. Then he told me that if my functionaries, who had been paid out of the same fund—like his family—weren't giving everything back to the people, there was no reason I should. And when I tried to tell him that his father had told me I didn't need to do this, not really, that it had been my idea, he said, "Mom and Dad have an amazing ability to make you have the ideas they want you to. Not that I have anything against them. They're both honest, dedicated people. World's worst parents, mind, but that's because the great cause leaves so little room for it. But all the same, I'm not comfortable with this, Luce. I don't like it. It's your private property, and you shouldn't be giving it to anyone."

"I don't need the property, Nat. I don't want it. Once I'm . . . We're going to have elections. Well, at least we will if things ever calm down enough and if it even looks like we're winning the war. And then this palace will be for the elected representative of the people: president or leader, or whatever they want to call him. And I'll move out. I'll find some place to live. Don't look like that. I'll still be rich beyond the dreams of avarice. The poor women . . . Anyway, I've inherited enough that could only be mine. I was thinking of investing in a lot of robots and going and clearing some acres in the North American protectorate."

He smiled at me. "Goldie will like that," he said, and then, "I miss him."

"Yeah, me too," I said. "But what do you propose to do about Circum Terra?"

He looked at me. "Curiously, exactly what you said we should do. You have a knack. That's why I thought you're the face of the revolution, more or less accidentally, and perhaps we should let you actually run it, if we could ever unclench Dad's and Mom's hands from the tiller."

"What do you mean what I said we should do? I said we should go to Circum. I was joking. We'd be shot out of the sky before we get there."

"Not . . . precisely. I was talking to Simon today."

He proceeded to reel off what sounded like a fantastic tale. Athena Hera Sinistra, Good Man Sinistra's daughter and, as far as it was known, the only fertile woman bred from a Good Man anywhere in the universe, had come to Earth in search of the writings of the legendary Jarl Ingemar.

I hadn't heard much about Jarl, because most of it was erased in the turmoils. It was as though the Good Men had a particularly vicious vendetta against him. Perhaps they did. If the story I got is right, he was one of those Mules who actually left Earth and made it to the stars in their starship. The ones left behind to die or claw their way back to the top as best they could would not be forgiving. Well, not if they were the lovely bunch I'd come to know as Good Men. But once upon a time Jarl Ingemar, who, as I understood it, was also a Mule, had been a well-known scientific genius, as famous for it as Einstein in his time. It is impossible to believe all the inventions attributed to him, from the power trees, those biological solar collectors in space that provide energy to all of the Earth, to some of the more sophisticated ways of bioengineering humans.

But Nat swore Jarl had existed and that, in fact, Athena Sinistra's husband—born on a colony left behind by the Mules on their way to the stars, in a hollowed asteroid somewhere in our system, the people we know on Earth as the mythical Darkship Thieves—was a clone of Jarl's, gene-modified to pilot the darkships. As someone who had always assumed darkship thieves were the harvesters' way of fudging the accounts, I held my peace. I supposed she was a friend of Nat's and if she'd married someone, it couldn't be someone imaginary. I mean, I might have had Ben by my side for fourteen years, but I never expected him to be visible to others.

Anyway, for reasons that were even more nebulous but which sounded like the darkship colony was in as much trouble as Earth, Athena and her husband and some other girl, whom Nat dismissed with a wave of the hand and a mutter about her being a mechanical genius, had come to Earth in search of Jarl's writings. And now they were going back to Circum Terra on their way home. "We can go with them," Nat said. "They have a ship and they're ready. And we can go aboard because it's a short hop and there's no problems with weight. They would appreciate the backup and we—"

Over a cup of coffee, which I'll admit was much better than what I had ever made with the sock, he explained the idea.

We'd provide reinforcement for them, and Zen, who was the girl who had come with them from Eden—the darkship colony—was apparently some type of communications genius and she had told Simon—who Nat thought, between the two of us and not for public consumption, was more than half gone on her—that she could rewire the communications stuff and also retrofit one of the ships left behind in Circum Terra—that part he never explained adequately—so they could go back to Eden.

Most of the details were beyond me, and those were the ones that sounded like they might be even remotely plausible, but what stayed behind in my mental map was that this meant Nat and I—and Simon and the Zen woman, whoever she was—were about to go and have a grand adventure.

The idea that I was going to be allowed to get out of Olympus and go do something, instead of recording mealy-mouthed broadcasts to keep the restive masses quiescent was enough to make me interested. But beyond that, Nat would be with me. There would be—for some days, at least—no perusing casualty lists, in living fear that the next name I read would be his. Better yet, I wouldn't be wondering every time I sat down to dinner if he was starving. I wouldn't be wondering when I lay in bed if he was sleeping rough, or worse, not sleeping at all, but in some desperate situation, fighting for his life. I looked at him, and I told him the absolute truth. "It sounds wonderful."

The corners of his lips went up, and his eyes sparked with mischief. "Yep," he said. "Lunatic. Certifiable. I tell you we're going to invade and take over a well-defended place, in a desperate bid to change the tenor of this war, and that the chances are we'll fail and if we fail we're dead men, and you react like I just invited you to a Sunday school picnic." He shook his head. "You have a screw loose, Luce, and you need a minder to make sure you don't end up living with three pigs, one of whom wears an apron."

A Few Good Men and
Not a Few Women

SO WE WENT TO CIRCUM. OKAY, IT WASN'T THAT EASY. ON THE
other hand perhaps it was. Going there was easy in itself. We
went to this place in Central Europe, in the middle of the zone
that got the same treatment as the North American continent.
Okay, minus the nukes, but the difference was more academic
than not. Bacteria had eaten everything and here there was, as
yet, no regreening.

Nat said that was where the Mules were raised, after being
created, but I think he got something wrong, because I've looked
up the history of the place and it was a resort of some sort, until
it was bought by the famous Jarl Ingemar and kept as a private
sort of resort, where he could—I presume—hide out from the
world, and perhaps from the fact that he would never feel like
a normal human.

It was locked with genlock, and it had a bioshield on both
entrances, and though I'd never trade it for the Longs' farm, it
was a wondrous area that various earthly paradises of legend
could be based on: trees massive as houses, wildlife of a non-
man-eating sort, fishes that leap into your hand, and a climate
that was kept warm year-round. The only thing marring it was
knowing it was artificial, a sort of playground for the very wealthy
and eventually for the wealthiest man of his time.

Nat did manage to secure access to the genlock code. Don't ask me how. I got the impression that Athena Hera Sinistra was very fond of him. We plan to go there, now and then, for privacy and rest. If we live long enough.

We'd met Athena Sinistra and her people there—well, her husband who...I'll confess I try not to be prejudiced, and there's a lot to be said for someone who is bioengineered himself not casting stones, but look... The man's eyes looked like cat's eyes, and I found I couldn't look at him straight on. It read to my back-brain as some sort of horrible deformity, and it was no use telling myself it was perfectly normal.

Mind you, he seemed to be a good man, and he went with us to help us take Circum, and there was no evil or malice in him, but it would have taken me months to get used to his eyes before I could look at him straight on. It gave me another insight into how we, humans, are wired not to accept those who are too different from the norm. It seems to be baked in, and while it can be overcome, it is part of how humans aren't perfect.

There was also Zen, leggy and reddish-blond, that color that used to be called Titian blond. I never looked at her straight on, because if I did Simon would probably have growled at me. There was a growl always hovering at the back of his gaze, and in the pinched setting of his mouth, and I don't think it would have done any good at all to tell him that while she was aesthetically pleasing I had no more personal interest in her than in any work of art. When a man gets it that bad it's no use being logical with him. I have reason to know.

Athena Sinistra, herself, was tiny and dark-haired. I remembered her father, a crusty son of a bitch to whom the term sawed-off-bastard could be applied with very little remorse. I saw the resemblance between them, of course, as I should if they were male and female clone. Twins of a sort, I suppose, but in Athena, what had been sullen distrust in her father became... boundless energy, a sort of determination always on the verge of erupting into action. I thought that she had a lot in common with Nat and it didn't surprise me at all that they got along, nor that now and then I found them with their heads together and whispering. It only disturbed me when Athena then proceeded to look at me and smile a secretive sort of smile, like she knew something I didn't.

The fourth member of their party was called Doc, and if one is to believe them he was Doctor Bartolomeu Dias. Yes, the Mule of that name. While I couldn't understand why he'd have stayed behind in Eden instead of going on to the stars, and while the rejuv job that would allow someone to live close on to four hundred years was hard to buy, he looked at least that old, and looked startled when he saw me, and mumbled in the way people do when retrieving a long-forgotten name, "Keeva, now. Another one, I suppose."

The trip to Circum was uneventful, and we landed in an area of Circum that hadn't been used in a long time. Part of me wanted to go through everything in that area to examine ships stored there since the *Je Reviens* had been built. They'd been meant to take everyone to the *Je Reviens*, but the contingent had been vastly diminished, between the Mules who were deliberately excluded and those bioed people who'd been caught and killed in the turmoils.

I tried to imagine what that had been like for my "father"— being left behind as the most important train of your lifetime departed without you. How it must have felt to know that your closest friends, your associates, the only people on Earth like you had left you behind; considered you unfit to live and departed to build a new life without you. Worse, they'd left you behind to face the turmoils and the almost certainty of getting killed in a horrible and public way.

I shuddered. No wonder they'd left all these air-to-space vehicles here, mothballed. No wonder they'd never tried to do anything about them or repair them in any way, or even use them for anything. Frankly, if I were them, I wouldn't even want to think about these, or anything related to them.

I'd have done exactly what they had done, in fact. I'd have left them here, and built other chambers onto Circum Terra, and done my best to pretend this area doesn't exist.

"There are legends," Simon said, in a hushed tone. "That a lot of these areas are infested with AI robots hostile to mankind or . . . or worse." He took a deep breath, almost shuddering, then said, "But I wonder, truly, if it's just . . . you know . . . ghosts. And I wonder if it's the ghosts of those who left or those who stayed. I think it would kill you a little to be betrayed this way."

I nodded. I was sure it would kill you. Even I might have become just like the creature who'd called himself my father.

Nat's hand touched my arm, and he said, "Not a chance," as though answering my thoughts, but I had no time to enquire what he meant, because Doctor Bartolomeu Dias said, "We thought we were doing it for the best. That they couldn't be trusted, you know, around...normal humans. But since I've wondered. Mind you, these men were by no means angels, but neither were the rest of us." A brief pause. "We did what we thought we had to do."

We had to let that serve as epitaph as we moved fast through the area.

We in this case was myself, Nat, Simon, Doctor Dias and Athena's husband, Kit. I would like to say I liked him better for volunteering to help us, and I did, but it was all a liking in the mind. At the same time I felt bad for cringing when he looked in my direction with his odd, feline eyes, and got impatient at myself for feeling bad. I told myself it would take months to get used to it. But we didn't have months. And he appeared to be a good person, and for that I'd honor him.

The women stayed behind working at outfitting one of the old, boomerang-shaped work platforms used to assemble the *Je Reviens*. They thought they could fit it for the trip to their world, Eden.

As for us, we walked through several compartments.

The part of Circum in use came up with startling suddenness. We went from an area covered in dust and cobwebs, through two doorways and a sealing door, and we were in shiny, air-conditioned corridors. And two men were running towards us.

My first reaction—Nat's too—was to reach for the burners on my belt. But as the men came near and slowed down, it turned out they were holding their thumb and forefinger together in a circle. Jan had sent messages ahead, he said through the grapevine, to Usaians aboard the station. And they were coming to meet us.

After some negotiation we armed them. The negotiation was such even I didn't understand, but it seemed to hinge on whether they were members in good standing and could be trusted. Simon deferred to Nat in the decisions, so I assumed none of these scientists were Sans Culottes.

About a third of the scientists were Usaians and almost all the harvesters were.

Yes, I know what you've been told. That we took Circum, the three of us, and heroically rewired the communications devices.

It wasn't that easy. And we were nowhere near alone. There were maybe sixty-five harvesters, and they were armed. Mostly homemade burners, but effective. They waited for us in the next area. After we armed the Usaian scientists, we advanced on the larger part of Circum where we were told almost everyone was at that time.

There were a hundred or so scientists and technicians, in a vast room partitioned in a hundred different cubes and sporting enough apparatus and machinery to stock your average continent.

Simon ordered everyone from the cubes, an order reinforced by harvesters running up and down the hallways with unsheathed burners. But two of the men who were, Simon whispered to me, guarding the equipment we needed, the communications equipment that had in them the kill switches that controlled communication on Earth, refused to come out. It looked like they'd have to be shot where they were.

This is when I got to see Nat in action mode, though he told me later on that this was not how he behaved in actual war, unless it was in very specialized circumstances. He'd brought with him a gun large enough that anyone who didn't know him would think he was compensating for other issues. The burner was massive, normally called a ship-killer and he had worn it in a holster slung across his back. It had become a joke, I think started by Athena, to say "Don't let Nat use the shipkiller."

The reason it was called a shipkiller, of course, was that if fired inside an air-to-space—or for that matter *at* an-air-to-space—it would tear it in two like a nut shell, which was why I was fairly sure that Nat had no intention of using it. But he unslung the shipkiller from his shoulder and at the first sign of resistance went into a good impression of a maniacal killer, yelling, "I just want an excuse to use this, okay? We're at war on Earth and they're killing my people. Mere children. People under my command. I've seen them die." Something like the horror I'd seen in his eyes when he'd come out of the night into my room, made it all more believable. "And I would love to get a little back, in revenge and in their memory." He pointed the ship killer at the two scientists and added, "If I shoot you, we'll have a hole in the hull, but there's probably another room behind and I don't care."

"Nat," Simon shouted. "Don't, you might hurt the machinery."

Nat told him, in loud and clear terms what he could do with the machinery. Comprehensively. Simon stepped back, and I thought his fear wasn't feigned. But even I was feeling a little concerned, except before I could intervene, the scientists put their hands in the air and allowed themselves to be shepherded into a group of others. Which was when Simon disappeared, after muttering he was going to find Zen.

But he was back by the time the scientists had been herded into two groups—those, who while not being Usaians were vouched for by the Usaian scientists, and those who...weren't.

Nat, striding about casually brandishing the shipkiller, looked as forceful as Abigail had been and managed to convey the impression he was about to burst in fire at any given moment. Only I knew that his short fuse was more of a put-on veneer than a real lack of patience. "What are we going to do with you?" he asked, even as Zen disappeared into the compartments the two scientists had tried to guard.

"Make them breathe space," Simon said, casually. I wasn't sure if this was an act, but it didn't sound like it to me.

It mustn't have sounded like it to Nat either, because he looked over his shoulder and, for just a moment, let us see a very shocked face. If the scientists had seen that, it would have destroyed all our chances of scaring them with Nat.

But at the same time, Doctor Dias clicked his tongue and said, "No. No, we don't act like them." And, looking intently at Simon, he said, "And you should be particularly careful not to act like *him*." I understood that by "him" the doctor meant the man from whom Simon had been cloned, one of the men who had been judged neither stable nor human enough to be trusted aboard the long-distance ship to the stars.

I shivered, thinking that my father, too, hadn't been trusted and wondering how much I was like him.

But the exchange had served its purpose; the scientists were cowed. When Doctor Dias said to the harvesters, "Herd them into one of the air-to-spaces in the unused portion. When we're secure, we shall send them down. They can land wherever they feel safe and good luck to them," they didn't even try to resist. Probably because it was all reinforced by Simon saying, "This is misguided. They will come back with a strike force."

But then Athena's husband, who'd been very quiet until then, looked suddenly haunted and shook his head. "No," he said. "No. Can I have three or four of you more...ah, technically inclined gentlemen?"

And as about a dozen of the loyal scientists approached him, I heard him say, "I will show you how to rig a defense system, so any ship trying to attach, without your specifically allowing it, will be burned on sight. Any ship trying to leave unauthorized, too."

"We don't have weapons here," one of the men said. "The harvesters have some, but..."

"You have a lot of discarded pieces, from the building of the *Je Reviens*," Athena's husband said. "And you have unlimited energy, in harvested pods."

His manner was different, his voice slightly higher than normal, his speech oddly accented in a way that reminded me of Doctor Dias.

For the next two days, Nat and I and Simon—though he was likely to disappear to go help Zen—kept the friendly scientists and the harvesters under eye, because we had to ensure no treason occurred.

Food was from rations and largely tasteless, but not unpleasant. Certainly more pleasant than pink mush and green mush.

After the two days, Zen announced that the machinery was rigged in such a way that it would not only no longer suppress communication on Earth, but that any attempts to suppress it again could be circumvented by bouncing the broadcasts off Circum and it would disseminate it to the whole Earth.

And Nat, Simon and I took our leave of Athena, Kit and Doc and left with instructions to release the ship with scientists a set time after us. At the last minute, before our air-to-space closed, Zen joined us. She said she'd decided she was more useful to us and Earth than to her native Eden.

At any rate, I didn't have much time to think about it, because shortly after we entered Earth's atmosphere, we found out we were in trouble bad.

Our Beloved Home

I'D BE TEMPTED TO SAY I'D FORGOTTEN HOW INSANE EARTH'S system of defense was, except I'd never known it. In my entire time as heir to Olympus, I'd gone to space three times, all of them before the age of twelve, with Mother and Father and, the last time, with Ben as a guest to keep me company.

We'd visited Circum twice, on state occasions, and once the Luna station on the moon, on some sort of inspection. The last trip was the only one I remembered, and most of what I remembered was the gratification of being able to impress Ben with going to space and show him space. By then, we'd watched quite a few holos of space adventures, and we'd spent most of the time by the viewport inventing and telling each other stories of space pirates and spaceships from other worlds, filled with strange creatures.

On the way back, all that I remembered was that we'd landed. But, of course, father's air-to-space had had the right broadcasting signals, identifying it as the traveling vehicle of the Good Man of Olympus. And the other Good Men would never dream of interfering with that.

Which brought us to our return to Earth now, on an air-to-space—probably the same one we'd taken up—which had no information as to its origin and no traceable identifiers.

And this was when I found out that the Earth had a defense

problem. For one, there was no such thing as an Earth defense mechanism. There wouldn't be, right? How could there be when all of the Earth had no one to fear from the outside? Even if all of Circum, all of the moon, and possibly all of mysterious Eden had come to attack Earth they'd not even be noticed by most of the Earth's population.

No, the only thing that could threaten Earth was Earth itself, and it turned out, once you entered the fields of alarm and defense of the various territories ruled over by Good Men, you found yourself in the crisscrossing path of several alarms, all of them threatening you with missiles or with robot-ships coming to arrest you.

For me, the cacophony of shrieking alarms came as a total surprise. For the others, I took it that it was also unexpected but not because they hadn't thought of it.

Zen said, "I thought I'd rigged it with your signal," to Simon.

And Simon had said, "You probably did, but it's probably broadcasting another signal, from when it was built three hundred years ago."

And Nat just went very stern and determined and I knew that he hadn't expected this, and didn't want this, but understood it, and was determined to out-pace it.

He nudged Simon, who was sitting at the controls. "Simon," he said. "Let me have those."

Simon looked up at him, in surprise. "What?"

"Let me have those. I know all the safe zones, where they can alarm but they won't be able to hit us." He continued, to Simon's disturbed look, "I had to. We fly transports, you know?"

Simon, clearly, like me, did not know. But he got up and let Nat take over the controls. Nat sat down, as new alarms echoed "You are invading the air space of the principality of Duachen, stop now or we shall—" "You are flying over the territory of—" and "Desist now or we shall have to—"

I took the copilot chair, but it was largely ornamental, because I cringed at each sound and had a hard time keeping my mind clear. But Nat's hands flew deftly on the controls, just as he'd done when broom fighting, and he brought us down to within sight of Olympus Seacity.

I could see it on the visor, tall amid the blue waters. And then I realized those waters were so full of air-sea transports as to look black.

Which was when the ship suddenly shuddered and a loud thud echoed under us. Before I even had time to blink, Nat had said, "Shit." He'd unbuckled himself and was diving, full body, out of the control chair.

He unstrapped me too, somehow, and took me along in his dive, an arm hooked around my middle. Just in time for the control chair to erupt into flames.

We'd dressed in a way that worked for brooming and I picked myself off the floor, to find that Simon and Zen were clutching brooms. And I went into my fast mode, diving for the closet where we'd stashed the brooms. Mine was the only one left. I grabbed it, then dove ahead of the others, to slam the emergency trap door on the floor open, by kicking the lock to release it, then stomping the door open.

Nat was the first one through on his broom, quickly followed by myself. By that time, smoke followed us, and as Nat signaled, *away from the debris, as fast as possible,* I saw he was signaling to three of us.

But we'd no more escaped the falling debris of the air-to-space, which sank into the sea like a torch in a bathtub, than I saw Nat signal, *Lucius, we're going to have to swim to approach. Those are enemy transports.* At that point, I stopped tracking where Zen and Simon had gone.

And the War's Desolation

HAVE YOU EVER WONDERED WHAT KIND OF MADMAN DIVES INTO a house on fire, or crawls into a collapsed mine to save those caught within? Look no further. His name is Nat Remy, and you'll probably read about him in the history books as Nathaniel Greene Remy. Oh, I'll probably be mentioned too, but I'm not that kind of idiot. If I'd been alone, I'd have flown my broom very far away from there and then come back, in a week or whenever the fighting calmed down, to bind wounds or do what I could.

Because as we flew our brooms near the seacity two things became clear: *surrounded* didn't begin to describe what was happening to my homeland. There were rings of vehicles around the island, vehicles parked in the plazas. There were explosions and smoke, and from the color of some of it, it wasn't just smoke but the kind of poisonous gases that incapacitate or kill everything in its wake.

It was clear as day that the other Good Men had decided to make an example of Olympus. My mind and my heart seized, thinking of everyone on the island, but most of all of Nat's family which had become, in a way, my own family in those last few weeks, at least as far as my looking after them, and they after me.

But what could two men, just two men do on the occasion? Nothing, right?

Fortunately, I never managed to say that. Because Nat seemed to guess my thoughts, and, flying alongside me said, *We have to save the children, Lucius. They'll be alone in the house.* His fingers flicked on, in their leather gloves, relentless, *No way we can get in this way, but we can swim and get near the tunnel to your house. It will be occupied, but we can fight through it.*

So, the kind of madman who will do this is also the kind of madman who will, without a second thought, fight through the most occupied part of the isle on the way to another, less occupied part. Fortunately I had a better idea, and I flicked at him, *No, follow me. I have a way into the garden.*

I expected... not quite an argument, demurring. There was none. He signaled. *Lead.*

It involved dropping into the sea like a stone, still, and swimming around, past all the easy harbors, where ships were anchored, and to a beach around the side, so narrow that there was barely space to put your toes on.

We had to swim beneath troop transports. Without the oxygen masks, we'd have been unable to breathe by the time we arrived. As was, we were at the limit of the oxygen concentrators, and we'd brought no bottles, but we made it.

Nat emerged first, since he must be part fish. As he balanced on the tiny ledge, he gave me a hand to climb up to it, then he removed his mask. "How do we get anywhere from here?" he asked. He looked up. "It must be a good fifty feet. Oh." The "oh" was because he'd seen them.

Years before our arrest, desperate for a way into the garden that could not be tracked by my father's guards, Ben and I had hollowed holes in the dimatough—by force of burner—and into those we'd forced tiny, transparent dimatough pegs. I could see how, in a situation like what we found ourselves in, it was a foolhardy risk, but we'd never thought of that, and to be honest, unless you knew what you were looking for, or, like Nat, you were looking straight up, you'd never see those pegs.

Climbing still wasn't easy. Some of the pegs were missing, but, more importantly, they were set for my height or Ben's, neither of which fit Nat. He managed it nonetheless, keeping pace just beneath me. We didn't have ropes, which worried me, but we had our brooms, in case we fell. And from a certain level up, they'd even be effective.

The greater danger was that the people below could pick us off the wall. There was nothing for it but to be like a fly on a wall. Fortunately, our suits were dark, and the wall was black. It was possible to see us, but unless you knew who we were, it was unlikely you'd pick us off. Surely, one would think we were invaders?

We made it all the way over the wall of my garden. And into a pitched firefight. I cannot and will not attempt to describe what I saw. There were . . . several burner fights going on at once. Several trees and bushes were ablaze. I recognized some of Sam's and Betsy's assistants, and I tried to take out their opponents, when I could identify them.

Which was easier said than done, as Nat had—ignoring the firefights, and several times coming close to running through a tree that had become a bonfire—taken off at speed through the garden, headed for Remy house.

Even with my fast-speed, I fell behind a few times, as I took time to kill someone or other. When I took out Royce's opponent, Royce must have recognized us, because he took off after Nat, also. Well, Royce was many brands of annoying, but he was no traitor, so I let him run with us, across the garden and over the wall, to the broad street that divided my house from Nat's.

This is a little harder to describe. People had barricaded themselves behind flyers. Other people were flying brooms. Burner fire crisscrossed in the street and since none of the people on the street were in uniform, the militia from our side was, and the several attackers wore all sorts of different uniforms, all you could say was that it was very hard to tell friend from foe at a glance. The only safe thing was that if it looked like a uniform and it wasn't sky blue you should burn. But even that wasn't safe, since as I tried to shoot the enemy, I realized the snappy red uniforms were those of Simon's militia, and I didn't even know on whose side they were, since he was obviously not in control of his own guard.

I found out afterward they were on both, adding to the mess of an extremely messy battle.

I have no idea how we made it across the street, or through the gates of Remy House. The gates—clear dimatough—were blasted open and charred by an explosion. My heart fell to the vicinity of my feet and stayed there. I was thinking of little Debra. I'd read to her ... just four days ago. She looked forward to my reading and waited for me, every night. I thought of James, who looked as Nat must have at fourteen, with longish, awkwardly cut hair, and a problematic complexion, but tall and limber, and full of fighting spirit, and no more knowing what to do with it than a puppy knows how to defend his pack from wolves. And Patrick, ten, who looked as much like Ben as Abigail had, and who was as eager for stories as Debra, though less willing to show it. And Tom, who favored his father and, at five, was just learning to read.

Nat was running up the steps ... and into pitched battle.

Burner fire was everywhere. We dropped to the ground, instinctively, and I heard Royce drop behind me, but it wasn't until I looked from the floor that I realized this entire fight was James, who stood in front ... of a wall. Was it just a wall? Why was he defending a wall? And holding off fifteen of the Good Men's best, in their dimatough-scale clothing, and their regulation burners. There were dead men all around, so he was doing a good job of it. But why?

There was no time to ask. I started burning men, from the back, careful not to aim where if I missed it might hit James. Royce and Nat joined in. Then Zen and Simon who came in running, helped. The men turned around. They burned at us. We burned back. A burner ray singed the top of my hair, and someone else took out the bastard.

Suddenly, from pitched battle we went to standing, five of us amid a pile of corpses. And James was collapsed against the door.

"James, hold on!" Nat yelled. He stepped unheeding over dead bodies to his brother's side. I noticed there was a dark wet patch on James's leg. Only one wound? Surely he could afford to lose a leg? It could be regened.

"James," Nat looked up at us. "Royce, for the love of heaven, call a medical transport." Then, without waiting, he said, "Why didn't you go in with them?"

James looked up at Nat, his eyes unfocused. I was now very near and could see and smell that the patch on his leg was blood. And I could see it bubbling out. Surely that wasn't right? Behind me, Royce was talking earnestly into some sort of link.

"They saw the kids go in," he said. "They saw them go in. They knew where the safe room was. They could have blasted through. I had to defend them."

Then he gave an odd sort of hiccup and sagged even as Nat was trying to lift him. At that moment, Royce said, "They're here," and a shadow obscured the doorway. Nat ran with James all the way in to the medical transport. But James died before they could take off. A burner cut had opened his femoral artery. He'd been hit before we arrived and remained at his post until we relieved him. Possibly by will power alone.

Nat opened the safe room and got the other children out. And two days later we had a family ceremony in which we wished James Madison Remy's spirit godspeed to a world where he could live as a free man. He had died as one.

Dearly Bought

ROYCE EXPLAINED TO US—BEFORE SAM AND BETSY GOT BACK TO the house, and long before the fighting was done with over the island—that we were actually winning. In fact, the attack on Remy house was the last stand of desperate invaders, trying to secure hostages for their retreat.

Because we'd freed the communications, when the Good Men attacked Olympus, we could call for help, not just to our allies but to Usaians and men of good will everywhere. Only half the transports were enemy, and the fight for the island, though bloody, was a victory. James hadn't died in vain.

The war was nowhere near over.

But after that communications on Earth were free. The first broadcast, in which I addressed the people of the Earth at large and told them what had happened and what our struggle had been in Olympus, together with the fact that now any private citizen could address any other number of other private citizens by text or voice and not be traced started a ball rolling that the Good Men simply couldn't stop. They still had the power, the armies, the Secret Services, but we were gaining. We weren't isolated anymore.

And the news that eventually leaked out—Betsy told me it wasn't her doing, but I was never sure I believed her—that the

Good Men were actually Mules, turned the battle of public opinion our way, though because of my visibility, my presence, and the fact that I am clearly not one of the old ones, I'm hoping most of the sons of Good Men will be spared.

Are Good Men shunned because of our blood? Perhaps, but it won't last. There is a war to be fought, a revolution turning ugly over in Liberte, and everything is in too much turmoil for anyone to worry too much about some artificial genetic markers, and the inability to reproduce with normal females. The Earth, held artificially under the same overarching and corrupt regime for years, is taking several paths to liberty and people are too busy with surviving and rebuilding to care too much that my genes were assembled in a lab. In fact, of all the surviving Good Men or ex-Good Men I am probably the one in best shape, as I am the image of the revolution. Or at least the Usaian part of the revolution.

At any rate, getting access to the energy shipments of Circum, as we now control access to the powerpods—even if the Good Men have managed to get sources of it going, enough to hold on against us, one can't help but think the war has turned. And having new recruits pour into our ranks, fresh as new paint and raw as steak though they are, doesn't hurt either.

After we cleaned Olympus, cremated our dead and bound our wounds, Nat went back to the war, and I went back to my work, and I won't say there weren't many days of perusing casualty lists ahead, but Nat was never on them. Somehow, through the next few months, he came through fire and hell alive and relatively intact. He says that, like Tom Sawyer in the book of ancient writer Mark Twain, he was born to hang and short of that nothing can kill him.

I'm sure the Good Men would gladly have hanged him, if they'd known, so I'll be grateful they didn't.

Oh, one other thing, which I'm not sure I should mention, as it has very little to do with the revolution and is purely personal, is that three nights after he came back from the Massacre of Broken River, Nat gave me a bracelet. It was a simple silver arc, open on the end, so it was adjustable. It had a stylized engraving of a tree with an ax resting against it. On the back it had my name, and underneath, Free Man, and the date I had joined the Usaians and the Sons of Liberty.

"I had it made," he said. "I had one made for myself, after the raid, and when I was ordering I thought you might want one too, and at any rate I owe you my life."

The ax and the tree were drawn by Nat and were supposed to symbolize George Washington, or something. I treasured it because Nat gave it to me, but later on, after they were noticed, a lot of people made up a whole story about it.

It appears that with my being the public face of the revolution, at least in broadcasts, and the whole thing being perceived as starting from my escaping Never-Never, a lot of the more fervent and prophecy-inclined Usaians have decided I am the foretold George who would come to restart the wheels of freedom.

It is no use at all telling them that my name was spelled Lucius and that none of my supposed ancestors had even been named anything with a G. And it is no use telling them I had done nothing except exist to start this pebble rolling. All they do is shake their heads and make some pronouncement about the mysterious ways of God.

I mention this because the bracelet is taken as corroboration of this ridiculous idea, and Nat finds himself greatly amused by it, though once he told me, "Has it ever occurred to you that you wouldn't know if you were him?" I suppose he's gotten a little loopy. It must be all the responsibility.

The Point Turns

I'VE BEEN STRUGGLING TO KNOW HOW TO FINISH THIS ACCOUNT. I've been told that my view of the war is important, since many people still think I was instrumental in starting the whole thing. I've been told that this might provide clues on how to avoid future tyrannies, how to create a revolution if needed, how to turn revolution gone wrong to revolution done right. I don't think so. Looking back at this, it all seems intensely personal and particular and I don't see how anyone can use it.

At any rate, after the raid on Circum Terra and the battle for Olympus, Nat went back to war, in command of a larger force than ever. He was in Herrera's private staff by then, Herrera's inner circle, who, like Wellington with his trusted men, he called his family. I didn't find out Nat's rank for sure till the next time he visited, and I don't know when the promotion happened.

As for me, I went back to making broadcasts and propaganda, but this time seriously and not just trading on my image. I found that as well as the super speed trick, superhuman memory and correlating ability had been engineered into my ancestor. Or, at least, Doctor Dias told me so. So I used it. I studied all the revolutions, including the French, and I started tailoring broadcasts and arranging things to bring people to our cause. Somewhere along the line I found that I was in charge and that Betsy was working for me. Fortunately her devotion to the cause allowed her to ignore the personal demotion. If it was a demotion. Like her son, that woman can always make sure what she wants happens, and the rest is only incidental.

And Athena Sinistra came back to Earth yet again, and then there was all the mess with the juveniles of my kind. But none of that is mine to tell, and as for how I turned public opinion in my favor, I'll eventually write about it. When the war is over. If the war is ever over.

And so, because this has turned into an intensely personal account, I'll finish with an intensely personal moment.

It was the next time Nat came home, after the raid on Circum. We'd just captured Sea York, in the first indisputable victory for our side, and he got sent home for real rest and recreation. He hadn't even gone to his parents' house but came directly to the palace, where he found me presiding over a staff of ten people, each of whom did their best to help me and mostly succeeded in driving me insane.

He waited at the door to the office, which I kept meaning to have refurnished, but which still looked like my father's, because it was a war and resources were scarce and I'd been divesting my attics of accumulated stuff to furnish other, more important offices than mine. After a while one of my secretaries, a timid young man from Liberte, had ventured to tell me that General Remy and "a big shaggy dog" were waiting for me. Yes, Nat had Goldie with him. And I managed not to make a spectacle of myself right there in the hall, because it had been almost a year since I'd seen Nat and every time I see him, truly see him, is a moment of wonder and joy that I haven't missed his name in the casualty lists. As for Goldie, he leapt at me, put paws on my shoulders and forgot all the proper behavior Nat had taught him.

After my face was thoroughly licked, Nat said, "It's as safe here as anywhere else, now, and most of the children are busy with the war, so I thought you could keep him."

I dragged them both off to the terrace outside my room, and Nat and I sat on the wall facing the sea, while Goldie put his head on my knees and Nat talked to me of strategy, of victories, of troop movements, of some of the weapon caches they found, of bits of documentation the Good Men had suppressed and which would come to me in time.

It was a beautiful spring day, with a soft breeze blowing, warm

and salty around us. I told him a little of what I was doing, and
he said, "I know. You're well on your way to becoming a living
legend. Forget the generals and everyone who actually fights.
When historians write about this period, it will all be Lucius
Keeva. Lucius Keeva came up with the idea, created the revolution and fought the war singlehanded."

I'd smiled at him and shrugged. "I just can't wait till there are
elections, and a legitimate representative of the people is elected
to take over this place, and I can be just Lucius Keeva, without
anyone associating me with being a Patrician or thinking I want
to go on being the Good Man."

"Ah. How goes the constitutional republic project?"

I made a face. "The convention is a howling mess. But I did
manage to get them not to outlaw homosexuality... Which considering that's been a crime in Earth's code for so long, with
death penalty attached many places, is a minor victory, and the
only time I got involved... for cause."

He grinned at me. "Minor victories, but personal."

"Of sorts. I don't like it, though, Nat. I don't like getting
involved in that sort of discussion. And I don't want them to
change their minds because it's personal."

He looked serious, again. "But it's all personal, isn't it? That is
the whole point of individual liberties. The right and the duty to
have it be personal, to have it count, to be the best person you
can be, no matter how easy or difficult for you, particularly."
He sounded pensive. "I think the beginning of the end, for the
republic, before, was dividing people into groups and buying into
collective guilt and collective innocence. In the end, all each of
us has is himself, and no regime will be perfect for everyone.
But particularly for us, the odd ones that don't quite fit in, the
regime that respects the individual most is always the best."

Silence fell and he smoked, quietly. After a long time, he cleared
his throat. "So, you don't want to go into politics? Because you're
quite good at it."

"No. I don't want to go into it. I hate it. I hate being on display, and my life observed from every angle."

He was quiet a longer while. "What do you intend to do,
after you pass on the governorship of Olympus and the North
American territories, and the war is over?"

"I told you before," I said. "I will take my money, if it's still worth anything, since your father is flapping about fiat currencies and a gold standard—"

"Oh, yes, one of Father's old hobby horses. Mind you, I haven't studied it enough to say he's not right, but..."

"Yeah, so if my money is still worth something, I'll buy an awful lot of robots and go cut down some of those fast-growing trees and start a farm. Close enough to the Longs that I can go to the Fall Festival, if they still have those. And then grow chickens and pigs and cows, and maybe even a couple of kids, because there're going to be a lot of them orphaned when this is over, and I've found I'm fond of reading bedtime stories."

"Are you really?" Nat said. He looked at me, examining my face, as if he were looking for something. I didn't know what, so I just looked back at him, waiting for him to say something like that I had a wart forming at the end of my nose. It was that sort of intent scrutiny.

But instead, after a long while, he flicked his spent cigarette out to sea and sighed. "And here, I'm a thoroughly urban man, but I don't think I can let you go and settle in the wilderness all alone. For one, you'd be making coffee with socks rather than learn to use the proper appliance—" I started to open my mouth to protest, but he didn't give me time. "For another, I remember you had the hardest time telling the cows from the bulls, and for yet another because even if you do adopt a couple of kids, eventually they will leave, and it's a sad thought that you'll end up like old Rogers, living with three pigs and talking to them as if they were people."

"So," I said, confused, "what are you saying?"

"When the war is over, *we*'ll go to the wilderness and start a farm," Nat said, firmly. "And *we*'ll have an attic room with a window at either end, so the breeze can flow through in the summer. And *we*'ll raise chickens and pigs who don't wear aprons, and cows, and kids if you insist, and a whole lot of golden-haired dumb dogs." He took a deep breath. "And I'll operate the kitchen machinery because, Lucius, honestly, you're pitiful."

I looked over at him, trying to determine if he was teasing me. But, even though his lips were curved in a smile, his eyes were deadly serious and a little anxious, as if he were afraid of what I might say. So I did what I had to do and tried not to look like I'd just won the lottery.

I said, "Yeah. Let's do that. I'd like that."